# ALL ABOUT
# ~~NOTHING~~
# BUT ABOUT
# EVERYTHING

By Nelle W.

# Content Warning:

*There are mentions of:*
*Abuse, Addiction, Loss of a loved one, and Grief.*

# Illusion

by Nelle W.

His eyes
Her heart
Green and Red
Her eyes
His heart
Brown and red
Two different lives
Two different people
Two different souls
Two different expectations
Intertwined by coincidence
But held together by force
He knows nothing
She knows nothing
But destiny knows everything
Their hearts yearn for something
beyond their understanding
Their eyes bleed darker shades of each other needs
Love. Fear. Hate.
Love upon a scale but the same with the flip of a coin
Bleed, bleed, and bleed
All about nothing But about everything

# Contents

6

| Free-Style | Playlist |
|---|---|
|  |  |
|  |  |
|  |  |
|  |  |
|  |  |
|  |  |
|  |  |
|  |  |
|  |  |
|  |  |
|  |  |
|  |  |

*This is a heartfelt dedication to young women who may not have experienced love yet yearn for it deeply, captivated by their romantic fantasies and desires—especially those who find themselves drawn to chaotic, passionate love stories. It is also in dedication to my loved ones who inspired some of the characters. Thank you truly!*
*I am with you—N.W.*

# Prologue[1]

I walked as fast as possible, passing each street sign, block, and building. It was my twenty-third birthday, and I always spent it with my nana. Since I was three years old, we've had a tradition of going to a diner that has been around for about fifty years. We both loved ordering our favorite: spaghetti with cilantro and extra sauce, but it was my nana's favorite first, and she introduced it to me. Dragging my feet against the pavement, I thought about how I should explain to her why I was so late, at least two hours. I hated making her wait, but the insufferable traffic jam made it hard to cross over. I always disliked how, in the city, people crammed together like rats.

I couldn't shake the feeling that something was wrong with her. Lately, she looked paler, smiled less, and always seemed exhausted. I had planned to ask her what was happening, but I knew she would likely brush it off like always. It reminded me of my mother's behavior - loving, yet emotionally distant, always holding onto her secrets and problems. After turning right, I finally arrived at my apartment building. Pausing at the crosswalk, I proceeded to King's Diner. From a distance, I spotted her engaged in conversation with a man. Watching her connect with anyone she found intriguing or from out of town was fascinating. Nana was genuinely curious about how others lived. As the crosswalk signal turned white, I rushed across the street, hoping she wasn't too disappointed with my lateness.

I could feel the weight of my long hair brushing against the fabric of my coat as I hurried along the sidewalk. Initially, I intended to style my hair into a neat bun, but this morning, amid my rush, I lacked the energy for such a task. All I managed to squeeze in was devouring a banana and quickly sipping from a small glass of orange juice. My outfit for the day consisted of a snug rose-pink dress with delicate floral patterns, complemented by my beloved vintage ocean blue coat that I had found at a thrift store. My well-worn black leather boots, a cherished Christmas gift from the previous year, were paired with it. Although they had seen better days, my affection for them hadn't waned. As I briskly walked, my golden hoop earrings swayed in opposing directions with every step, and my dainty initial necklace gently clung to my skin. The city's noise grew louder as the wind picked up speed. I reached the diner's door, took a moment to compose myself, and then pushed the heavy black, rusted doors open using their gleaming golden handles. Inside, I caught sight of Nana, engrossed in conversation with a stranger, her radiant smile lighting up the room. At times, we affectionately called her Nana because, as a child, I struggled to pronounce "grandmother." Much to the chagrin of my family, who attempted to teach me the correct term, the nickname stuck. I always found it amusing how her face instantly lit up when I called her Nana, as if the entire world lay within that single word.

"Nana!" I eagerly shouted from the entrance of the diner.

She turned toward me, her joyful grin revealing a charming gap between her front teeth. Her hair was elegantly styled in a curly bun, and she wore purple glasses, a matching turtleneck, a denim skirt, and the same black boots I had gifted her the previous Christmas. She sported a pedicure in a grape shade. Purple was undeniably her color of choice, evident not only in her clothing but also in her surroundings. Her obsession with the hue was endearing; she didn't merely wear purple—she embodied it. Nana's fair complexion contrasted beautifully with her cocoa-colored eyes, her enthusiastic spirit shining through every purple-hued ensemble detail.

As I walked towards the table, I caught my breath and smiled. It felt like my face would be sore after all the smiling. I acted like a child around Nana because she brought it out of me. I loved her just that much. I was excited to hear about her day and to tell her about mine. I practically skipped to the seat across from her, and when I arrived, I ranted about feeling bad for being late.

"Nana, I'm sorry. The traffic was hectic, and people were such assholes. It was like fighting through a crowd of imbeciles, you know. However, I made it. I love you, and I am so sorry. I hope you are not too mad at me. I wouldn't say I like it when I let you down. Please say I did not waste your time, and you have to go."

My nana looked at me with enduring affection and giggled softly. I knew she wouldn't take me seriously, but I also understood there was no need to stress. My nana has never been disappointed in me.

"Oh, baby, why do you stress so much? You know, I could care less about how late you were and more about how you made it to me safe and sound," she smiled, "Besides, you left me two messages about how late you would be, but it is no fuss. I only want a kiss and to wish you a happy birthday. Sounds good?"

I giggled and said, "Sounds good, Nana. Sorry for overthinking. It is my specialty. A kiss would suffice with me."

I kissed her on the cheek but cringed at how warm she felt. Luckily, she did not notice and kissed me back.

She turned sideways and said, "By the way, this is Dawn. He is new to the city and kept me engaged until you arrived. You can thank him for keeping me company," I stared at the man with a baseball cap and a brown trench coat. He had white sneakers paired with brown joggers and a regular white tee. You could barely see his face or how he held his head down, but his eyes. His eyes were captivating; they reminded me of the Emerald City. He was reclusive.

"Do not be shy, baby. Please introduce yourself to my gorgeous granddaughter. Go ahead now." He smiled, nodded, then said, "Hello. I have heard so much about you in such a short time. Your nana is such a conversationist. She is a real delight and deeply knowledgeable. I mean, I might survive in the city with her expertise. Your name is Aira, right?"

I twitched at the echo when he called me "Aira." Only people close to me use that name; my grandmother knows that. However, she believes that everyone should call me by my first name. Although I preferred "Moon," I remained polite. "Yes, my name is Aira, but I prefer Moon. Thank you for keeping my nana occupied until I got here. I am sorry if we took up too much of your time. You seem nice, and our King Burger is good if you want to know the best thing to eat here," I trailed off and asked my nana, "Should we go ahead and order? I know you are starving like me, and I am ready for our usual ritual if Mr. Dawn here does not mind."

He nodded in agreement as his food made its way to his table, which was good because I was over the conversation and did not care to converse with people I did not care to know. Maybe it was a city thing because my nana was from the south, so she had better hospitality, apart from my straightforwardness.

"Um, no, I do not mind. I do not want to take up any more of your time. Thank you for the lovely conversation. If you don't mind me asking, what should I call you, Nana, if we cross paths again? This will be my last question, I promise. Then, I am out of your hair." he chuckled.

I sat in front of my nana, tired and flipping through the menu as she answered the strange man.

"You were a joy to entertain, baby, and you can call me Jane Moon, but my people call me Janey. I consider you my friend because of how sweet you are. If no one has told you that you have the cutest dimples when you smile, they are crazy. If we cross paths again, do not forget to remind me that I owe you a tour of our fabulous city," she winked at him.

"I will, and thank you again for the lovely talk, Janey," he said, lifting his head slightly and smiling.

"Enjoy the pie." She said, ending the conversation.

He looked back at his plate as he ate, and I let out a small sigh at the fact that it was just me and Nana now. I wondered why I looked at the menu as if we did not get the same thing as always. I sat up straight and smiled.

"So! We can finally order, and yes, I know to ask for extra sauce," I said playfully, rolling my eyes and looking back at her, "How was your day, Nana? Anything new besides attracting strangers," I said, laughing.

She pulled down her glasses and looked at me. "The only thing "new" I do is talk to strangers. Also, add cilantro and ask for some parmesan, baby. You know how we like it, but how was your day?"

"Okay, I will." I tapped the fork on the table. "How have you been feeling as of late?" Evening out her denim skirt with her hands, she said, "What are you talking about, baby?"

"I mean, are you feeling well? These days, when I see you, you look different."

"Different, how?"

"You look tired. Sometimes frail. I want to make sure you are doing all right, Nana."

"I'm fine, baby, don't worry about me. I need rest, that's all. It's probably all that volunteering. Don't worry; you're pretty- little head over it."

"Are you sure?"

"Yes! Now stop interrogating me before I knock some sense into you. I'm already hungry, child." She said, exceptionally annoyed.

"Okay, okay, sorry. I'll leave it alone." I didn't believe her, but if Nana says her health was spectacular, it was. In time, I would know the truth.

"Thank you."

She called Marleen, the waitress who had worked at the diner her whole life. Marleen and Nana have known each other since Marleen moved to the city thirty years ago. They spend time together now and then. I saw her from time to time because of it, but we were not close. She liked to call me Mo, which is short for Moon. Luckily, she gets a pass for the nickname because I have seen her around most of my life.

"Mo! Janey! My girls are here! Oh, happy birthday, baby. How does it feel to be the big two and three? Just let me know if you need anything or life advice. I used to light up the city at that age. Good times. Just ask your nana."

When we arrived, she had already placed our order in the kitchen, knowing we always ordered the same dish on my birthday. She was a petite woman in her sixties, with platinum blonde hair, blue color contacts, and long blue acrylic nails adorned with grey and gold star designs. She had a light beige skin tone and pale blue eyes. Her waitress outfit didn't fit as well as it used to; it was too big, and she wore shoes that were a size too small, making it obvious that it hurt her to walk.

I smiled and said, "All the advice I need, Nana, has already shared. When did you become a motivational speaker? As I recall, you hated sharing the facts of life because it reminded you of your age," I giggled, and Nana reached across the table to give me a love tap. "I'm sorry, Marleen. I would not mind some wisdom in life when you have spare time. I also love the new hair color. It gives supermodel!" I said, eyes wide and sarcastic, but she could never tell; on the other hand, my nana could and gave me a look.

Marleen smiled and blushed at the model's comment, placing the bread and two lemonades on the table. She knew our order by heart and was always punctual. "Oh, doll, that was so sweet of you. Aside from the gentlemen behind you, you are the second person to say that today. Also, I will take you up on that offer, but it will be unexpected, like in the movies. It would be bleak if you asked me straight out, and I hope I was not the only one to find him cute. Janey! If only I were a few years younger," she said, blushing and looking at that guy named Dawn.

However, she knew she was older than him by a couple of years unless he was interested in older women. I could barely make out his face because of his baseball cap, but he must be handsome if people say so.

Nana laughed and said, "Now, Marleen, leave the boy alone and bring us parmesan and put the extra sauce in the spaghetti since Aira wants to chatter about nothing with you. Also, we must meet this week and have a gal's day out. It has been so long, and Mo can join in, too, so you can shed light on life, huh?"

It hurt that she lied because I would lie about having plans before going out with Nana and Marleen again. Imagine older women gossiping and thinking that what they saw on the 9 o'clock news was gossip, along with discussions about certain brands changing their recipes.

Marleen jumped for joy and agreed, "Nana, you are such a doll because you are right. It has been forever since I saw my girls outside this pigsty, and we can plan out an entire day or week as we used to when Mo was just a baby doll," she said, squeezing my cheeks, "It would—" She gets cut off as her boss, Joey, called for her to help another waitress who drops her tray of orders. She blew each of us a kiss as she walked away. Marleen will always be a spark of light to me because she cannot help but be herself and love life as much as she does. I see why Nana and she became friends, no matter how annoying they were together.

"My day was pretty average. I went to work at the flower shop, wrote some new poetry, and caught up with old friends. Besides that, I need to clean my bedroom, which I've been putting off for two weeks. Also, I have a poetry set at the club on Friday, and I was hoping you could come after you're done volunteering at the shelter," I said, making a pouty face for extra persuasion.

She leaned back and smiled at me. "I will see if I can make it. You are spoiled, you know. I am surprised your Papa, and I could raise you." She took a sip of her lemonade. "I missed you. I have not seen you in a week, and I know you are busy, but we should spend more time together," Nana said as she looked down at her hands wistfully, but I interrupted.

"Yeah, of course. Just let me check my schedule. I would love to hang out more as well. We can ride the ferry for fun like we used to and go to the amusement park. I miss riding the pony no matter how old I get. Oh! I bought it. Do you want to see it?"

She nodded, and I reached into my coat pocket and pulled out a lighter and a candle shaped like the number twenty-three. I planned to stick the candle into my spaghetti and light it. They used to count in the past because they thought I was too young to have a lit candle near me, but as I got older, it became a tradition. I didn't care much for sweets or cake, so we stuck to spaghetti instead.

"You be careful, now. I do not want your pretty dress to get ruined—And if I'm not mistaken. Is that hers?"

Nana noticed it was my mama's dress. She had left us fifteen years ago. We barely talked about it because Nana's heart broke whenever she thought about it. I used to be like Nana — my heart couldn't comprehend why she would do such a thing.

Some people aren't meant to be parents, let alone mothers. My mama did have taste in clothes. She left behind many things that surprisingly fit me, so I would say we are the same size. As for my daddy, he died before I was born. He was a good and gentle man, I heard. Nana said he was average but had a charm that had all the girls, even my mama, fawning. She assumed that after his death, she checked out of being a mother, as they spent most of their lives together.

It always made me sad when she told me such truths because I never really knew my mama; she was a shell of herself by the time I was eight. Nana attended my events, tucked me into bed, and tended to my needs. She was there, but my mama would come home drunk and spend her money on that. Nana would pick her up off the floor, passed out, cold, and she would be flat-out drunk. This has happened ever since I was six years old. My mama never healed. Her name was Angel Moon, but I do not know how. She was the most fallen angel I ever met.

"Yes, it is hers. She left chic stuff behind, which fit me, so why not? It's not like she needs it. I love you and what you have done for me, and I promise never to disappoint you. You are my love, and since you raised me, you know about people who have broken my heart. I am just glad you haven't, Nana. No matter how spoiled or bratty I am, you could never leave me." I said, trying not to cry. "I just wanted to say thank you for giving me my twenty-third birthday."

Marleen came out with our food and set it down. Nana reached over and wiped a tear from my right cheek while Marleen was on the left. They sang "Happy Birthday" quietly to me to avoid attracting attention. I sat there singing along in my head and smiling. I felt like a blessed child to have a family that cared for me. I would never take it for granted.

Nana interrupted the song. "I love you, baby girl. I understand your sorrows, hopes, love, and dreams. You deserve the strongest blessings in your life, whether earned or not. You are the heart of my life. If you were broken, I would not know what to do. You have grown into such a beautiful and talented woman," she said as tears rose. "You have your whole life ahead of you—a good one. Venture out, fall in love, and make permanent friends. I am here with you every step of the way. Happy birthday, now blow out your candle."

Marleen stuck my candle in the spaghetti and lit it. I blew the candle out, and we all smiled and clapped. Marleen wished me a happy birthday again before returning to tending to other customers. Nana and I started clearing our plates with the speed of our forks. We talked and talked about everything and nothing at all. It felt so good to be with her again. I've been so busy with my life that we haven't had time to hang out, especially since she has been volunteering a lot lately. She seemed so weak since the last time I saw her. I figured she had a cold or needed to eat more. I don't know what it is, but she still seemed happy. Peace was always the goal of her life and family. She was traditional but open-minded, although our family was not too religious.

I am so grateful to Nana for everything because Grandpa was a devout Catholic. He passed away of natural causes when I was just eight years old, shortly after my mama had left. Nana believed he died of a broken heart, even though he didn't show any signs. She felt it was more his spirit than his heart.

I was closer to Nana, but I loved when Grandpa snuck me candy, read bedtime stories, and playfully tossed me in the air. He was like a substitute for the father I never had. To this day, I still wear the initial necklace he gave me for my seventh birthday. It feels like a distant memory, and it's the only time from my childhood that doesn't bring tears to my eyes. I had so much fun that day - a towering cake, a bouncy castle, presents, and my mom wasn't drunk. She was trying to be sober at the time. For once, it felt like we were a real family. Papa detested it when Mama got drunk and when he came home to find Nana picking her up off the floor. He repeatedly swore to kick her out and teach her a lesson. It pained him to see his daughter, someone whose actions he was ashamed of.

Our plates were clean, glasses emptied, and laughs settled. Our bellies were packed and ready to burst. Nana asked for apple pie to go as I shrunk down into my seat. I noticed the guy she introduced earlier was gathering his things and getting ready to leave, which I found odd. He had been here the whole time. He only had a salad and apple pie. I sat up and flipped my hair, grabbing a hair tie from my pocket and pulling my hair into a bun like Nana. It did not look like hers since I didn't have curly hair. My arms burning, I leaned back into my spot, and Nana headed for the restroom before we left. I turned to look out the window, taking in the sun and passing cars. I zoned out on how fast the vehicles passed each other. The car wheels and colors became a blur of flashes. My fingers tapped my left leg as my arms crossed on my lap. I began to take comfort in it as it eased my anxiety in public places.

Three minutes passed, and I snapped out of it when I heard a voice. I thought it was my nana, but it was the guy who sat behind us. "It was nice meeting you, and Happy Early Easter!" he said as he left.

I replied, "Thanks! You too!" Though Easter had already passed, what a weird thing to say. Maybe he just likes to hear himself talk.

Later, when Nana came out of the restroom and we headed to her parked car, I mentioned the strange man who wished me a happy Easter. She thought it was sweet and hoped they would see each other again, which led to one of her lectures about being nicer to people. She needed to understand people who weren't inherently friendly or hospitable. She wouldn't have moved to the city if she knew it would be like this, but she had hope for people. She considered me one of those people.

Nana used the car keys to unlock the door and rubbed my back as I entered the passenger seat. As I buckled my seat belt, I settled in and saw my Nana through the rearview mirror. As she walked around the car to the driver's seat, she dropped the bag of apple pie and the keys. Suddenly, her eyes rolled back, and she fell hard on the ground. Quickly, I unbuckled my seat belt and ran to her side. She was unconscious and burning up with a fever. Her left leg was tucked behind her right, and her body was bruised from scratches on the concrete. She was bleeding, and I didn't know how to help. I cried out and tried to call 911, but my eyes were so blurry from the tears.

I was at a loss for what to do. All I could do was hold her and cry. I felt utterly powerless and insignificant, like a child. The situation was so confusing and overwhelming. Unable to wait longer, I called Marleen, and she rushed out of the diner to help. We got Nana into the car together, and Marleen agreed to drive us to the hospital. She seemed remarkably calm, showing no fear, confusion, or shock. It was as if she had encountered a similar situation with Nana before. I didn't care whether she knew what was happening, but I was concerned about Nana's well-being. During the drive, I sat in the back with Nana, filled with tears and holding her hand. My entire life flashed before my eyes.

*Why did she fall? Is she sick, and if so, why? I should have met up with her more when she wanted. I focused too much on the big things that didn't mean anything to the little things in the grand scheme. I don't want her to go. I am scared.*

I couldn't help but panic. Marleen reached back and double-tapped my knee with her hand. It was her way of saying everything would be okay and that she loved me. It's her signature move whenever I'm hurt, a way for her to express her concern even if she can't help. I wish I could do the same for Nana. The only thing I could do was cradle her.

It was as if she was lifeless—a doll to be played with—something gone. A rose was dying.

# Prologue[2]

Nana was unconscious in the hospital bed. I had never seen her so vulnerable and exhausted. Though she still looked pale, her body temperature had decreased. She had medical patches across her chest to monitor whatever was happening and an IV in her arm. The hospital room was freezing; everything was white, beige, and somewhat old. She had been in and out of consciousness since Marleen brought us to the hospital. The monitor kept beeping as if it could determine whether she lived. The whole experience creeped me out. The fact that she could die any minute or hour, and I had no control over it, scared me.

I sat beside her bed, holding her hand. My head rested near her thigh as I picked at the blanket covering her. I listened to the beeps from the monitor, waiting for her to wake. We had arrived four hours ago, but I told Marleen to leave to get some rest. I promised to stay with Nana and let her know if anything changed. The room was quiet, aside from the machines and our breathing. The darkness of the night seeped through the gigantic hospital windows with no curtains.

The room contained a hospital bed, a bathroom, a closet, a TV, and two chairs. It had minimal decorations, which felt quite bleak. Perhaps only wealthier hospitals have more inviting rooms. The room's enclosure made me feel like darkness was closing in on me, as if Nana's life was hanging by a thread. When she was admitted, the doctors were unsure what affected her. They conducted chest, brain, and full body scans and drew blood. They said she would be in and out for a while, but if she did wake up and if I felt something was wrong, to hit the nurse button. The nurse and doctor checked her vitals constantly, but nothing changed much, and her blood pressure decreased.

Her right hand moved frequently for some time, which I deemed good because she wasn't entirely gone, right? I had no appetite. I couldn't sleep, and I grew restless for the results from the hospital. She had to know something was wrong. I felt it this past week. She rarely left the house other than volunteering; she was pale and always short of breath sometimes. There were apparent signs, but I was too selfish and caught up in my little world, and Nana was hurting. However, Marleen didn't seem shocked, so she had to know something, or at least Nana confided in her. I would ask her tomorrow; maybe she can give me answers alongside the doctors about what my grandmother had been hiding.

This situation infuriated me so much because she had to know she was sick and didn't tell me. I would have driven her to the doctor and supported her through this process. People in her generation are so stubborn about their health. It's always "I'm fine" and "I'm okay" until their body parts are being chopped off and they're being disintegrated in an oven to be turned into ashes for their funeral. She knows I hate to be around death, but never for her. She and I were stubborn, but she had to know that I would always be there for her.

I sat up and let go of her hand, my eyes looking over at her heartbeat. I smiled as I remembered how, as a baby, I would always crawl onto Mama's or Nana's chest and listen to their heartbeat to fall asleep, or so they say. I faintly remember it, but I could remember how hot and rough their bodies felt against mine. It didn't disturb me too much because it felt like a calling to do so—Mother Nature at its own will. As a baby, I couldn't understand what they smelled like, but It was human. I left the chair and paced around the room, thinking to myself while keeping an eye on her.

The door was open, and I could see out into the hallway. I could see nurses, doctors, patients, and the commotion. Some people were crying, laughing, bleeding, and wounded. It was like a circus for the best spectacle. It wasn't so awful as I could see children running around and playing. It made me smile that even in death, there could be happiness, or at least when faced with it. I walked and stood in the doorway, looking out into the cold and sterile world of the hospital. I wondered if they felt how I did or worse. Everyone's diagnosis was different but scary. Everything about life was horrifying.

You never knew when you would drop dead or live to the end of time.

I was terrified not only for her but also for myself. I wanted my nana to be a part of my life for a long time. I hoped she would be there to witness my personal growth, my falling in love, getting married, having kids, and even becoming a spinster if none of those things happened. It was something I had thought about countless times; it was beyond my control.

It would cause me pain, but I had come to terms with it. I had nothing else to do but to endure the pain, not as much as her, but still, I was hurting. I pushed the door up and sat in the chair beside her bed. I gazed at the ceiling and then closed my eyes, wondering if the darkness I saw was the same darkness she saw. If she saw anything at all, but who was I kidding? She was dreaming.

My phone chimed with a notification, and I quickly opened my eyes to check who it was. Marleen asked if there were any changes, but there weren't any. I exhaled and replied with the latest updates. Poor Marleen, Nana, and she were like sisters, and seeing a friend like this must have been crushing.

Being by her side like this and me had taken enormous strength. Also, for my grandmother to be sick like this with my grandfather gone and Mama far away, who knows where, I grasped her hand and kissed it, hoping that it would let her know that I was there, but I feared speaking to her. What if she couldn't hear me or understand what I was saying? Janey Moon, who would have thought you would be in this position?

Another hour passed, and a nurse checked on her again, but there were no signs of her waking up. I forced myself to eat within that time to not drop from exhaustion. I plaited my hair to find something to do other than being consumed by my thoughts. It was 10 pm, but it didn't seem like it. Time seemed to stop for me when she dropped to the ground. The disgusting, wet, dirty concrete ground. I rocked back and forth as I continued to plait my hair. Interestingly enough, the sounds from her monitor could match the beat of a song, distracting the mind.

Clueless, I plaited too fast and cut my finger with my nail and screeched in agony. I sucked on the blood on my finger. It was only a little blood, but the cut stung severely. I walked to the closet to see if they had antibiotic wipes and band-aids. I used my dominant hand to search, but it appeared to be only blankets and useless junk.

So, I closed the closet door and turned around to see Nana's eyes open. I jumped in shock at first but then smiled as I gradually called her name. She checked her surroundings, squinted her eyes, and moved her body. I walked over and grabbed her hand. "You're awake, Nana!" I said happily.

She was confused and drowsy as she tried to focus on me. I whispered, "It's Aira. Your granddaughter." She smiled and gripped my hand tight, not happily, but in fear. She tried to talk, but her tongue seemed to be in the way. "Do you need water? Is your mouth numb?" I panicked and pressed the nurse button.

I kissed her hand and said, "It's okay. I'll pour you some water, and they will check you out."

"Mm," she said, as if in pain. *I do hope she wasn't in pain.*

The nurse entered the room and checked her out by flashing a light in her eyes, checking her vitals, and asking her questions. She then called on the doctor, who did the same. I poured water into a cup, raised her bed, and let her sip small amounts. "She appears to be adjusting, but her vitals are normal."

"What does that mean?"

"It appears she passed out due to dehydration, so she will need to become coherent again."

I had a look of fear written all over my face. "How should I put it? She must regain her senses; it varies depending on the person, but hopefully not too long."

"She drinks water more than the average person. How can she be dehydrated," I said, shocked.

"That is what we are trying to factor in."

"How long will it take her to come to her senses?"

"It depends. It might take a few hours or two to three days."

"That long?"

"I know, but it's up to the patient."

"How did I not know this?" I said, anxious.

"Yes, um, we discussed it with— a Marleen Cusack. She didn't tell you?" He said, looking down at his medical board, then back up at me.

"No. I sent her home without asking—I've had so much on my mind that I didn't even think about it." I said, teary-eyed and tired. *I don't even know why she didn't tell me herself.*

"It's okay. It can happen to anyone."

I looked down at my grandmother. "Not to me."

"Well, she did appear to be dehydrated for some time. It's good that you gave her water, at least. Nothing to worry about too much right now."

"Okay," I said, relieved. "What about her test results?"

"I'm still ruling out some factors, but you should have a diagnosis by the morning."

"Does it have to take that long?"

"I'm sorry for the inconvenience, but I have a lot of patients and will try to get to everyone as fast as possible."

'No, it's okay. Do what you have to." I smiled anxiously.

He nodded and did a tight lip smile. "If you want, we'll get you a bed to rest."

I shook my head. "No, I don't think I will be getting rest anytime soon."

"Okay." He sympathetically touched my arm. "We'll keep you posted."

"Thank you again, doctor—"

"Phillips. Call on me if you need anything."

"Okay."

Doctor Phillips asked the nurse to administer a 30 ml/kg IV dose after the first bag for dehydration, which might help her recover and eat some food. She had drifted back unconscious, but this time, she was just asleep. I sat back down beside her, feeling the soft strands of her hair under my fingertips as she peacefully slept. The quiet room seemed to amplify my sense of solitude, and tears welled up in my eyes as I watched her rest. She looked so serene, yet the weight of responsibility weighed heavily on my shoulders. It shouldn't have been just Marleen and me here. Mama and Pa should have been here too, but somehow, it always seemed to be our duty to take care of everything.

The entire family was falling apart, and we relied on avoidance to cope. Our lives were in shambles. I could sense death looming, but I always tried to avoid it. When my Pa passed away, I couldn't bear to see him being lowered into the ground. It unsettled me deeply. A grave is more than just a deep hole. It can be a hospital bed, a bottle of liquor, old age, or slaving away at the same job for the past 30 years. Everyone's death was different. I pondered what mine could be—family, love, or loneliness.

I slipped into bed next to Nana within a second. I pressed my ear to her chest, listening to her heart. It felt irregular and didn't sound as strong as when I was a baby. But I didn't care; she would live until she was 205 if I willed it. I could take anyone else leaving me behind, but not her. She had to be next to me. She may not have been my mother, but she was my true love. She was my nana. I held her hand for comfort, but she would need it more than anyone else. As I closed my eyes, I felt my body slowly relax. The only sound clouding my eardrum was the rhythmic throbbing of her heart. Her chest's gentle rise and fall beneath my ear was calming, and I was completely wrapped in the still moment.

# 1. The Date

**It** was somewhat funny. All the love in the world could not save her from disappointment. Things crashed around her. She was doomed since birth, and even the love of the ones who took pity could not suffice. A lonely existence, no matter what anyone called it, was lonely. She was alone, and that was all she knew in the present. She could never truly love herself as others have not done the same. She had love come and go. She felt thawed out, as if she had been cold for a long time. Images and images of disappointment and sorrow were what she had left over. She was drained, incomplete, and left alone. She liked to think she was special. She had this hidden destiny to save the world or find a purpose for herself; it always dawned on her. A chain latched on so thick she could not think straight—a burden she never understood nor wanted but would come to appreciate in time. Not realizing lonely is never really lonely and she would not carry it all by herself; she still does not know how to exist in the world anymore.

She moved as delicately as the air in the room. Her thick brunette shoulder-length hair swayed as she did. Not a strand disturbed as beautiful as when she was born. Her caramel skin glistened when a stray light broke from the sunset within the white curtains hiding the balcony. Her brown eyes were going in circles as she dropped eye drops into her eyes. It was almost fall, and her eyes tended to dry out on occasion. As her bear-shaped nose sniffled as a reaction, she examined herself in the nearest mirror in the living room. Her heart-shaped lips kissed each other to expand the overspread of lip gloss. She was pinching her round face to make her cheeks blush for effect. The cherry red nails went perfectly with her cherry red dress. A fitted dress with a neckline reaching the shoulders and ankle length with the back out. She had black leather boots to pair with them. Chanel #5 oozed out of every pore of hers as she had sprayed it about six times earlier in the day.

Her purse lay flat on her lap. It was black and encrusted with white and grey flowers. It had a faded gold handle and pouch. It was a vintage purse her nana passed on to her. Truly the style when she was alive. Her grandmother wore it everywhere like a prize. It warmed her heart to have such sentiment in a jarring moment like this. It comforted her. She hated makeup. She could only convince herself of lip gloss or lip balm. Her eyelashes were long and black, so mascara was unnecessary. The same is true with her eyebrows; they were not too thick, but not thin. She had a set of 5 piercings on her ears. Two piercings on the left ear and three on the right. All were occupied with gold studded earrings. She had one tattoo: a small trail of roses on her wrist, three to be exact. As each rose led to another, at least one petal and leaf fell. She also wore a thin gold initial necklace with the letter M to bring it together.

Her eyes had fallen heavy. It felt like they could not move. They were piercing through an all-white apartment. It made her feel out of her mind. She was surrounded by such a cut and clean white space with minimalism down to the foundation, which was even bone white. She never understood the fear of personality. She missed how houses had character. She always had a fondness for cluttered spaces as they give insight into someone's habits, comforts, fears, hopes, dreams, and memories. This place was like a ghost, hidden, cold, and unmemorable. It had dimmed lighting, so you needed a magnifying glass to see anything.

That is why she couldn't move—stuck in one spot at the edge of a white leather couch. It was sleek and clean without a crack. The pain she felt every time she tried to find comfort in that one spot. It pricked her with every movement she made. Her body's friction created heat the more she moved. He was nowhere to be found. The more time passed, the more nervous she became. She did not know him, which was reflected in his home. All white, everything down to the nonexistent dust in the air. She wondered why she agreed to meet him. He is not even her type. He is decent-looking and has an excellent style. He was a mystery. All she could think about was his marshy eyes and profound dimples. That was the most normal thing about him.

Everything else about him was unusual. She never liked men with pitch-black hair. She never liked men who were as pale as the moon's light. She never liked men with perfect smiles. She wanted her men to be present, imperfect, and predictable. He was none of those things.

She could not put a finger on it, but the feeling did make her stomach burn. It was not butterflies. They barely said two words to each other.

They passed each other every day outside their apartment, and nothing. She did not know why he was confident to ask her out now. If anything, they were strangers and nothing more—but here she was. Growing impatient, she tapped the tips of her boots together, humming a song she did not remember the lyrics to. He appeared in the corner of her eye, and her heart skipped a beat. He stood in the bedroom doorway with a black turtleneck, black high-waisted suit pants, and an alluring dark cherry-red suit jacket with matching shoes. His hair was a medium to long haircut. She liked to call it messy hair, but it was combed out of his face this time. She noticed he fixed his bright green eyes on her and began to mutter something. She focused on his chiseled chin more than his words. Wondering how perfect a jawline could be and how sharp it was. Trying to reflect on his words, she asked, "What did you say?"

He moved closer to her and did a spin. He asked, "How do I look?"

Feeling bad for not listening, she laughed nervously and said, "You look lavish." She could not call him handsome because he wasn't her type or all that attractive, but she could not help but admit he knew how to dress.

A big grin appeared as he said, "That is a new one. Most people call me handsome or charming, but never lavish. Not to say offense is taken. It is just new, and I like it. Oh—um, where are my manners? We never introduced ourselves, now that I think about it." He chuckled afterward. She agreed with him. When he asked her out on this date, he never once mentioned his name, nor did she. That spoke volumes.

She forced a nervous smile. "That is okay. Neither did I. My name is Aira Moon, but I prefer people to call me Moon—

only that. The people who called me Aira are either dead or removed from my life. All I ask is to be called Moon. And you?"

He put his hands in his pockets and looked Moon in her eyes without batting an eyelash. "The name is Dawn. Nothing more. Nothing less. I do not care for my last name, so I like it when people call me Dawn. The only people who know my last name are me and me!" He let out a small laugh. Moon laughed too unexpectedly, but she knew he had to have parents or friends who did. She could save the significant questions for another time unless he is an orphan.

"You look exquisite, by the way. You will have all eyes on you tonight, including mine. I have to say, you are very gorgeous." He blew a whistle afterward and smiled, "I just got to grab my keys, and we can head out. Okay?"

Moon reassured him with a smile and said, "Okay."

Dawn headed towards the kitchen to grab his wallet and keys. Moon decided to stretch her legs by standing up. She never felt more comfortable relieving herself from such a stiff couch. Her couch might have been thrifted, but it was softer and made you feel light as a feather. She stood by the door to get another glimpse of her outfit with the mirror on the far right. *Gorgeous. Exquisite.* Those words swam through her mind. No one has called her that in such a long time. Well, only her nana. She looked down at the purse again. This time, gripping it tight, hoping to get the comfort she felt earlier, but *nothing*. Her eyes shifted to Dawn as he put his black trench coat on and grabbed her shabby, deep blue vintage coat that reminded her of the ocean sea. Most of everything she wore was vintage, passed down, or thrifted. He stuffed his wallet in his pants and let his keys hang on his index finger. He had a class ring on. The stone resembled the blood moon and was encrusted with his class years in gold. She always saw him with it on. *It must be sentimental.* Like everything else in his apartment, his kitchen was white, with only a toaster and appliances in sight. *Unmemorable.*

He went to Moon, helped her put her coat on, and opened the door.

He said, "Ladies first."

She thought of him as a real gentleman and polite. Who would have thought they would walk side by side to go on a date? She certainly did not. She stopped in her tracks once they arrived at his car. She was stunned to see that he had a 1967 black Chevy Impala. However, she did not show it and did not want to seem impressed. It was a nice classic car, one she would love to have if she had the money. Dawn opened the door for her to get in and headed to the driver's side. He stopped when he received a phone call and stood outside the door talking to whoever it was. Moon couldn't help but admire the car's features. All black leather seats, a cross hanging from the rearview mirror, and an air freshener hung on the inner car vents. It smelled of vanilla, which she didn't mind. She thought at least this smell did not make her queasy. One thing she hated was fragrances that made her nauseous because of their potency. She wanted to snoop in the glove compartment, but it felt intrusive. However, he had his back turned while pacing on the phone.

What he doesn't know wouldn't hurt him, and her curiosity would be satisfied.

She leaned forward and opened the glove compartment. She made sure to check occasionally if his back was turned to her. Inside, she found small Ziplock bags, each labeled with something important. She carefully searched to avoid disturbing anything that he might notice. Looking at each label, she couldn't help but wonder why a "perfect" guy like Dawn would want a 1967 Chevy Impala. It seemed too old school and imperfect for him. He did not seem edgy to her, or at least a guy who knew about cars. Maybe he thought it was trendy or bought it to show off; that seemed more plausible. Turning her attention back to the Ziplock bags with labels of little interest, like sanitize, documents, and utensils, she noted that at least he was organized. However, one bag had no label, thickness, and dates on the back of a plain white surface. She was about to reach for it, but the call he was on was ending, so she had to hurry and put everything back in place; so much for figuring him out even a little bit.

She sighed as she leaned back into the seat and buckled her seat belt. Oddly, she was calm and not scared of being caught. Dawn got into the car and dropped his phone into the cup holder. He looked over at Moon and smiled.

"Sorry about that. I had some business to take care of. I hope it did not spoil the mood."

"No, it didn't. I didn't mind at all. Who was it?"

"It doesn't matter. It's all been taken care of. Besides, I am more focused on being nervous about our date than anything. I am surprised you agreed to begin with. We passed each other every day, and not one glance you gave me, so I am shocked I am even sitting here," he said as he started the car.

Moon knew the ride would be long, agreeing that she did not glance too much toward his way whenever they passed each other in the building. This made her want to proceed with the questions, having given him this chance and not wanting to end up in a Hitchcock film. She adjusted herself to be comfortable and began her interrogation.

"You are right. I barely noticed you, if we are being honest. I mean, I did but didn't. I usually do not go on dates since the passing of my grandmother a month ago. Ever since then, I have kept to myself. I kept to the shadows, not attracting attention I didn't want. When I saw you confront me, I figured it was an opportunity to get out of my stuffy apartment and get to know someone." She tried not to make eye contact. "I find it funny because before my grandma died. She made me promise to put myself out there and find my people. Whatever that means. She told me to "maybe fall in love" as if there were no bigger issues to worry about. That was my grandmother, you know. A big heart no matter the circumstances," she awkwardly chuckled.

Moon held back tears as she realized she was sharing too much. She gathered her emotions and continued the conversation. "Sorry if I was rambling. Sometimes, I get caught in the wind of it all and get carried away."

Dawn kept his eyes on the road while flashing his pearly white teeth.

"No, it is okay. I do not mind the rambling. I like getting to know you. I mean, we are going on a date to get to know each other, and I admire how you value family. It is sweet. Also, sorry about your grandmother, my condolences if I did not say it before."

"Thank you. How about you? Do you have family and friends? I mean, I always see you alone. I could have sworn you are a loner by choice like me," Moon wanted to poke fun at him, but she wanted to know more about this mystery man who had her trust. "Also, where are you taking me, and how far is it? We were on the road for a minute—don't answer all at once," she chuckled to assess if the mood was still light and not heavy from her little rant.

"I did not know you were so curious about me. I can answer all at once if you like. Anything for a pretty lady." He side-eyed Moon with a smile. She wondered why he smiled so much and if it hindered his true feelings. Was he genuinely happy? It irked her to the core. She could never be that smiley, at least never again.

"Well, our destination is not that far, about 20 minutes longer. As for the date, I cannot reveal it because it is a surprise. As lovely as your charms are, you are not getting that out of me."

He winked at Moon with his dominant dimple prominent. "I value family and friends just as much as you. I have had my challenges. Not to go into detail. Family is a sore subject, and I don't like talking about it. I would happily answer if you had asked me two years ago about family, but not tonight, okay? As for friends, I have two people in my life I consider my best friends. Their names are Enzo and Star. We have been friends since we were in diapers. They have been in my life for as long as I can remember. Enzo moved to Las Vegas last year, and Star is a newlywed, so she has been building her own family. I do not get to see them much, but we keep in contact now and then. I love them with all my heart, and they are my family. Anything else you are curious about?"

Moon pondered on one question she was hesitant to ask but gave it a shot. She had been dying to ask him since they met at his apartment. "Yes. Why did you ask me out? Why did I catch your eye? There are other women in our apartment complex, real beauties. From the life you live, they would be more of your type. But I hate to jump to conclusions."

She looked out the car window after asking such a question. Usually, she would not ask anyone why they liked her or not. She tended not to care but was burning to know about Dawn. That same burning knot appeared in her lower stomach again. She started to think about what he would answer. She did not know if he would say he was bored, his friends bet him, or if she looked easy compared to the other women. He had not answered her question. She started to think he took offense. The car had driven up a hill as they closed in on their destination for the date. She did not know whether to repeat the question or sit quietly and cluelessly. She became impatient, and then the car came to a halt.

Dawn said, "We are here. Give me a few minutes to double-check things, and I will come back. Okay." She agreed with a nod while still looking out the window. Before she knew it, he was out of the car and up the path. As far as she could see, they were up on a hill. On the outskirts of the city. She noticed the city lights, buildings, and cars create twinkles like the stars in the sky but brighter. She could see a greenhouse from a distance. It had lights, but she could not see anything else until she was closer. It reminded her of an igloo. It was an old greenhouse based on its faded color. It looked green but had blue hues when you stared long enough. She was in the middle of nowhere, not one person in sight.

Dawn headed back towards the car. She prepared herself and had an ounce of hope that it was a pleasant surprise. She would hate to be on a boring date when she could have better things to do. She crossed her fingers and left it to the universe. Dawn opened the door. She noticed he had something in his hand. It was a silk cloth. She backed up and had a look of confusion on her face.

"Do not worry. It is a blindfold for the surprise. I promise it will be worth it, but I understand if you feel uncomfortable." He looked concerned.

Moon leaned forward and made sure to state the obvious. "I am not comfortable. Your nice dawn, but it is the first date, and we are in the middle of nowhere."

He bent down to her eye level on one knee. Looking gently into her eyes, he said, "I respect that. As an alternative, how about you put your hands over your eyes? It would make you feel better and make me feel better if the surprise were not spoiled." He gave a sincere smile and put his hand out.

She put her worry aside and let him guide her. If this were a trap, she would have her mace and taser if he decided to get out of hand. No matter how cute her date's dimples were, a girl like herself needed to be cautious. He trailed behind her, and he guided her along. She could feel the dampened ground as she walked. The chilly wind made her shiver, but she had kept her eyes covered. The sounds of cicadas blurred her hearing while she tried to identify where Dawn was leading her. As they got closer, she got hold of a familiar smell. It gave her flashbacks to her childhood when she and Nana tended to the local kids' community garden. She guessed it had to be planted, but roses, to be specific.

They came to a stop. He walked in front of her, and she heard the creak of a door.

He asked, "Are you ready?" The suspense was building, and Moon was excited to see the surprise, predominantly since she smelt roses. Roses were her favorite, and they always made her smile.

"Yes. I am ready."

"Are you sure because it does not sound like it? I need better enthusiasm than that." He taunted.

"Dawn—come on. I promise I am excited. Show me already."

"Mm—I do not know." He taunted again.

"Dawn!"

"Okay, okay! Open your eyes," he laughed, waiting to see her reaction.

When she opened her eyes, her face melted with glee. She was in awe of the place. She saw a greenhouse filled with red roses that filled the entire room from back to front. She could not believe it. She loved roses because they reminded her of her childhood and made her feel at peace. She noticed an open space in the middle with a small dining table set for two, with a candle centered on the table and more candles here and there for decoration. Her eyes couldn't help but wonder. It was everything and more than what she expected. No one had done this for her before. She turned and smiled at Dawn. He closed the door behind him and stood next to her.

He asked, "Do you like it? I hope I outdid myself and did not let you down." Moon responded by kissing Dawn on the cheek. It was a small and soft kiss on his dimple as he smiled. His skin had a glossiness to it, but not overpowering. She could not help but think how smooth his skin was as her lips parted from his face, something she also liked about him. Grabbing her by the hand, he gently led her to the table, pulled out the chair, and helped her with her coat, placing it on the back of the chair.

As she sat, he asked, "You want to see a magic trick?"

Moon raised an eyebrow and smiled, hoping this trick came with food because she was starving. Her nerves took her mind away from only eating a banana that morning. She had a habit of not eating until the end of the day. It was her thing, and she barely questioned it. She assumed it was her mental state and how it filled the belly. Moon nodded with a polite smile. He told her to pay attention to his hands. He walked over to one of the roses and pricked a petal. He put the petal in his hand and had the other on top. He circled his palms together and opened them up. The petal was gone.

She watched his hand while giving him the benefit of the doubt. She did much hoping tonight. She hoped this trick was not him making a rose petal disappear alone. It would take his points down a notch, not that he had any. "Just keep watch and wait." He was so gleeful doing this trick. He seemed so content doing these things for her. He was like a schoolboy, finally getting his chance with a crush. How odd, she thought. That school crush would be her. Zoning out with her eyes falling onto the roses behind Dawn, a bouquet of them appeared in his hand. She looked over instantly and was confused. He did not move from that very spot. She remembered he was rubbing his hands together, barely paying attention, but she could still see him. Confused about how he did it, she asked, "Are those for me?" *I wanted them to be. Roses are my weakness.* She gave him a longing look with her doe eyes.

"Of course, they are for you. I would not have done a trick if they were not. Only for the prettiest girl in the room."

He handed the roses to Moon. He glanced back longingly as she continued to smell the roses and smile. She could tell he was surprised by how much she was smiling, and internally, she felt like a *little girl* kicking her feet. Dozens of roses pressed against her heart as she held them tightly with her nana's purse. She was the sentimental kind.

"Thank you, Dawn." She paused and looked down at the beguiling roses. Then, she raised her head, looking at Dawn, and said, "I could just hug you," giving him an adorned look. He was starting to charm her, or at least his actions were. She wanted to know how he knew her so well. She decided to ask him later because she would be smitten if he kept behaving like this. The hug would have to wait, and a kiss would suffice because she was starving and didn't want to leave her chair.

He mentioned putting the food in the storage room and that he would have to bring it out. He stepped away briefly while Moon placed the roses on the table. She sat silently, her elbow on the table and her face in her hand, admiring the roses, candles, and table. The table and chairs were made of mahogany. The white tablecloth was cotton with lace patterns of embroidery. The candle was black and held in a bronze candle holder. Her index finger traced the patterns on the table over and over. Feeling a slight breeze, she got goosebumps down her arm. She was someone who preferred the spring. She disliked the cold of fall and winter and couldn't understand people's fascination with those seasons. She found them depressing and isolating, even the holidays associated with them. The memory of her nana passing away last month sent a tremor down her spine. It always made her feel dull, as she was the only family she had.

Her nana was the only reason she enjoyed the holidays. Christmas was special to them for a time, even though her nana's favorite holiday was Easter. She celebrated because her nana knew she needed something similar to a childhood.

She remembered how early it would be on Christmas morning, and she would sneak into her nana's bed. She loved the smell of flowers that came off her and the warmth of her embrace when her nana realized she was there. It was easy to fall asleep near her nana because she felt safe. It would always be sore for her. An ache of pain for a person who was always there for her, loved her, and raised her. Fall would always be too cold for her.

She lifted her head when she heard the squeak of a door shut behind her. Dawn appeared with a tray of food and drinks, setting them on the table. He placed the bread and salad on the side of the table next to her roses. He placed covered plates on each side and opened a bottle of something she couldn't identify. It turned out to be red wine, the sweet kind. He also had water, which she was grateful for because she didn't drink. He placed two glasses on the table and poured wine into one shakily but didn't pour any into hers. Instead, he poured water into her glass. She sat up straight and looked directly at him.

"How did you know I did not drink? People barely know that and assume I do."

Half his dimples emerged as he struggled to suppress a grin and said, "One thing to know about me is that I tend to pay attention often. I tend to watch others and their habits. Whether it was by coincidence or by being observant. I just noticed that on occasion, when passing by each other, you either had water or juice, never alcohol. I assumed you did not prefer it. Whether I was wrong or not." He made a conscious effort to avoid eye contact as he didn't want to seem strange.

She smirked, "I am the same way. I observe out of my weird fascination with humanity, whether it is willful or not. There is nothing weird about it. Thank you for being considerate," she said.

Dawn started blushing as she saw him turning redder than a ghost pepper. After serving drinks, he removed the metal cloches from the plates, revealing spaghetti with parmesan and cilantro.

*I wonder if it has extra sauce. I always forget the extra sauce; maybe he did, too.* It was her favorite dish, and she ate it every Friday at this sweet and forgotten diner named Kings across from their apartment building. *It was my nana's favorite, too; I would not even eat it if it were not for her.*

She could see that he took his notes seriously. As he sat across from her, she realized how observant he was. She wondered if he had intentionally chosen to wear her favorite color, as his suit jacket was the exact shade of red that she favored.

As they began to eat, she took the first bite and closed her eyes as her taste buds relished the goodness. She licked the leftover sauce from her lips, not caring about the heat. She was starving and thirsty, so she drank water from her wine glass to wash away the savory taste of onion and caramelized tomato. After a few more bites, they resumed their earlier conversation from the car. She wanted to hear his response to the question, but she realized she was becoming nervous, her palms starting to sweat, making it difficult to ask again. "So, will you answer my question from earlier, or will we hear the scraping sound of our plates the rest of the night?" she said invitingly.

"No! We would not want that, would we," he said teasingly with a flirtatious smirk.

She did a slight eye roll while twisting spaghetti on her fork. "I did not know I was in the hot seat. If I had known, I would have answered more quickly, but there is nothing like a little tension," he smiled. "I would hate for you to jump to conclusions. It would break my heart. Better yet, it would ruin our night," he said as he smiled again.

She felt like all the smiling and hesitation would kill her before she finished her food. He sat up straight, placed both elbows on the table in a prayerful manner, and looked directly at her with his deep emerald eyes. His gaze traced every detail of her face and every movement. He appeared to be contemplating his response, which was essential to her. She didn't want just any words to leave his lips. She had never really noticed his lips before, and she found the shape of his cupid's bow fascinating, although not particularly pleasing to her. She usually preferred men with fuller lips but not excessively so. They had to be just right, not too overpowering, but still capable of bringing her pleasure. Soft lips had the ability to warm her at night, something she was weak for. She didn't enjoy making out, but with the right person, it was worth it. His lips were soft, moisturized, pink, and slender. They were not too thin; they had a certain liveliness to them. With the right expertise, she believed a woman could work with them. As he considered his response, his ring finger gently traced his lips.

She continued to eat her meal while he lost himself in thought. As she reached for a piece of bread, she noticed him pausing, making her stop. She pulled her arm back and placed the bread on her plate, wishing she had some butter. She thought to herself, *"Who forgets butter?"* He then rested his arms flat on the table.

He looked at Moon again and said, "I went over the question you asked in my head. I thought of a million things I could say, but I want to stay as close to the truth as possible." He used his ring finger to make circles on his thumb.

"I was new to your part of the city. I had already decided to move there, and once settled, I decided to familiarize myself with the block. I tried to find places I knew I wanted to become a regular, whether it was a library, coffee shop, theater, or diner," he smiled, looked down, and said, "One day, I was tired from exploring most of every shop on the block that I decided to get something to eat. Lo and behold, a little rundown diner across from our apartment building was open. Most days, I would think it was abandoned because of how worn down it was." Looking back up at Moon, his fingers moved more intensely. "I walk across the street and head into King's Diner. I sit down and try to figure out what to order. I called the waitress, and she asked me what I wanted to eat, so I told her I wanted a salad and apple pie. She takes my order and heads off. I settled down in my seat, and I heard this voice. It sounded like the older voice of a woman, and she said, "Eating healthy, are we? How will you come to our part of town and not order our famous king burger." Mind you, I do not know her. I figured I would converse with the locals since I was to be living there."

Moon found the story irrelevant to what she had asked, but she continued to listen to understand what he was trying to say. She wasn't sure if he didn't know himself or if he didn't like her. She believed that attraction alone would not be enough for her.

He leaned back in the seat but kept his hands on the table. "To keep it short, I asked her how she knew I was not from there, and she said it was my attitude aside from the ascent. I laughed, and then she laughed. I told her I did not eat meat much, but I would take her advice on the famous burger since she was the fifth person to recommend it. We kept talking till my order came, discussing the city's restaurants, museums, libraries, and theaters. She welcomed me to the city and said I was the most handsome young man she had seen in a long time. Around that time, my food came, and a young woman came rushing to her as soon as the plate hit my table."

He pulled his hands into his lap and started looking at her endearingly. "She was telling her grandmother how sorry she was for being late and getting caught up. Her grandmother did not mind and requested a kiss; as she did, her grandmother made a brief introduction. After that, a thought of me left their minds as they talked. If I remember correctly, they ordered spaghetti with cilantro with extra sauce. Mind you, I could not help but overhear how gentle, loving, and enamored with each other they were. Something I have always wished to have with my family. Her granddaughter had the most beautiful brunette hair. It lay thick on her shoulders, but that was not the best part. She had these big babydoll eyes that could make you melt, how every expression she made came through her eyes. She would frantically curl her index finger in her hair to distract from her burst of energy. It was just so refreshing seeing love like that," he smiled slightly, "It was a love so agreeable," he paused, "Who would not want that kind of love? I did not think I would be passing by that love every day. I did not know how badly I yearned for love until it sat right before me, just as you are now," he said.

Everything burned in silence. Everyone and everything froze in time. The roses stood still, the wind slammed through the greenhouse's rotten cracks, and the glass scratched from the sounds of cicadas. The concrete floor was so sandy that Moon boots could grind a hole into the shoe's sole. The distant sirens of the city could not even leave a tap on their eardrums.

Everything burned in silence. Their eyes were not leaving one another. It felt treacherous to do so. Their lips ached to move but were wired shut. *My eyes—My eyes. My nana. My love. Our love.* These words pounded in her head and heart. How could she not remember? He struck a blow so hard even her pride could not fight. Her shield was down. She felt wetness consuming her cheeks. She hated it when she became teary-eyed and red. It made her feel so vulnerable and silly. He met her nana. He talked to her. He knew her, but not as she knew her. She could not fathom him learning of her in this way. Two strangers who did not flinch at each other's existence was a better ideal in her head.

She burned inside. Her feet and body wanted to find the nearest exit. She needed to escape. She felt heartache. She felt rage. She felt tenderness. It was not his fault. She asked for an answer, and she got it. She wanted to feel relief, but she was mixed up. Every fleeting minute, she tried to calm herself; he would be sitting across from her, staring with fondness. It was a fondness someone with deep affection for someone would have. It was like he was following her lead. If she moved, he moved. If she was quiet, he was quiet. If she made a sound, he would make a sound. Such a gentleman, she thought to herself. The tension lay thick in the air with a side of hesitation. She had no words, only thoughts, and those she did not want to share.

Her lips ran dry from crying, and she could feel the middle of her lower lip crack. She held on to the glass of water and drank from it as if her life depended on it. Swallow after swallow, she tried to think of what to say, but nothing. She felt as if her throat was closing. He leaned forward and placed his hand on hers. She jolted back. How dare he touch her, she felt. He hid this for so long. He passed her every day with the knowledge of this. He knew of her nana and her momentarily, nor showed an ounce of support.

The thought irked her as if something grimy brushed against her. He barely knew them, but he knew how much of a wreck she was after her nana's death. She barely had friends or family, and she just needed an ounce of love when she was nothing but a black hole consuming itself. She did not know whether to *yell, be quiet, or cry.* All she wanted was water. She grabbed the pitcher and poured glass after glass. Eventually, Dawn snatched the glass and pitcher from her. He sat it down on the floor behind him. She was burning so badly that she needed to cool off. He did not make it easy, and it drove her crazy.

"I—" He started to say. "I am sorry. I did not mean to upset you. I thought it could convey how I feel and help you understand why I asked you out. I did not mean to upset you. Your grandmother is a sore subject but a beautiful memory, nonetheless. I would have never said anything if I knew it would make you hurt," he said softly, "I would never want to hurt you." Moon stood up from the table and walked over to a patch of roses. As she used her index finger to trace the petals, she couldn't help but dwell on what had prevented him from expressing his feelings a month earlier. She would have been more receptive to him at that time. She can hardly remember what she was like before Nana's death and before her childhood began to unravel. That's why she prefers to be called Moon. The moon was like an ocean, deep but distant—an untouchable beauty yet felt and cherished.

She stared at the petals she was tracing, and all she could say was, "I know. Hurt is its own entity. It hides. It lingers. You never know when it strikes because the playing field is never level. It is just something that exists but is never controlled. A person can't outrun it. It has been around before we even existed. So, I know." Her back was still turned to dawn, and he walked over and stood next to her.

He looked down at the roses but still watched her from the corner of his eye. He let out a small sigh. "I know what you are thinking. Why didn't I say anything before? The only thing I can say is that it was not my place," he paused for a moment, "before I was scared. I did not think a woman so down-to-earth and beautiful would go for me. You already knew me as the aloof bachelor who flirted with the women in our building. Also, there were rumors of your grandmother being sick; then she passed, so you needed space. Room to breathe. It was chicken of me not to acknowledge that moment and a potential need for a shoulder to lean on," he moved closer next to her, "Trust me. I missed you every day since that day. Love from afar can be scary, especially the pursuit of it. I did come to the funeral and put flowers on her grave. You had already gone by then. She had this rare kindness and welcoming presence. I knew I had to say goodbye," he said.

She calmed her nerves and looked up at him, noticing his strong jawline and intense gaze.

"Sometimes saying goodbye is not enough. Not for me, at least. Thank you for going to her funeral and saying goodbye. She would have loved it," she stepped back, "These roses are beautiful. It is heartbreaking how they fade after a time. Love can be the same way. It can be loving yet fleeting, but who could tell the difference? I did not mean to get angry at you. I am all jumbled up right now. I hope I did not ruin this night for you because it was beautiful, though I tried not to show it. Thank you."

He reached for her hand. She felt the roughness of his dazzling ring. The jewel seemed to look right at her, she thought. He gently grabbed her hand and led her back to the chair. As she sat, he kneeled on one knee and put his hand on her knee, moving towards her inner thigh.

"Are you going to be okay?"

She took a minute to answer. "Yes, I think I will be okay," she said as she breathed in and out.

Reassuringly, he said, "If not, let me take you home, but if so, we can continue our date and enjoy ourselves," his hand softly caressed her knee as if she were a delicate thing to break. She nodded slowly in agreement. He removed his hand and went back to the storage room. When he returned, she was still in the same spot. He placed a small, blue, chipped speaker on a shelf and connected it to his phone. Moon unzipped her boots, practically ripping them off. Dawn put his phone next to the speaker and rushed over to her. He pulled her up from the chair to dance, and she was glad. If they were going to dance, it was better for her to be in less pain with bare feet than tight shoes. She appreciated how he tried to cheer her up in these small, inconsequential moments. She was about five inches shorter than him and had to stand on the tips of her toes. She placed her arms around his neck as he placed his around her waist. The song sounded familiar as they danced, but she did not care to ask what it was because her throat still felt dry after all the crying. She felt awkward and small in his presence, but he did not see her that way. As close as she was to him, she could hear the pitter-patter beats of his heart. It was as if chaos erupted on how his heart would stay on beat, then off. Her feet started to hurt from standing on her tippy toes, evident in how she winced because of the concrete floor.

She felt his hands lift her gently onto his shoes, and he said, "There—is that better?"

Moon nodded in response. She didn't care if he did all the talking for the rest of the night because her head and heart hurt too much. She knew she was being a bit dramatic, but she couldn't even form a word, let alone a sentence. She didn't care what her actions portrayed anymore. She laid her head on his chest, listening to the profound movement of his heart, and it calmed her mind as she calmed his. Their bodies moved as the music grew louder, drowning out the burning silence they had before. They moved fluidly as water. They were connected like magnets, like cats on a hot tin roof. One of his hands rubbed up and down her back. She assumed he felt it would make her feel better, and it did for a while. They danced in circles near the rose patches, not too fast or slow. His grip around her waist became more assertive, but he did it in a way she didn't notice. They kept going around in circles as the songs changed, and she grew complacent, becoming immersed in his essence. His smell hinted at white musk and floral scent but wasn't too strong. It was exactly right. It was perfect for her to fall into his arms. She removed her hands from his neck to his chest, and he repositioned himself. It was like she was a cradled baby, pure in all forms and safe. His chin nuzzled into the top of her thick hair, consuming her smell and basking in their comfort for one another at that moment.

Her cherry-red dress dragged across the floor, collecting dirt at the ends of the hem. Her eyes closed as she listened closely to the music, which matched the rhythm of his heart. She was forcing herself to cry as she thought of all the events in her life. She slightly adjusted her head under his chin as she could feel his facial muscles move. She figured he was smiling or smirking when he finally got his hug. This was the most peaceful she had felt since her nana died. The pain and restlessness in her had become quiet. She did not know if the mere dancing or Dawn kept her at ease for such a night. Most nights, she would cry, eat less, and find anything to distract her mind from the waste of life she felt she had. Moon had goals, plans, and drives that came to a halt for her nana. Constant doctors' appointments, bill upkeep, house upkeep, and medicine kept her at bay from those dreams. She would never regret taking care of her nana to her last breath, but by God, she wished she had leaned on others more and didn't cut everyone out. It was hard for her to embrace another, even with such vulnerability. She didn't want the dance to end but knew it would.

Abruptly, they came to a stop. Peeking from under his chin and looking up, she saw him looking down at her. They were in the same position; their eyes met, and Dawn smiled. She hated it when he smiled so much, not because it was an ugly smile, but because his smile could melt her down to her soul. He had this aura that made the inside of her stomach boil, her heart race, and her mind clutter. She tried to resist because it always made her want to cry. It made her feel safe and open. Not knowing the reason made her scared and hateful towards that ever-so-lovely smile.

He was easy on the eye and on the heart. What could she do but run? The strategy did not work, even when she passed him daily without knowing who he was. How could she not remember those forest green eyes that could stare at her for hours in passing and pierce whatever she had left of a soul? As they made eye contact for two minutes, the music stopped, and

Dawn broke whatever unspeakable silence they had between each other.

"You have such beautiful eyes. They flutter so nicely, big and brown. Anyone could get lost in them. Fading into you would be everyone's fate if they stood as close to you as I do now." He said, pining.

"They say you can tell a lot about a person by their eyes. What do my eyes say? If you faded into me, what would you lose, and what would you keep? Some might call them windows to the soul, but to me, they are just eyes. Unfortunate for what they have seen yet treasured for what they have not seen."

He tightened his grip on Moon and moved his face an inch away from hers.

"They show me you. I see you, and I fall without hesitation. I would lose all of me in you and save nothing. The only thing I would get to keep is you, a sacrifice worth everything, including my heart. Even if you do not see the same in me, it would make no difference; it would be my fate."

Charmed, she stared into his eyes as if in a trance, taking slow breaths.

"You bring light. That scares me because I would either gain or lose something of myself to keep it. It is such a bright light, too. Pastoral it is. It crushes me to question everything. I do not want that light to leave; I want to call out to it, cherish it, and have it with me forever. It would be my fate, and—" She stopped speaking midway as he planted a docile kiss on her.

She kissed him back with her eyes wide open from surprise. Though not in shock for too long, she closed her eyes just as he did and let everything else disappear. It became heated in the room, like their bodies were on fire as he held her, and she had him. The kiss became a bit firm and rough. It was like they needed every breath they gave each other. She thought he was a good kisser compared to her. She kissed but never like this. She kissed boys at her school, but who counts adolescents as experts?

Moreover, they were nothing special. She was not in love, but this moment contained it. She basked in this love, this kiss, his embrace. She had not felt such passion for anything in such a long time. She wondered if he thought the same, though he kissed her first. She became hotter, as if she were suffocated in a mesmerizing way. It felt as if their lips were going to bleed. This kiss had to say what they could not. Their kiss slowed to a stop.

They caught their breath and smiled slightly with enjoyment. His hands left red handprints on her back, their lips were swollen and red, and their faces were blushed with the deepest pink. As the heat dissipated, Dawn lifted her, and both of her hands held onto his shoulders. High in the air within his arms, he spun and spun, making her laugh with joy.

Moon laughed and said, "Dawn, put me down!"

She was glad he didn't because she felt like she was in the highest heavens. The brisk wind blew through her hair, making her feel different and more present.

Dawn took in the moment and said, "My rose."

He kept repeating it until that was all she could hear. The thrill spread through her entire body and mind as if she were on a high she couldn't come down from. As he swung her higher and in circles, she couldn't help but think that every rose had its beginning and end, whether in rain or sunshine.

## 2. The Magic Question (flashback¹)

**B**oth of my legs slid back and forth past each other while my back arched improperly, and both hands sat firmly on the brim of a bronze pot. It held a three-foot-tall cow plant. I wanted to spice up my apartment with something I loved that could remind me of Nana. Seeing such a plant daily would bring me hope that I would no longer wake up crying in the middle of the night. It was her favorite plant. I wondered if it was bad to hope. I wondered if it was bad to miss a loved one so much that you ached every moment. I wondered if it was bad to give up on life. I knew consciously it was not, but my mind made me feel otherwise. The sink and countertops overflowed with dirty dishes, and I had neglected the laundry for weeks. My dining room table was covered in takeout containers, emanating a pungent aroma that couldn't attract even a stray cat. It had been two weeks since Nana's death. *Livid I was. Sad I was. Lonely I was. Scattered, I was.* Neighbors and random people brought offerings of prayers, pies, cakes, casseroles, and alcohol to my door. I wanted to be alone with my grief but was constantly disturbed by well-meaning visitors wishing for my recovery.

During the first week, I couldn't help but vomit and cry on the bare tile of the bathroom floor. I am grateful that it stopped, but the tears will always come. I understood the pain would not go away entirely, but it would still be there, even if the crying did. In a way, with Nana's death, I felt like I was making up for my Papa and Mama, even though she was not dead. Yes, my mama. I wonder if she knows her father and mother are dead or if she ever cared. She did not come to either funeral, but who knows, she might have died as well. It would save me money and all the planning. I hated her. She never was there, not even today. I think an insane asylum would suffice because she was out of her mind when she left. It seems plausible to me.

At least Nana had a full funeral, just like her life with so many friends, family, and love. I didn't think I would have the same. Marleen might come If I did die, but not after I ignored her calls and texts. I wanted to be alone, and space was what I needed. I didn't just ignore her but my so-called friends too, who, by the way, did not show up to my grandmother's funeral because they were hung over from a previous night of partying. It was an excuse. *Imbeciles.* City kids at their finest. It was like my body stood solid when thinking about these things. I couldn't escape my mind due to constant headaches, as my thoughts crowded my head and made me dizzy as they do now.

I used every muscle to push the plant through my door, but it did not move an inch. I left all my strength at the grave with my nana. I kept pushing and pushing, but it just would not move. It was an obstacle like anything else, but it would not move. I took it as a sign from the universe that nothing I avoided would go away so quickly.

My back sank back in, and my legs bent down into the bare floor beneath me in the hallway. I felt the coldness rise through my body. It was as if I was a hostage to my emotions as I just bent there, crying and crying. I could not stop because the plant would not move. I felt as if the entire world hated me.

My apartment door was wide open, painted a god-awful yellow because I was going through my Pinterest phase. It had streaks of dirt from my hands, and my windows from afar in the living room were closed off, with sunburned curtains blocking out all the light. It was like I could not see, move, or escape myself—all signs, I say, cruel and cold.

I heard footsteps echoing through the building, tapping on the Mediterranean staircase made of dark blue marble with black trim decorated with white flowers and fruit. The bronzed and old railings sounded like sandpaper as someone's hand slid across them. They would shake as you move past them. The apartment hallway and downstairs reigned in cream color and brick. It had big Victorian doors with windows for eyes as white satin curtains hung from them. A welcome mat that spelled welcome as "*we come.*" The two side tables by the door were bronze and iron. They had two vases with petunias in them. The front door had these cowbells that would ring so annoyingly that you wanted to drag yourself across the floor just for it to stop. Each black apartment door had a gold number listed out of order. It was an old apartment, but I never understood the numbers as being out of order, other than laziness.

The sounds were a short distance away. I raised my head from dropping tears on the bare, dark blue tiles. I turned my head, and a man was standing there. He looked at me expressionlessly. I felt embarrassed as tears trickled down from my face to my neck. I wore an orange, ripped dress that fit my bare-chested hourglass body and bunny slippers. My coarse hair was damp and down my back, but luckily, it was curly when wet, so I didn't have to do much with it. The only accessory I wore was my small initial necklace. I felt a tear slide down my upper lip as I wiped my face, leaving a speck of dirt from the plant pot.

He stood, dressed in all black, with keys hanging from his ring finger. The ring was gold, with a red jewel in the center and numbers encrusted. He wore an all-black suit and trench coat. His dress shoes reflected off the light from the mirror over the petunias downstairs. He wore a gold medallion necklace with small writing, but I would have to move closer to see what it said. His hair was messy, but it was cute that way. It flowed freely. It was jet black like his clothes. His eyes were indescribable. I have seen people with colored eyes, but his were dark virid that could not go unnoticed. His eyes appeared never to blink.

He walked closer to me and smiled. "Is everything okay? If you need help moving that pot, I don't mind volunteering. I hate seeing a pretty lady like you crying, especially over a stubborn plant." He smiled again. This time, I noticed his ever-so-sweet dimples.

I gathered myself and stood up, and he pulled a handkerchief out of his coat pocket and handed it to me. I take the offer and grab the handkerchief. Our hands brushed against each other as I did. His hands were oddly soft but lovely. He stood out to me. He was peculiar.

I wiped my face and said, "I am sorry you had to see that. I have been going through a lot lately, and this stupid plant pot was insufferable, but I would not mind some help. Of course, if your offer still stands."

He quickly put his keys in his pocket and threw his coat over the railing. He smiled and agreed to help move the plant, and I forgot how messy my apartment was and flinched at him.

I ran ahead of him and blocked the doorway, saying, "Sorry. My apartment is a mess, and I wanted to warn you. I am not a slob; it's not that your opinion matters; it's just that I don't want you to be surprised. Thank you again for moving this for me, so— I will get out of your way." I moved out of the way and smiled awkwardly at him.

"Aren't you just a character?" he asked with a perplexed smile.

I stood out in the hallway as he moved the plant. He assumed a football position. He used more of his knees than I did. I mean, I was smaller than him, but not skinny. His muscles bulged out of his dress shirt. His hair fell before his eyes as he clenched his jaw shut. His eyes looked down, but I could see a hint of green. He picked up the plant on the count of three and put it in the corner nook beside my bookcase between the kitchen and front door. He set it down and caught his breath. His face turned pale red, so I headed to the kitchen, found a clean glass, and poured water from the pitcher in the fridge. I walked over and handed it to him. He thanked me as he drank from the glass.

I noticed his eyes scanning my apartment, taking in what he could before setting the glass on my dining room table. "If you need help with anything heavy, please don't hesitate to ask, okay? I don't want to sound pretentious, but we don't want you hurting yourself. And I must say, your apartment looks great; I've never seen such character." he said, smiling again.

I proudly walked around the table and smiled, saying, "Well, thank you. It is on account of my grandmother. She always had such style, so it rubbed off on me. What is an artist without art but an empty canvas?" I knew my apartment needed cleaning, but I wondered if he was being sarcastic or giving an actual compliment.

"Poet too, I see."

"Maybe." I shrugged. "Do you live here, or are you just visiting?"

I knew he lived here, but I wanted to be polite and start a conversation to show appreciation.

"I live here," he smiled. "I am the door down from you—I was on my way until I saw you upset."

He acted like he saved my life, but in a way, what is a man without a woman to boost his ego?

"Sorry again. I did not mean to startle you like that. It's just I rarely run into neighbors here, not since—" I looked away before I mentioned Nana, so I changed the subject, "It just wasn't a good week, but If there is any way I could thank you, let me know." I smiled forcibly, knowing I would rather he forget this encounter and pretend I never existed and I could go about my day.

He walked over to the door and put his hands in his pockets. He turned sideways in the doorway, leaned, and looked me dead in the eye, studying me sternly.

It lasted about a second, and then he said, "Okay, let me take you on a date."

I stood in place, blinked, and bit the right side of my inner mouth. He could have asked for anything, and he said a date. It made my blood boil. I thought he was nice but only wanted to sleep with me. He thinks I don't know who he is. I hear all the commotion from the women in our building arguing and fighting over him. He had the gall to stand in my apartment and ask for my time. I don't have time. I had more crying scheduled, unfortunately, and I could not stop grieving to go on a date. Who does he think he is? He is not my type. I wouldn't be dead caught with a douche like him, especially one in a suit. From what I hear, he spends money and breaks hearts. I'm not going to be another notch on his belt.

Even worse, I am standing in a sheer orange dress with damp hair and bunny slippers. I am practically naked, and he asks an inconsiderate question like that. I don't know what to do. He doesn't look like the type to get mad or chop me into pieces if I say no. However, he could become one of those neighbors who make it known that he does not like you because of something you did. I have no time, but it's not like I left my place, anyway. I remember Nana saying I should make friends and find love and adventure. I didn't promise her outright, but she knew I would try no matter if she asked or not. If you were here, Nana, you would know what to do; we would laugh at it all.

He was not bad-looking. He had lovely eyes, dimples, hair, and stylish clothing. He seemed to have his life together, and he did help me out. I even asked him what he wanted. Who was I to get mad at the outcome? Why didn't he want dessert or cash to make this encounter quicker? He was the subject of discussion among the women in the building, but at the same time, we barely knew anything about him—his life, career, and even his apartment were a mystery. Everything about him seemed to scream secrets. I felt lightheaded and warmer than usual, and that's saying something since I'm always cold.

He smiled and said, "You do not have to answer now, or you could just say no. It would not be the end of the world. I asked a pretty lady out, that is it. I would not want anything else from you nor require it."

I found myself frozen in place and needed to sit down. I walked over to my pink sofa, covered entirely by a white throw blanket. Unsure of what to say, I realized it had been forever since I had been on a date. I went over possible responses in my head, trying to calm myself down. I thought that leaving the apartment wouldn't hurt. It would be better than standing on the sidewalk, coming back in, or reading books I've read a thousand times. Leaning forward on the sofa, I gripped the ends of the cushion and turned my head to see where he was. I rested my head on my shoulder, saying, "Yes." It sounded better than being sad, and the word radiated positivity.

A spark ignited in his eyes, and he winked at me, saying, "It's a date! Let's meet this Saturday, either at your apartment or mine. I will plan the date, so no worries, and it will be fun. I'll be in touch."

He seemed rejoiced as he could not stand still in the doorway. I remained on the sofa, unamused, saying, "Okay. It's a date, but somewhere nice, okay." He nodded and agreed, then backed into the hallway and grabbed his coat off the railing. He leaned on the door for two seconds as he wrote down his phone number, leaving it on the dining table.

I left the sofa and closed my door slowly to avoid being noticed. I slid down onto the wooden floor against the front door. Pushing my knees to my chest, I rested my head sideways. As I traced circles on the walnut wood, I thought about my upcoming challenge.

The date was just two days away. I didn't know exactly why I had agreed to it, perhaps to fill a void. I didn't want to get his hopes up; I'm not sure a guy like that would have any, but I hated lying. I could say I was sick, but he would probably attempt to bring me soup. I could say I broke a leg, or even better, my neck, but he would find any reason to try to take care of me.

He gave me chills, which was odd. I say odd. Everyone was curious about him, and I was too. We passed each other every day outside the building, but he didn't notice. I did. His head was always down—walking fast as if someone were out to get him. I am unsure. I know he made me feel strange, which is the only way I can describe him.

My hands played with my toes as I counted each one. I thought about what happened and how I should approach the situation. I made a choice, and that meant I had a date. It could be my adventure. It would be different from my usual routine. I don't plan to spend my life sitting on the floor in this apartment without really living. I needed to leave this emptiness behind but not carry it with me. As I stood up from the floor, I realized I didn't even know his name, but I did know his apartment number: six. The only thing he knew about me was that I was a mess. I decided to pass the time by cleaning. I started by washing my face and changing into an oversized white t-shirt with my hair pulled back into a braid. My focus was on the kitchen and dining table. I removed the takeout by putting everything in a black garbage bag and cleaning all the dishes and counters.

The apartment needed to be more spotless. I swept, sprayed air freshener, and added a hint of perfume just in case he decided to return to my apartment for the date. I grabbed his number from the dining table and saved it in my phone contacts as number six. While playing music on the TV, I searched through my worn-out walnut wooden closet, which I got from a thrift store. I needed to replace it because it's falling apart. I danced to the music while searching for something to wear for my date. Finally, I found my favorite pair of shoes - a pair of black leather boots I received for Christmas two years ago. Despite feeling unsure, I couldn't find an outfit date-worthy for the occasion. Then, I remembered the other closet in my apartment, which contained clothes my mama had left behind, in the hall, near the TV and spare bathroom.

I yanked the painted closet door open. As I threw garments out of the closet, my eye caught something red in the pile. I didn't know how it looked but planned to reach for it. My right hand grabbed a silky piece of clothing, and as I looked down, it was the red I had seen. Lifting the dark red dress in front of me as I stood up, I couldn't believe it was the one, so I walked to the mirror in my room. I didn't have to try it on because my mama and I wore the same size. Also, I had lost a little weight in the past two weeks, so it should fit well.

I held the dress against my body and stood up straight. I stepped back from the mirror and then moved closer to it. I placed my boots next to the dress to see if the colors would work well together: black and red. I accessorized the outfit with some jewelry, and it looked nice. I had found the outfit I would wear, and the apartment was clean. Everything seemed to fall into place, and I shouldn't worry. However, that hollow feeling came and went. I needed to learn how to overcome it. I needed to stay strong for Nana and, most importantly, myself. Life had to go on, but it was difficult—a lonely journey for a lonely girl. I planned to call Marleen and explain what had been going on. It wasn't fair for her to be kept in the dark. She was a woman I had known since childhood, a friend of Nana's, and like an aunt to me. It was unfair of me to shut her out. Everything needed to be mended.

I looked at the dress again, and I had the dress on this time to get a feel for it. It couldn't have looked any better.

"Perfect," I said happily.

# 3. The Moon

The skies became overcast with the puffiest of clouds. They did not form anything, but clouds like these weren't for seeing but more for feeling. Encompassed in indigo blue, the sky looked down on the clashing of rocks and water. Two miles from the towering bridge they called Crimson Pass because of how ruby red it was. Her feet trailed through the grass atop the hill as the shore splashed water on them while her eyes fixed a gaze on the beauty of the sky, which gave her a melancholy feel. Far behind her was Dawn as he leaned across his 1967 Chevy Impala, which reflected the night's gloomy light, painting him blue against his pale skin and pink lips appearing pitch black. The breeze was much colder since they left the greenhouse. She could not resist taking in the night before they returned to the city.

The prickly texture of the grass tickled her toes. It smelled wild and green. She always loved feeling the earth beneath her, the wind in her hair, and nature in all its splendor. She heard Dawn open something with a metallic sound, followed by the smell of smoke. Turning, she saw that he was smoking a cigarette, an uncharacteristic but strangely attractive habit. Watching him lean against the car, smoking and pushing back his hair with his right hand, she noticed a small silver hoop earring in his ear. It added to his aura of mystery, and she often learned about him by observation rather than conversation. As he caught her staring, he walked over and kissed her on the cheek before embracing her from behind, their hands and fingers intertwined. His scent was heavy with smoke as he continued to shower her with kisses, exploring new spots and stopping at her lips.

He stared at her lips, resisting the urge to kiss her once more, and said, "I'll save the best for last," he then pulled away and walked over to his car trunk. She could still taste the tobacco, thinking she should object next time. But what's more romantic than a bit of distaste? He pulled out two blankets and laid them flat on the ground. He sat down, pulling Moon by the arm into his lap while wrapping the other blanket around them.

56

She positioned herself comfortably on his lap and leaned into the crook of his neck. She smiled and gazed into the distance, hoping the moment would never end. The warmth of his embrace gave her butterflies; it felt settling but different, like a new adventure to experience. She wanted to embrace it, live it, and love it. As they cuddled, basking in each other's presence, she felt his gaze, so she turned and caught his eye. His eyes seemed different this time, not pure or devoted but entrapping. They appeared dark and desireful, and she wondered what he desired, dreamed, and felt. *What were his deepest fears? What was his life like?* She did not know, but he knew about her. She wanted to understand all of him and hoped he could see that in her eyes. She longed for him to stop being a mystery.

Her eyes left his gaze, pushing his arms off her, and she leaned forward to say, "I want to know you. The real you. I want to know all of you and to see all of you. Whether for all my life or a season, I would enjoy all of you and leave you complete. Nothing short of the truth. Cross my heart, Dawn." She waited for his answer, pushing her knees to her chest and resting her face on them. Her toes wiggled in the dirt of the grass. She waited as if she would not wait forever. She thought about how low-toned his voice was and how every syllable falling off his tongue, whenever they talked, sunk in with depth but was clear enough for you to listen forever. *His voice. His voice* - she was dying to hear him speak. It weighed heavily on her how his voice could make her smile, and like the high seas, big and profound, it went almost unnoticed. She did not think he would have this much effect on her at this stage as if they were still strangers. Love on a whim, love fearful, love hopeful, love unknown. She started to twirl the ends of her hair and kept staring down but felt a finger lift her chin.

He had hurried near her, using his finger to make their eyes level.

He smiled and said, "Ask anything, my rose, nothing short of the truth, cross my heart." Raising one eyebrow, he pulled her back into his arms. He covered them with a blanket, brought her hand to his lips, and kissed them.

He cleared his throat and said, "I'm cool with sharing my life with you. Just ask me whatever you want, and I'll try to give you the best answer possible. I always knew we'd get to know each other, the little and big things. I was worried for a moment that you'd changed your mind, but I was relieved you were just curious about me." He displayed relief on his face. "Ask away."

She felt fuzzy inside. She did not know what to ask but dove into it. She ran her tongue over her tiny teeth and bit her lip. "Let's keep it simple. I will ask you a question, and you will answer, but I will also answer the same question. Okay," He nodded and kissed her forehead to give her the go-ahead. "Okay, what is your favorite color? This will be an icebreaker." He squinted at her in disbelief at the first question but indulged her. "White and black are my favorite colors, you?"

"Cherry red, but you knew that," she slightly giggled, "You also know my favorite food, and I don't care for anything else but juice and water. You?"

"I have a taste for sweet wine, whether red or white. As for favorite food, it would be as simple as mac and cheese," he chuckled, "You can never go wrong with that dish."

"What made you want to move to our city? I mean, like, where are you from?" She nudged her nose against his cheek. No matter how often they passed each other without interacting, she always tried to guess where he was from. She meant she was not like her nana with intuition. She thought about how she would imagine what specific state his ascent and attitude matched but never had luck because he could be from any part of that state. She even researched, which is odd for someone not curious about another person.

She nudged her nose against his face once more, smiling. "California," he said.

"What part of California?" He pulled her closer and said, "Sacramento is where I was born and raised. That is where I got my car; It was a gift. We can go together one day, but first, we should explore your city together for fair advantage."

She smiled, thinking about spending all the time with him, traveling, and enjoying each other's different worlds. She meant Boston, Massachusetts, was not much of a rave, but it is different for people not from there.

"By the way, I never asked, what part of the South was your grandmother from?"

"She was from Nashville, Tennessee, and my grandfather was from Mississippi. They never said what part he was from. That is all I know." She said, shrugging her shoulders.

"Now that we got that out of the way. Why don't you talk about your family? I know it's a sore subject and how that feels, but it would be nice to know if we will be serious about each other. The small and big things, remember?"

She could tell he was uncomfortable as he clenched his jaw and sighed. His eyes wandered off to the side, and she felt the energy shift. It got even colder, and his hug was less warm and looser. She thought the subject would be a future problem and did not want to walk on eggshells about it. He knew her past a bit and pain, so why can't she? She planned to tell him about her mother and father when he told her about his family. That way, nothing could be a secret. She hated secrets; telling the truth was her standard and nothing less. She thought it could not have been that bad between him and his family, but her family was not the Brady brunch. Everyone does not get Sunday dinners, smiling faces, and rainbows in their house.

"I meant what I said: my childhood friends are family. I love them, and they love me. I have family beside them, but you probably won't meet them, and I am barely in contact with them. They were controlling and manipulative and never let me grow as I should have. I have not seen them in 6 years — but that's how life goes. I tried to make things work again, which they did for a while, but things turned unpleasant because of major conflicting differences."

Moon looked at him with understanding and pity. No one should have to be alone, even though he was not, but to be away from family that way. She could not fathom being out of contact with her nana, but now she would have to since she was dead. "I have a mother and father. They are probably divorced by now, but if not, it is not a surprise. They are like mirrors to each other—traditional, loveless, and small-minded. Both were born and raised in California. I have two older sisters. I would not say they are like my parents, but they share one or two ideals and values. They are complex to me because they can be sweet yet cruel. All of us grew up in the same house and lived there—well, at least I do not," He looked out toward the shore and rocks, watching them clash against each other. He smiled slightly, then took a deep breath. "I was a momma's boy, always attached to her hip. I would follow her around, play with her, and do much more. I never got along with my father; he always thought I was like my mother - weak and naive. My siblings and I were close when we were younger, but things changed as I got older and started thinking for myself. They used to push me around and take advantage of me, but nothing too serious; that's just what families do, right? I love my family, but we are just too different. I don't think I could ever go back, and if I did, it would be as ashes in a box." His face turned hateful, and it churned her stomach. She wanted to change the subject and said, "I couldn't imagine you as a child— adorable and innocent. But I mean, you still are adorable."

He chuckled and said, "Yeah, you would not. I was so skinny and big-eared. My teeth were too big for my mouth. You would have run," he smirked as he looked at her, "On the other hand, I feel like you would have been captivating among the masses on the playground. I probably would have been obsessed with you then. I love how you curl your hair with your finger, sniffle when it's too cold, zone out when you're too anxious, and smile with so much fire you could set the room ablaze."

They talked until their lips turned blue from the cold. They discussed each other's lives, dreams, hopes, and fears. She could not fathom how interesting he was. She judged him too soon and figured he was a womanizer with no personality, but he was enthralling from his thoughts of the world to his movie taste. She could not help but fall little by little and without regret in sight. He made her smile, laugh, and hope. The most significant things any woman would want. She could not understand how he was the black sheep out in the world and his family. She knew she could not understand because she was an only child and a golden child. There was no competition and pressure upon her daily other than to live. She loved how the muscles in his face tensed when he wanted to make his point, how his eyes became chameleon with the moonlight, and how his hair fell to the right of his face. He was helpless, smiling when he spoke and listened to her. They could go all night like this, and the world would not be interrupted. It would just be still in their eyes. The night dragged on, and it got even later. She did not want to go home. She was having fun for once and loved it.

"There is no way you own a bookstore!"

"I swear I do! It is the small store next to the alley by Peppers coffee shop on Third Street."

"You own the bookstore called Little Reads! I always go there to read or at least find something of taste to read. Too bad you folks do not sell smut. Your name would have been on the grapevine," she said with a smile that reached her eyes.

"Yes. That is the one, and I saw you a few times, but cowardly of me, I watched from afar and stayed in my office. You always come on Thursdays and Sundays looking for the same book."

The only thing she did was understand. It crossed her mind how much he was afraid of himself, how he let her pass him every day without a clue how he felt for her and why. She didn't need space or understanding; she needed his presence and for the crying to stop. He knew everything about her like a secret, as if she were his secret. She did not like it. This sweetness he had she needed a month ago, but she was with him now. If only her nana could see them, an apple and orange in the garden.

"A man of observation, I see."

"That I am."

"What book?"

"I can only remember the author, Anne Rice."

"Your memory is a little bit too good."

"If it helps, my guilty pleasure is Harry Potter."

"Okay, not bad. I'm into wizards." She said teasingly. "And I'm into the unhinged supernatural."

"I thought you said you only knew the author's name."

He smirked, "I never said I didn't know her work, either," he said as he winked.

"Okay, smooth operator," she rolled her eyes and elbowed his chest.

"What is your music taste? That way—I can brace myself for the unknown when we ride in your car. It's rare to find good music, and I like dating people who can influence me their way a little."

"Wow! Influence you! I mean, I might not live up to your expectations."

She giggled. "Come on!" she said pleadingly.

"If I had to say, I would need something that touches me." He thought for a moment, then said, "I listen to all kinds of music, stuff like the neighbourhood and Kaleo."

"Nice! Dark and heavy." She joked.

He chuckled. "What about you?"

"I don't have favorites either, but if I had to choose, it would be sad-pop and hip-hop music. My mind is too blank for an artist right now. Um—You might not know him, but Joesef. He touches me, you know; he can pull the sadness out of a person. He speaks to the artist within."

"I'll take note—because I don't know who that is." They laughed. "It's okay, but just imagine being loved by a writer."

"Imagination is never far from reality," he said as they fell into each other cavernously. "Actions in love often follow closely behind words of love." He winked, and she rolled her eyes.

They both started to yawn as it was getting late. Dawn decided to head back to the car and get warm. Moon did not want to go home just yet. She wanted to explore his bookstore even more now that she knew it was his. She would come up with any excuse to be one with the night and take in the ambiance. As he slipped the blanket off them, he took her into his arms and carried her to the car. He kissed her on the lips. She grew small in his arms and let that tingling take over. When the car door opened, he sat her in the seat and opened the glove compartment. He opened a Ziplock bag of wipes and cleaned off her feet. He was so gentle and patient as he cleaned every crevice. Once he was done, he put his things back and kissed her on the cheek, and she did the same to him as he closed the door. She put on her shoes and coat. He opened the driver's side door and turned on the car. He put the heat on, then closed the door to pick up the blankets.

She sat there in silence, feeling content as he got everything together. She shifted her body to the right to look at him, imagining what the rest of her life would look like with him in it. Would she get married, have kids, find love, go on adventures, have time for herself, and feel secure? All these thoughts filled her mind, giving her the biggest butterflies. She couldn't help but smile and bite her lips at the thought of waking up next to someone she loves, feeling protected, and having the life she wants. He was a poet, and she was a poet. He was a reader, and she was a reader. Time was fleeting, and she fell for him. She no longer tried to force him into a box. She didn't need to. She knew him now, and he knew her. Her biggest regret was not getting to know him sooner. Her body was filled with deep affection, a new feeling for her from head to toe. It was as if she was blossoming. She sat there with her mind *calm and quiet*, taking in the sounds of his dress shoes stepping on the grass and the slam of the trunk, sending ripples through the car. The sky was dark, and the stars were bright. As she felt the car door open, he started the car, and she couldn't help but stare at him. He was like a piece of art. His green eyes, cupid mouth, chiseled chin, dimples, and silky black hair. He was like a Roman statue before her, no longer a ghost but a whole being.

They hit the road again, and she mulled over her desire to go to the bookstore instead of heading home. She wondered if she needed to convince him. When she tried to take in the scenery, he stopped. *What would change now?* It meant more time together, and they had nothing better to do. If they went their separate ways, she knew she would spend the night thinking of him as she had been doing all day. She felt a rush of giddiness. It would be a long drive back, but she cherished their moment before breaking the silence. He was lovingly holding and caressing her hand, and smiles were exchanged here and there. They caught each other's eyes whenever they could. The radio was playing "About Her" by Malcolm McLaren.

Unexpectedly, Dawn sang along with the song as she stared in disbelief. It was a different side of him she had never seen before. He would smile and laugh occasionally but generally had a serious demeanor. Singing was far from her mind, but she took a mental picture to keep along the way. She planned to tease him about it later, but for now, she joined in and sang along. She couldn't keep up with the lyrics since she didn't know them very well. They bopped their heads back and forth to song after song as they rolled down the car window, letting the air rush in. Dawn noticed Moon was feeling cold, so he turned down the vehicle's heat and advised her to remove her coat. She then brought up the idea of going to the bookstore, nervously explaining her desires and giving him her signature puppy dog look. However, he shook his head and suggested they head home before it got too late. Despite his refusal, she continued to pout and shower him with kisses as he drove.

"Moon, we should be getting back," he said firmly.

"I want to go to the bookstore, please," she pouted.

He sighed and thought about it for a minute. "Fine, but only for a minute. It is just that the cold has tired us, and you want to play still," he said smugly.

Moon jumped joyfully, kissed him, and then returned to swinging her hand out the window. She was confident she could convince him. She knew he would understand, and they would get along well.

"Thank you for everything," she said.

He winked at her while keeping his eyes on the road. Everything moved fast outside the window, but that was life—never-ending. As long as she was with the right people, in the right places, and feeling the right feelings, she didn't mind. So far, he was right for everything. She had to follow her heart, not just for Nana, but for herself. He revved the car and squeezed her hand to show off, and she went with the wave of it all. Without much thought, she followed wherever the wind would take her.

# 4. Rose Petal

The bookstore had a concrete exterior painted over with a faded Oxford blue. One large window was present, clear at the bottom and foggy at the top, bearing the name "Little Reads." The door was big and bulky, with a small window at the top, and the round handles had two lions as their base. The bookstore had two floors of bookshelves, which were lined up from wall to wall. They were six feet tall and brown. Some books were modern, while others were old, and dust was visible to the naked eye. The Checkout counter was to the store's left, and the office was behind it. The counter was mahogany. The register was digital and white with a card reader. It had one stool chair that was hand carved, mahogany brown, and western.

There were about three other big windows—no curtains in sight. One was in the lounge area near the back of the bookshelves upstairs, and the other two were downstairs. They all had sayings and poems written by readers and poetry heads. Each month, a poet or writer got the chance to cram their thoughts into the window. Once another year came around, they were cleaned, and the words flowed again. Moon tended to be one of the participants of such writings—posters placed evenly on each wall of classic movies and book covers. One poster was for the movie Seven, and another was for the book Alice in Wonderland.

His office had a solid blue door that was open halfway. The room had a dark academia vibe. Two bookshelves were on each side of the walls, overflowing with books piled on the floor. A simple black laptop sat in the middle of a marron-timbered desk. The desk was neat and organized, with books stacked neatly alphabetically. Two gold fountain pens with the name "Dawn" encrusted were placed on the desk. A small black journal was also on the desk but had water damage. A similar table was situated behind the desk, with photo albums and picture frames of people in them. A dusty old fan with tulip flowers for lights hung from the ceiling, and a Roseto lamp was on the table and the desk. A Western-style leather chair with one leg and cracks on the seat was in the corner of the room. Behind the door, there was a wooden and reddish-brown coat rack. Rainbow-colored bean bag chairs were scattered throughout the bookstore, both upstairs and downstairs. The lounge area featured a green Eastbourne couch, a small fake plant on a glass coffee table, and a yellow vase. A brown mini-fridge sat next to the sofa, stocked with refreshments and snacks for customers. Across from the couch sat a vinyl player with bronze legs on a high glass table backed by the staircase railing. The staircase was constructed from iron with twisted railings decorated with flowers. The light fixtures were tulips made of translucent glass with no fan. Piles of vinyl records could be found under one of the big windows downstairs, across from the checkout counter. The floors were covered in frieze carpet and were bright red.

They both ran into the bookstore, and Dawn shut the door behind them. They were wet from the pouring rain. The windows became foggy, muffling the sounds outside. She felt at ease as he gently removed her jacket and walked towards the bookshelves. The room was chilly, and she hoped the heat would be turned on. She saw him put their coats on the coat rack behind his office door, then bend down at his desk to search for something. So, she turned her head and began to explore. Her fingers traced each book, opening and flipping through pages, her eyes hoping to find something enticing, her fingertips hoping to find familiarity. Standing near one of the windows with writing, she got a sparkle in her eye and headed over to it. She tried to find her handwriting, smiling as she considered each expression. She reminisced about where she was at that moment in her life, knowing it was an entirely new year and those meaningful words would disappear soon.

She walked towards the office, hoping to find him unoccupied. She hummed as she leaned in the doorway and saw him writing in a journal while he stared at the laptop screen. She raised her eyebrow and said, "I thought we were on a date. I did not know you came here to work?" She bit her bottom lip as he lifted his eyes from the screen. *Those eyes.* He closed it midway, sat his pen down, and walked to her. He put one arm up on the door and leaned. "And I thought you wanted to explore."

"I want to explore but still have your attention at the same time," she said teasingly.

He pulled her close by the waist, her arms crossed, eyes only on him. Their faces were an inch away, their eyes and mouths craving each other, and their bodies pulsing.

"I promise to give you my full attention once I finish this one task. Then, I am all yours. We can talk all night and even kiss if you want," he said, biting his lip as he laughed softly while Moon playfully punched him. "Very funny, but okay. I will explore more, but I want you upstairs within fifteen minutes, no less. If not, then I have to issue you a punishment." she said, blowing a kiss as she walked off slowly, hoping he saw the flow of the back of her dress. He backed away, staring at her backside and curvy hourglass figure as she walked upstairs, managing to sit back at the desk and continue his task.

The stairs screeched with each step she took as she gripped the metallic railings. She turned the corner and noticed a vinyl player and stacks of records. After sitting on the couch and removing her boots, she went to find something to play with. She discovered a record of Sade: The Ultimate Collection, set it in the player, and let the music fill the room.

She noticed a mini-fridge in the corner of her eye. Opening it, she found cold drinks and snacks inside. Despite feeling full, she grabbed a cold bottle that looked like juice. It smelled fruity and tasted overly sweet. She ended up drinking two bottles while dancing to a song called "No Ordinary Love" by Sade. As time passed, she started feeling dizzy and noticed a change in her demeanor. She became extra cheerful, giggly, and alluring and continued dancing with her hands in the air.

Not noticing a book near her feet, she tripped, and all she could hear was a thud. She lay on the floor laughing hysterically, but the music stopped. All she could see was the room moving, and she did not know why. She thought to herself about what she had drunk earlier and concluded it was alcohol. She wasn't afraid, and she didn't judge herself harshly. She did not want to be a copy of her mother, the person who traumatized her in the first place, which was the only reason she did not drink.

She realized that fifteen minutes had passed, and he had broken his promise. Her body felt weightless and free, making it difficult for her to move. She thought she was being whisked away, even if she managed to sit up. So, she just lay there with her thoughts and feelings as she did every day. Somehow, her mind created its own music, and she began to sing. It was as if the angels were dancing in the clouds above. An ethereal, high-pitched sound came from her lips, and seraphic waves coursed through the room, landing on Dawn's ears.

She was singing at full blast when she heard his steps and him saying, "Moon? Moon?"

She wanted to make him wait for her just as she had. Swiftly, her little feet moved as she got up from the floor and ran into the stacks where she was hiding, eager to play. She could hear him calling her name repeatedly, so she covered her mouth to stifle her laughter. She hid near the farthest bookshelf and said, "If you can find me, then we can play, pretty boy!" She peeked from behind the shelf to see his response, and he seemed perfectly content. He was smiling and shaking his head, saying, "Okay! I am sorry for losing track of time, but I do not feel this is fair. But you did warn me," he licked his teeth and smiled again, "Let's play!"

He looked through the stacks, and she moved, paying close attention to him. She noticed he had almost found her a couple of times. She could see he began to become frustrated, so she knocked a book over to give him a hint. His body turned instantly from the noise, and she ran quiet enough for him not to hear, and he ended up standing over the book. He became more frustrated as she had him going around in circles from upstairs to downstairs, so she decided to give him a break. She ran upstairs, her feet sore from the iron, and played more music. She sat on the couch with her legs crossed and hands rubbing the cushions. She liked how soft it was and matched the color of his eyes. She felt as if he was already there with her. Looking towards the stairs, he stood, out of breath and jaw clenching.

He walked over slowly as if she would run away again. His eyes were fixed on her as if she were prey. She wondered if he felt she belonged to him. She had never been in a real relationship or in love.

She cared for boys she liked but never loved them. It was rare for her. There was something about him being out of breath and needing her to be in one place. He had one strand of hair hanging and a wrinkled sweater. She smiled villainously as if he were all hers through and through, which she could see he was. Their eyes focused on each other; he stood over her, then bent down. His face was near her lap. She leaned up, with her dark hair covering the shape of her face. "What took you so long?" she said, glowing and lustful.

Dawn caught his breath. "You are tough to keep up with; how fast you move and so beautifully. I don't know how you got away," he said, admiring her figure.

Her dress left an impression with the way it emphasized her breasts and how good she smelled. Her charismatic doe eyes and smile overwhelmed him every minute. He didn't know what to do with her. He moved closer to her, and she moved closer to him. The kiss was intense as he leaned over and embraced her. He switched positions and sat her on his lap, kissing repeatedly until they traced over each other's body parts. The aura in the room appeared pink when she opened her eyes to look at him. He put both of his hands on her hips, rubbing up and down her body, leaving red marks as if he were marking his territory.

She mumbled words as they kissed, suddenly feeling the urge to dance. Her mind was scrambled from the drinks. She knew he didn't think she was drunk but would catch on soon. It was funny – he thinks it's her, but it's the poison pumping through her veins. The adrenaline rush she felt from his touches and the alcohol combined made her feel all over the place.

She pushed him back onto the couch, then caught her breath and smiled. "I want to dance, Dawn."

He looked at her, obsessed, and said, "You want to dance now?"

"Yeah, I want to dance to see the stars," she said, looking up at the ambient lights. "Can you help me reach the stars? Do you have that much power?" She placed her hands in the air as the room spun more, but she didn't care because she liked the feeling of being so light.

She left his lap and ran to the center of the room, reaching her hand toward him. She moved impatiently to the music, waiting for him to join her. Her caramel skin had an olive undertone that looked orange under the lights, and her hair was rich and radiant, with thick strands cascading down her back, giving her the appearance of the sun. He nodded and eventually joined her in dancing. She ran into his arms when he approached, and he carried her around in circles to the music. Their smiles were endless as she mumbled about anything and everything.

"All I can see are the stars, but I want to be the moon amongst them."

"Why must you be amongst them? You shine bright all by yourself."

"It's just a feeling."

"Maybe I could give you the stars and moon?"

"That would take a lot of power."

"Yes, it would, but anything for you."

"Can I have the biggest of stars? Can I dance upon the moon? Can I have them?"

"Anything is possible. We could dance on the moon all the time."

"And what would you like? I may not have as much power as you, but I will give if you ask for anything."

"Anything?"

"Anything," she said, burping before covering her mouth and laughing.

"The only thing I could ask for is you."

"Me?"

"Yes, it is nothing better. I have wanted to be around you for the longest time and breathe the same air as you. This day has been nothing short of what I want."

"Aww," she said before kissing him.

She could not see anything but a faint resemblance to his face. She thought he figured her out, but it did not matter because she was with him. Their foreheads and noses touched, and the night was going smoothly. She leaned back into his arms as he held her. They giggled endlessly, and she began singing again.

"How drunk are you?" He said with a concerned face.

"I had only two drinks that I thought were juice, but I should have paid more attention," she slurred her words. "I—I am fine. I need to—" Moon began to close her eyes as she talked. He called her name three times, picked her up entirely, and she woke slightly. "No. No—no! I want to dance. I am not that tipsy!"

Her doe eyes opened to prove a point.

"Moon, it does not matter what you say; we need to get you sober; you cannot handle your alcohol. They were just coolers." He smirked and looked down at her, captivated by how adorable she looked.

She felt herself being swung gracefully onto the couch. He placed her down gently as if she was on clouds, and she moved into the fetal position. All she wanted to do was sleep and nothing else. She heard him open and close the mini-fridge, looking for something, and felt his presence at the end of the couch. He kept calling her name, trying to wake her, but she did not want anything. She wanted to sleep. She felt his heavy hands lift her from the couch and sit her up. She leaned onto his chest and bawled her legs up on the couch. She felt her lips dampen, so she squinted her eyes to see what she was drinking, and it was water. She took tiny sips because she felt nauseous.

She realized she could not hold her alcohol, especially since she only drank amateur coolers. It left her drunk, which made her internally amused. She was not her mother's daughter because it took the strongest of liquor to get her mother drunk. It made her hopeful that she would not develop an addiction like her. As she sat up, she felt ill because her food had worn off, and her eyes were droopy, so she drank the water he offered her.

"I am sorry. I should have put a sign up about what is in the fridge. I don't have one because most people who drink know the difference, but I should start thinking about the people who don't," he tilted his head and looked at her with guilt. "Are you feeling better, rose?"

She loved it when he called her "rose." It was not like most pet names other men used for her—nothing cliché or weirdly gross. It just rolled off his tongue, which made her hope to be his "rose" for a long time, whether forever or for some years. Only to be his. It was deemed unimpressionable on the first date, but it would be something to laugh over later in life. He took the bottle away, and she blinked twice to process everything. Her throat was less dry this time, but she felt like she was coming down with a cold. She lay back on his chest while he caressed her hair.

"I did not mean to worry you. I am here, then I am not. I thought it was non-alcoholic. I feel embarrassed."

"You do not have to be. Whether it was intentional or not, everybody gets drunk, but in your case, I understand."

"My mother used to drink, and I don't want to be seen that way."

"I will not see you that way, especially after what you told me. I wouldn't, okay, even if you decide to drink eventually."

"I'm glad my father didn't see her like that, but in a way, he did in spirit. I can't imagine loving someone so much that drinking would be the only way to cope and make life worth living."

"Love is what you make it. Your mother was in pain like anyone. It's just that she didn't know the healthy way to cope."

"Healthy way to cope? — It was a bottle down her throat. She lived and breathed it. I was her child, and I needed her; Nana needed her, and Pa. She was selfish to leave, especially after leaving a mess," she said, her face drenched in tears. "It's great that she left because I could not deal with her falling into the bottle for both funerals. And believe me, she would crawl to the casket if it meant she would be seen. She is a drunk and always will be, and if not, then fuck her for not picking up the pieces."

He rubbed her back while she cried. "I miss Nana. I miss her so much; everything would have been better if she had been here. I would not be so fucked up! I would not be sitting here crying. I feel like shit. I would not know what to do if you were not here." She looked up at him with tenderness and warmth.

He looked back at her, rubbed her hair, and said, "I am here and glad to be."

She ranted to him about her emotions as he sat and listened. His acceptance made her feel safe. It was a decent human thing to do, and he made it ten times better. He was kind, doting, and there for her. She couldn't believe she was in this situation on a Saturday at a bookstore with a man she didn't know. They talked about their lives and things, trusting their words to be true. Her cheeks' plumpness soaked with the tears' stains, turning red.

"Have you ever been in love or felt a love so deep that it messed you up in ways from which you could not come back? I hope you haven't, but that would be impossible for me to ask. It would hurt me to know you were in someone else's heart and mind. It's overwhelming to think about. You make me feel a certain way, and I like it. Initially, I rejected it, but now I don't want the feeling to stop."

"I have loved but not on purpose. Love can come with regrets and moments you never want to lose, but love is many things on the spectrum. It is never just one thing." He looked away and stared outside the window as the rain stopped. "I like you too," he said.

"So, you have been in love. I have not, but I would want it to be you if I were. We have things in common, and I feel safe with you. It's like we've known each other for a long time and have this intense attraction to each other."

She placed her hand over her stomach as it settled. Nausea came and went, but she was still tipsy. She slurred her words but managed to get her points across.

"The women in our building: were you serious about them or toying with them? Since I met you, it does not seem like you would, but—" He cut her off and said, "No. I was not serious nor toying with them. I told them that I was not interested. I hung out with them a few times, being friendly and flirting, but I never got their hopes up. I always waited for you. Undoubtedly, I wanted you."

Relationships were a discovery for her because she had never truly experienced one. She had small crushes and short relationships in high school. She had hoped to experience what others did in college, but it didn't happen. Boys were attracted to and pursued her but didn't see her for who she was. They only seemed interested in her virtue and nothing else, treating her like an object. However, Dawn was different. He made her feel like a woman and safe enough to embrace it. He allowed her to take the lead, which she appreciated. She hoped he wasn't just another lesson from the universe but a gift to lighten the load off her shoulders and be free.

"How old are you? We never discussed our ages."

He turned his head, and it caught her off guard. His face seemed more visible as shadows cast from the window. "Curious, are we?"

"There is nothing wrong with that."

"You are right. There is nothing wrong with that. I am surprised you asked after all this time."

"Well, as you can see, I've been busy," she said to be funny, but her words fell flat from her drunkenness. She tried to stay awake.

He snickered and said, "You are out of it, but it's cute. Please, do not drink again. It's not for you."

He smiled, and she poked his dimple.

"I am thirty, but my birthday is in five months. I am close to the big three and one."

"I am—I am twenty-three years old. I will be twenty-four this month," she said as she burped, then laughed.

"Seven years."

"Between us—who would have thought? You look my age, not thirty."

"Not the first time I've heard that. But it's not too bad. It means I won't age terribly." he winked.

"You would make a handsome dilf."

"Would I? Because That is the ultimate title for a man."

"Sure," she said, closing her eyes.

"I'm only thirty. The title would be flattering but not earned quite yet."

"So, you say." She giggled.

"Feeling better?"

"I feel tired, but I also want a kiss. I think it will make me feel better," she said cheekily.

"Did you ask for a kiss while not feeling well?"

"Yeah"

"No. I need to take you home to rest, but first, I need to get you more water to drink."

"I don't think lecturing will help, but a kiss will."

"No."

"I want a kiss! I want a kiss! I want a kiss!" She said pleading.

He looked at her with pity and a frown but shook his head. "You need to become sober," he said.

She needed to convince him to kiss her, so she turned on the charm. She figured he would rethink if she burst into tears, but that felt like too much. She couldn't believe those ideas would work. She wanted to kiss him and hoped he wanted the same. It felt unfair to her that he did not kiss her. It was her right. It was the only thing on her mind while he was across the room, straightening the records and picking up books off the floor, but she waited. She would fake a stomachache once he returned to her side of the room, and then she would capture her kiss.

She dozed off again, unable to resist the effects of the alcohol. Despite her strong desire for a kiss, thoughts of his soft lips, minty breath, and enticing scent consumed her. Picturing his gem-like eyes and dreamy dimples, she felt a rush of heat throughout her body, starting from her head and traveling down to her toes. She pressed her thighs together and let out small whimpers.

He called her name out of curiosity about what was going on, but she did not care what he saw. His soothing, low-tone voice made her even hotter. She kept chanting that she wanted a kiss. She could not take it anymore and caved in. She felt him collide with her mouth while her eyes were half open. And it was not her imagination. The kiss was addictive—raw and like shockwaves. He attempted to pull away, but her arms locked around his neck. She kept him in place while she kept kissing, and he followed suit. Moon's hands moved from his neck to chest, caressing every peck and muscle. His tongue entered her mouth, and she sucked on it.

He repositioned his body, and his bulge moved between her legs as she spread them. Their kiss was intense and sweaty while his hands stroked her body, moving from her thighs to her breast. He rubbed her bare nipples in circular motions but not too rough. Her moans echoed while she arched her back as they dry-humped. He pulled back her dress while he traced her white cotton panties. He teased her as he lightly brushed against her folds with his fingers, making her moan louder. His mouth moved to her neck and suckled it, leaving his mark as her head fell back on the couch. She hiked up his sweater and saw his toned abdominal muscles, tattooed words across his chest, and a beauty mark next to his belly button. They moaned louder as their lower halves moved against each other.

She pulled him back into the kiss and used her hands to massage his penis. He yanked down the top of her dress, and it sent a surge through her body. Her eyes widened as he sucked on her breast, using his tongue in ways unimaginable, while his other hand pushed her panties back. He slipped a finger past her folds into her vagina. She arched her back more as his finger moved slowly in her, and then he added another.

*I didn't think that it would happen so fast. I have been a virgin most of my life, and here I am, getting fingered on a couch. It feels good. It is what most of the girls talked about in college and high school. I always felt they were exaggerating and did not think sex would be that great, even if you were in love. I wondered if it would go past this point. I am not afraid but more intrigued. I know how it feels for my vagina to be spread by a finger, but what about a penis. His penis. His kisses are sweet, but I want to go further. I want to be claimed. I want to be loved and make love.*

She pressed her hand down on his to force his fingers deeper, making her gasp and her eyes roll into the back of her head. Then, before she knew it, her dress was down on the floor, and she was utterly naked down to her panties. He gripped her tight as he flipped her onto her stomach and pulled down her underwear. He kissed her spine as she arched her back, moving down to her bare ass. He briefly kissed each ass cheek and then sucked on her neck and back.

He left behind as many marks as possible on her body. He spread her legs wide as his mouth met with her vagina. He licked her clitoris gradually as he curled his tongue in her entrance while he moved his fingers in and out. He toyed with her. He sped up his pace, then slowed it down. She could not help but push her hips against the sensation. He used one hand to press down her leg and another to hold her hand.

She couldn't move while his pace kept fast. She tried not to moan so loud, but her body felt like ecstasy. She was experiencing a fiery sensation in the pit of her stomach, and she knew what it could be; it felt exciting to experience her first *orgasm*. Leaving her mindless, her body shook as the orgasm spread through her. She wanted to scream at how electric she felt but moaned into her hand. He left her vagina alone and kissed her all over her body. She caressed his bulge as she wanted him to know she was ready to have sex, fuck, to make love.

He whispered in her ear, "Aira."

She whined and said, "Pl—plea—please, I want you to make love to me."

He stopped kissing her and asked, "Are you sure? Have you had sex before?"

Wasn't it obvious to him that she was a virgin? Most men she encountered were shocked when she told them and often assumed she was not a virgin, and she didn't know why. It was different with him. He was genuinely curious. There were times she would have lost her virginity, but most of the boys she met didn't know where the clitoris was and kissed like fish gasping for air. It was primitive—they knew nothing about a woman's body or desires. The attraction did play a part, and if there was one flaw, she was out.

His eyes, mouth, and everything about him caused her to fade away. He made her brain rot and her vagina throb. "Yes. I am sure. I want you to be my first." She whispered.

He seemed hesitant at first but agreed. "Okay."

He pressed a kiss against her forehead and left the sofa. He took off his clothing and pulled a condom out of his wallet that was in his pants pocket. His penis was a shade darker than his skin tone, and the tip was pink. It was lean but thick and nine inches long. As it hung, she could see how hard he was as he put the condom on, almost stretching the rubber thin. He had a handsome penis, though she appeared mortified.

She braced herself and held her folds open. Dawn kissed her passionately and sloppily as he teased his penis at her entrance. He took pleasure in hearing her whines and then gently pushed his penis inside her. The pain left a sting, and she knew it would cause some discomfort, but not like that. She whimpered when he tried to move. They stayed in place for a few minutes before he moved little by little inside her. He tried not to moan about the wetness he felt between her legs. She tilted her head back and arched her back while he slid in, a drop of sweat trickling down his face.

He kissed her. "I'm going to move slow, okay," he said as he laid his head in the crook of her neck.

She nodded and said, "Okay." She could feel the pain subside.

He moaned deep in her ear the more he moved, and the more he moved, the better she felt and wetter. Her moans grew louder, leading to his pace picking up. The kisses, bruises, and hotness consumed them. He held her legs to her chest as he pounded into her. She left scratches on his back as his penis hit her G-spot, and she held onto him.

*I hope I didn't stain the couch. Otherwise, I would feel bad for those who wanted to sit on it.*

Their kisses were messy and hungry. They maintained eye contact to revel in each other. She tried to keep up with his pace but couldn't. "You're so beautiful," he said, looking deep into her eyes.

His pace was out of control, and it felt exhilarating. She was losing her mind as he went deeper and deeper. Only their moans were heard. She rolled her eyes, her mind blank and crazed. He quickly changed positions by sitting her in his lap with her back to him. She spread her legs, and he entered her again.

"Dawn," she moaned as she held onto his arms, then turned to kiss him.

Smugly, he said, "I know rose."

In ecstasy, she arched her back as he pressed down on her hips and thrust slow, then fast, leaving her speechless. "My rose," he said as he kissed her neck.

"Don't Stop," she whimpered.

The atmosphere intensified as he felt a tightening sensation, and she noticed his movements becoming more erratic. She leaned in for a kiss just as he hoisted them off the couch, picking up the pace and going deeper, leading to their release.

They fell back onto the sofa, with Moon resting on his chest. *I lost it and do not feel wrong, ignorant, or regretful. I feel satisfied, wanted, and loved.* He gently caressed her back as she lay breathless on him, basking in the silence.

After lounging on the comfortable couch, they slowly got dressed. As she prepared to leave, she couldn't help but notice the faint blood stains on the sofa, remnants of virginity. Meanwhile, Dawn went downstairs to gather their belongings. As she stood there, her gaze fixed on the stains, she felt a pang of reluctance, as if leaving a small part of herself behind. Deep down, she knew he would take care of it, but the stains were a tangible reminder of their connection and the memorable events of the night. Feeling drained from the excitement, she made her way over to one of the cozy bean bags, sinking into its softness as she closed her eyes.

*It all happened so fast. It felt like fate. It's something that happens all the time in the movies. I lost my virginity to someone I genuinely wanted, but does that mean we're obligated to each other? It's okay if we don't last, but would it hurt? Will I cry night and morning as I did for Nana? Would he leave now that we've had sex? I knew he always wanted me, but is that a terrible thing? Wouldn't that mean I'm obligated to him? Is he my boyfriend? My man? Do we even have a relationship, or do we need to go on more dates first? I don't know what love is or whatever we have with each other. I felt something. We have a connection. I don't want to be used. I don't want to be pitied. I don't want to get hurt.*

# 5. Wolfe

At midnight, he carried her up the stairs as she slept in his arms. She felt as free as a bird, as if she were flying. His smell and the touch of his hands reminded her of this sensation as he lightly carried her upstairs, his footsteps echoing on the steps. His presence reassured her. She could feel her feet swinging and her hair being pulled by the air. She needed wings, but he would suffice for the moment. She could feel and hear everything but see. Her eyes were sensitive to the light, and her head felt like someone had slammed a hammer against it. It was evident she was sobering up. Everything around her was a nuisance, even the sound of the key entering her apartment door.

She knew she was home. The smell of coconut butter and roses filled the air. The round bed was covered in white sheets with a red knitted throw, all matching the white bed skirt and five pillows in coordinated white and red. On the nightstands, there were family portraits and two antique Victorian lamps. The lamps were gold, red, and blue, with the bottom resembling a blue puddle sitting on leaves, the middle featuring a green jewel and smaller ones, and the top shaped like stars wrapped in red lace and gold, adorned with dangling green, red, and blue jewels topped with a large red jewel.

She had a handcrafted mirror in the corner of her room, next to the window. It was made of wood and walnut, with cracks covered with pink lace tied into a bow. On the right was a photo of her grandparents, and on the left was a photo of her parents. Beside the mirror was a red chair with a stuffed cotton candy-blue bunny holding a gold bracelet with the inscription "Little Rosie."

In front of the bed was a black vanity desk with a marble top, yarn, and a sewing machine. A black laptop decorated with stickers of the moon and inspirational sayings sat on the edge of the desk next to a white diary labeled "Ari." The room had a cream carpet and various awards on the wall for poetry and academic achievements. A miniature collection of turtle trinkets lined the windowsill.

Centered in the bed, she felt him remove her shoes and coat. His words felt like whispers as he spoke. She did not know if it was a dream or reality. She was either there or not at all. She was sobering up, but it felt like hell. Everything near the frontal lobe hurt. She could barely open and close her eyes. She was dehydrated, and her body felt heavy but weak.

Despite her feeling weak, she focused on what he said.

She could feel him lying beside her on the bed. He asked, "Do you need anything?" His fingers traced her cheek as she forced her eyes open despite her headache. Her voice was hoarse because of a dry throat.

"Water," she said. He leaned in, kissed her temple, and then went to the kitchen for a glass.

He helped her sit up and brought the glass to her mouth. Her wrist was too weak to grab it, but she drank the water as if it were the last on earth. She drank about two more glasses of water, which gave her some strength to sit up for a little while before laying back on the bed. She saw Dawn take off his coat, toss it on the back of the chair, and walk back to her.

He smiled, leaned onto the bed, and said, "You feel a bit better?"

"Yeah, but my throat is still a little sore."

"Okay, rose." He looked around the room and smiled. "So, this is your domain. It suits you. It has a coquettish vibe."

"Thanks. Whatever you said, I assume you are saying I have style."

"Welcome. I enjoy being in your space, which is far from my boring taste. It's probably what you were thinking when you saw my place." He winked.

She felt uncomfortable and constricted in her outfit. Pulling at the fabric, struggling to remove it, she wanted to scream in frustration at her inability to move properly.

"Do you need help?" He asked, worried. "I can help you remove your clothes and bathe— because you smell of alcohol and sex." He said as he licked his teeth.

"Ha! Ha! Very funny, but I am okay. You can leave if you want. I am sure I can do it. I am okay," she said, nodding.

He didn't look convinced. "I don't know if you have a blindfold, but you can't. I don't have a problem helping because you seem weak. It's not like I haven't seen you naked, and I asked you to respect your boundaries."

"Point made, but it's just that I don't want to be a burden. What if I fall asleep again?"

"Moon," he kneeled by the bed. "Burden or not, that is my cross to bear. I have no problem lending a hand; you should not have a problem asking me for things. We saw each other in the rawest forms two hours ago, and you think I do not care about your needs."

"I—"

*He wanted to help, but I had never asked for help for most of my life, except for Nana. This would be hard, but we had had sex, so it was nothing new. I felt scared. This vulnerability was different from just colliding bodies. It was rare and emotional. I did not know if my mind would torture me for it later. I could be at war with myself, which would be my cross to bear. He is an angel. My angel.*

"Don't answer that. I am helping, and at this point, we are more than strangers, you know."

"Okay, but be gentle."

"Okay."

'Sleeping beauty found her prince," she said playfully.

"A prince?"

"Yeah, my handsome and loving prince," she said with a weak smile.

"I'll be the best prince you've ever met," he said as he made a silly face and stuck out his tongue.

"If you do fall back to sleep, it's fine, as long as you get some rest and stay clean. Let me know if you feel uncomfortable or like taking over."

"Okay," she said with a wink.

"Smooth move."

*I haven't had a dream in so long. They stopped when my mama left. At first, I was scared, but then it became my thing. It was mine not to dream but only to sleep. I've always felt like a sleeping beauty, doomed to an existence of twisted fate. If I could, I would dream of my family and places that were not in my world. It could answer all my problems but not fix them. Maybe that is why I never honestly tried in life. Every time I closed my eyes, it was dark. Amnesia. I would dream of him and what we are. I hated dreaming with my eyes open. It was unfair, unjust, wrong. This was something my mama took. I had imagination and ambition but never the privilege to dream. If anyone asked me what I dreamed of, it would be to dream. I went to the doctor, but there was nothing they could do. It was all on me and my psyche. I was not wired right; I was broken because of my mama.*

He brushed her hair aside as he took off her dress. Removing her panties and jewelry, he casually tossed them into the dirty hamper in her bathroom. She lay on the bed, feeling exposed and vulnerable. She could hear him moving around in the bathroom, running water in the tub. She adjusted herself in bed, shifting the pillows to the other side and curling up in a fetal position. She closed her eyes and pulled the blanket over herself. She had a moon-shaped birthmark on her lower back, her nipples were sandy brown, and she had tiny stretch marks that looked like lightning bolts. She had no moles, cuts, or bruises. Her feet were tiny, and she had cherry-red painted toenails.

"Sleeping beauty— my beauty," he whispered in her ear. "It's time."

"Mhm, is it morning yet?"

"No, it is still midnight, but I will need you to sit up so you can get into the bath."

"Please give me five more minutes."

"You can get more than five minutes if you get out of bed, but it seems I'm going to have to do that."

He kissed her on the wrist. "Rose, please make it easy for me."

She peaked from under the throw cover as if she were a baby bird. He swooped her up and carried her to the tub. In her drunken stupor, he eased her into the hot bubble bath and reached for the washcloth to wash her. The bathroom walls were the color of grapefruit with unfinished tiles that seemed unfamiliar in color; only white and black, faded. Her shower and tub were one. The shower head and knobs were dusty gold. The tub was a white Cambridge with golden feet.

There was a big white round sink with a mirror that glowed with a bright white light. There were drawers and cabinets on each side of the sink with two windows above them. They were purple and blue with a hint of red in the middle. Pink and red towels hung in the bathroom. Light pink slippers stood beside the bathroom door, and a yellow robe hung behind it. The carpet in front of the tub was shaped like a turtle. Its legs were brown, but the shell was cream and patterned in circles.

He knelt with both legs beside the tub, placing a towel behind her head, and she awoke. The hot water was soothing but boiled her skin as the bubbles covered her neck. She couldn't help but smile a little when she saw him. She reached her hand out of the water, traced a heart on his lips, and then looked back at her toes as they played with the bubbles. "Awake, are we?"

He dipped the washcloth in the water and spread the soap across it. Then, he moved to the end of the tub and cleaned her feet. "That feels nice," she said as she twirled her wet finger in his hair. He went as gently as he could with her body, knowing she felt unwell. It was like he knew her feet were her hot spot, but in an affectionate way. She liked it when her feet were rubbed. It relaxed her, as anyone would, but it was usually ticklish.

He bit his lip. "I hope so, but I'm glad you're awake. I was worried you would sleep forever," he said as he cleaned her thighs.

*I was curious about his love language. Suppose it was touch, acts of service, gifts, affirmation, or quality time. I could not pinpoint him but assumed it was all the above. For me, someone's time and acts of service would win me over through and through. I had been prominent on those since abandonment in my childhood. I would always make people prove themselves and if they would stick around.*

"Why are you so caring?" She asked as he lifted each leg, scrubbing and cleaning. The sincerity in her voice rose as she asked again. "Why are you so caring?"

He remained focused on the task and said, "I can be caring. That's just how I am. Depending on my feelings, I go as far as I can with my care toward someone. I like you."

Her hand lay softly on his, stopping him from cleaning while she sat up and scooted to where he was. She filled her palms with water and spread it in her hair, causing it to form into curls. Then, she rested her chin on her shoulder. "Both of us know that you like me. You have always had feelings for me, but why me? Earlier, you mentioned seeing a unique love within me and wanting to experience it with me, but why? There are plenty of people with the same kind of love." Sincerity bled from her eyes as the intensity of wanting to get inside his head grew. This was something she always did: overthink. She wanted to question everything because she could never be too safe. He was good to her but too good to be true.

*He's bathing me, which is sweet but weird. I'm fully awake, and my head still feels like shit. And it dawned on me how fast we are moving again. It feels right, but I cannot trust myself. I want to be sure.*

"Everyone has love, but it is rare to find it and keep it. I could have chosen anyone, but it does not mean they have the same love as you. They are not you, and I wanted you. I do not need anyone to love me, but I want it. Enormous difference, so if you want to hear about how I need you. I do not, but I want to love you and have love between us."

Taken aback, she laid back and thought. Their eyes locked. "Fair enough." She was at a loss for words. "What's with the questions—hmm."

"I wanted to know where your head was at."

"Understood. If you want to know how I feel or what I think of you, ask. I will show you nine times out of ten rather than tell you." *Nice overthinking. I know he is right, but I don't have an answer. I know I have questions that fill my head every minute we are together, and I want to prove my negative thoughts wrong.*

"I have these thoughts. They always overwhelm me. It's always negative for me. I used to be optimistic and loving, but now I can't. It's so hard to accept things I know I deserve. I fight and fight, but it's inevitable." The air and the water were cold around her. She turned on the hot water, and Dawn used his hand to mix it. She smiled, and he smiled as he sat on the carpet and laid his head against the tub with his other arm.

"See that! You do things for me without me asking."

"Moon." He chuckled. "You just haven't had a guy like you enough to do these things. Which is crazy considering the things I would do for you."

"That makes sense," she said as the realization crossed her face. "And what things would you do for me?" His eyes shimmered in the light. "Anything and everything."

She felt the intensity in his gaze. It was obsessive, but she chose to ignore it. After all, who isn't a little bit mental? She was aware of her quirks. When she noticed the bathtub overflowing, she turned off the water. She washed the areas of her body that he hadn't gotten to. He observed, but she didn't mind. It felt like she was a piece of art on display, and she enjoyed the attention. She couldn't reach her back well, so she asked Dawn for help.

He moved to the front of the tub, knelt behind her, and placed her wet hair to the side. "I didn't know you had a birthmark on your lower back." He leaned close to her ear and whispered, "Very sexy."

She giggled and said, "You are making me blush, and I did not know I had one until I was fifteen. I mentioned it to my family around that time, and they would say, "We thought you knew," but I digress."

"A moon birthmark"

"I know it's very ironic."

"Very."

He finished cleaning her back gently while tracing her birthmark. She unplugged the tub; he handed her a towel and a robe. Wanting to mix a cure for her hangover, he headed to the kitchen but kissed her before doing so. She turned off the lights in the bathroom and walked back into the bedroom, feeling relieved from the stuffiness and heat. She tossed the towel into the hamper and opened her closet to decide what to wear to bed. As the closet doors opened, she looked past one of them and saw Dawn, and there he was, finding fruit and veggies to blend. It was cute, and it felt great to have someone in her apartment again. Usually, it would be her nana in the kitchen whipping up her famous Southern concoctions. Oh God, she missed her. Her nana would slap her on the backside, congratulating her for having a man.

She turned toward the closet to find something to sleep in and spotted an oversized, plain, light gray T-shirt. After closing the doors, she tossed the shirt on the bed and went to her nightstand by the window to look for panties. She picked out a pair of light blue cotton panties with a rose design and placed them on the bed. Then, she went over to her vanity, used a comb to detangle her hair, and applied coconut oil to her scalp and hair. After putting her hair up into a bun, she called out to Dawn to see if he had finished making the cocktail. Although she didn't know what was in it, she planned to find out.

She walked over to the kitchen as he poured it into the glass. "Do not worry; I will clean up after myself. Before you ask, this is a hangover cocktail, as I said before. It consists of two oranges, two carrots, two celery sticks, a beet, a lemon, and a piece of ginger," he slid the juice toward her. Come on, try it."

He smiled. "I promise it is not too bad."

"Okay. I am trusting you."

"Never doubted it."

"By the way, can you spend the night after you clean? I don't want to be alone since it was my first night intoxicated. I tend to overthink."

"Like I said, all you have to do is ask. I will take a shower first and change."

"Okay. I will miss you until you return; this cocktail is so gross." They laughed. "Yeah, it is, but it's to help the hangover more than to taste good."

"Kiss, please."

He looked at her, smiled, and kissed her before cleaning up his mess. She returned to the bedroom, finished her cocktail glass, and changed into her clothes on the bed. She heard him finish cleaning and head out the door, but not without saying, "Do not go to sleep without me, beautiful. Also, get something in your stomach; it might help more."

The door closed. She could only think about getting some sleep. Perhaps having some dinner would give her more strength. The kitchen walls were covered with white tiles, and the floor was wooden, with a chestnut fur carpet. The countertops were made of white marble but were worn down. She had two wooden shelves. One shelf held food recipes and a teapot; the other had seasonings and tea packets. She had a picture frame of her family on the counter, a small lamp, and two wooden cupboards. There was also a glass vase of roses and a bowl of fruit. In the center of the kitchen was a red gas stove between two countertops, with kitchenware hanging from the rack above it, and a vintage two-door cream-colored glossy refrigerator with silver handles. The dining table was wooden, with three wooden chairs, a white tablecloth covering it, and a bowl of uncracked walnuts in the middle.

The fridge door swung open as she fixed her gaze on the leftover tomato soup she had made earlier in the week. It had no meat or vegetables, just plain tomato soup. She placed the soup on the counter and grabbed a pot from the cabinet. After setting the bronze pot on the stove, she poured the soup into it and placed the handmade red clay storage bowl in the sink. Turning the stove knob to medium heat, she went back to the cabinet to grab a light sapphire glass teapot shaped like Aladdin's lamp with an elephant's trunk, filling it with water from the faucet and placing it on the stove next to the soup. Then she grabbed parsley, pepper, and salt to add flavor to the soup this time. Finally, she dragged her feet to the chair at the dining table and sat down, waiting and hoping that everything would be ready before she got sleepy again.

Moon could not tell the time because she didn't have her phone; it was in her purse in the room. With a sigh, she went back to the bedroom, retrieved her phone, and sat at the dining table. She checked the time and saw that it was two in the morning, but since she had all the time in the world to sleep and spend time with Dawn, she didn't mind. She briefly scrolled through her social media, watched some funny videos, and checked on the soup and tea she was preparing. Feeling bored, she decided to watch a horror movie; she loved watching scary movies as they were her favorite way to relax. She added seasoning to the soup, mixed it thoroughly, and poured it into a medium-sized yellow glass bowl. She also poured boiling water into a matching teacup, added two tea bags, and sprinkled a small pinch of sugar into the cup.

Before starting her meal, she cleaned up after herself, leaving the kitchen spotless. Then, she placed the soup and teacup on the coffee table before the television and sat on the sofa. She laughed, cried, and even got a second cup of tea while watching her movie.

*It's taking him forever to come back. I'm nervous about it. I worry that he changed his mind, not that he didn't have the right. He said he would return. I expect him to keep his word. I'm trying not to overthink and be irrational. He is coming back; before I know it, he will walk through the front door. I know it and see the night, the date, and my losing my virginity was not all for nothing.*

She yawned, realizing it was time to go to bed. Waiting for him was no longer an option since he had left an hour ago. She turned off the television and gathered her dishes to clean.

Letting the lukewarm water run over her hands, she zoned out while washing the dishes. She tried to look away from the water and the repetitive circling of the towel in the bowl but snapped out of it when one of the seasonings fell off the shelf. Turning off the faucet, she put the seasoning back in place and entered the bedroom bathroom. She opened the medicine cabinet, took out the soap and rose water, and started washing her face. The soap felt silky as it filled her hands, gently scrubbing her face. Splashing warm water across her face, she felt sleep overtake her. She quickly applied rose water to her face and brushed her teeth with her pink toothbrush to speed up the process. She didn't have to do much to her face since she had flawless skin, but she maintained a routine for her health.

She turned off the light in the bathroom. She was happy to be back home and finally able to rest. She left the door open for him, but another hour passed. She wasn't worried about safety because the building was occupied mostly by older people and women, and the main door required a key to open. She trusted that she would be safe during the night. Aside from her date, it would have been the second exciting thing that had happened to her. Even being haunted would be more comforting, as she wouldn't be alone. She chuckled at the thought of what would keep her from feeling lonely at night and sad in the morning. She appreciated it when her thoughts could provide her with some comfort. She hoped for a text or a call to explain why it took him two hours to return. She was sure he hadn't changed his mind, as he had shown much interest before she realized it. She believed something must have come up, causing him not to come right away.

She decided to text him, *"I'm going to bed. The door is unlocked. If you come back, please lock it. Goodnight. Kisses."*

She turned off all the lights and closed the curtains in the bedroom, leaving only a lamp on. Then, she sat on the bed and opened her nightstand to pull out a silk bonnet. After placing her bun in the bonnet, she curled under the covers, trying to get comfortable. Lying on her right side and facing the bedroom closet, she rested her head on the pillow, put her hands under her chin, and curled up under the covers. She lay there with her eyes open, surrounded by silence and her haunting thoughts. The other side of her bed remained empty, just as always.

*Why hasn't he texted me yet? Did he fall asleep in his apartment? Did he get cold feet? Did he not genuinely care, and it was all a hoax? Was he bored? Did the date go as well as I thought? A fool. Maybe I let my guard down too fast. He used my nana to have sex with me. I'm stupid and naïve. It had to be it; otherwise, the problem was just me. Nothing more, nothing less. I know I can be loved, my family did not abandon me, everything was in my head, and I could think happy thoughts. Maybe—*

She dozed off to sleep, feeling snug in her bed, surrounded by the warmth and softness of her sheets that smelled so fresh. As she faded into sleep, her eyes became heavy, her body felt smooth, and her heart and mind were calm, leaving her in a trance-like state. She was leaving her room and entering darkness as her eyes closed. A notification came from her phone as she fell asleep, but she did not care. She did not care what he had to say or why he took so long. She was exhausted and seemed to be dreaming. When her mother left, all those dreams she had disappeared, leaving her behind. It was strange. She tried to figure out what she was dreaming about and needed clarification. She was excited. It had been so long, and she wanted to know what her dream was telling her. Whatever emotion it evoked, she was willing to experience it, as it was all new to her again.

# The Nightmare

She stood in a grass field next to a big, intertwined tree. The clouds were enormous, almost unreal, as if someone had used a magnifying glass. Different shades of horses ran wild, and she could see a giant castle in the distance, with kids playing "ring around the rosy." At the corner of her eye, she spotted what appeared to be her nana and papa. They were so far away and dancing, which made her smile, but they went farther and farther away when she tried to walk towards them. She stopped, feeling heartbroken that she could not reach them, and decided to walk towards the castle. As she walked, her hands took turns touching the tall grass as she spread her fingers. She was wearing a dress resembling a wedding dress, made of white chiffon fabric with two snake-like patterns covering her breasts and poofy at the bottom. She had two gold rings on her right hand, a head full of curls, and no shoes.

Upon passing the children, who were dancing and laughing, one of the children ran to her.

"You came, rosie." He said cheerfully.

She didn't understand what was happening but felt like she knew him. He had fluffy black hair with slight curls and the cutest dimples. He wore white tennis shoes, black slacks, and a white T-shirt. He felt so familiar, but she could not put her finger on it. He grabbed her by the wrist and took her to the castle. They ran and then walked the rest of the way. She was curious about where in the castle he would take her. She wanted to stop but couldn't. He called her Rosie and said he had been waiting for her.

"You look fantastic." He said, out of breath. "We have been waiting for you, but why didn't you come sooner?" Moon shrugged. "Everyone was sad, but I'm happy you are back. I missed you, Rosie."

She smiled. "Why do you call me Rosie? The only person who called me that name was my mama." He didn't respond. "She always called me that because I would steal roses from her garden."

She felt them getting closer and grew weary. Something felt amiss, but it intrigued her.

"That is what she told me to call you. She always talked about you and said how beautiful you were. We almost thought you were a myth, but you are here. You are a rose, Rosie."

Her feet bled, but she felt no pain as she walked, noticing she was the only one leaving bloody marks on the black tile of the steps. "Where are we going?" She noticed her feet only bled when they touched the tile, which she found strange. She looked at him. "She wants to see you. She missed her little rosie."

They were standing in front of a large iron door. It was black with a wolf's head and a handle in its mouth. She knocked and knocked but received no answer. He looked up at her with *those eyes,* and she shivered.

"You don't have to knock; it's your home." Moon smiled in confusion. "My home?" she mumbled.

As they entered the castle, they held hands. The castle was large and made of gray-cream-like concrete, with two black railings on the side of the steps. Two figure statues held up the balcony: a man and a woman. Above the balcony, a giant wolf sat and howled, moving its head menacingly. The castle roof was black with green architecture. Trimmed trees and bushes with dark red roses adorned the sides of the steps, with pearls seeping out of them. Everything seemed blurry and significant, as if she shouldn't have seen more. Despite his small size, the little boy pushed the door open with surprising strength. Looking to be about ten years old, he held her hand as they walked in. Inside, the castle was an open space with a woman sitting at the piano and a tall figure of a man dancing in circles with two little girls. Outside, she could see identical little girls playing with the boy.

"She's been waiting. Come on."

The little boy led her to where the music was coming from. A shiver ran down her spine as he released her hand and ran over to the man and little girls, dancing and happy.

"Wait, where am I? Who wants to see me?" she yelled.

But it seemed as though he couldn't hear her and was in a trance, dancing. She glanced at the woman playing the piano, then back at the boy, and gasped. They were a blur—hidden figures.

It seemed like she was wearing glasses, with everything around her appearing transparent. Then she heard a voice say, "Little Rosie, you came." She turned around to look.

"Little boy!" she called. The voice called out again. "Little Rosie, can you hear me?"

She saw the woman at the piano, who had dirty blonde curly hair, slightly tan white skin, and long natural French-tipped fingernails. She wore the red dress Moon had worn earlier, with red heels and a gold crest pattern on the back. The woman played the piano beautifully, and the melody sounded familiar. "I am glad you came. I missed you, my little Rosie. If only you knew how much I missed you."

*That voice.*

Her heartbeat accelerated as she approached to see the woman's face. Shock overcame her as she realized it was her mother. She felt astonished, sad, and in disbelief. Her mother had deep brown doe eyes, a sharply upward nose, a small mouth with a full upper lip, and a round face. Her eyebrows were thin, and her cheekbones were sharp, reminiscent of a goddess.

She gathered her thoughts, but before speaking, her mother stopped playing and patted her hand on the seat. Moon sat beside her, and she could feel the anger and tears welling up. She wanted to speak, but her mouth stayed shut. Instead, she cried. She wasn't crying to be dramatic or because of how much she was hurt but because of how beautiful her mother was. She was Angel Moon, nothing more, nothing less. She could hate her for the rest of her life and still love her just as much. She reached out to touch her to see if she was there, and her mother smiled.

"You grew up. I kept an eye on you. If only your father could see you, he would have loved you so much. He would have loved you, Rosie."

"Yeah, he would have," she said as she wiped her tears.

Her mother touched her hair, her dress, and her face. "Little rosie, I know you are mad at me. I did not mean to leave you like that, but I had to. What mother could I have been? All the screaming, drinking, and hurt I caused you and the family, I just thought it best." She smiled and said, "I understand if you have nothing to say. It is not like I am here, but for you, I am. I do and did miss you."

"You missed me for fifteen years as much as a spider missed its web. I was nothing to you, but I thought I was. I get you were hurting over Daddy, but what about me? Yes, Nana and Pa cared for me but didn't call once. I have been hurt most of my life, but now I am just angry because you left me. I have no one now. Are you here for me, or just here to torture my consciousness because God knows I need that?" Moon said heatedly. Her face was red and hot. Her emotions were pumping.

"I know," Angel said softly. "A mother should be a mother, but I am a person too. Yes. I should have considered that you would be more hurt by me being gone, but your father died while you were in my womb. He only felt you kick once; he did not see your first walk, hear your first word, or see you. He did not get to meet you because he was a sad man. Sad as a man can be, I could not save him as you could not. I had to do that myself, so I got the courage to leave you," She paused for a minute, then said, "I thought it was the best choice, and even if I am not here, you are my little Rosie. I could not lose anything, so I had to leave you behind. I—"

Moon interrupted her. "What about Nana and Pa? Did you even know they died? If you did, why didn't you come to the funeral? What excuse do you have for that?"

"Oh, baby, I was there in spirit, even though not in body. They were my parents, of course. You couldn't handle me being there, but I kept you all in my heart."

"You kept us in your heart." Her face tensed.

"Rosie, do not be so angry, hmm," she said, fiddling with the curls in Moon's hair, then placing her hands on Moon's. "It leaves wrinkles." She smiled, and so did Moon slightly.

*I was not too fond of my mama saying that whenever I got angry because I knew it was to get me to laugh. She always said, "Do not get too angry, or it will leave wrinkles, and then you will wonder why you're twenty-looking forty-five. It happened to me."*

"Oh, sweetie, I would never want to intentionally hurt you or Nana and Pa. I just felt bitter for a while, but you will see that bitterness has faded with time. I was heartbroken, just like you, when my parents died. I don't want the same for you, especially. If only I were there to comfort and support you, I am here for you now."

"If only for many things. Why am I here? Why did you want to see me?"

"Well, I missed you, and that sweet baby brought you to me. I hope he did not scare you. Nana and Pa love him and wanted to say hi, but they wanted us to talk."

"Nana and Pa? You talked to them, and who is the little boy?"

"Yes, I did, Rosie. We were happy to know you were coming, but like I said, they had to go. They told me to tell you to stop being afraid of everything that is meant for you, to be calm, and that they love you."

"And what about you? Is that all you have to tell me? Because I could say so much more?"

"Little Rosie, the only thing I have to tell you is that you are resilient, and you will always be my daughter, my baby," she said fondly with such sad eyes. "Oh, that little boy is a friend of sorts. Do not worry about him, but did you notice he had such pretty eyes, just like your daddy."

"Yes, Mama, I did see. The angels themselves would descend if they knew he had them." She said sarcastically. "Yes, they would."

Her mother turned to the piano and started playing again, swaying to the melody, while the man danced in circles with his little girls as if there was no other place to be.

"I'm listening, baby." She wanted to say more. She tried to shout everything she thought of when she was a child. Imagining this very moment, she knew, in a way, it was not real. It was a dream, though it felt like it wasn't. So, she just sat there with her, trying not to be upset, and asked her questions to which she knew she had the answer.

"Mama, how much did you love Daddy? Why did you let it consume you? It wasn't fun to be around you when it seemed like he had power over you. It broke my heart."

Her mother looked at her and smiled.

"Honey, that's what love does. It can make or break you. I tried to help you understand when you were a child, but you didn't know love from my perspective. You knew love as Nana giving you a cookie before dinner or taking rides on Papa's back. You never knew love as I did. Getting to know someone and all their flaws, seeing them every day, and embracing them in intimate ways, and then that love is gone. How could I explain that to you? I mean, you were a child, and I was broken. Yes, broken is the word for such a long time."

"I knew exactly what you meant as a child. I loved you, didn't I?"

"Yes, you did. I just—"

"You assumed I couldn't comprehend love like an adult. I did, and it broke me, but I never let it run my life. Like you."

"Fair point, I could have done more."

"Besides—Love? What is love anyway? I do not want to sit up thinking about someone else. How would it benefit me? How is love going to benefit me? I could imagine the most heart-wrenching, sinister, and all-consuming love and, in the end, still not want it. Maybe that is just for me, but seeing you in that much pain would make me curse love. I hate it for what it did to you and our family. I can only come so close to love, but I am scared. I will always fear it. Oh, mama, if you knew."

"Love is so many things, but it is never hugely beneficial to the person unless they want it to be. Baby girl, love is love. Humans express it in so many ways. Love is art. Love is history. Love is words. Love is the world. Love is us. Love is just here. I can defend its case, but the very soul you possess is love. Love is love, nothing you can see or grasp but feel. The hardest lesson anybody has to learn is that you will feel it whether you want to or not. In this life or the next. At this age or later. In a person or a book. Love will always be there."

Moon ran her fingers along the piano keys and played a tune. She was silent for a moment before speaking. "Then, why did Daddy become so sad?"

"He was sad. He just was. I cannot give you this grand explanation of why, but you know why."

"I do because you are here, but not here."

"Exactly."

"Maybe later, then."

"Maybe." She smiled.

"You have his eyes, and knowing that kept me alive. You were the best thing he ever gave me. Our love took shape through you."

"I know. It was like you grew a rose of your own. The sun and the garden worked together. Daddy is the sun, and you are the garden. It rained and rained, and then the sun appeared and, working together, created a seed. It nested and grew until it blossomed into a rose. It had all ten toes and fingers. Big brown eyes and skin that glistened in the sun. Your little rosie. Mama, you have told me this story since I could walk."

"At least you know it by heart." She chuckled. "Play with me a little longer."

"Okay."

Time seemed to stand still as she felt the music on her fingertips. Her ears picked up the sound of her blood coursing through her veins as she played the piano. It was an uncontrollable and all-consuming feeling. She loved it when her mother took her to the basement, where they had a piano and played for hours. It was not her passion but an excuse to be closer to her mother. As she absorbed everything around her, she felt never-ending and loved. Her mother stopped playing, watching as she bent the piano to her will, emulating what she knew.

"Perfect baby."

"Thanks, mama"

"Remember the song I used to sing to you?"

"A little, why?"

"Sing it for me, baby. Please."

"Little rose, little rose.

Trampling in the garden

Little rose, little rose.

Where have you hidden?

Little rose, little rose—"

"Ah yes, little rose, I will try to find you.

It took the sun and the garden to plant a seed.

The rain is a blessing but a burden to be.

We want you to grow; look how big you came to be.

Little rose, little rose, we planted a seed.

It took the sun, the garden, and the rain for you to be," She sang happily, moving her hands side by side. Moon hummed along to the same song that was her lullaby, the very song that sent her off to sleep. She hoped her mother knew the rest because it was a blur to her.

"Little rose, little rose, how can this be?

Little rose, little rose, I need you next to me.

Little rose, little rose, come home so I can tuck you in safely.

Little rose, little rose, a gift meant to be.

Pausing at the final line, her mother said, "My rose, little rose, has left the garden."

Suddenly, she couldn't hear her mother, but her mother kept singing. It was an empty sound. She could see that her mother knew she couldn't hear her, but her mother kept singing the song repeatedly, which drove her crazy. She tried to understand what happened, saying, "I can't hear you, mama!"

"I can't hear you!"

"I can't hear you, mama!" She cried out loudly, and her scream echoed through the castle. In an instant, her mother vanished.

In shock, she got up and looked around the room. It was empty. She ran through the castle, repeatedly calling out, "Mama!"

However, no one was in sight, not even the man and the little girls. The little boy with green eyes somehow appeared at the top of the stairs. He looked pale when the sun shone on him, like a bright light.

"Where is she? Where did she go?" she whispered in a low and sad tone as tears filled her eyes once more. "Don't cry," said the little boy as he descended the stairs. "She will be back, not now, but she will."

His piercing green eyes locked onto her, and his gaze was familiar and comforting. As he reached the bottom of the stairs, he sprinted toward her and embraced her. She hesitated momentarily before returning the hug. "I am sorry for your pain. It will be over soon. Do not worry, but I have to show you something before you can go home." She nodded in agreement and let him lead the way.

When they left the castle, the wolf howled so loudly that the sky magically turned into night. They walked and walked; it seemed like forever. Her grandparents were gone, and there was no sign of her mom or that family.

"Where is your family? Why didn't you go with them? They might get worried."

"They never worry. I am here to guide you so you will not be alone. Though it is my fault, you are alone."

"I don't see how I'm alone because of you—but okay." They came to a halt. He leaned over and said, "The name is Wolfe."

In response, she said, "Nice to meet you, Wolfe. I am Moon, but I think you prefer little rosie."

She smiled, hoping that wherever he took her was neither scary nor dangerous. She checked her surroundings and saw they had stopped before a bed of roses. There was a grave named Lincoln Bowie—her father, mystery man, and mother's heart.

"What are we doing here?" She went and sat in front of the tombstone, wondering what her mother meant when she said he was a sad man. She knew he died, but they never did say how, and she did not question it. She did not need to think hard about it. She could see what her mother meant, and it felt haunting to know. She turned her head and asked again, "What are we doing here, Wolfe?"

"I thought you should see him before you go."

"See what."

There was an echo of silence as she turned to see Wolfe gone and everything in her sight misty. The tombstone eulogy stated, "*A loving and caring husband and son. He was beloved. Gone too soon, but forever in our hearts.*" A sigh left her mouth as mist surrounded her, and it became cold. She did not know the man, but he impacted her. She knew of the great Lincoln Bowie, who made her mother tremble at her knees and left an everlasting impression on the family. Her mother told ghost stories of him to her at bedtime when she could function, making her sad and hopeful he could come back from the grave and be her father. She would pray at night just to tell the universe to send him back because her mother was lost without him, and she needed a daddy to tuck her in at night, not knowing it would fuck her up later in life.

Moon started crying again. She wished they had visited his grave more often. At first, it was every day, then every two weeks, every two months, and eventually, they stopped visiting altogether. She lay on the flat, dirty, grassy earth with her father beneath her. It all felt so real, as if he was there. She wondered if he could see her during her poetry nights, getting an A on her math test, or her first kiss with a boy she had a crush on. He missed all these moments because he was sad. She never knew anybody in the family could be that sad. She had thought her mother might have left this world due to all the sadness that oozed from her. She believed it was just her consciousness playing tricks on her. She did not know how he died, but suicide seemed so farfetched. She used to write poetry about this man every chance she got. Journals stained with her tears and a broken heart. If only she could ask Nana and Papa; they were gone, too. The only one left was her mother, but she did not know where she was, and for all she knew, she was dead, too.

She had Marleen, who was like an aunt but had her own family and issues. She did not want to burden her. The roses felt so soft, like a bed against her skin. She was cold but felt happy to be near her father. Her crying turned into small sobs of love that she never got to experience or express. He was not just an ordinary father to her but a towering figure. Whether he was sad or not, he was her everything besides her mother—merely the side effects of being a child with absent parents. There was no choice but to hold onto hope and love. She could hear footsteps approaching. Reacting quickly, she sat up, and her eyes were watery. She couldn't see clearly in the dark. It was a dark figure. She couldn't make out their face, but he wore a black muscle shirt, grey square-patterned suit pants, black dress shoes, a gold watch, and a gold wedding ring. His hair was cut into a fade, and his skin was chestnut brown with a red undertone. As the person came closer, she could see their eyes were simple brown, their sculpted chin with a dimple, average-sized lips, and a wide nose that was sharp at the tip.

The figure in the shadows was her father. She could not move, and she did not know how to feel. She wanted to run towards and hug him, but she was confused, a bit scared, and did not understand. She used the tomb as leverage to stand up.

She reached out her hand and said, "Daddy?" She did not know whether to smile or cry, so she did both. She said, "Daddy, it's me, Aira, your baby girl."

"Please say something."

He opened his mouth, and yellow liquid fell out. She became worried and ran to him, but her feet could not move as the rose's vines wrapped around her leg. Her father was stuck in that spot, far away from her. She yelled, "Daddy!".

Dirt was coming out of his mouth as he spoke. She was filled with adrenaline and fear as she attempted to pull away, tugging at the vines, leaving marks on her legs instead.

"Help him! Help!" she screamed as tears ran down her face and her voice faded into silence. Wolfe appeared in the mist, watching but doing nothing. She couldn't yell anymore but looked, hoping he would help. His green eyes glowed in the fog, but he did not.

It seemed as though she was on a mission. Her feet ran and ran as her father gradually faded into the mist around them. She angrily tore at one of the vines, then fell and stabbed the ground with a shovel that appeared out of nowhere, screaming out of anger.

"He is gone! He is gone because of you! He is always going to be gone!"

Breaking free, she sprinted and reached for her father's hand. By a slim chance, she touched him and smiled. Unfortunately, a force pulled her into the air, making everything below look tiny, and her father disappeared. She moved higher and higher from the ground, her body dangling with nothing to hold onto. When she opened her eyes, she saw the dim light of the bedroom and noticed that Dawn was sleeping across from her.

*I felt confused, silent, and awake, yet not entirely alone.*

# 6. Goldilocks (flashback²)

## "Aira!"

My mama shouted disagreeably and with great passion. I knew I was going to be in trouble again for hiding her bottle of whiskey. She had four usual spots: the car, my room, the kitchen, and the bathroom. Whenever I found any supply, I would smash it and get rid of it. If I didn't know any better, she would have been one step closer to the grave, just like my daddy. I knew she would be angry, but I didn't care. I was seven and a half years old. I needed a mother, not a drunk. She hadn't acted like a mother since I was six, but her parents took over. It was sad. I still held onto hope for our relationship, but at this rate, she might as well be dead. Uselessness and heartbreak seem to be the only things going for her. I ran to my room and hid in my closet, knowing she was coming and dreading it. All she would do was yell and demand I hand over her drug.

It numbed her to whatever she was feeling. I'll never understand what kind of mother puts her addiction before her child. I know my daddy died before I was born, but she has been stuck in the same place. Her heart should have healed by now. I knew I would never be like her when I became a woman. Love would not control my life. It would not hinder me. My life would be mine. My heart would be mine. It was not like it hadn't withered from her abandonment and lack of having a daddy. She would never be my mama, not really. Her mama was my mama, more than she could ever be. Angel Moon, ladies and gentlemen. A class act of toxic motherhood and trauma.

My hair was in a bun with a red bow wrapped around it. Two curly strands of hair hung in front of my face. I was wearing a grapefruit-colored sundress with red tights. I had on black Mary Jane shoes to match. I was wearing small gold hoop earrings and a gold bracelet that says, *"Little Rosie,"* a gift from Mama. I was sitting on the sunflower cushion I always reserved for hiding in the closet. My legs were close to my chest, and my arms were crossed over them. The closet door was made of thick wood with a gold knob bearing my

Mama and Daddy's initials. The closet contained toys, clothes, and forgotten items such as my baby crib and photo albums.

"Aira! This is the last time! Where are you?" She yelled.

I rolled my eyes at the thought that I was the one hiding, as if she wasn't in the wrong. My grandparents had left for church, but I didn't go this time because I couldn't stomach religion. It wasn't my thing. I knew I prayed, but that was only on my mama's behalf and belief. I wasn't an atheist, either. I believed in a higher power, but I didn't think it sent a man to die for our sins on the cross. That sounded like something adults came up with to avoid responsibility for their actions. Nana felt the same way, too, but she didn't say it to avoid starting a debate with Papa. Always pleasing a man, once again, and with my mama, it was beyond the grave.

If only others could feel what I feel right now. Dealing with Mama's screaming, crying, puking, and occasional blackouts has become a routine. It was ridiculous. Sometimes, she found me in the closet, but I hoped today wasn't one of those days because I was not up for it. I couldn't wait until Nana and Papa returned home – they always saved me from her tantrums and screaming. It's the screaming that really gets to me. I was never immune to her drunk slurring. She was like an angel with no wings, but all her beauty faded. Sometimes, I called Mama "Angel" when she made me angry. Today, she was irritating, like a little child looking for a lost toy.

I am proud to be an only child because I wouldn't want the trauma to be passed down to any siblings. I even wondered if I wished to have kids or a husband when I got older. It is not needed in the 21st century. Keyword need, instead of wanted. When and if I decided, hopefully, I would be in a good place because I would hate to damage anyone how my mama was doing me. I know church lasted for about two hours. It had only been an hour. Mama was sleeping on the couch, passed out, when I smashed all the bottles of whiskey she had hidden. I wanted her to get better and enjoy it, too. I will say it was risky but worth my sanity and hers.

In the long run, this helped her even if she didn't see it now. I realized I didn't lock the closet door, so I turned the lock. I tended to do that so she wouldn't get in, and I would be safe from all the yelling and throwing of things in my room. One time, she broke my collection of turtles. It took me a year to collect all of them, but Papa came to the rescue and bought me more. He rode to antique stores for two days to find turtles I would like to collect as a surprise. He brought them to me in a blue gift box with a white ribbon. He said, "A gift from your ma. She wanted to apologize but was too embarrassed to give it to you herself." I knew Mama didn't get me the gift, but it pleased Papa to realize I would pretend she did. I had an achy heart when I knew someone loved me more than a bottle. He leaned down, put his hand on my cheek, and said, "Forgive your mama, for she does not know what she does." Cliché, but a father at work for his child.

I heard my bedroom door open. The sound of the door scraping against the floor was so loud that my heart skipped a beat, but I think it was just my heightened senses. I heard my mother's footsteps slowly shuffling across the floor. I knew she was wearing that same old blue robe my father used to wear, the pajamas she never took off, and the same black house slides. It was surprising when she took showers most days. Her hair was always down and curly, and her face looked sad - it was her everyday look, whether in or out of the house. Each step she took made me more frightened.

I knew my mama wouldn't physically hurt me, but in other places, she could.

"Aira! I know you're here. Baby, come out and tell me where you put Mama's special drinks. I promise I won't yell like last time."

I sat in the same spot and stayed quiet. She said this every time, and I always got yelled at for saying I poured them out. I should wait it out and wait for Nana and Papa. I could hear her dragging her feet all over the room, searching through my things and throwing things. I heard nothing break, so I assumed my turtles were okay. She stopped at the closet door. She began to yank on the doorknob and stopped because she noticed it was locked.

I could hear her deep breath as she said, "I know you're in there, Aira." I could hear the impatience in her voice. Her hands started to beat on the door and pull on the doorknob. I sat there, still unfazed. As I said, it was routine at this point.

Her banging turned into her fists slamming into the door. Yelling at me, she said, "You're a little nuisance! You know that. How dare you touch my shit! Sometimes, I wish I could get rid of you!"

As usual, my eyes moved ahead of my emotions, and I started to cry. I rocked back and forth, hoping the beating on the door would stop. I hated it when she became like this. She wasn't my mama in this state. I could envision her hateful expressions while repeating, "I should have aborted you!"

It tore through me every time it happened. I was expecting it but didn't understand why my body hadn't gotten used to it by now. I took a vow of silence with my mama. I hadn't talked to her in a month because she was a shell of herself—nothing but an empty husk. She never smiled or laughed. All she did was cry herself to sleep and drink. It was all she was—nothing. It was a repeating cycle.

I spotted my blue bunny in the far corner of the closet amidst all the chaos. I grabbed it and hugged it tightly. It was the only source of warmth in my life. My daddy had given it to me before I was born, or so my mama liked to say when the angels descended on earth and planted me in her womb. I knew the truth about sex, but I let her continue with her fables about my birth. Whenever she spoke of the garden or angels, I just listened. Even though I've had chances to tell her to shut up, I knew it helped keep her mostly sane, no matter how sadly poetic it was. She was my mama, and all I had to do was wait it out. There I was, rocking back and forth as if in a cradle. It kept me calm. I wanted to shout back badly and explain how she ruined me, but it would be like talking to a brick wall.

The next thing I knew, everything was quiet. I stopped rocking back and forth and put my ear to the door. Based on some clues, I figured out she was up to something; if she was, it meant trouble. She never backed down. The door shook with a direct hit. I didn't know what it was, but I jumped back, scooting behind the clothes in my closet to the wall, gripping my bunny for dear life. It turned out that it was my mama hitting the door with a metal bat. I recognized the bat - it belonged to Papa when he used to play. It had the name "Vic" written in big black letters. That's what the other baseball players used to call him from time to time – "Big Vic." I used to watch him swing it in the afternoons when he felt he didn't have the game in him anymore, but he did. When that big metal bat swung, it was the size of a nuclear launch against Mother Nature, so I knew it could do some damage to that door.

It felt like I was experiencing a heart attack; my body was overloaded, and I didn't know what to do. Although she had been angry before, it was nothing like this.

She continued to shout, "Give me my shit, Aira!"

I was in disarray and afraid of my mama. As a child, I felt powerless against an adult. All I could do was scream and cry. Suppose I had to damage my voice and snatch out my lungs for her to leave, then I would make sure that door rattled with my pain. Swing after swing and crash after crash, I exploded. The size of the hole destroyed the door.

In all my might, I screamed past the terror and tears, "Stop it, mama! Stop it! I want Nana! I want Papa! You're scaring me! I don't have anything!" She kept hitting the door no matter what I did. So, I said, "Daddy! Daddy would protect me and hate you for this!" as the hot tears stung and burned my eyes from the constant crying.

I recounted what I had said and noticed the bat stopped hitting, and the door became still, even though it was damaged. Seeing through the clothes covering my face was difficult, but she looked terrible. It was as if she was a monster lurking in the shadows. Everything about her exuded darkness and horror. She wore the same robe and pajamas, and her dirty hair was disheveled. Her eyes were crazy, and her hands were bleeding from banging on the wooden closet door earlier.

"What did you say?" she asked as she stumbled back onto my bed.

"I said daddy wouldn't like you hurting your little Rosie. You're Aira, his Aira."

I lay on the closet floor in a fetal position. My big brown eyes could see Mama start to cry on the bed. Her hands were covered in blood from hitting the wood, and the bat was also bloody.

She just cried and said, "I'm sorry, baby. I just wanted to numb the pain." She stared at the closet door, unable to see me. "You look so pretty in your dress." Wiping her tears, "Did you know I picked it out? I thought it would pair great with your eyes and hair color since we couldn't find red," she slurred.

I put my stuffed bunny to my mouth to fight the urge to cry again and respond. No matter what she said for those few minutes, I lay there silent, incapable of loving her or forgiving her at that moment. "As I said, I'm sorry, baby. I got ahead of myself and didn't think. You're just a child." I still didn't respond. She fell quiet as the bat had in my mind. All I could hear was our breathing, one after the other: daughter and mother.

Some time passed, and I lay there until I fell asleep. This wasn't part of our routine. She usually shouted and banged on the closet door, then left and passed out on the couch. This time was different. I loved Angel, but she could be difficult and weak at times. I had never experienced grief and didn't want to. The only time I had felt that kind of sadness was when my pet turtle died. I found it next to the school playground, half of its shell torn off and barely alive. I nursed it back to health; I considered it mine from then on. I loved that turtle. I still miss it sometimes, but one day, it closed its little eyes and was gone. I had named it Bowie, after my father. I figured if he wasn't here physically, why not in spirit? That was a long time ago when I was obsessed with who my daddy was, but now I am not.

I wanted nothing to do with him or anything related to him. I wouldn't say I like the thought of enduring Angel's daily torment filled with drinking and rage. I miss the person she used to be. I know people change and grow, but this is not the same. She used to smile, laugh, hug, and be kind. She used to bake, dance, and create memories but suddenly stopped. As I turned six, she began to seem distant and erratic, just as she is now. There have been times when I've considered running away because of it, but I always knew that Nana and Papa were here to protect and guide me. I wanted her to leave if this was what it would feel like without them. I knew that if I told them, she would be sent to rehab or something even worse. I had to think about it because she was my mama.

Who knew what a foreign place like that would do to her? She wouldn't be home, and it would be like a prison. As much as I hated her right now, I didn't want her trapped in a cage and left alone. Even now, I could leave this room, but I don't want to leave her alone. It would be a betrayal, in a way, sadly. She was my mama. If I could time travel, Daddy would still be here, and she would be the happiest woman on Earth. I hated to admit it, but I would never leave her; who could?

A loud thump woke me up. I sat up, stretched my arms and legs, and a pile of clothes hit my face. I hurried to the door and peeked through the big hole in the closet door. I saw Angel passed out on my bed, with a whiskey bottle nearby. My room looked neat, so I assumed the bottle had come from somewhere else. I was shocked because I thought she didn't have any money. Nana and Papa had stopped giving her money because she kept buying alcohol. I unlocked the door as quietly as possible, rubbed my sore backside from sitting on the floor, and looked around. The only thing out of place was my bed.

I took a closer look at the bed and noticed some liquid and what appeared to be vomit at the edge of it. I didn't pay much attention to it because I was used to such things. I removed my Mary Jane shoes, neatly placed them in the closet, and then put my bunny on a chair in my room. After that, I searched through my clothes for my favorite pajamas, which were pinkish-red with small, funny-looking creatures on them. I had bought them from a thrift store, so no one else in the house recognized them.

I untied the ribbon bow from my bun and let my hair down. I picked up my bunny and pushed the door against the wall. To cover the hole, I threw an old blue blanket over it so it wouldn't be noticeable for the next fifteen years. Then, I took the thick pieces of wood from the closet door and threw them in the garbage can outside. After that, I looked around my room for the bat and found it in the hallway. I dragged it behind me to the bathroom, cleaned off the blood, and then returned it to Nana and Papa's room.

I re-entered my room and sighed as I headed over to the bed. It reeked of alcohol and whatever smell came from Angel.

I decided to lie beside her, so I crawled lightly onto the bed so as not to wake her. I brought my bunny close to my chest as I lay beside her. I was so close I could smell the liquor on her breath. I knew that when Nana and Papa came home, they would smell it on her from a mile away, and I would only want her to get in trouble for that rather than for putting a hole in my closet door. I knew I would have nightmares for some time, but who doesn't? As I said, I'm used to it. I could see every breath she took as she slept. I could see the dry blood on her hands and prints on the bottle in her hand. I could see the tear stains on her face and how her clothes needed to be washed. I could see the greasiness of her hair. I could see so many flaws in Angel, and it still couldn't stop me from loving her.

She looked so peaceful as she lay there. I didn't know what to say or how to act. I just wanted to cry again. I hated how I cried so much. I couldn't help it. It was all I could do for her, me, and our situation. I wouldn't tell Nana and Papa about what happened hours ago. I knew they would be home soon. I kept calm and turned over onto my back. I looked up at the ceiling. I wondered. If I made a wish for it to collapse, would it? I didn't love my life exactly, but I loved my grandparents and Angel. I wondered if it would be better for us if we were dead. I couldn't let her die alone. It would be betrayal, and I knew she counted on me. If I squinted hard, maybe it would work.

It would be sad and heartbreaking for my grandparents to come home to that, but it would be the best. Our bodies would be demolished. It would be bloody. It would be satisfactory. We needed to move on, and being dead would fix that. It would be freeing and chaotic, but it would work. I always imagined what it would be like. Would our souls leave our bodies quickly, would we suffer, or would it be quick and unmemorable to our souls? At least we would be with Daddy and be in what we called heaven.

As I thought of us sitting in an open grass field, surrounded by rose beds, during a picnic, I couldn't help but cry. Mama and Daddy showed their love for each other while I played. I could imagine the peace and beauty of the scene, and it made me happy. Trying not to cry out loud, I bite my lip. Angel was snoring next to me. My thoughts were screaming for everything to fall apart. I liked to think I would die before Angel because I was smaller, but she was drunk, so she wouldn't feel a thing. Instant impact. Wham!

I let out a giggle. I thought I was going crazy. Maybe that's the only thing she had managed to give me – nothing good, something wrong. I felt my sanity slipping. I couldn't express this to her or my grandparents because they would worry too much. I stared at the thick, white ceiling. It was clean and smooth. It would be like heaven caving in on us. Maybe that was how you got there. A dense, white ceiling.

Smooth it was, but you had others that weren't so smooth. I thought we fell into the other category in life.

We were like a ceiling. It either stayed put or fell. Ours seemed smooth from afar, but if you looked closely, you found bumps here and there. I was tired of selling myself short about having a happy family. I lived in pure hell, even though I didn't believe in it. The concept fitted my life, at least. It did not fall. I knew it wouldn't, but in my imagination, it did.

My nose started to run, and my throat became scratchy from all the crying. I felt Angel's hand grab mine and pull me closer to her chest. I looked over at her and said, "Mama?"

She didn't respond at first, but I lay there, head near her chest and knees balled up with my bunny between us. I could mockingly say that Daddy, Mama, and I were together again.

"Aira," she whispered.

"I'm here," I whispered back.

She grinned slightly and said, "I knew you would be." I rolled my eyes at the remark.

"Lay here with me, will you? Just for a little while. I don't want to be alone."

How could she ask that? Of course, I would lie with her, but I drew a heart on her lips to let her know. She always did that to me as a baby to say, 'I love you.' I smiled, and she smiled.

"Love you too. I'm sorry, baby girl," she whispered again.

"It's okay, mama," I said meekly.

I took in her presence; I couldn't bring myself to say I forgive her because I couldn't. I could clean up after her and take care of her mess this time, but it had created a wedge between us. I loved her, but I didn't like her. In time, things would get better, but not at this moment. I breathed into my stuffed bunny to escape from the smell of alcohol. Angel kissed my temple without warning and said, "My little Rosie." I couldn't help but look at her with my doll-like eyes and cry.

# 7. Sweet Dreams

He was lying about three feet away from her. His face was partly covered by his beautiful black hair, which resembled that of a black stallion. He wore no shirt, and she saw his toned and prominent muscles. She wondered if he wore boxers, pajama pants, or nothing under the covers. She smiled at the thought of the last option. Slowly, she reached over and pulled the covers back a little. She saw that he was wearing Calvin Klein boxers, which she found to be an exciting choice. The dim light made him look a bit yellowish due to his paleness, but he still looked handsome. She turned around and picked up her phone to check the time. It was only around 4:00 am, which meant he had been by her side for about 40 minutes. She was still concerned about him being three hours late but decided to address it later.

She had a great view. She wanted to get closer but didn't want to come off as creepy by staring at him while he slept. It made her wonder if he watched her sleep. She hoped she didn't snore or talk in her sleep. It had been so long since she dreamed that everything felt new to her again. It was nice seeing him. He was near her, and she dared to dissect his character. He slept gracefully as if he was defined and royal. He slept as if he owned the world, tossing and turning in such a fanciful way. It was as if he wasn't real. He seemed like such an unusual person to her, but then again, in life, she questioned everything. Her big doe eyes flickered endlessly as she watched, finding the courage to get closer and move his hair out of his face.

All of him was in her view. He shone like the sun with such dim light in the room. She took comfort in knowing someone was next to her. She grabbed his arm from his side and placed it around her as she snuggled underneath him. She moved her face near his. Their noses were an inch apart. She thought how cute it was to nuzzle him, so she used the tip of her nose to rub his. She did it three times before he smiled.

"Psst," she whispered.

His eyebrows furred in response, and his body moved closer to her, pulling her into his chest. He let out a small sigh and said, "Hello, Rose," in a mumble.

She giggled and said, "Are you awake?"

There wasn't a response, but after a few minutes, he said, "What do you think?"

"I don't know."

"Then, "don't know," and go back to sleep."

She nudged his chest with her fist and said, "Dawn!" in a whiny voice.

 He smirked and opened his pretty green eyes, eye to eye with her.

"I'm just kidding. What is it, lovely? You couldn't sleep?"

"No."

"Then what?"

"I think I had a nightmare, but it might have just been a dream. I haven't dreamed since my mama left me fifteen years ago, and today, of all days, I do." She said, looking down.

He kissed her forehead and said, "You never told me about the dream thing, but no matter. Maybe it was both. What was it about?"

"I don't know. It seemed like a distant blur, but my Mama and Daddy were there. It was this weird little boy, a wolf; day turned into night. I don't know; it was just weird," she said, concerned. "All I know is I didn't like it, but I liked how I saw my nana and papa. It was soothing in a way. I think that is the only thing I liked."

"I know you expressed this disdain for your parents before, but did you not enjoy seeing them at all?"

"You're the one to ask," she said, smiling and tracing circles on his chin.

"Well, obviously, it doesn't diminish my love for my parents. I just don't like them."

"I never knew my daddy. Seeing him was eye-opening. In terms of opening old wounds, I thought I put away, but it's no secret I have issues with my parents. Who doesn't on this planet."

He reclined on the bed, allowing Moon to rest on his chest while his fingers traced her back beneath her shirt. "And your mother? How did it feel seeing her."

She fell silent for a moment, thinking of what to say and how to say it. My mama was always a mix of good and bad. You can either love or hate her, so I would say both. However, I feel like my love for her prevailed. In the dream, at least, she appeared to be sober.

"Maybe your dream was trying to tell you to face your fears. Have you tried to get in contact with your mother? I'm not saying you have to, but it could mean closure."

"Closure?"

" Yeah, closure."

"I've thought about it for about fifteen years, but my grandparents always brushed it off. They would say they didn't know where she was, but somehow have presents from her on holidays and my birthday." She laid her hand flat under her chin and turned her head to look up at Dawn. "Marleen, I'm not sure if I mentioned her, but she is like an aunt to me, and she almost gave away where she was, but my nana put a stop to that."

His eyes filled with pity as he said, "That's sad." They laughed.

"Yeah, but I'll have to think about it. Now that Nana and Papa aren't here, I could ask Marleen. See what comes up."

"That's good. If you do, make sure to tell me all about it. Okay."

"Yeah, sure. I'll have a party," she said sneeringly.

"Be nice." He said firmly. "I'm just saying I will be here for you, that's all."

She scrunched her nose and blew a kiss. "Okay, sorry. When it comes to my mama, I get defensive, but I will think about it. I might even visit Daddy one of these days."

"I understand. My parents make me lose my mind, too. Family, right?"

"Yeah, don't you just love reunions?"

She moved from his chest and sat against the pillows on the bed. She didn't have a headboard. She was a bare-wall type of girl. She didn't have the money to get the bed she wanted, so this circle bed alone would do. He sat beside her, and she said, "And, speaking of reunions. What took you so long to come back? Three hours, to be exact."

"I knew I would be in trouble. If you will it, can I be honest?"

She had a look of confusion on her face as she said, "Well, I wouldn't want anything less of the truth."

"After I showered, or whatnot. I got a call from my sisters, not my parents, but that is their style."

"Yes."

"They wanted to invite me to my uncle's engagement party."

"That's nice, but I thought you weren't in contact with your family."

"I'm not, but my number hasn't changed. Sometimes, they will call to catch up, but usually, it's my uncle. We have been close since I was a teenager. He gets me, you know." She nodded her head.

"I told them I love Uncle Bronte and wouldn't mind coming. They said I could bring a plus one—so I was hoping you could come."

"I do not know. They really wouldn't mind, would they? I wouldn't want to impose on such a family event."

"No. It would take the pressure off of returning after six years."

"Well—"

"Pretty please!" He begged playfully.

She laughed, elbowed him, lay on his shoulder, and said, "Okay, okay, you big baby."

He grinned in victory as he played with her curls a little. "Wow! Uncle Bronte is engaged. That's a first. Who would have thought."

"Why would you say that?"

"Let's say he was an adventurous bachelor when I was a kid."

"Oh."

Dawn smirked. "Yeah, he used to rant about love not being for him, only family. He would detest things that dealt with love or relationships."

"He sounds fun and just like me." She joked.

He pinched her, and she said, "Ouch."

"He was worse than you, but you are not an anti-love person, but then again, I can't read your mind."

"Exactly," she said, pinching him back. He flinched and smirked again. "He's cool, and you will like him. I don't know how you will fare with the rest of my family, but they might have changed over the years."

"Maybe."

"Um, that reminds me. It took me so long to come back because my parents overheard my sisters and me, and then they joined the call. One thing led to another."

"I see."

"Yeah. Let's say everyone is all caught up."

"I'm happy to have started a reunion between you and your family. Who knew I was that kind of girl."

"Yeah, who knew I had such a lady on my arm," he said as he tickled her. She laughed endlessly as she tried to pull away, and they ended up in the middle of the bed and him on top of her. Her legs wrapped around his waist and arms around his neck. "If you wanted to go more rounds, you could have just asked." She rolled her eyes and said, "Don't flatter yourself; I just like it when you are close, my cuddling buddy."

"Cuddling buddy, huh?"

"Yeah," she said, biting her bottom lip.

"I can work with that." He said, looking down at her lips.

He leaned in for a kiss, and they kissed sweetly, then stared into each other's eyes. It was delightful, quiet, and drowning. It was like talking without speaking a word. At that moment, Moon had no fears or worries. It was just the two of them.

*Love. It was the only word popping into my head. Not to say I was in love. I mean, wouldn't that be too fast? I can't be in love. I like him and care for him. I'm sure he feels the same way, but who knows? Love. It was the only word I thought of. I wonder what he had said about me to his family and if they would like me. It was not in my playbook to be thinking about these things. I wondered what his family looked like and if they could be nice to me. I didn't have a big family like Dawn, which made me nervous. I don't want to overthink anything. His family probably was less of an embarrassment than mine was. I'm not saying they were, but it was no fairytale.*

She disrupted the moment as she removed her arms from his neck and moved to the other side of the bed, and he did the same. She sat back up and said, "So, what did you say about me?"

Dawn stared at her. "What did you say about me to your family?" she said, raising her eyebrows with intrigue. "OH!"

"Yeah."

"I said I met a gorgeous young woman that I had my sights set on for a while and that we went on a date."

"Okay." She sat on her legs, suggesting he tell her more.

"I said, Father and Mother, you should see how breathtaking she is. She has these big brown doll eyes that could make you melt on the inside, and this strong personality that doesn't make her too agreeable, but rather approachable." He said jokingly.

"Hey!" she said, punching his stomach.

He laughed and said, "I cannot help that is how you are. Don't worry, they will love you. My parents are not too critical of others. They like their children to an extent. And I like you; that is all that matters."

He pulled her off her legs and then closer to his chest.

"Anything else you want to ask?"

"No."

"Good."

"I will go with you on one condition and one condition only."

"What?"

The condition would sound childish to him, but she had followed it since childhood. It was a reasonable condition, and who wouldn't agree to it? She trusted him, but she needed to be cautious about such events. This way, everyone would be on the same page and not left hanging high and dry. It was simple and concise.

"We need to have a signal for someone being uncomfortable or ready to leave."

"Sure—Like what?"

She had the urge to laugh, but instead, she smiled. Her gesture might seem silly to him, but it was something her grandparents came up with that always worked. It was cute, funny, and straightforward, and it inspired her. She demonstrated the gesture by raising her middle finger and index finger together, twisting them once, bringing them close to her nose, and pretending to sneeze. He looked at her like she was crazy but then burst into laughter.

"I'm not doing that. What is that?"

"It's the signal."

"You came up with that all on your own?"

"No, My grandparents—whenever I wanted to leave or felt uncomfortable, I would signal with that."

"It's very outdated."

"Hey! I happen to be proud of that signal. It used to work." She said with a pout.

"Keyword "used" too. How about we wink at each other."

"Oh, yeah, um—that sounds more plausible," she said as she and Dawn laughed.

"Yes, it does. My sisters and I used to do that for a signal whenever we wanted to leave certain situations."

"Well, I guess that is solved." He pulled the covers over them as they prepared to go to sleep.

"Are you sleepy now?" he asked, smiling softly. "Yes," she said in a baby voice, shutting her eyes.

# 8. Birthday Candles

Two vivid red candles flickered in a warm glow on a moon-shaped cake. The cake was vanilla, but the icing boasted a creamy, buttercream texture in a soft cream hue. It sat proudly on a gold gilded plate with a "Happy 24th Moon" written in red icing on a crystal coffee table in Dawn's apartment. A gold cake cutter sat right next to it on a napkin. It had been a few days since the night with Dawn. In the following days, they kept in contact by calling, texting, and visiting each other's favorite spots. They planned to celebrate Moon's birthday at Kings Diner, but unforeseen weather changes happened and ruined tradition. It rained heavily and had been raining for about three days.

She sat on the same white leather couch that had poked and prodded her the last time she was there, but it could have been her nerves. Not too far away from her was her birthday cake, which would have been spaghetti if not for the weather. She wasn't upset, but it was different. She hadn't had cake in a while. She wasn't really into sweets, but it was nice that Dawn tried for her. She sat there looking like a work of art. Her thick pink sweater, folded at her shoulders, kept her warm. She wore a dark brown cheetah print skirt that gracefully reached her ankles and six-inch black heels with two diagonal straps and a pink orchid centered on them. She wore gold hoop earrings and a necklace with her initials around her neck. Her nails were painted a vibrant cherry red, and her hair had large, bouncy curls.

The faint light in his apartment highlighted the darkness of her caramel skin and brunette hair. Her celestial aura was powerful yet calm, a shade of magenta that outshone the milkiness of the walls. She sat comfortably on the couch, legs crossed and one foot swaying, while he frantically gathered the presents for her birthday. The thought of him feeling such pressure brought a big smile to her face, though it wasn't significant to her. She would have settled for a cake. Her forte was to like simple things - a caring note, a cake, or someone being there. She found sentiment to be a small gesture that did not have to impress her but move her in such a way that she knew someone cared. There was no need for big-headedness or a war to be waged.

She wanted what she liked and could care for. It was as simple as that. He came stumbling into the living room with three boxes. Two boxes were miniature and wrapped in gold packaging; another was huge in a black suede box. He sat all three on the coffee table beside the cake and fell onto the couch. His arm gracefully rested behind her shoulder on the couch's surface while his body remained pointed toward her. Noticing his weariness, she tilted her head and said, "Tired, are we?"

"Nope. I'm just mesmerized by your beauty." A smile spread across his face, revealing his charming dimples. She felt her heart race and admitted, "You're making me blush."

"Is that a bad thing or a good thing?"

"A Good thing," she replied, kissing him sweetly.

"I missed you for twelve minutes."

She smiled. "I missed you too. For all of twelve minutes."

"I think my heart skipped a beat, my dear rose," he admitted.

She rolled her eyes playfully and scoffed, "Yeah, yeah, I bet it did."

"I'm serious! I can't get enough of you. Last night, I couldn't get you off my mind, and because of that, I was up until about 2 am."

She cupped his face and said, "Weirdly enough, you have been on my mind, too. It's tantalizing for someone like me because this is a first for me apart from you looking handsome with those lovely dimples when you smile." She said with a pouty face.

"No, I never noticed." He teased, puckering his lips for a kiss. She happily obliged, releasing his face and kissing him. They ended up in a make-out session before he pulled away from her gently.

He smiled with a loss of breath, "We should blow out your candles before the cake becomes inedible with candle wax," he said with a red face.

"You're right. Make out later. Cake now, especially since I'm hungry for a slice."

His attire caught her attention as he carefully positioned the cake within her reach. He wore blue denim jeans, a white turtleneck sweater, and white Reebok sneakers, complemented by a gold medallion necklace and his class ring. His hair was messy as usual but appeared darker in the dim light.

Dawn joyfully started singing a birthday song for Moon, which made her happy. Anxiously, she placed her hands in her lap, and he inquired, "Make a wish." Closing her eyes and blowing the candles out in seconds, he asked, "What did you wish?" She smiled hesitantly and said, "That's something I'll never tell."

He reacted disappointedly to her answer, but it was for the best. She did make a wish, but it was never to be known. It wasn't that she didn't want to tell him; it was the rules, and it would not be very comfortable if he knew what she wished for. It would be a secret between her heart and the universe. That is at least what Nana taught her: that every wish belongs to the sender, never the outsiders or granter.

*"May you rest in peace, lovely, and I wish you were here for this."*

Anxious by the state of the room, she said, "Let's cut this baby up and open some presents."

He smiled and said, "Okay, the first slice goes to the birthday girl!"

"Yay!" she said in excitement, eyes locked on the cake. "I want a big piece."

"Anything for you. It's your day." He winked.

"When should I start packing my bags for your uncle's engagement party?"

"In five days," he said, licking buttercream frosting off his finger before handing Moon her slice of cake. "Is there a theme? Do I need to wear specific attire?"

"Something casual. Something fancy, and we can always go shopping if you don't. We are going to be there for a few days."

"No need for shopping. When you say fancy or casual, I have fancy and casual love."

"It's settled then."

"Also, what do you mean by a few days?"

"Yes, we will be there for a week. I thought it would be great to get away."

"Like a vacation?"

"Like a vacation." He repeated. "I'm just so excited for us to get away and for you to meet my family that I forgot to mention it." He sat his cake plate on the table. "I hope you don't think we are moving too fast. In the city, we have work and life in the way sometimes, but at my uncle's engagement party weekend, we get more time together."

"Love, I didn't want to make you feel bad. I was just asking. I love the chance to experience some alone time in a new place and with you."

"You know it's all right if you are undecided about this trip."

"I never said I was."

"That's the thing. You don't," he said sadly.

"I'm sorry," she said worriedly. "My mind sometimes moves faster than my mouth, so I keep it to myself. I am excited, really. It's new territory, that's all."

He sat there silently, waiting for her to speak, hoping she would share more than a few words.

"Look, Dawn. I like you and might not express myself as much as you, but I'm getting there."

"Enlighten me then."

"Okay, what do you want to know?"

"I don't know, you tell me. We spent a week getting to know each other but still are, and I have yet to know what you are thinking or feeling when it comes to us, sometimes."

"Ask me two questions that will help you get to know me better, and I will do my best to answer them."

"Sure," he chuckled. "Go ahead."

"Two questions, huh?"

"Kill me with the suspense, why don't you?" She hoped she wouldn't put her foot in her mouth because her nails dug into her hand from anticipating what he would ask.

He playfully rolled his eyes, laid his head back on the couch, and contemplated. He raised his head again and asked, "Do you think this will work?"

"Do I think what will work?"

"Us?"

"Dawn—"

He sternly said, "Aira."

Her eyes jumped to his. She's heard him say that only once, and it's when he's grave with her. She hated vomiting out her emotions. It was like a fresh wound for her, and she knew if she didn't rip the scab off, she wouldn't have anyone to share those emotions with.

"I do not have the answer. I would like for us to last and make more memories. You make my heart burn passionately, and my stomach flutter. I get nervous when you don't text or call; I toss and turn in bed at night, thinking about our future. I become disappointed when I don't see you in the apartment hallway and daydream all day about your kisses. Your sweet butterfly kisses, so it is safe to say there is an us. I cannot promise, but I hope."

He didn't say a word but asked, "Butterfly kisses?"

As she twirled her finger in her hair, her eyes sparkled with tenderness while she tried to keep her mind and words focused. "I know. It's the very opposite of what I think."

"And what is that?"

"I call your kisses that because they make me feel like I'm flying. They make me feel like I'm the only person in your world, heart, and mind. The rarity of those kisses makes them even more special."

He gently took her in his arms and showered her face, neck, and hands with kisses until she was laughing and in high spirits. "Okay! Okay!" She gently pushed him away and said, "Next question."

"You got it, beautiful." He said, kissing her one last time.

"I want to let you know that I think this will work; we just have to give it a chance and communicate." She smiled, waiting for him to continue. "Where would you go if you could be anywhere in the world right now?"

The question took her aback. He chose this one out of all the questions he could have asked. She wasn't sure if he was joking or not. She didn't answer right away because she had never considered being anywhere but the city. It was all she knew. It was surprising because she wanted to know the answer but had never thought about it. She let out a breath, sat quietly for two seconds, and said, "I wouldn't know, but I can say that I wouldn't mind going anywhere in the world with you. I do not mind having an escort to show me the delights of the world I haven't seen."

"What makes you think I've been around the world?"

"Well, have you?"

He chuckled before saying a word, then said, "Yes, I have been to about three countries."

"Which ones?"

"Italy, Guatemala, and Ireland, why?"

"I expect to be taken there, maybe Morrocco too."

"Duly noted." He nodded as he chuckled.

"If you had to choose one of those countries for a romantic getaway, which would you pick?

"Guatemala. Antigua, Guatemala, to be exact."

"Why?" she said, stunned at his response.

"It's not your stereotypical romantic place and a culture so enriched that it's sometimes taken for granted and looked down on. It makes you appreciate it more. If I wanted you to learn anything, it would be from a place like that."

"I hope so because, as I said, I do not mind traveling the world with my boyfriend, especially to such a cultural place."

"Boyfriend?" He said, flattered. "Are we assigning labels now?"

She sunk onto the sofa in shyness and said, "Yes. I guess we are. You are my boyfriend."

"And you are my girlfriend." He winked, and she responded with a blushing nod.

"See how conversations can lead to progress."

"Yeah, yeah." She rubbed her fingers together.

"I would have done the full show and pony if I knew we were becoming boyfriend and girlfriend." He tickled her neck.

"Why is that?" She giggled, pushing his hand away.

"Well, I mean, it's something to take seriously, and it would have given me the chance to ask you properly to be my girlfriend."

"Mm-hmm," she shrugged. "Well, you know better than me. I've never had a boyfriend." She giggled. Dawn smiled and rolled his eyes, scooting a bit closer. "Aira?"

"Yes, Dawn." She replied sweetly.

He chuckled. "Will you do me the honors of granting me permission to be your boyfriend?"

She blushed and sucked some frosting off her pinky and looked him dead in the eye, then said, "Yes, Dawn. I happily accept the pleasure of you being my boyfriend."

They looked at each other smitten.

"That being said, you don't think we are moving fast?" He asked, hopeful.

"Um—"

He nodded. "Yeah?"

She nervously laughed before munching on a mouthful of cake to dodge the question because it seemed like things were moving too quickly. But in truth, she's just someone who tends to overthink everything, and she had already answered two of his questions. She became hopeful he wouldn't ask again, so she said with a mouth full of cake, "Who made this? This is good cake."

He wiped some frosting from the side of her face with a napkin. "I made it, but I'm too lazy to cook sometimes." He shrugged. "I learned from a friend." Licking the frosting from her teeth and setting her plate on the couch, she said, "A friend?"

'A family friend, who happens to be a chef, taught me how to cook after I begged him to."

"Aww! I would like to see you in the kitchen one day."

"Yeah, that will be the day."

"And why didn't you tell me? I would have helped. I have some grease in these elbows." She winked.

"You will not have to step in the kitchen as long as I'm around." *It sounds like a threat to me.*

"News flash! I already did when I made nachos in my place earlier." She laughed.

He stared at her enduringly and smiled. "I know what you meant. Now kiss me and tell me about home."

He kissed her swiftly and asked, "My home?"

"Yeah, the house you lived in as a child."

"Ah! The forbidden mystery."

"Dawn!" she whined.

"Okay, okay, I'm kidding. Of course, I will spill the beans about my asylum. Come gather around the campfire." She couldn't help but giggle as he pulled her onto his lap, snuggling her head into his shoulder. It was a comfortable and cozy embrace, and she couldn't have been happier to be there.

She couldn't stop thinking about his home, family, and life, knowing it was messing with his head. Every time she brought it up, he looked like he'd been hit by a truck, and she felt terrible about it. It was like reopening old wounds, and she knew she had to be more careful about how she talked about it. She understood him but wanted to know his wounds as he knew hers. She felt they could lick over each other's wounds if he wished to. She disliked comparing scars but was curious if his childhood was worse. Not that having a drunk for a mother is not terrible, but she needed to know what made him run away from home.

*I often conjure up conspiracy theories, imagining the most diabolical scenarios. What if he was a prince hailing from a faraway kingdom? What if he was secretly a member of the mob? What if he belonged to an international spy family? What if he was a billionaire on the run from the IRS? What if he was a villain or a superhero? That theory is the last one on my list because it sounds a little too childish.*

Her mind was often a casualty, vacillating between nothingness and chaos. It was too much. She endured herself for as long as possible but did not want to ruin things between her and Dawn. She kept it light with him. She knew he was an enduring man and loved that about him. He was a breath of fresh air. He was straightforward and knew his desires but often still distant. She had never been a great thinker and didn't want to be. She loved her simplicity and how he complimented her. She couldn't look away from him. He had an incredible way of describing things that left her in awe. There he was, clenching his jaw to get his point across. He moved his hands whenever he needed to demonstrate, which made him think more because his eyes never blinked. But then again, that could be something people with colored eyes do.

She was deeply infatuated with him and appreciated everything he did and how he did it. She genuinely believed that by being warmer and more welcoming towards him, they could have a chance at experiencing love together. It wasn't like they needed it; at least he didn't. On the other hand, Moon required it in a way only a mother could give. It didn't mean she shouldn't experience another form of love that wasn't parental. *"Isn't it my right?" He will think that I overthink too much. Wait? He already thinks that.*

He noticed Moon smiling as the conversation continued, but that was her.

"I was raised in a pretty huge house."

"How huge?"

"Use your imagination."

"The size of the white house!" She didn't think it was that big, but she always imagined that he grew up in a big white house—the classic American dream.

"It's about half the size of that."

"Is it really?" She laughed a little, knowing he couldn't be serious.

"Yes, it is." He smiled slightly.

"I bet that was fun." She played with his fingers. "I couldn't imagine a house that big and playing as a kid. It would have been fun."

"Growing up in the Wolfe household had its challenges."

"Wolfe?" It sounded familiar to her.

He laughed, looked up, sighed, and then looked back at her, saying, "That's right, I never told you my last name. It's Wolfe."

"It sounds so outside of the box," she said, staggered. "Who would've guessed."

"Yeah. if only you knew." He said, looking down. She didn't want him to clarify, so she changed the subject. "Dawn Wolfe, it sounds sexy," she said, tracing her thumb over his medallion with a wolf on it. "Thank you. I still prefer just Dawn."

"I never said you didn't." She smirked. She could see he didn't like the name, which, again, sounded familiar to her.

He smiled sadly and said, "It wasn't just enormous. I don't know if it still looks the same because the place has been renovated over the years. When I was a child, this big wolf head was outside the front doorway that hung over the balcony. It was creepy. It felt like it would eat me, but I was an imaginative child. These angelic statues, a man and a woman, held up the balcony that belonged to my parent's room."

It appeared to her that his childhood wasn't so sweet compared to how extravagant his house was.

"We have a big garden. I do not know how big it is, but it's like separate land in front and behind. We do have flowers, fruit, etc., which are grown sometimes. But as I said, I do not know if they still do these things. Surprisingly, my father cared for the garden's upkeep; he loves nature. My mother prefers renovations and décor."

"Me and your father would get along, you think. We like gardens and such, so we have something in common."

"I don't know. Maybe." He said as he rubbed her cheek.

"The mystery awaits." They laughed.

"Stepping into my parent's house feels like entering a museum. Every corner is garnished with art from different eras and cultures, and antique furniture adds a sense of history and tradition. Overall, my parents' house is a true masterpiece, where every element has been carefully curated to create a beautiful and functional space. Never homely, just perfect on the eye."

"Wow! That sounds lovely. It sounds beautiful but bittersweet."

"Yeah, it's a grand palace."

"If you're not feeling it, we can stop. I can sense that this might be making you feel uncomfortable, and I don't want that.'

"It's all right, my rose; I tend to highlight the flaws of home life despite romanticizing it."

"Okay." She said, smiling lightly.

"Our house has a horse stable, which we use for storage. When my mother was riding a horse, unfortunately, she fell off and sustained some injuries. The incident made my father quite worried about the safety of the family. Therefore, he decided to ban horses from our property to prevent any such accidents from happening again."

"Yikes. She wasn't too severely hurt, was she?"

"No, she just had some bruises but was fine."

"That's good; continue, please," she said in a baby voice.

"As you wish," he said playfully, "The kitchen was quite spacious, almost as big as the hallway. It was the only room in the house adorned with black and gold decorations. While I faintly remember my siblings' rooms, I could not enter them. However, my room was like any other boy's room. It was filled with everything related to outer space, stars, the Cartoon Network, and two bookshelves, the most important part of my room."

"Well— I cannot wait to see it, and why didn't you tell me from the beginning that you lived in a mansion."

"I wouldn't say it is a mansion. It just resembles one. Trust me, it's not that big. It's how I remember it from the last time I was there."

"Okay, whatever you say." She sensed he came from a higher social class but didn't disclose it. She'd have to see for herself.

"What about your childhood home?"

"Oh, I don't know. It's been so long since I stepped into that house, and Nana did move, but I could tell you."

"Well, before you do that, I want you to open the presents I got you for your birthday."

It slipped her mind about the presents he had gotten her. That showed he was either a good storyteller or she needed to be more present-minded. She almost forgot her birthday but hoped for gifts worth cherishing. She moved off his lap and sat upright on the couch; she closed her eyes and opened her hands while he reached for the first gift. He began with the small boxes, handing her the first one. She eagerly tore off the wrapping. The box was small and made of shiny Venetian red. On top of it was a golden paw print. She examined the box from all angles, searching for the brand name. However, there was no brand name, only the brand logo.

"Open it." He spoke.

As she slowly opened the box, her eyes widened with amazement as she beheld a stunning piece of jewelry. It was a bracelet made entirely of pure gold. The metal was perfectly polished, gleaming in the light, and felt heavy in her hand. But what caught her attention were the roses that adorned the bracelet. Red as blood and with petals of gold, they appeared to be blooming on her wrist. The delicate details of the roses were breathtaking, and they looked as if they had been plucked from a beautiful garden. She couldn't help but stare at the bracelet, admiring its beauty and craftsmanship.

He helped her put on the bracelet, and she said, "I love it."

She admired his dedication to gifting her roses in many ways because of her love for them. It was admirable. She took the bracelet in her hand and felt it. It was smooth and full of love, and again, she said with her heart on her sleeve and smiled, "I really love this. I will cherish it forever."

"I'm happy that you like it, rose. I had it made for you especially."

She joked, "I hope I didn't break your pockets." He responded with a laugh and said, "Open this one; you'll love it the most."

Opening her next gift, she asked, "How long did it take to make this? Not that it matters. I've always been curious since I have only had second-hand jewelry most of my life."

He smiled gently with a hint of cockiness and said, "It took three weeks to make the product as every piece needed to be placed correctly and even illustrated. The cost was quite high, but luckily, I knew some people who could do it for me free of charge."

"That sounds like some cutting-edge moves. I wish I knew people like that but avoid them too much. If I didn't, I would have connections and friends."

"You have me."

"And that is even better." He leaned over and kissed her on the cheek.

It was a box like before, but a miniature turtle statue was inside this time. She couldn't help but be mesmerized by the intricate details of its glossy green exterior. The surface was perfectly smooth and appeared to have a glimmering sheen, as though it had been polished to perfection. Its ruby rose-colored eyes were like two tiny jewels that seemed to glow with an inner light, and the way they were set in the green shell added a touch of elegance to the overall appearance. But it was the purple shell that caught her attention. It was unlike anything she had ever seen, with a deep, rich hue that was almost mesmerizing. The shell seemed to have a subtle, iridescent quality, reflecting different shades of purple depending on how the light hit it. As she studied it more closely, she realized that the shell was covered in intricate patterns and designs, each more intricate than the last.

She ran her fingers over the delicate turtle statue, and he said, "I had this custom-made to add to your collection."

She took the turtle, closed her hand around it, and placed it close to her heart, trying to contain her emotions. "I love it and will make it a part of the family. Thank your friends for me too. I'm happy they helped you with this because the craftmanship and elegance are breathtaking." She knew he had been showing his dedication to her for the past few days, but she had never received such extravagant gifts. The thought of the last gift to be opened made her feel uneasy, as she wasn't sure if she could compete when his birthday came around.

*Maybe I was more important to him than I thought, but the gifts he gave me didn't necessarily prove it.*

"Yes, they're good at their job. That's why my uncle recommended them."

"That's sweet of him."

"You worth it, so why wouldn't he."

She smiled confidently and said, "Dawn!"

"What? You are worth everything, even my love. Nothing is wrong with that."

"No, there isn't. I'm just not used to being this way with someone."

"It's all right. I understand that dating can be new and confusing. I'm willing to wait until you feel comfortable."

"I love how patient you are with me. I'm sorry if I smile awkwardly or stare when you say lovely things like that. I promise you I am trying."

"No promises needed. You have to get used to it, that's all."

She nodded and smiled, then enthusiastically kissed him while twirling his hair.

She loved playing with his hair, which was her way of expressing affection besides kissing. She had developed stronger feelings for him over the past few days and was confident about it. She secretly prayed to the universe, an unknown being, hoping that what they had would last forever. It was one of her deepest desires, and she was sure it would come true. Although she couldn't express it openly, she loved it when he told her he wanted her to be his. She had a mix of emotions when it came to him that were a guilty pleasure, and she couldn't let them go. It did not matter if they were healthy; they were different. It made her feel good. She thought it was better than being sad all day like a character in a Sofia Coppola Movie.

She needed to put more effort into the relationship because she felt he wouldn't have invited her to meet the family if they weren't in a serious relationship. She could rationalize and say it was too early to meet his family, but love had no time frame or rules. *Do I love him, or do I like him a lot?* She didn't know. She had never been in love, so how could she recognize it? She was unsure if it was a feeling or a sign. A realistic, hopeless romantic she was. She felt like a dummy when it came to these things.

He sat there, looking absolutely perfect. She couldn't help but wonder if there was a hidden side to him that she didn't know and if he would eventually prove her right. She was worried that he might be insincere and that she would be the fool. After all, who would want to love her? Her mother was an alcoholic, and her father was deceased, as were her grandparents. She felt like a complete mess and had never been in love before. She second-guessed everything that seemed too good to be true and couldn't help but be suspicious of any man who called her beautiful.

She could feel the first-hand embarrassment in her bones. It was too late to reconsider because she was here. She had a relationship and a duty to herself to accept the love and adventure she had never experienced. She held herself back, but not this time. It was her day, and she deserved it. The negatives would have to sit on the bench this time. She wished herself good luck.

"Okay! I'm ready for the big one. Hit me, love!"

He smiled widely. "Okay, beautiful."

Feeling a little giddy, she couldn't help but be curious about the last present; it was tempting and eye-catching. He quickly placed it in her lap. It didn't seem to weigh much, no matter how easily he did so. She tried to guess what was in the box before opening it, which was amusing. She was like a mouse that found cheese. The box was more prominent than her thighs, made of black suede, and had a black ribbon wrapped around it. It was smooth to the touch and odorless. She untied the ribbon thoroughly and opened the box; it had white paper wrapped around an item with the same paw logo. After pulling back the translucent paper, she was taken aback to see that it was covered with brown fur. She initially thought it was a dead animal, but he knew better. She carefully opened the box and found a faux fur coat inside.

The coat was crafted with soft and luscious faux fur, a combination of several shades of brown. It stood tall and proud, displaying an impeccable posture that exuded confidence. The femininity was apparent in the curves. The coat was impressively massive and sturdy, exuding an aura of elegance.

She couldn't believe it, but she knew she had to say something other than sit there with her mouth wide open. If he couldn't find the coat at the thrift shop, he would have to spend much money on it because coats like that are expensive. Unless his friends did him a favor, which she doubted, he would have to take out a loan for it, which he probably didn't need. She had to run her hands all over the coat to make sure it was real, and it was. She thought she would try it on to avoid shock, and Dawn helped her.

"How does it feel? Is it too tight? I couldn't get your measurements but guessed with luck."

"What such luck. It fits perfectly."

"That's the luck of being a Wolfe." He winked.

"Lucky you."

"Well? Do you like it?"

"No." She stared blankly, then laughed and said, "Of course I like it. NO! I love it!"

He smiled and laughed with relief. "You almost had me there. Hilarious, baby."

She wrapped her arms around his waist and whispered, "I like teasing you." She gave him a gentle kiss on the nose.

They shared a series of tendered kisses, savoring every moment of their affectionate embrace. She pulls away from the kiss, her eyes sparkling excitedly. She rushed to the full-length mirror, her new fur coat flowing behind her in a soft, luxurious flutter. She stood before the mirror, admiring how the coat hugged her curves and accentuated her figure. She ran her hands over the plush fur, reveling in its warmth. With a satisfied smile, she turned to Dawn, who was watching her with adoration in his eyes. She gave him one final kiss, feeling beautiful and confident in her elegant new coat.

"I'm happy that you like it." He whispered seductively into her ear before picking her up, with her arms and legs wrapped around him. "I thought you wanted to hear about my childhood home?"

"I think that can wait, don't you?" She smiled and said, "What about the cake?"

"Moon. It can wait, don't you think?" He kissed her again.

"I mean—" He smacked her on her ass, and she giggled in surprise.

"Do you think it can wait or not?"

"Well, now that you mention it, I think it can wait."

"Good girl." He spoke.

He carried her to the bedroom; she smiled ear to ear. They kissed endlessly, full of passion. Their bodies intertwined in the heat of the moment. She might have never been in love, but she knew what it felt like to make love. He was the first to touch her and, presumably, the last touch she would ever want. She didn't know how many times in a day they would have sex, but it was often. They had this immense attraction to one another and, by force, pulled them together. It was exhilarating to have someone like that around who listened, loved, and loved being loved. It was terrific in her eyes.

She desired a love that would consume her entirely, that would obliterate the world, and wipe out the entire universe, leaving behind nothing but smoke and ashes. It wouldn't be a fleeting emotion that would come and go; it would be a love that would keep her warm at night and guide her through the darkness in life. And, if that love led to consequences, it would be worth it. She would choose death as the only penalty for loving someone and for love to do so in return.

She desired a freeing love that would have the ocean waves consume humanity and destroy anything that stood a thousand feet tall. It wouldn't be a fleeting emotion that would come and go; it would wash her of all her sins and carry her over the threshold of harmony. And, again, if that love led to consequences, it would be the price. She would choose death as the only penalty for loving someone and for love to do so in return.

She desired a plentiful love that would fill her with pureness to see the world in a new light and vision to understand it. It wouldn't be a fleeting emotion that would come and go; it would give her a clear mind to make decisions and hope to be laid to rest in a bed of roses. Lastly, it would be worth it if that love led to consequences. She would choose death as the only penalty for loving someone and for love to do so in return.

He had her pinned against the bed; her legs were wide open and eagerly ready to receive him. When his penis entered her, she let out a low whimper. His pace was slow but steady, kissing her in between. The heat of their intertwined bodies grew intense, leaving sweat imprints on the bed and a mixture of their love and scent in the air. His back had deep, bright red scratch marks; her body was traced with passionate kisses that would later turn into dark purple hues of hickeys, which she felt was his way of saying she was his and her way of expressing belonging to someone. Their moans bounced off the walls, and bed creaks dispersed to each door throughout the apartment hallway, but she didn't care. She loved it and admitted the defeat of their affection for each other.

# 9. Bronte

He inquired with genuine concern, "Are you okay?" She shifted her gaze away from the taxicab window and replied, "I am okay as I can be," followed by a nervous chuckle.

"That's good to hear." He smiled.

"Question."

"Yes, my rose."

"Are you sure this is a good idea?"

"Stop it!" he said softly. "They will love you; stop overthinking it so much. I wouldn't have brought you along if I thought for a second that they would not like you."

"I know. It's just that I'm nervous and do not know how to calm down," she said, her palms sweating. She showed him her hands and said, "See!"

She sighed. "I think I am losing my mind, but now it's worse."

He chuckled and said, "Baby! You are okay. Just breathe in and out. I promise they are not as scary as you think, okay."

"Okay, okay, you are right. I'm sorry," she said, her face flushed and red with panic.

"This is why I adore you. You cannot help but be so you, you know."

"So, me?"

"Yeah, you are you." He smiled enduringly. "I love all of you. If that means I must love your tendency to overthink, nervousness, baby talk, and intense passions, I will be more willing to do so."

"Aww, baby! —You are not helping. Now I'm even more nervous."

"Sorry," He laughed, "I was trying to help."

She started laughing with Dawn. "I need to calm down before I explode. It's not every day you meet your boyfriend's family. I want everything to go smoothly, that is all," she said with twinkles in her big doe eyes.

He rubbed her chin and said, "Trust me, my family's opinion of you will not matter. Any of their opinions do not hold too much weight on my consciousness." He smiled, "Not like it used to."

He gently grabbed Moon by her waist and pulled her into his arms, her head resting on his chest. The sound of his heartbeat calmed her down as she counted per beat. "Relax now. I promise no one will upset you, not if I am around. My rose." He kissed her on the top of her head as he held her on the ride to the airport. Dawn looked straight ahead while Moon looked outside the taxi cab's window.

The taxicab was dusty yellow. It had a taxi light that would turn on but surge out occasionally. The seats were faded black leather. A window with a sliding door in the taxi separated them from the taxi driver. The ceiling had newspapers covering holes: They had various stories from over the past few years. A Snoopy bobblehead sat on the dashboard, and prayer beads hung from the ceiling before the cab. Each prayer bead was blood-clot red, but one cross was silver and gold. The names were written on each one but smeared in black lettering. The cab smelled of fresh lemon with a hint of mint. The cab had an optimum temperature, though it felt as if her blood had run cold.

She felt each bump as the cab approached its destination. She didn't know how she would live this down. She wasn't scared for the right reasons. He thought she was scared because of what his family would think of her, but she knew it was what he thought of her and the possibility that this trip would make him realize he didn't care for her as much as he thought.

*What if he spends too much time with me and grows tired? What if he doesn't like the everyday Moon? What if he finds the little things about me more tiresome than intriguing?*

She had many flaws, but more major ones than others. It would drive her crazy if he saw them, not for the sake of perfection but for her sanity. She never really liked anything about herself, especially her defects. She cherished her charm, solidarity, and caring side towards others, but never the parts of her that made her cry or veins run black.

She was aware that her nastiness could run wide and long. It was heavy knowing that, giving her shivers through her body, but she hoped he could love her biggest flaws even more than the smaller ones. She disappeared gradually into the atmosphere outside the window as Dawn conversed politely with the taxi driver. She drowned even the faintest of sounds out. The cab was driving a mile a minute. The cars, the trees, the people, and the buildings vanished with each passing moment. She closed her eyes to feel the movement of the cab. It was soothing to her and made the time go faster. She didn't know why Dawn wasn't as anxious as her; he hadn't seen his family in six years, but he was serene. She didn't know how this trip wasn't killing him on the inside, but it could be a sign that the trip would go nicely. Maybe she was overreacting like usual.

The cab arrived at a stop at a red light, but it wasn't the usual stop. The cab had swerved a little, and she opened her eyes to the taxi driver and Dawn yelling at a lime Honda vehicle. The car had a dangerous turn and almost crashed into them. She moved to the left side of the passenger seat while he screamed at the top of his lungs more than the driver. She had never seen him so angry. It was like he was another person, and she was curious if he would become like this if they ever fought. His mood changed when they were in danger or just her.

He kept yelling, "You could have fucking kilt us! You could have hurt my girl! What the hell were you thinking." She was spacing out as she felt the sensation of throwing up, and her hand came up to her mouth.

She said, "Dawn!"

The anger dropped from his face as he rushed over to her and asked softly, "What's wrong? Are you hurt?"

Her hand still close to her mouth, she held on to his jacket strap and attempted to keep from vomiting. She said one word, "Puke!" as she shoved the cab door open. He held her hair as she hunched over, allowing her nerves to work. She knew she was a bit uneasy, but not to the point of vomiting, not since she was a child. She felt him caress her back in support, and she felt comforted, but it felt like it was a disaster. It didn't help that she did not have anything to eat. It was clear like water, had no smell, and spread out on the road. Her eyes were red, and she was able to breathe. Dawn passed her his handkerchief to wipe her mouth.

"I knew you were nervous, but not to this extent." He rubbed her back in a circular motion.

"Mm-hmm," she said. It hurt too much for her to talk. It was like her stomach was in knots.

"I don't want to urge you to speak. You can lay on my lap until we reach the airport."

She nodded in agreement. She sat back in the car seat, and he closed the door behind her. Dawn gently placed her head on his lap. "Sir! Can we go now? There is no damage, and obviously, this idiot likes to argue. My girlfriend is sick, and we need to get where we are going."

"He almost crashed into me!" The driver said with confusion.

"Are we not in the car too? I know! If there is damage, I will reimburse you so we can get to where we are headed, okay?"

"Uh —Sure!" The driver said with defeat.

"You fucker! It was his fault!" The other driver said.

"You are an asshole! You almost collided with us, but it doesn't matter! I know how to handle people like you!" he said with a sigh and threw a finger sign. "Drive off now!"

"Yes, sir."

"By the way, what is your name?"

"Younes Scarr."

"Well, Younes, thank you. Forget that asshole. You're doing an excellent job."

"Thank you, sir. My pleasure."

He repeatedly caressed Moon's hair as she remained on his lap. Her stomach was still in a knot, but she liked being pampered. "I hope you feel better, ma'am," Younes said sincerely.

"Thank you, she will. She cannot talk right now because she doesn't feel good. Isn't that right, my rose?" She moaned in agreement. "I take that as a yes, but Younes listen. Once we reach the airport, I want to talk to you, okay?"

"Yes sir, will do."

"Please, call me Dawn."

"Okay, Dawn." He smiled. "You make a handsome couple. Makes me miss my wife." He chuckled. "Where are you headed to, if you do not mind me asking."

"We are going on a week's trip to my parent's house. My uncle invited us to his engagement party."

"I wish the happy couple a blissful engagement."

"Thank you. I will make sure to tell them."

"Where are you from?"

"What makes you think I'm not from here?"

"The accent."

"Yes, the accent." He smacked his lips together.

"Well?"

"California"

"Oh! A California man."

"Yes, that's me."

"I'm from Boston, born and raised, but I'm sure it's obvious."

"It's the accent." He said, laughing, and Younes laughed with him.

"No offense, but your girlfriend is a beautiful young woman."

"None was taken; she would thank you if she could."

"Is that right?"

"Yes. She is the moon to my sun. She is my rose to my thorn." Moon's index finger traced a heart on the top of his hand, and he smiled.

"Never let the world forget how much your woman means to you—not for a second, even her. If it means you have to swallow your pride and let her win every fight or always be right, do it," he said as his eyes smiled.

"I'll keep that in mind for the future."

"Good. A woman's happiness is everything."

"Isn't that the truth? I know firsthand from my mother."

"A man's first love is always his mother as a father is his daughters."

"Hmm. Something like that."

"What's your last name? Maybe I know some of your people from down there. I know many people in California."

"You wouldn't know us and wouldn't want to, honestly."

"Maybe," Younes said inquisitively.

Dawn sighed and said, "Wolfe, Dawn Wolfe."

"Wolfe? Wolfe?"

"I told you."

"Oh! Wolfe! Are you related to a Summer Wolfe?"

"Yes, she is my older sister."

"I told you I know people down there. I visit sometimes and do a side job, and it can lead to me driving certain people. Your sister hires me to drive her to places when I'm down there. It's like clockwork. You look just like her. You could be twins."

"Hmm— I see. People have told me that my older sisters and I always look alike. You can't escape a Wolfe if you tried." He said sarcastically.

"No, you cannot."

"How much further?"

"About an hour, Dawn."

"Okay."

"If you ever need a private driver, call on me, okay," Younes said cheerfully.

"Why don't you give me your card, and I'll keep in touch."

"Yes, sir! Mr. Wolfe— I mean Dawn." He said, jittery as if he were in the presence of royalty.

It became evident to her that once Dawn figured the driver knew who he was, the tone in his voice changed, and he became agitated. She didn't know why, but it wasn't as sincere as before. She knew he would end the conversation one way or another and retreat into his head.

"Please, call me Dawn." He said coldly.

"Yes, I know that's why I corrected myself," Younes said hesitantly.

"Good."

"My rose." She rubbed his hand with her index finger to let him know she was okay.

"Nickname, huh?"

"What?"

"Rose?"

"Oh, yes. It's a term of endearment."

"I call my wife honey or marshmallow because she is sweet on the tooth."

"Hah! Sweet on the tooth. Nice one." He said with a slight chuckle.

"Yeah, my one and only. How did you and your lady meet?"

"Oh, now that is a story for the books." He smirked.

"I'm listening."

"Not right now. I think Moon is ready for us to stop yapping." She was happy he finally realized that no matter the bro moment they were having.

"Come on. I'm a sucker for love stories."

She moaned to let Dawn know it was time to shut up and side-eyed him.

"Scarr."

"Please!"

"Mr. Scarr, I doubt you will want to hear it. It's not that our story isn't beautiful, but I think Moon needs rest and quiet. But I'll be happy to tell you once the ride is over," he said with a slight annoyance.

"Sounds good to me," he said, motioning his fingers over his lips as if zipping them up.

"Baby, we can try to find something to soothe your stomach pain once we get to the airport, okay? I need you to hang in there," he said, kissing her head again. "Love you," he whispered in her ear.

She didn't know if she misunderstood; maybe the sickness made her delirious, but she could have sworn he said, *"I love you."* She couldn't react because she felt terrible, but her heart quaked. They just made it to boyfriend and girlfriend titles, but not "*I love you.*" She assumed he was in the moment. The cab was almost in a car collision, and all the yelling might have confused him. He might regret it as we speak.

However, it was like sweet nectar dripping off his tongue. It seemed unreal. It was a faint dream she couldn't comprehend. That word had to be nesting in every bone in his body. She would hate for him to be a liar. *Did he want me to say it back? Did he expect me to feel the same? Did he want me to know?* It wasn't kind of him to take advantage. Yes, he thought it to be enduring, but she felt it to be painful. It would have been kind if he had given her the chance to defend herself. *I didn't even know if I loved him. It was an unfair advantage.* The pain increased inside of her. It was as if the pain had spread through her entire body.

She turned over in his lap, and their faces met. She had tears in her eyes from the pain, hoping when they got to the airport that, it could be fixed; she didn't want to let him down. She wanted to go on the trip, but he asked, "Are you sure you want to do this? We can turn back and take you back home. It looks like you aren't going to make it."

She said weakly, "No. I want to go. It is just a stomach bug; nothing a little rest and medicine can't fix."

"Are you sure, rose?"

"Yes, baby, I got this."

"Okay, I love you and wanted you to get better, so do not look at me like that."

He repeated it. She was so weak she couldn't even give a dumbfounded impression. She smiled, and he kissed her on the lips. "Don't worry, it's not the end of the world. You do not have to say it back. It is just how I feel, and I have been dying to get it off my chest for a while now. Rest, okay?"

Dawn asked the driver for a bottle of water, but he ran out before they requested the cab, so she was out of luck. She had to endure it and hope for the best. She knew he would tell the driver to turn around in a heartbeat, but she didn't want him to miss his uncle's engagement party because he would not leave her alone in such a state. Has he ever?

"Try not to speak and preserve your strength. Who would have known you would meet my uncle in this state? A funny story for the future." He said with a chuckle and a smile.

"My uncle loves herbal tea, so he should have some to make your stomach feel better; he always did when I was a kid. It was homemade, and he carried it everywhere just in case."

She had hearts embedded into her gaze as she fondly listened to him speak about his uncle and healing her.

"You know I will have to carry you onto the plane," he whispered.

"Try not to break me, okay." He winked, and she laughed. "Ass!" she quietly shouted.

"There is that joyous laugh. How I longed to hear it for the past hour." He smiled, and she smiled back. "Never leave me without that pretty smile again."

Although he did not cure her, she felt relief from the pain. His hand rubbed the side of her cheek, easing her into sleep. She heard him say, "Sweet dreams, rose."

She came to, realizing she was on the seat and there was no sign of Dawn. Her stomach simmered down, but she hoped she would not need medicine by the end of the flight. She sat up and saw Dawn and the taxi driver speaking outside the cab. He appeared to be having a deep conversation with Younes and handed him a roll of money. It was a thick stack, which she had only seen in movies. She wanted to know if they discussed how he and she met or more pressing matters. He would always be a mystery to her; everything he does is something she never knew him to do or out of the blue.

She fixed her clothing and composed herself. She could see they were not at a regular airport. She was confused. She was sure he said they were going to the airport but was not parked in front of one. They were in an oversized garage with men and women wearing safety jackets that were yellow and orange, yet one plane was in sight. Not a plane. A jet! She knew he had some explaining to do because she did not expect to ride in a plane for about five hours. It wasn't as if she wasn't intrigued but wanted to know why he would lie. She wouldn't have been mad if she knew they were riding in a jet.

She could see that the jet was private since they were the only ones there. It was porcelain milk chocolate with a light creamy underbelly. The legs and stairs of the plane matched. The circular windows, captains' windows, and wings were silver. She thought it was a brown thrasher the size of a building.

Dawn and Younes were all smiles. He pulled him close as he held his shoulder firm. He made sure that Younes could hear whatever he was saying. The conversation ended, and Younes headed for the cab trunk to get their belongings. Moon sat there like a deer in headlights as he opened the door.

He crouched down by the cab door and said, "Hello, sleeping beauty." He smiled.

"All this time I have known you, I have seen you sleep more than we have had talked to each other, but that is the perk of dating sleeping beauty."

She rolled her eyes and punched his chest, and he kept her hand there, "What's sleeping beauty without her dwarf of a prince, right," she said, smiling.

"Ouch— Dwarf prince." He smiled. His dimples were ever so hypnotizing.

"It's all love, baby." She said, kissing him. "What were you two talking about?"

"Who?"

"Younes and you?"

"Oh—We were discussing some damage to his cab and the misunderstanding from earlier. Why?"

"Nothing. I was curious, that's all."

"He's taking our things to the jet. And, before you say anything, we were going to the airport originally, but last night, I found out my uncle had our tickets refunded and demanded we take the jet he was sending. I wanted to tell you last night, but you were already nervous."

"It's okay. At least a plane full of people can't watch me be sick, and I can be more comfortable."

"The private, the better," he said as they smiled.

"But he can do that?"

"You will be surprised what a Wolfe can do, but it's all love on my uncle's end. He wanted to meet you so badly, so here we are."

"Well, I'm just as excited to meet him, especially if he's as handsome as you."

"What can I say? It runs in the family," he said, caressing her hand with his fingers.

"Also, he's on the jet, so don't be surprised by a hidden figure in the shadows." He laughed.

"What is he? A mysterious being because if so, I think that runs in the family, too."

"Yes, it does, but I know I give you vague answers here and there. I thought it was for your good because I wouldn't see my family for a while."

"I understand, Dawn." She said, removing her hand from his chest, caressing his face, and looking deep into his eyes. "I'll tell you all you need to know about me and my family. Give me a chance, too, okay?"

"Okay." They smiled at each other.

He kissed her on the temple and leaned into the cab to pick her up into his arms. Moon smiled as he carried her to the jet. "You know I love it when you carry me."

"I know." He spoke. They both smiled. "Maybe I should do it more often if it puts you in a good mood."

"Maybe." She smiled.

"I have a surprise for you when we get on the jet."

"What is it?"

"It's a surprise."

Dawn walked up the jet stairs carefully while carrying Moon. He placed her in one of the seats, kissed her on the cheek, and said, "I am going to make sure our belongings are being put away correctly. Are you fine here for a few minutes by yourself?"

Before she could answer, "Of course, she is, nephew. Why wouldn't she be?" A huge smile broke out on Dawn's face, and he sprinted toward his uncle, almost sending him off balance with a warm hug.

"Wow! You have grown since I last saw you." He said, holding both sides of Dawn's face.

"What can I say? I eat a lot," they both laughed and hugged.

"Wolfe mentality at best, son! How have you been?"

"I've been great. I opened a bookstore, took up new hobbies, slept more, and met someone."

"I see D. I know you said she was gorgeous, but she is a real goddess. Where have you been hiding her?"

Moon began to blush after what Uncle Bronte said. She felt he was exaggerating. Her beauty couldn't be compared to a goddess. Well, at least she thought so. "Yes, she is a goddess."

"And does this goddess have a name?" Expecting Dawn to answer for her, he looked back at her, and she said, "Aira Moon, but I prefer Moon."

"Aira Moon." He said, contemplating. "A beautiful name. Moon suits you just fine."

"Thank you, Mr. Wolfe." She smiled, and Uncle Bronte laughed. "Please. Please. Call me Bronte. Mr. Wolfe is so formal."

"Oh yes. Right." She said, her nerves starting up again.

"Why does it feel like you are putting the moves on my girl."

"I do not know, D; maybe it's because no woman can resist the Wolfe charm."

"My girl can."

"Well, I wouldn't say that if she is with you." They all laughed. "God, I missed you, D."

"I missed you too, Bronte." They hugged again, and she smiled.

"Bronte. Do you happen to have any tea for Moon to drink? Her nerves got the best of her, and she ended up car-sick. She is a little better, but I hoped your concoctions would make her feel better."

"Yes, yes, she can have some tea. I can see now she does look a little pale," he said, looking concerned. Some food would do her good, too, son." He smiled, and a gold front tooth appeared.

Dawn looked back at her and smiled. "Yes, she does, but can you keep her company while I ensure they handle the luggage properly? They never do every time trips like this happen, and it always makes me lose my mind."

"You only lose your temper because you like to be in control, especially when we have the means to buy new luggage anyways, but okay. I'll keep our radiant goddess company! We can get to know each other while you play the ship's captain."

"Don't start. If I don't, who will get it done, especially with how cozy you are."

"Whatever you say, son." Dawn winked at his uncle and Moon and walked out of the jet. "Make sure they do not lose my happy hour suitcase because I will be severely torn!" Bronte yelled, and Dawn said, "Sure!" from afar.

The jet was chocolate-brown inside, just as on the outside—fluffy white pillows on the seats to even out the tone. Bottles of white wine sat in buckets of ice, and three wine glasses were on the table. The windows were tinted black outside the jet, but you could see everything outside. The seats were cream-colored and leather with A wolf logo on them. It was the same logo that was on Moon's presents. At least she knew who Dawn's connections were now when getting the gifts.

Uncle Bronte seemed to be the opposite of Dawn. He was more intense, aggressive, and carefree. His favorite color seemed to be brown because he had an all-brown entire on. His slacks were dark brown, His leather loafers, his checkered high socks, and a silk shirt that was open enough to display his hairy chest. He had a gold Cartier bracelet and a watch on his right wrist. He seemed to be in his forties. He had a Roman nose, a rectangle chin, and an extended goatee. His eyes were a light green. His hair color was pitch black but had a few strands of grey. He had brown transparent sunglasses, but they had gold trim. He had a gold front tooth that would show anytime he smiled and a small upside-down cross tattoo behind his ear.

He called the flight attendant to order some food and for her to heat some of his famous healing tea. He snapped his fingers, rushing her to do what he said, which Moon found rude, but what did she expect?

"So, you are the secret my nephew has been hiding for months."

"Months?"

"Yes, he would mention this girl he had a big crush on but never said whether he pursued her. Now, I know." He smirked.

"Yes, we know now." She smiled nervously.

"You do not talk much, do you? Or are your nerves getting the best of you again?"

"No. I am completely fine. I'm just hungry and tired from the long ride. I'm not good with strangers much."

"I understand. It is best to observe others than talk to them to see if they are worthy of talking to."

"I wouldn't put it like that, but yes."

"I hope my tea makes you feel better, or it would be like letting my ancestors down." He chuckled. "It's a family recipe passed down."

Moon nodded and said, "Great! I'm sure it will do the trick."

He winked and said, "It should—wait, no it will."

Moon smiled, "Are you excited about the engagement?"

"Oh yes! I finally met the love of my life. My soulmate. And I will marry her in front of all the people I love. It's nerve-wracking and exciting at the same time. It's like snorting cocaine for the first time." He laughed, and she laughed nervously with him.

She hoped that he was kidding, but then again, he was not.

"Well, that's good. You are excited. Congratulations on your engagement."

"Thank you, thank you." He rubbed his nose. "Have you done drugs before?"

"No—no, no!"

"Good! It is not good for you. Make you cuckoo." He laughed hysterically.

"Oh, yeah."

"Oh, don't be so scared. I swear I'm on my best behavior. Now, tell me, Boston girl. Are you excited to be around us, Cali natives?"

"Yes, I am. Your city seems so beautiful. I can't wait to see it up close."

"If you ever get tired of Dawn showing you around. Do not hesitate to call on me to show you a good time around the city."

"Okay, I will." She smiled. "Such a pretty smile. Did anyone ever tell you that you look like a baby doll?"

"Yes. I hear it all the time."

"Good. Everyone needs compliments now and then."

"Are you his mother or father's brother?"

He sighed. "Sadly, his father's brother."

"Oh, okay."

"Do not get me wrong. I love my brother, but he takes life too seriously, just like his son. Luckily, I had a hand in raising Dawn somewhat, so he's lighthearted, unlike his parents."

"And his sisters?"

"I love my nieces, but they are a fucking chip off the old block." He ran his hands through his hair. "You will grow to love them." He winked.

"Okay, that's a relief."

"When the Wolfe family wants to, we can be pretty lovable. We care deeply for each other, and we value loyalty the most. I'm unsure if he shared this with you, but we're from a wealthy background, even if he tries to escape that reality."

"He told me you guys had money and that you and he are close, unlike the rest of his family."

"Yes, we are close, thank God. The family and him have not seen eye to eye for years. I tried to mend it on occasion, but six years ago, that changed. I hope they can settle their differences for the weekend and do not scare off my fiancé."

He took a wine bottle and popped it open. He poured some into a wine glass, threw about three ice cubes into it, and drank some. "Where are my manners? Do you want me to pour you some?"

"No, thanks. I do not drink."

"Oh well, your loss."

"What happened six years ago? He doesn't tell me. I've tried asking, but he always changes the subject."

He took more sips out of the glass. The flight attendant approached them with food. She sat down a bowl of Caesar salad and fruit.

"The tea is still heating up, Mr. Wolfe; it should be ready shortly."

"Thank you."

"Anything else, Mr. Wolfe?" He looked at her, and she said, "A glass of water, please, Ma'am."

"Yes, Ms. Moon."

She walked back to her station. He sat back in his seat and crossed his legs.

"That is between you and him." He used his pinky to stir the ice in his wine glass.

"Why?"

"Because he's my nephew, and his business is his business. I think you should hear it from him. Simple as that."

"Oh, come on, Bronte. Not you, too," she rolled her eyes and shoved some salad in her face.

"Aren't you the sassy one?" He smiled. "Look, gorgeous. Talk to my nephew if you want answers. I like you a lot, but I'm not the one to gossip with." He said firmly. She was unsure what to think of him. All she knew was that he was serious, and she would have to find answers herself. He was no help, and she was back to square one.

"I didn't mean it like that. I would like to know more about my boyfriend, and—"

"Aha! So, you guys are serious."

"I guess you can say that."

"Boyfriend? I cannot wait to tease him about this the whole week." He laughed. "Also, no matter how you word it. It's not my place to tell you, okay." He blew a kiss. She got frustrated and decided to eat. The flight attendant brought the water and scolded the tea. "Drink up! We have five long hours together, and I think we will need food and rest."

"What do you do?" She stabbed her fork into the fruit.

"As in?"

"Work?"

"I am the CEO of a jewelry company."

"Oh, wow." She smiled.

"Yes."

"What company?"

"The name of the company is Elegant Gems. A Wolfe's legacy."

"It seems familiar."

"I can see. Seeing as you are wearing the rose bracelet he had customized for you."

She twisted the rose bracelet on her arm, "Yes! I love it. It's the most beautiful thing I have seen. I didn't know you made it."

"I wouldn't be a Wolfe if I didn't, anything for D." He smiled, and she smiled, "Thank you."

"You are very Welcome," he said as he drank the rest of his wine.

They sat in silence, waiting for Dawn to return. The jet was getting ready to take off. She began to yawn after eating her fill and drinking hot tea. Bronte requested a blanket for her, and as the flight attendant placed a bright orange blanket on her, Dawn walked in.

He sat next to her and kissed her hand.

"What did I miss?"

"Nothing much. Your lady and I were getting to know each other."

"You guys didn't fight, did you? If you did, please, for my sake, kiss and make up."

They all smiled. "Dawn, of course not."

He kissed her on the lips and said, "Good. I couldn't bear my two favorite people in the world not getting along."

"That won't happen, D." Bronte winked.

He poured himself another glass of wine and passed Dawn one.

"Baby, I can move if you want to lie down."

She yawned and said, "I can move. You don't have to."

"Nonsense! Lay down. If you don't want to move nor him, just put your feet on him."

"Good idea, Bronte." He said sarcastically. "Why didn't we think of that." He winked at Moon, and she smiled. Moon placed her feet on his lap and her head on a pillow. Bronte placed something into Dawn's hands.

"Put these in your ear to block out the noise."

With a smile, she slipped the pink buds into her ears. It was a pity that she couldn't hear anything, especially since she was curious about the tension between Dawn and his family. Hopefully, she could piece things together after they landed, but she figured it was best to get some sleep for now.

"She asked about six years ago."

"Moon?"

"There isn't a ghost in these walls, is it?"

"Very funny." He said sarcastically.

"What did you tell her?"

"It wasn't my place to say; I said she should ask you."

"Okay, good."

"Why haven't you told her?" He asked, concerned.

"Because I do not want to dredge up old feelings. I love our family, but if I told her, I feel she wouldn't be so welcoming to them and wouldn't have agreed to come this weekend."

"Don't stop progress on our behalf, but I understand." He sighed. "Sooner or later, you will have to tell her, or she will find out on her own."

"Yes, I know how informative the Wolfes can be."

"I love you, D, and I can tell you are serious about her, so tell her."

"I will, and I am serious about her."

"Great."

"I'm in love with her."

Bronte choked on his wine and caught his breath. "In love! You haven't known each other that long," he whispered.

"Are you okay?"

"D!"

"Yes, I know, but you know me. I'm a hopeful romantic."

"Hopeful romantic. Don't you mean hopeless romantic?"

"No. Hopeful romantic." He chuckled.

"Whatever you mean, please think this through. I do not want to see your heart broken again and another six years go by, okay?" he said, annoyed, as he placed his glass on the coaster.

"Yes, Uncle Bronte. I can say the same about you."

"Not quite. I know she is the one, and we've dated for three years, so I think we have proven ourselves to each other." He smiled confidently.

"Does Moon feel the same?"

"She will soon," he said unsurely.

"D."

"Do not start. I do not want to hear it. I know she loves me, and I won't rush her."

"This is not a repeat of last time, is it?"

"No, Bronte. Let's drop it, okay."

"D?"

"Bronte!" he said with massive annoyance.

"Okay, just be careful," Bronte said, waving his hands in the air as a surrender.

"I will." They smiled. "Well—isn't love in the air for us."

"It is. It is, most definitely."

Dawn sipped some of his white wine and gazed out of the window. The captain announced to the speaker that they were planning to take flight, but Moon was still asleep. Bronte ranted about his love life, money endeavors, and the family to catch him up. Dawn provided vague answers here and there while hoping that the trip would be successful and that it wouldn't test the waters between him and Moon too much. They were headed to his prison, but more so his sore wound called "home."

# 10. A Beating Heart

The jet hit some turbulence, jolting Moon awake. She pushed the blanket aside and stretched her arms, rubbing the sleep from her eyes as she took in her surroundings. She noticed Bronte sleeping with his headphones on, covered by a blanket. At first, Dawn was hard to spot, but she soon caught sight of him across the aisle. He was talking on the phone, his voice low and tense, turned away from her and gazing out the window. To announce her wakefulness, she coughed lightly. Startled, he turned to her, offering a smile that she returned, though her expression quickly dimmed as he made his way to the restroom for more privacy. As always, this piqued her curiosity about who he spoke to and why he needed to be secretive. She could think of numerous reasons for his behavior but decided to hold off on speculating until he finished his conversation.

She took out her phone to check for messages and found just one: a text from Marleen. It read, *"Have fun, Moon! You only live once! Worry less and love more!"* A smile spread across her face, but she couldn't respond since her phone was in SOS mode. Shifting closer to the window on the far right, she looked outside and sighed. She realized this short vacation was her chance to let go and embrace some fun. All she needed to do was set aside her fears and insecurities; it would feel like turning over a new leaf. Marleen's words resonated, and it was time for her to make the effort. She heard the restroom door click shut and the sound of Dawn's footsteps approaching. Turning her head towards the main entrance, her wide doe eyes took him in.

He dropped down into the seat next to her. His finger twirled the curly ends of her hair, and he had no expression. It left her worried. She knew something was wrong, so she stopped his hand from fiddling with her hair and said, "What's wrong, handsome?" scooting closer to him. He looked away for a moment without a response, fiddled with his class ring, and said, "My parents."

"What about them?"

"They are happy about me coming home."

She smiled. "What's wrong with that? I would give anything to have family excited that I was coming home for a visit."

He clenched his jaw and rubbed his face. "Baby, I love your open mind, but please do not have one when it comes to my family. They are like parasites that will eat you out from the inside."

"That's harsh."

"It is. They are only happy that I'm coming because they think they can convince me to stay permanently."

She grabbed his hand, turned it over, and traced hearts. "Do you want to stay? Permanently— I mean."

"No."

"Okay, good." She smiled. "How do they feel about me coming along? What I mean is, do they know of me or know me?"

"A little bit of both. I did not go into detail about you because I wanted them to meet you instead of hearing about you. Words can only express so much about someone, let alone help others envision."

"For a family that is so parasitic, you sure did tell me not to worry on the cab ride over here. Or did you tell me they would love me to ease my mind because you're contradicting yourself?"

"They will love you—I was just——I mean, of course, they make my blood boil, but they have their positives. I'm sorry to make you worry. I can't promise, but I know they will love you like Bronte."

"I know you have no control over what your family does. It's just that I do not want to be taken aback if they start crucifying me at the stake."

He chuckled.

"Dawn!" She whined.

"I swear I will put out the flames before anything happens, and I'll be by your side. Do not worry. I'm just venting."

"You said you would tell me everything about you and your family. I am ready to listen if you're ready to tell me." She insinuated.

"Rose, do not worry, honestly." He tossed his head back toward the seat and sighed.

"Dawn. You have given me vague answers. I want to know what has driven a wedge between you and your family. You speak of them as if they held you down and burned your favorite toy in front of you. I want to know."

He brought her wrist to his mouth, kissed it, and said, "Okay." He smiled.

He took off his black trench coat and wore a white filmy shirt, which he rolled up the sleeves. He wore black slacks, white tennis shoes, and his usual wolf pendant around his neck. His hair was wild, like a pearl bouncing off the night's light.

He gestured for her to move closer, and she did. "We have about two more hours in the air. I might as well tell you everything like I promised." He appeared dreadful at the start of their conversation, but at least she would know everything and not be left in the dark. They barely knew each other, and that was entirely too much.

He turned completely, faced her, and said, "I used to be naïve when it came to love and wanting to be loved." He looked into her eyes, trying to find his words, "Remember when I told you that I and my family could not get along because of our differences?"

"Yes."

"Well, six years ago, it went further than it should have." She didn't like where this conversation was going because his eyes grew red, and he had to take breaths after each word. "I had no luck keeping relationships, partly because I could not come out of my shell, and I was a Wolfe. I had to watch out for users, someone not of my status, and stalkers."

"Mm-hmm."

"Yeah." He smiled disappointedly. "My friends and family used to tease me about it. Most of my family had no relationship problems due to being prejudiced anyway, except for Uncle Bronte. He gave me advice sometimes. I couldn't even talk to a girl. I was so used to being to myself. I like to think I even had more life in me, too. I did not have the confidence I did with you, but I would say the only reason girls have been attracted to me is because of my aloofness." They smiled at each other. "Who could deny that and your good looks."

"Anyways, out of the blue, I had luck. Her name is—was Rainy Crow. We ran into each other at a drive-thru movie theater. We both were with friends. She was your average California girl. Blonde hair, blue eyes, spray tan, and skinny enough to be healthy but look sickly for the runway. She strived to be a model, but it wasn't surprising. She had my heart before you. She didn't care for it well."

"What drew you to her?" She said with intrigue.

"Straight to the point, huh?"

"What can I say." She shrugged.

"I ventured from my friends to buy more popcorn, and she was at the snack stand. I do not know what drew me to her, but I would say it could have been the kindness in her eyes. I did not have to try so hard with her. Every word from my mouth was like butter to her, making me feel seen. She didn't have money to get popcorn, so I offered to pay, and one thing led to another." If he felt the girl who had broken his heart was easy to be with, did he feel the same about Moon? She wondered if she made him feel seen. He made her feel seen; it would break her heart if she made things difficult for him. *Did that mean she was his first love or something else?*

"Her and you started to date?"

"Yes, we did, and quick. We practically hung out with each other every day. Dinner dates, movies, parties, you name it. It was an interesting time in my life. My parents were happy I was leaving the house and experiencing life. It got to a point where we both confessed our love to one another. In my mind, I thought this was a big step and would be a good time to introduce her to my family. So, I did."

"And, what happened?"

"The Wolfe mansion almost burned down, figuratively, of course."

"Omg," she chuckled. "Yeah, my parents hated that I was dating a wannabe model. She was white trash in their eyes as far as they were concerned. Uncle Bronte was the only one that welcomed her with open arms."

"Is that why you haven't seen them for six years?"

"Oh god, no. It was bigger than that. I could keep them in check about her status. She was an angel of a specimen in my eyes, so that did not bother me."

"Then, what was it?"

"I was naïve on both ends. They wanted to prove a point, and I let them. I loved her to the point that I thought of marriage. She was my everything. It hurt I couldn't see her true colors, not to say she was a bad person, but she was not loyal."

He smiled painfully. "My parents persisted that we test her, and I wanted them off our backs and to prove them wrong, so I agreed." He looked away and stared at Bronte. "They gave her two tests. They offered her money and a modeling career if she broke up with me. I stayed in the shadows and watched from afar through a camera. She said yes to everything." He paused. "My heart shrunk in my chest and fell into my stomach. I couldn't believe it. It had to be a joke, so I ran into the room and demanded she say she was lying. That she was joking, but she wasn't. If anything, she was sorry she got caught, even asked if it was over and if she could keep what they offered."

"What. That is so—fucked up. She loved you."

"I thought she loved me too. She shouted it from the top of her lungs, but I didn't believe anything else she had to say." He sighed. "If that wasn't awful, imagine the second test. It was the cherry on the fucking top."

She didn't know what to say. She felt terrible for him. His family turned out to be right. His heart was placed on the butcher's table, chopped into tiny pieces, and sold to the highest bidder. She hugged him and kissed his cheek. She could never think of doing such a thing to him. They belong to each other. Nothing would come in between that- she had hoped.

"If I felt a hug so genuinely back then, maybe I wouldn't have fallen off the deep end." He said, kissing her on top of her head.

"What happened with the second test?"

"Without my knowledge, they paid a servant of ours to seduce her, and well, you know the rest. They even had my uncle flirt with her, and she flirted back, but I didn't care; she fell for it. I cared that my family went through all this trouble to show me such flaws in her that I would come to know on my own. It was the principle. I was angry at both parties, even Bronte, for a while. It wasn't long after they tried to set me up with someone from a high-standing family. I couldn't take it and told them how I felt."

"Was she cute, at least?" She smiled." Not as cute as you, rose." He smiled.

"My family and I got into a big argument and said awful things to each other. After that, I left for good. I haven't seen them since, but like I said, we slowly began to get back into touch."

"How?"

"Uncle Bronte. He never stops meddling in people's affairs, so it wasn't shocking he broke the silence between us." He smirked. "Now you know the whole story."

"Yes, that wasn't so bad, was it?"

"No, but it didn't feel good either."

"Old wounds, I know."

"Yeah, but the worst part was that she never said sorry. She left with it all to plummet her career in two years with drugs and bad relationships. Last I heard of her, she was pregnant and in rehab."

"That sucks."

"Karma's a bitch." He smirked.

"Dawn!" She whined.

"Dawn." He mocked.

She knew she couldn't tell him how to feel, but it just felt wrong to bask in someone's downfall. It might be hypocrisy on her part, she thought, since she has wished her mother dead so many times.

"Did she happen to be your first love or your first everything? Maybe vice-versa, too."

"She was a young love I had, not a first love or true love. She doesn't deserve that title. I didn't lose my virginity to her, if that is what you are asking. I did experience girls before her, so I did gain experience."

"Okay, good to know. It will help me sleep easier at night." She joked.

He smiled. "Anything else you want to know?"

"Yes. Did she act differently when she found out you were a Wolfe?"

"No, I will say she enjoyed the perks of being with one until she needed more. It would have been better for her to marry one than use one for money."

"It would have been disingenuous either way. It would have been best if she broke it off with you or been upfront about loving money more than love."

"Yeah." He kissed her, and she kissed him back. "How did you know the second test was real and that your family did not make it up?"

He kissed her again. "As I said, all of it was unbelievable, but I saw it with my eyes and felt disgusted. It took me a year to come to terms with it. I went to therapy and started journaling, but I was open to love once again."

"I'm sorry, love. I'm glad you worked through it and distanced yourself." He smiled.

"I would never want to hurt you and will not." They both smiled and hugged each other tightly.

She will show him her love the best she can. She will try not to be a downer. He had done much for her, and she would return the favor. She needed this trip to determine her feelings in the long run and not leave him clueless. It doesn't help that his family is snakes looking for prey. She hoped they would not attack her all at once. She wasn't prepared but could be just as snappy. She had to endure this for him, her heart, her destiny. She could not let him down or herself. She hugged him tightly. She didn't want to suffocate him, but if she had to, to show him she cared, she would.

He laughed, "Baby, you're squeezing too tight. Let go," he said as he kept laughing.

She let him go and laughed nervously, "Do not feel the need to act differently because of the story. I do not doubt your affection for me; besides, it was six years ago, and though it still hits a soft spot, I won't judge you based on past relationships. You are two different people." He said as he caressed her chin.

She smiled with relief but was still worried. "Okay." He winked at her and smiled.

"I have a present for you."

Her eyes widened. "Dawn," she whined, "Another gift? You gave me so much already."

"What? I like spoiling you, and it's my love language, even if it is not yours."

"I didn't say that. It's just that I have yet to get you anything."

"I have everything I need in the world, so do not worry your gorgeous mind, okay?"

"I will trust me." She giggled.

"Oh, I do." He laughed.

She rolled her eyes and said, "Okay, let's see this present."

"Say less."

He rushed to the flight attendant section of the jet and returned with a purple box with a silver bow. He handed her the box, and she unwrapped it slowly. "The suspense." She laughed.

She opened the box halfway and saw something move. She slid two fingers across it, and it moved. She jumped back and asked, "What is it?"

He laughed, then said, "Open the box and see."

She gathered the courage to open the box and saw it was a baby turtle. It was the size of a penny. It was sea green like the earth. She placed it in the palm of her hand and rubbed its little shell. She couldn't stop smiling. Her brain began to process names for the turtle. She had a soft spot for turtles since she was a young girl. She never knew why, but they comforted her; maybe it was their way of life. A community within itself, a family. Dawn knew her well, but what would possess him to buy her a pet turtle?

"What made you buy me a baby turtle?"

"I do not know."

"Really?" She looked at him with skepticism.

"I mean, I thought it would be nice for you to have company besides your TV and me at home." He said as he smiled, "I know we get busy sometimes, and I wanted you not to be alone."

She smiled widely. "You are so sweet and thoughtful." She looked down at the turtle, smiling. "How could I not just want to kiss you."

"Me or the turtle?"

"Turtle, of course."

"Ouch." He teased.

She rolled her eyes. "I give you enough attention."

"What are you going to name it."

"Depends on what's the sex. What's the sex?"

"I didn't ask." He said, unsure.

"That's the first thing you ask, baby," she whined, letting out a sigh.

"How about Dawn Jr.?"

He smiled. "Are you serious?"

"Maybe. It can be practice for our future children," she said playfully.

"Is that right?" He smirked, licking his lips.

"Yes, that is right." She continued to rub the turtle's shell.

"We can get practice right now," he winked.

She laughed and put the turtle back in the box. He grabbed her by the waist, and they kissed passionately. She pushed him back lightly. "No—no, baby!" She squealed playfully.

"What?" He laughed.

"Your uncle is across from us, and I'm sure we will land soon. There is not enough time nor any space in here for that." She laughed loudly while covering her mouth so as not to wake Bronte.

"We can manage." He smiled seductively.

"No, baby. After we land, okay. You are not the only one in the mood." She smiled shyly.

The captain announced on the speaker that they were landing as soon as Dawn tried to kiss her again. They giggled and sat properly in their seats, each buckling their seat belts.

"I'm happy you chose not to consummate your love before me." They were shocked and blushed as Bronte spoke.

"Please do not stop on my behalf." He said, half-awake, and pushed the blanket off himself, staring at them both.

"Sorry, Bronte." Dawn laughed.

"No worries. I get the same way around my woman." He winked at them both.

"I heard through the grapevine."

"And who would that be?" He asked as he took off his headphones and sat up straight.

"Oh, I do not know. Your family."

"Who per se?"

"Your nieces."

"Those snitches." His gold teeth showed as he laughed.

The captain announced again to the speaker that they should buckle their seat belts and prepare for landing. Bronte buckled himself and smiled at them both. "Get ready, beautiful. You are about to meet the family."

"I am as ready as I am excited." She smiled anxiously.

"That's the spirit."

Dawn and Moon kissed before bracing themselves for landing. Meanwhile, Bronte embraced the view of their love and said, "Love birds."

It was the middle of the night when they landed, and a black SUV was parked outside the jet. The driver placed the luggage in the trunk. Moon stood beside the jet door, waiting on Dawn, her mind elsewhere. Unexpectedly, he picked her up into his arms. She was shaken at first but smiled at the gesture of it all. He loved to give her what she wanted. If she said she wanted to buy Greece, he would find a way to hand it to her on a golden platter. She liked the fact that he wanted to give her the world sometimes. It was nice to feel important and wanted. That is why she knew she would fall in love with him soon enough, but there was no rush. He made her laugh and feel safe; that was a start in itself.

"Are you going to carry me everywhere now?"

"I wouldn't say everywhere." He winked. "Why? Would you prefer to walk because—"

She cut him off mid-sentence. "No." She laughed. "It is lovely that you carry me. I like it when you do small things like that. It's a less strenuous activity for me. It took me by shock, that's all." She smiled ear to ear.

"Sorry to have to tell you this, but your life will be full of surprises being around me. The perks of being with such a devoted boyfriend." He smiled. "When you put it like that." She smirked.

"Do you have any complaints, madam? We love feedback and reviews," he said with a terrible fake French accent. She chuckled and looked away. "Madam?"

She looked back at him with a blushing face. "No complaints, Mr. Wolfe— sir."

He kissed her eagerly while holding her at the end of the jet stairs. The kissing didn't stop. It was as if they were deprived of each other. The driver mentioned twice that the car was ready, but they did not hear.

Bronte yelled, "Lovebirds! Time to go!" shaking his head in disbelief. "If anyone wouldn't like to walk to the mansion, then please place your asses in the car." He thumped the side of Dawn's head. Dawn released Moon from the kiss. She laughed, and Dawn looked at Bronte playfully, irritated. Bronte looked back at Dawn in a tempting manner, scoffing his way into the front seat.

They got into the car. "You didn't have to strike me, you know."

"If I didn't, your feet would still be molded to the ground and your face to Moon."

"Maybe." He smiled sarcastically as he placed gum into his mouth. He offered her some, but she declined.

"No gum for me, D?"

"Not for aggressors, no."

"Aww, I'm hurt. We were just so close." He chuckled. "Stop being a big baby."

Dawn threw up a finger sign and rolled his eyes. Bronte smirked and motioned for the driver to head to the Wolfe mansion.

"See Mo! If you don't mind me calling, you Mo."

She smiled. "No. Mo is okay."

He smiled. "This is what I have to deal with. A knucklehead."

Dawn laughed and lightly punched Bronte's shoulder. "I love you too, Uncle Bronte."

"Mm-hmm." They all laughed.

Bronte slipped on his headphones while the driver turned to Dawn and Moon, asking if they wanted to tune into the radio. They both shook their heads, preferring the quiet as they felt the nerves building up about reaching the mansion and meeting everyone. Sitting across from each other, they held hands, boredom creeping in as they stared at one another. It felt like their eyes might dry out as they traced the outlines of each other's faces and compared their eye colors. They found themselves wondering what it would be like to swap eyes. Would he have those stunning green eyes like a lush forest? Would she have those adorable, heart-melting baby doll eyes? They were communicating without saying a word, which was refreshing. Sometimes, it was exhausting to let a bunch of words dictate the mood. They exchanged smiles and turned their gazes back to the windows, their grip on each other's hands tightening. They never wanted to let go.

The black SUV's transparent sunroof let her gaze at the starry night. She found herself staring up, feeling a bit more at ease. Suddenly, the car stopped, and she shifted her focus back on Dawn, gripping his hand firmly. Her stomach was churning, and she didn't know if it was nerves or something frightening.

*Could the Wolfe family smell fear? What if they had a handful of tests prepared for me that I didn't know about? Not that I wouldn't pass, but I couldn't take it. I was strong by mind but weak by heart. There is so much I can take.*

Bronte happily leaped out of the car and ran to hug two women outside the mansion. She didn't see who they were but assumed they were family. She turned to Dawn and smiled anxiously.

"Breathe, it's just my sisters." He kissed her cheek. "Are you ready?"

She knew she had to be ready. She didn't have more time not to be. Taking a deep breath, she exhaled slowly, then gave Dawn a nod and a smile. "Okay. Let's go meet the family."

When she exited the massive SUV, it hit her just how short she was. They walked hand in hand toward everyone, and his uncle smiled and giggled. It annoyed her a bit because she longed to have that kind of self-confidence he had.

*What if they hate me? What if they made snarky remarks, and I have to be on my toes to catch it? What if they think I'm ugly? What if they shun me, and I have to leave on the spot?*

It killed her not to know what they would think of her. Her palms got sweaty, and she hoped Dawn wouldn't become disgusted but would understand. She gazed at him for a second, and he shot her a smile. She smiled back, horror in her eyes, as they stopped beside Bronte.

Dawn wrapped his arm around Moon's waist, and she clutched his hand almost too tightly. She realized she was squeezing hard, but he didn't flinch. He just smiled at his sisters, taking it all in stride. As they got closer, she could faintly hear their names, catching only the letter S. The sisters looked to be in their early 30s, with the oldest being the blonde. She wasn't a fake blonde; instead, she was tall and slender with subtle curves. Her striking blue eyes stood out against her square-shaped face, which featured a small, sharp nose. Her top lip was slightly fuller than her bottom lip, and she had a thin scar above her eyebrows. Her straight hair was neatly tucked behind her ears. She wore flared black pants with a simple white belt and a white strapless tank top with a black trim and a little bow. White and gold Tommy Hilfiger sandals were on her feet, and her nails were polished with a clear coat. She accessorized with large gold hoop earrings and a class ring that looked much like Dawn's, except hers had a deep-sea-colored stone.

The second oldest sister was quite the contrast—she was short, bowlegged, and skinny as a pencil. Her hair was a mix of auburn and ginger, and her eyes were a plain brown. She had a petite, sharp nose and an oval face. Compared to the blonde sister, she was as pale as Dawn. Her hair was styled in a braided ponytail, and she sported light makeup with a glossy finish on her lips. She wore a dark-pink long-sleeve polo, loose light jeans, and dark-pink leather ankle boots. Her only accessories were a Tiffany necklace called "Summer" and a silver Italian bracelet adorned with pink-gold charms, each representing a different activity or city. Her nails were short and painted bright pink, hinting that pink was her go-to color. Each sister had their aura, but they stood together. Summer was more relaxed and approachable, while the other sister had a more severe and distant demeanor—always observant and a bit aloof.

Moon felt like the odd man out while everyone was dressed nicely. Thinking they would have time to change before meeting everyone, but it looked impossible. She wore cheetah-print Uggs, a black skintight romper, a messy bun, and her boyfriend's old college grey hoodie. She wanted to make an excellent first impression, but it didn't appear to be that way and his sisters continued to observe her. They had to be looking for something; otherwise, they wouldn't stare. On the inside, she knew everything would turn out okay. They would fight for each other despite his family's opinions. She would follow her heart.

Everyone looked at each other without saying one word. Someone would have to break the ice, and she would hate for it to be herself, especially since his sisters seemed happy before they arrived. She wanted this weekend to go smoothly for Bronte and his soon-to-be bride. Also, Dawn didn't need any more stress added to his feelings about his family. She wanted to get to know her boyfriend peacefully, besides what he chose to show her.

She tugged at the ends of her hair while the silence intensified among everyone. What felt like an eternity was only three seconds passing, and she was willing to gather the guts to speak if no one would. However, one of his sisters broke the tension by speaking.

"Well? Are you going to say hello or stand there like a statue flaunting your new woman?" She said bluntly and hard.

Dawn smiled tensely. "Nice to see you too."

"Hi, D." the other sister said with candor and a faint sweetness.

"Moon. This is Summer and Crystal." Moon smiled.

"Hello." His sisters nodded and smiled.

"Summer and Crystal, this is Moon." They smiled again. "You are the beauty our brother almost lost his tongue speaking about." Moon chuckled, hand over her mouth.

"Really, Summer?"

"Okay. Okay, you lost a few teeth but kept your tongue."

Dawn stared at her, and she smiled back.

"Uncle Bronte, is it not true our little brother has a mouth on him? Is it our fault he can talk a person's head off?"

"No, Summer, it isn't." Bronte smiled big.

"I wish he would lose a few teeth talking to me." Moon looked at him enduringly.

"He rarely speaks. He's a mouse around me." She winked at him.

"Not true."

"Yes, it is."

"We talk a lot."

"Not as much as I would like."

"I can say the same thing about you."

They squinted at each other and lightly laughed. "Do not worry; being around us for a few days should help. We are big on helping our brother communicate," Summer said snarkily.

She could feel someone's eyes on her, and it was Crystal. She barely said a word but kept eye contact, which sent a chill down her body. "Crystal? What do you think?"

"Huh?"

Moon smiled and said, "What do you think about Dawn's yapping?"

Crystal stared at everyone for about five seconds before saying anything. "He's a Wolfe at best howling at the moon. He would make our ears bleed as kids, but what could we say? He was cute and our little brother," she giggled.

"I knew you were a sweetheart," Moon said as she smiled at him. Dawn blushed in response.

"Enough about me. How has everything been?"

"As good as it gets. Mother and father are happy. She has taken up horses again."

"Oh, really?"

Crystal smiled. "Yes, she has. She loves it, and it gives her something to do other than interior decorating."

Everyone smiled as Bronte ended up texting on the phone.

"That's good, and you two? How's the life of my beautiful sisters?"

His sisters smiled in unison. Oh, do not flatter us. Not when a goddess is standing next to you."

"Thank you." Moon and Dawn said at the same time, chuckling.

"Well? How have you been?"

Summer rolled her eyes at Crystal. "Well, I have been great. I took up Latin. I've started a small project to collect charms for the cities I have been to. I've been on a few dates but haven't met the love of my life. And yeah," she giggled with her hands behind her back and bounced a little. Dawn and Summer stared at Crystal.

She sighed and said, "For the love of God, I have been exercising more. I have been helping at the company—no love life or fun. The office has been my life for the past few weeks now."

"Has father been hard on you?"

"No—"

"Yes!" Bronte and Summer shouted.

"They are exaggerating." She nudged summer.

"I'm sure," Dawn said firmly.

"So—what can you tell us about you?" Moon was startled and nervous. She looked at Dawn. "Don't worry about him. We want to know what you two been up to besides what he told us, which was nothing." Summer winked, pulling out a piece of gum and throwing it into her mouth.

"I'm from Boston, born and raised. Most of my family is deceased except for my mother, but we are estranged. I like poetry and writing. I'm finding myself and trying out new experiences. That's all I can think of." She smiled.

"College?" Crystal quickly pressed.

"Yes, I went to a four-year and majored in arts with an understudy in creative writing."

"Which college?"

"Does that matter?" His tone was vexed.

"I was just asking," Crystal said softly while Summer grinned.

"We heard you liked roses, pasta, and nature. You could light up the sky like the moon, and no girl could compare to you, not even the goddess Hathor."

"Hathor?" Moon asked, confused.

"Words courtesy of my brother, and she is the goddess of beauty in Egypt."

She blushed. She never got so many compliments on her beauty. She always felt average. It made her wonder if she was more beautiful than she thought. "Aww! —Baby, you are so sweet!" They kissed for a minute.

"Ew! —No kissing in front of us, Dawn!" Summer nudged his arm.

"Hey! I don't believe that it's my fault you have never seen intimacy up close. So deprived, sister," he smiled.

"Ha—ha!" Summer rolled her eyes.

"Trust us, D. We have kissed men before. You are our little brother, but we even have to admit you are all grown up."

"You are just coming to that realization. Who would have thought."

Bronte put away his phone and joined the conversation. "Yeah." Bronte smiled.

"So—Bronte, are you excited about this weekend?"

"Ready than I'll ever be." He smiled.

"Good!" Moon smiled.

"Speaking of that, I know my nephew will be my best man, but I would love for you to be my finance bridesmaid. She doesn't have many friends. What do you say?"

"I would love to." Dawn hugged her from behind. "Another chance to see your beautiful face even more."

"Mm-hmm." Moon smiled.

"Great! I'm happy that you agreed."

"Aren't you just the cutest couple," Crystal smirked.

"Who else is going to be?" Dawn said confidently.

"Well, we should get ready to go inside. It's getting late." Bronte kept checking his phone and eyeing Crystal.

"We all have missed you." Crystal nervously smiled. "Come on, Summer."

"Good times, D. Missed you." Summer said as if she was reminiscent.

"I missed all of you too. I can't say much for Mother and Father. Where are they?"

Bronte's face fell with disappointment as he put his shades back on. Summer looked at Crystal, seeking her approval. Crystal nodded and looked away. "What is it?"

Summer smiled, lacking assurance, and said, "Mother and Father had an engagement for tonight. We will see them in the morning."

"You sure?" he said with vigor.

"I wouldn't have said if I wasn't."

"I doubt that."

"Excuse me." Crystal looked at Dawn fiercely.

"You heard me."

"Dawn." Moon's face tensed.

"I know they promised to meet you at the jet, then the house, but plans change. You will see them if that is your concern." Summer said calmly.

"No, it's the principal that they do not concern themselves with."

Anger arose in Dawn and Summer's voices.

"Hey. It's okay." Moon said softly.

"Stay out of it, rose," Dawn said, affirming, removing his arm around her waist. He stood tall in front of his older sisters and moved closer. Bronte pulled Moon near him with his arm.

"Stay out of it, okay?" Bronte said, smiling and rubbing her chin. He also moved closer to the argument.

"Screaming at the new girl already, brother," Crystal said.

"Shut up! You do not know what you are talking about, so stop changing the subject. They said they would meet us, but of course, they didn't unless it was to ruin my life."

"Stop being a baby!" The sisters echoed. "Don't call me that!"

"Why shouldn't we? Because It's Bronte's engagement weekend, and you are like a toddler crying about mommy and daddy not being here on your time!" Crystal chuckled. "As always! Spoiled golden child!"

"You couldn't wait to say that, could you? All my life, you both taunted me and made me cry about how our parents played favorites. If they did, it would have been with you two!" The anger ran him red and hot. She could see the steam coming off his body. "Always jealous!"

"How fucking dare you! Jealous? I wouldn't be jealous of someone who can't discern gold from a fucking penny when it comes to his life choices and WOMEN!" Crystal shrieked.

Summer stood there in all the chaos she had started, smiling evilly, making Moon want to cry for Dawn. She moved towards everyone a little, and Bronte quickly turned his head and said, "No."

She stood to the side, waiting for it all to be over, and to think she was worried about them judging her.

"You are such a BITCH! Like a fucking pit bull at my heel since I could crawl out of the crib!"

"Well, you must stalk your prey to last long in the Wolfe household. Sorry, we do not have a DICK!" Crystal smiled.

"Oh, please spare me the daddy and mommy don't love us because we are girls! I was under fucking microscope when you got to do what the fuck you wanted!"

"Wow, D! If anything, they went light on you! We had to become fucking pets on a leash to get to that point! I can't even change my toenail polish without them knowing!"

"Yeah! Yeah!" He waved her out of his face.

"Does your beloved know the full story, or do you cry to her at night about the shit you did before you even decided to leave this fucking house! Huh! Imbecile!"

"What the fuck are you talking about!" His face became distorted, just like hers. Moon had never seen such anger before, not since her mother.

"Hey! Moon, did you know-!"

"NOT IN FRONT OF MOON!" Bronte screamed ferociously. "LIKE FUCKING DOGS IN THE COURTYARD!" Everyone went silent. He took off his shades. "I wanted to let you all get the anger out, but this shit is just messy!" Everyone looked down. "Should be ashamed doing this in front of a guest, especially you, Dawn." Dawn barely turned his head.

"I'm sorry." He whispered.

"I couldn't hear you simply because of the fact you started this bullshit. Your mother and father have always been the same, and it's not an excuse to be fucking childish."

"Yes, sir." Bronte looked at Summer and Crystal. "Yes, sir, we are sorry," The sisters agreed.

"And Moon, we are sorry about this. This boy lost his wits for a moment." He patted Dawn's face.

She forced a smile. "It's okay. I understand." She didn't know if she should go over, so she stayed put.

"I'm going to tell the driver to unload our things, and we can finish this discussion like adults in the morning." He firmly looked at everyone. "Yes, sir." They replied.

Bronte walked towards the car. Summer and Crystal held hands as they stepped inside the manor. Dawn grabbed Moon's hand and kissed her on the temple.

"I'm sorry. I usually do not get out of character like that, especially in front of you." His voice trembled.

It seemed as if he wanted to cry. She wouldn't mind it, not at all. "It's okay, Dawn. I have my family squabbles myself or used to." She whispered gently.

He began to cry. His eyes burned with fever, and his demeanor weakened.

"I'm sorry."

He repeated it to her over and over.

"Shh." She caressed his face. "Let's go inside okay."

He sniffed and wiped the tears from his face. "Okay."

"I will see you both inside," Bronte said, patting Dawn on the back.

"Okay," they replied.

# 11. Yearning

They entered Wolfe Manor. The sight was indescribable. It was nightfall, so Moon couldn't gauge the size of the manor, but it resembled the pearly gates. The entrance was a dazzling white, almost blinding in its brightness. The marble staircase looked like scattered droplets of liquid, with a Victorian stair runner adorning its steps. The staircase arms were elegant black steel, twisting and turning like plant vines, with delicate gold leaf patterns and trim. A single yellow-lit lamp titivated the staircase wall next to a large, archaic European painting. Although she didn't fully understand the painting's significance, Dawn could sense a triangle of love, death, and loss within it. Below the staircase, a small circular window was framed by black steel shaped into a flower. A golden clock was positioned on the far right, alongside a bronze plaque commemorating the late Aygo Wolfe, with the years 1867-1916 inscribed upon it.

To the left of her, there was a classic black piano and a royal blue sitting chair. The dining room had an open entrance. The table was covered with a white tablecloth and decorated with various colored flowers ranging from small to big. The chairs had cream lining with espresso-colored cushions. The room was all marble white and featured a fireplace. The same flowers were spread everywhere, including gold candle holders, big old European paintings, and gold trims along the walls. A crystal chandelier hung from the ceiling, with each crystal light dangling and modeled differently. The space reminded her of Marie Antoinette, evoking a soft and coquettish ambiance.

To her right was the living room: spacious and serene, with tall arched windows with half a fan, low lighting, white-cotton sofas, and a white leather let-out chair. A Persian rug was in the middle of the floor, accompanied by a glass coffee table and three lamps. A wooden door opened onto a balcony with a white Victorian interior. All that could be seen was the ocean and nature: dark, wild, and beautiful. She couldn't wait to see the rest of the manor. She noticed two more entrances leading to other rooms, but the doors were closed. In spite of the earlier fight, she was ecstatic about the rest of the weekend and was anxious to meet everyone.

Bronte instructed the driver to leave the bags by the staircase and tipped him generously. He gestured to Dawn to join him, and they spoke in hushed tones so she couldn't overhear. In the meantime, she decided to sit on the stairs and wait until they were finished. She messaged Marleen to let her know that the flight had gone well and they had arrived safely at the manor. She took some photos to send to her and then wandered into the living room while Dawn was occupied. However, she didn't understand how everything in the manor seemed so lively and grand compared to what she was accustomed to. It felt spacious and unadorned, with hardly any curtains or shades. You could see everything. She stepped out onto the balcony, and all she could see was the ocean, vast and calm, with nothing else in sight. She thought to herself, what could be more alluring? She let her hair down to feel the wind and leaned over the balcony, standing on her tiptoes, feeling the ocean breeze on her face. She smiled and took in deep breaths of fresh air.

"Enjoying ourselves, are we?" Her eyes shot open as she heard an unfamiliar voice. She turned around and saw a woman hidden in the shadows of the dim light, but she could see fiery red hair. She knew it couldn't be Summer because the woman's voice wasn't as mature and raspy as Summer's.

"Who's asking?"

"Depends."

"On what?"

"Who are you?"

She squinted in confusion. "My name is Aira Moon, but I prefer Moon. And you?"

The woman moved closer but still could not see the other woman's face.

"That's a need-to-know basis. Are you here with Dawn?"

"For someone asking questions, you sure don't know how to answer them."

"What can I say? I'm not the open type."

"Me either—but if you are going to ask me questions, at least answer mine."

The woman remained silent for a while before saying, "My name is Ginger."

"Nice to meet you, Ginger."

"Likewise."

"Yes, I am with Dawn—well, I am his girlfriend."

"Mm-hmm—you are different than what I thought you would be."

"Meaning?"

"Why are you out here alone?"

"He's having a private discussion, and I got bored, so I came to look around."

"Yes, the manor is exquisite."

"It is— even more than that, but I assume you are here for the engagement party."

"Yes, I am."

"Are you the friend of the family, work here, or a burglar?"

"Burglar?"

"One can never be too cautious." She smirked.

"No—I'm none of the above. And, if you are wondering what I meant earlier about your being different—I meant you have impeccable beauty."

She froze and smiled. "Really? Thank you and you have stunning hair. I love red."

The woman chuckled. "Thank you. I hope you were taken care of and all is well."

"Yes, but still, who are you?"

"Like I said, on a need-to-know basis." She rolled her eyes. "Whatever you say, even though I could be in danger just standing here."

"Is it that obvious." The woman said sarcastically.

Moon leaned against the balcony. "Anything else you would like to know—stranger?"

"Maybe—maybe not, but for now, no."

"Good because I do."

"Ask away."

"Are you going to hide in the shadows all night or come into the light?" The woman attempted to move closer, but Moon's phone rang. "Excuse me a moment."

"No problem."

"Hello? Hello?" No one answered back, so she hung up the phone. Then she heard Dawn call for her. "I'm sorry about that."

She noticed that the woman was gone. She went back into the living room, which was now empty and bathed in light. Dawn appeared in the hallway. She didn't know who the woman was but hoped to find out. She shrugged off the encounter and followed Dawn upstairs. He and Bronte had the maid take the luggage into the guest room. He led her through the bright white hallways with old paintings and plants. They stopped at a wooden bedroom door with a black metal handle. "Here we are." He winked.

He opened the door and let her walk in ahead of him. The bedroom was different from the rest of the house. It was of average size, but it was filled with large white and pink peonies. The floor was made of light-brown bricks extending into the bathroom. To the left of the room was a desk with bookshelves on each side and above it, along with a small window in the middle. The walls were a dim, cream-like white with black trim. The bed had white sheets and linen and sat on a faded black bedframe with white curtains hanging from the top and two lamps on each side. The bathroom was also average, with a grey porcelain tub outside, a silver showerhead, a big mirror with two separate sinks, and a low-sitting toilet.

She found herself mainly thinking about the peonies. They were a bit of a surprise, not her favorite flower. They were so large and unruly. Roses, on the other hand, were simple, red, and elegant. Peonies were a bit unconventional, but they had their own beauty. He embraced her from behind.

"There's a note," he whispered as he kissed her temple. Releasing her, she reached for the note attached to the vase of flowers. Slowly, she unfolded it. "What does it say?"

*"Apologies from mother and father. See you soon. Love you, and I hope you like the peonies. Signed A and G."*

"How sweet. It's just like them." He said, looking down with disappointment.

She closed the note. "I don't like peonies, so who is it for, us?" she said, confused, and he smiled.

"They are for me. They're my favorite," he replied.

She kissed him on the cheek. "So, there are things I do not know about you."

"That is what this week is about," he said, and they both smiled. "I will have them clear it out."

"No," she said as she jumped on the bed. "It's nice, and I love sleeping with plants around."

"Why?" he snickered as he jumped on the bed beside her.

"I do not know. It brings peace in a way most living things don't," she explained.

He smiled. 'Okay." Moon smiled back and bounced on the bed.

"Do you want to unpack, get something to eat, shower, all in that order, or whatever you want to do?"

She sat there with a mix of excitement and fear in the pit of her stomach. As a child and teenager, she rarely had sleepovers, so this was a big deal for her. It wasn't exactly a sleepover, but staying at her boyfriend's parents' house for a week meant a lot to her. She didn't have any answers, but she had feelings, and she was happy to be near him, to breathe the same air, and to experience being with him.

"Hmm—I'm not too hungry, but I'm happy with whatever we do as long as I'm with you."

"Okay, let's unpack and shower, but I'm starving, so I'm heading to the kitchen for something to eat."

"Okay." She smiled. "Are you sure you don't want anything?"
"I am sure. Now go eat!" She said as she pushed him off the bed.

He turned around and kissed her, then left the room. She laid back on the bed and let out a sigh. It was a new experience, she thought. The energy and way of life where Dawn lived were different. She hoped everything would go great, and that drama would not arise because she was mortified; she couldn't stop the earlier argument. He looked different when angry. He had never gotten angry around her until this trip. She didn't think the trip would become a regret, but it might down the line. She undressed and took a shower. Afterward, she started to unpack her belongings. She threw on a grey tank top and blue panties with a small red rose on the front of them. She walked on the floor barefoot, filling her side of the dresser and closet with her clothes.

Dawn walked through the door and quickly changed into his boxers. He went into the bathroom to shower but wandered back into the bedroom. She stopped folding clothes into the drawers and turned to see Dawn staring at her. She just laughed.

"If I had known wearing such a skimpy outfit would grab your attention so quickly, then maybe I should have worn a T-shirt because I am distracting you from your shower."

"It doesn't matter. You always catch my attention."

"Even if I wore a potato sack like Marilyn Monroe?"

"Even then, and even if you were transformed into a worm. Only if you were a cute worm."

"A worm? You couldn't say a bird or cat."

"What's the difference?

"They're not helpless just as they are beautiful, no offense to the worm."

"What can I say? It was the first thing that came to mind." He smiled, revealing his dimples and causing her to melt. "Don't you have a shower to take?"

"Yes, but—"

"But?"

"I wanted to take one last look at you before I did."

"You can't get enough of me, huh?"

She stopped what she was doing and stood over him, leaning lightly onto him and his hands holding on to her waist. "No, I can't," she said. They kissed effortlessly in passion, but Moon pulled away and smiled. "And never will," she said as his body burned hot.

"I think it's time for that shower before we—I get carried away." She rolled her eyes and went back to folding her clothes, and he headed back to the bathroom.

# Settled

They were lying in bed with the open curtains, allowing nature to seep through. They lay on their respective sides until he reached between her legs and pulled her close. She rested on his chest, and he kissed her forehead twice. The cover was slightly hanging off them. The room was warm, which was okay for most people. However, she preferred the room to be cold. It seemed more fitting to her. What better temperature could your comforter be used at? She questioned her habits, wondering if what she liked was influenced by her parents. Maybe they passed on their everyday habits, not their destructive ones. Dawn preferred the room warm, but he did not like the cold or heat. It had to be just right, like spring.

They had opposite preferences regarding certain nuances but complemented each other like fire and a match. She held onto him tighter. She enjoyed the warmth emanating from his body, which could help her fall asleep as she was having trouble. Her nerves were high again because she didn't know what tomorrow could hold – the usual anxiety. She realized she wasn't the only one awake, as she had initially thought.

"Sorry."

"What are you sorry about?"

"I know you expected the room to be bigger, but my parents are still renovating, and this is one of the only rooms they haven't gotten to yet."

"That's okay. I don't mind. It doesn't need to be huge to be a bedroom."

"Well, aren't you just the enthusiast." They both chuckled.

"Besides, I do not see why they are changing the rooms. It looks great to me."

"My mother tends to think if she changes, then everything in the house needs to as well, or the problems she hides from would be all for nothing."

"It sounds complicated."

"It is. At least we get to spend more time together."

"Yeah, and I wouldn't want it any other way." He hugged her tightly.

"You should see my parents in person, hopefully at breakfast."

"That's great. I've been dying to get it over with."

"Don't worry. They aren't as scary as you think."

"Easier for you to say since they are your parents."

"Relax, rose. Remember, if you ever feel uncomfortable, we have our signal."

"I remember, and I hope it won't come to that. They will love me, you'll see."

"Not a doubt in my mind or heart," he smiled as he shut his eyes to sleep, "It will be only us two tomorrow before the engagement party. I wanted you all to myself before they go and steal you away."

"Well, baby, I'm excited, and I hope they do not try to peel too many layers, or I might seem scarier than I am." She took in his smell and smiled. "We'll talk about it more in the morning."

"Okay, love." She kissed his chest and closed her eyes.

# Mystery Woman

She stood in front of the bathroom body mirror, applying lip gloss. She could feel a presence behind her and turned to see Dawn. He stood in the doorway smiling.

"You're going to wear that for breakfast in the morning."

She wore an ivory-sheer, filmy, ankle-length, slightly plumy dress at the bottom. Her bare back and silk-thong panties could be seen, but her chest was covered with the solid color of the top of the dress. The click of her kitten heels and the small thump of her hair swayed as she turned to look at him.

"I felt daring—Why? Do you object?"

"No." She winked and turned back towards the mirror. "I wouldn't expect anything less."

He smirked. "Well, I'm ready when you are, so I will wait by the door."

"Okay, love." She blew a kiss and threw on jewelry as the last razzle-dazzle. "Wow!" he said when she entered the bedroom. "Oh, shush! I'm ready. Let's get this over with."

"As you wish, rose." They kissed and then headed downstairs, squeezing each other's hands tightly.

"Did I ever tell you I love it when you wear all black?" She bit her lip, and he blushed.

"Rose!" He whispered with an extensive smile.

As they entered the dining room, everyone stopped eating, and the clink of the silverware hitting the table could be heard. It amounted to nothing compared to Dawn's parents sitting at the table. Her confidence was on a thin string, ready to break, and she didn't know how to stop it. She felt Dawn place his hand on her waist for support. "Good morning," they said to everyone as they walked in. They took their seats at the end of the table. She couldn't help but notice how his mother had the same fiery hair as the strange woman she talked to the first night they got there. Could it have been? Was she Ginger? The letter G was on the note; it couldn't have been. If it was— that meant his mother secretly interrogated her last night.

"Moon, this is my mother and father," They both smiled, "Mother and father, this is Moon."

"It's so nice to meet you both. I've been waiting for a long time."

"Well, I hope it was not too long," His father said with a caring smile.

"Atlas and I have been on the edge of our seats, too," His mother said, delight spreading across her face.

She knew his mother spoke with her that night because she recognized her voice, but why would she lie and say she wasn't family? It was strange to Moon.

"You look well, son; all black suits you." His mother said with a sorrowful but pleading look of endurance.

"Thank you, mother." He said with an insincere smile.

"We missed you, D. Hopefully, we will see you more in the future," his father said sternly.

"I hope so too, Father." Summer and Crystal sat opposite them.

"Hi, Mo! You look great." Summer exclaimed.

Shocked, she smiled and said, "Thank you, Summer. It's nice to see you too."

"Yeah, Mo. You look great. I wanted to apologize for last night. We didn't mean to ruin your first night here."

"It's no biggie. I'm used to it. Family right." She giggled.

Dawn was still tense but smiled at her. She placed fruit and some eggs on her plate as she was too nervous to eat anything. "What happened last night?" Dawn's parents asked. Everyone's face turned pale at the table.

"Uh—" Crystal was at a loss for words, and Summer shoved food into her mouth.

"What did you think happened?"

"I do not know. You tell us, James." His father pressed.

"As always, your absence caused a commotion, but everything was resolved."

"You all know we hate when you fight. It's not healthy."

"You're the ones to talk," he said under his breath.

"I love you too, James."

"SO! Where is Bronte?" she asked, trying to change the subject. His father stared at everyone suspiciously.

"All the love in the world does not warrant his disrespect. We said we were sorry, and so were your sisters. You either can be a man and accept it or leave if you feel our presence is so disruptive, but you wouldn't do that to Bronte, right James?" He and his father were tense, but she could see the fear and vulnerability in Dawn's eyes.

"Yes, father. I do accept all your apologies, and I am grateful. Let's move past it." She placed her hand on the back of Dawn's head and rubbed it with affection. His body released the tension as he calmed down.

"To answer your question, Ms. Moon, Bronte went to meet his fiancé. They should be back by tomorrow morning, but we won't see them until noon of the engagement."

She nodded in agreement and ate what was on her plate as everyone conversed about their plans for the day and shared stories about the manor. The discussion even delved into how she and Dawn met, their relationship, and their future together. It felt invasive, but she didn't mind. She knew this conversation would come sooner or later. It's normal for a family to want to ensure their loved one is treated with love, respect, and care. During the discussion, the family mentioned the names of his parents, Atlas Wolfe and Ginger Wolfe. She was dying to ask if it was her, but she didn't want to cross any boundaries.

"Ms. Wolfe?" She whispered as she secretly got her attention.

His mother looked her way out of curiosity. "Yes, dear, and please, you can call me Ginger on occasion." She smiled.

His mother had intense red hair, green eyes, and pale skin with freckles. She and Summer looked the most alike. Crystal was a combination of their mother and father, but Dawn did have his mother's eyes and his father's looks. His father, Atlas Wolfe, was muscular, with black and grey hair and beard, brown eyes, sharp nose, small lips, and reasonably tanned. Both seemed to be in their 50s.

"Forgive me for saying this, but I could have sworn we had a discussion last night on the balcony, or at least someone who looked like you. But what do I know? It was very dark last night."

It seemed she questioned whether she should lie, be honest, or acknowledge it.

Her green eyes pierced Moon's face, "Yes, we did. I wanted to scope you out and not be known by the house that night."

"Oh great, so I wasn't crazy."

"No, you weren't. Sorry if I scared you. But I see it was worth it this morning." They both smiled.

"You should visit the horse stable when you get a chance. I'll let you ride my favorite horse. Let you get some practice in since you are a part of the family now."

"I would love that. I was planning to go there today with Dawn."

"Fantastic! You both can roam the grounds and take in some nature."

"I agree," they both giggled.

Dawn kissed her on the cheek, and she kissed him back. Everyone in the room went silent and smiled at each other. It made them feel out of place but the center of attention, not that they needed it. Breakfast ended; his father and Crystal headed to the office, Summer went off with friends, and his mother planned to change before going to the stables.

He seemed excited as he leaned over and said, "Told you, not so bad, and they loved you."

They kissed passionately, and he dragged her by the hand to the horse stables. Her kitten heels fought against the pavement until he carried her the rest of the way, but she was not complaining. At least her dress wouldn't get dirty, and she could be the princess she was or feel like one.

# Gypsy

She sat on a wooden bench in the horse stable. She put on some riding shoes that were left over from Dawn's mother's occasional rides. He also changed his boots and offered her a riding hat, but she declined. She thought riding a horse wouldn't be so hard and hoped it would come naturally to her. She loved nature and knew it wouldn't harm her. They noticed his mother walking towards the stable, and she braced herself. Dawn looked at her and smiled.

"Remember to stay calm, and the horse will have no problem with you. They feel what we feel, so stay calm, okay? But my mother will explain it better," he winked, "I'm going to let you ladies start your lesson while I catch up with Boa."

Before rushing off, Moon grabbed his wrist and asked, "Who is Boa?"

"Oh, it's my horse."

"You have a horse?" She smiled out of amazement.

"Yes, it's been his horse since he was a little boy." His mother smiled as she put on her riding gloves.

He kissed Moon on the lips and then headed off to his horse. Her nerves weren't in chaos; she was excited to receive a small horse-riding lesson. She knew it would be like flying in the clouds, yet grounded. She turned towards Mrs. Wolfe and smiled. "So, what's my first lesson?"

"I like a fast learner, and you being one is so cute." Mrs. Wolfe chuckled. "You're not dressed for the occasion, but that's okay. I like a challenge." Moon looked semi-flattered. "And I like to challenge others. Two peas in a pod," she snickered.

"Okay, the first lesson is to bond with the horse, or more so, get it to let you ride it."

"Okey, dokey."

Mrs. Wolfe pointed to two horses drinking from a brick water well. The water was sea green, and a small iron fountain was in the middle, with water springing out of it magically. One horse was umber-skinned, and the other was black but had vast white patches on its body and white hair. Mrs. Wolfe pointed directly at the horse with white patches and didn't expect to see anything more beautiful.

"What's the horse's name?"

Mrs. Wolfe smiled. "Her name is Gypsy."

"It suits her—beautiful." She said, smiling. "She is out of this world."

"Yes, she is. She is my light but aggressive and doesn't let just anybody ride her, so I am taking a risk, but nothing but the best for James."

"Nothing short for a Wolfe, right," Moon said as she looked back at Dawn feeding his horse an apple.

"Oh, absolutely, and nothing to be ashamed of. Everyone should want the best for themselves."

She knew his mother wasn't wrong. She looked at them as privileged socialites but never thought about it that way. From birth, they are taught to want the best, be the best, and do the best, while everyone else has their scraps, scars, and prayers. Some are more blessed than others, but it didn't mean Moon wasn't. She experienced the lowest of all things: an abusive parent, so she came to expect the worst and wasn't too optimistic about things. It was refreshing to be treated better than she ever had, but no one could hold her heart better than her Nana. She missed her dearly; she wished she could be experiencing this moment with her. Nana would always be in her heart and mind, but she only realized that it was until this moment that she hadn't thought of her. It was new to her and odd because she always thought of Nana. She didn't want to forget her face, her laugh, her wisdom, and their moments together. She would have loved the horses, the smell of manure, and wildlife. She slowly became gloomy, but that changed when- "Let's head on over!" Mrs. Wolfe smiled as she pulled Moon along toward Gypsy.

The horse already had reigns on. They stopped, and Ginger was faced to face with Moon. She held both her hands. She smiled, and Moon smiled back. "Okay, this is it. I'm going to take gypsy to the paddock so that she won't run, but it will give you room and space to feel each other out."

"Then what happens?"

"You ride." She was still gloomy. "Smile—smile!" Mrs. Wolfe held Moon's face with one hand.

She led Moon to Gypsy and allowed her to caress the horse. Gypsy was still drinking water and didn't seem to mind Moon's touch. Mrs. Wolfe smiled and said, "It seems she likes you or just doesn't pay you any mind, but we will see."

"I do want her to like me. I'm a sucker for first impressions, especially with things of nature."

"Nature girl, are we?"

"Something like that. Ever since I was a little girl, I have taken refuge in nature because it created me and all things living. So, I figured, why not bury my head in the one thing meant to protect and love me in the first place? It never harmed me and always calmed me in such hard times. It was part of me, and I was part of it, whatever nature took shape in."

"An extraordinary young woman, Moon. Who would have known by how quiet you are? I like it when you talk more."

"Really?"

"Yes, keep it up." Mrs. Wolfe let her pet Gypsy again, then told her to wait as she led Gypsy away.

She didn't know what was wrong but was happy until a few minutes ago. Grieving was a bitch, but she was ready to move on. However, it seemed not to want to move on from her. She started to second guess herself as Mrs. Wolfe brought Gypsy into the paddock. She called her over, but her feet couldn't move. She planned to run, though a cowardly thing to do, but she was exhausted. Her mood hit level zero, and she didn't know what to do. She didn't want Dawn's mother to see her as an on-edge person because it would slim her chances to none on the normal radar. "Moon, let's go!" She called twice.

She stood in the same place and then felt him wrap his arms around her waist.

"You got this. Give yourself a chance. I love you," he whispered and kissed her on the cheek. She almost shed a tear, but she kept her strength. "Okay," she said with faint courage. She was becoming accustomed to him saying, "I love you." It wasn't just sweet; it was honorable.

He let go of her and led her towards the paddock. As she reached the gate, she stopped, took a deep breath, and then exhaled. "It'll be okay, honey. Come on." She looked back at him, and he smiled, reassuring her. The gate opened with a slight squeak, and she walked through. She took the lead by approaching Gypsy on her own. Mrs. Wolfe seemed proud as she did not have to guide her, not to say she was a fairy godmother. But if she were, she would be more heavenly than her mother. Ginger and Angel are two opposite forces at play. Then, again, Dawn didn't think so much, but people grow and change. If his mother would, so could hers, not that she would want to know. The fact she could compare mothers was as if nature wasn't staring her down. It was very on point for Moon. She was as pure as any girl could come to be.

The wind blew forcefully, the grass was semi-muddy and wet, and Gypsy stood proudly in the middle of the paddock. She gazed down at Moon, not in intimidation, but with audacity. It was an audacity that welcomed and understood her desire for freedom from herself. She half-expected someone to shout that she was doing everything wrong, but every fiber of her being urged her to rush towards Gypsy. Not knowing what came over her, she swiftly walked towards the horse, took hold of the reins, and jumped on its back. She waited for an adverse reaction, but nothing happened. She petted the horse twice to double-check if she wasn't losing her mind. Unbeknownst to herself, she was right. Gypsy accepted her, and she didn't know how to process it. Shouldn't the horse have cried out, ran, or at least resisted? She often felt weighed down by heavy energy, so she was surprised that Dawn even took an interest in her. Maybe she wasn't as twisted and screwed up as she thought. She smiled as wide as the sun and eagerly awaited her next lesson.

"Good girl." She whispered as she felt the wind all around her. Mrs. Wolfe walked over to her, and Dawn still watched from afar on his horse. He gave her a thumbs-up and blew a kiss with his hands. She giggled and smiled. Mrs. Wolfe guided Gypsy in circles, trying to get her used to being carried around by the horse, and gave her tips on getting the horse to ride, stop, and slow down. They were easy lessons, and she was always a fast learner and independent. It was like a piece of cake to her.

"You're a natural, Moon." Mrs. Wolfe smiled. "Are you sure you haven't had any lessons?" Moon blushed with shyness. "I'm sure." She said ever so lightly.

She was eventually allowed to ride around the paddock on the horse alone. She could feel he was still watching, but then again, she could feel him everywhere she was. Slowly, she rode at first, but then the speed took consciousness of its own, and she owned the wind, horse, and path she was taking.

"She's doing great, Mother, is she not?" Moon's eyes grew hungry. She wanted to ride more freely than she was. "Yes! yes, she is James!" They smiled in amazement at her improvement on the horse, and before she knew it, Dawn's mother opened the gate wide. "Go ahead! Ride! Ride!" Mrs. Wolfe laughed.

Moon rode out of the paddock past dawn and into the woods, saying, "Keep up, pretty boy!" He rode right behind her, just as fast. They rode with the wind, letting nature take the lead, going faster and faster. It was majestic how she could see such vast land. It couldn't all belong to the Wolfes. No one should have all that land. It was too much to comprehend.

They came into a thick fog, which wasn't surprising because it wasn't that warm out. She could feel the chill approaching along with the wind. They came onto a big open grass field, and she let go of the reigns. Her body flowed with the horse, but her hair mangled her face, with only one of her eyes showing. Her nipples hardened, and her legs turned tender from riding in such a thin dress, but she did not care nor take notice. She was free and was finally in a place she didn't feel the need to control. What seemed freeing to her was chilling to Dawn because he rode near her and yelled, "Aira! Aira! — Take hold of the reigns, now!"

She couldn't hear him at first because she was so focused on all the green around her, the smell of grass, sky, and nature in its entirety, but she snapped out of it when the horse buckled a bit, and Dawn yelled, "Take control before you hurt yourself." She pulled Gypsy to a stop and laughed while taking heavy breaths. She flipped her hair out of her face. "I thought I told you never to call me that." She smiled, but he seemed serious.

"At this point, what does it matter."

"Oh, lighten up. I was having fun. I'm sorry if I scared you."

"Please, rose, do not do that again, and you did scare me."

"Sorry." She put up a heart with her hands and made a sad face. He just laughed.

"I forgive you. You want to roam the manor grounds and see a secret spot I've never shown anyone."

She bit her lip and jumped for joy. She and Gypsy were fatigued, but they would rest soon.

"I would love that. I like it when we have our secrets." She winked.

They trailed next to each other. The fog was still thick, but she trusted that he knew where he was going. It was nice taking a stroll with her boyfriend on his land. The peace of it all. They rode until he saw an inkling of what he knew to be his hidden place. He smiled back at her and said, "Slowly, okay."

"Okay, love." The pit of her stomach was screaming. She could feel the thrill coming on before she knew it; they were coming upon a soaring waterfall. It was taller than Mount Everest, and the waters ran deeper than the ocean. It was still midday. The open land around them, the water, had rainbows bouncing off it, and there were mountains of rock and green, but they were out of the fog. Edging the horses closer, Dawn gets off his horse and lets it get a drink and rest, but Moon takes Gypsy into the water for a cool down.

"Moon!" She looked back and smiled. "It's okay! I think she will like it." Worry had set in on his face, but she wasn't worried. He settled under Boa and watched her. Boa's legs buckled onto the ground, and the horse nuzzled Dawn's hair. His hand gently petted Boa's face.

She allowed Gypsy to lead the way. The horse drank some water first, then walked deeper into the water. Moon felt Gypsy knew she wanted to be closer to the falls. The water covered half of Gypsy's body and the lower half of Moon. They walked in circles until the horse led her to the falls. They moved closer and closer until she was submerged beneath the waterfall. She relaxed and let the water wash over her. Her hands ran over her hair and body. She felt shocks of adrenaline in her body as the freezing water engulfed her, causing her to fall off the horse and into the water.

The water wasn't too deep, as her feet could touch the ground. She stayed submerged as she watched Gypsy's hooves move away. The water was crystal clear, and fish the size of her toes circled her. She hoped they wouldn't mistake her for their food, but she enjoyed feeling them glide near her. Blowing bubbles, she swam back and forth before becoming bored.

She lifted her head above water, only her eyes showing, and noticed Dawn had disappeared. The horses were on land, nibbling at apples in the grass. She wanted to know where he had gone. She swam far to the left and right until she rose from the water. She looked around her and started to worry. She called his name about five times. "This isn't funny! Where are you!" She was stranded, lost, without Dawn to show her the way back. She was chilled to the bone from being in the water.

"Dawn!" She screamed.

Weirdly enough, when walking towards the horses, she saw a shadow trailing behind her, and before she could turn around, she was hoisted into the air. She screamed and screamed until she heard his laugh. Her eyes opened from the relief of panic as he put her down.

"Now, look who is scared." He sneered, the sun bouncing off his dimples.

She hit his chest hard with her fist. "You're an asshole!" She laughed out of place.

He grabbed her gently by the neck and said, "Yeah, but I'm your asshole." They kissed, and she pushed him off.

"Where were you? I called you plenty of times."

"I was watching from afar. I couldn't see you in the waterfall and got worried, then I noticed you underneath the water, so I trailed off." He smiled. "I got the idea to surprise you like you've been surprising me all day. Which seemed to have worked."

"That is so —" She said with frustration. "So what?"

"Childish!" Her eyes and body displayed disappointment. He dropped his smile and became regretful.

"I'm sorry to have scared you. I thought it would be a fun little joke, but it's not, I see."

"Yeah."

He took hold of her. "Hey—Are you okay? I'm here." He whispered affectionately.

Moon wasn't mad at him and knew he was only joking. However, she had people disappear from her life enough, and though it was not his fault, she was triggered. She felt it stung, and, at that moment, she was scared. She didn't know if he was hurt or decided he wanted to leave her. It was her wounds she had to bear, not his. She tried not to be so sensitive and cruel about the matter. It wasn't like she wasn't causing havoc herself, but it was as simple as enjoying the moment and doing something adventurous. She had to ease her mind and always pretended everything was fine. She hated that she often hid her true self from him, though she said she wouldn't. What would be the point of being a burden, especially when it was feeling so heavy it could be a nuclear bomb, and she was sure he had his own that he tried not to launch?

"I'm okay, love. I'm just ready to head back and get warm." She kissed him. "You have nothing to apologize for. It was just a prank."

He smiled with relief and asked, "Are you happy?"

She chuckled and said, "I'm—content, why?" questioning his meaning.

He shook his head and caressed the wet strands of her hair.

She gave him a sincere glare. "I'm happy, love."

He nodded and said, "Mm-hmm. I hear you." He kissed her on the forehead.

"Okay," she chuckled and then smiled.

"My sweet rose," he said as he locked eyes with her before he leaned in for a kiss.

Her arms wrapped gently around his neck as he carried her to shore. He placed her tenderly on the grass, her dress soaked and glistening, her hair untamed, and her lips rosy. Her honey-like skin, glowing in the midday sun, created a stunning golden hour light. It had a somewhat effect on him because before she knew it, they were making out in a field of grass, half-naked. She giggled as he kissed all over her body, but he stopped and hovered over her. They looked into each other's eyes for who knows how long, then decided to make love.

# 12. Over The Rainbow

She lay across Crystal's lap as she flicked the petals off the peony in her hands. Her legs swung off the bed, and the natural light bounced off every inch of white in the room, possibly blinding the sun itself. It was like a cloggy haze through a smeared glass. They had matching bikinis. Moon didn't bring any because it didn't cross her mind that his family had a yacht, and they liked to use it. She had never been on a yacht, but at least she can now. The ability to explore the ocean without drowning in it, she would be a passenger, and safe. She loved the water but feared the sea. It was unexplored and deeper than any human could imagine, especially old. It could give you strength or take it all away at once. But then again, nothing was ever easy.

He loves me; he loves me not. He loves me; he loves me not. He loves me, she spoke in her head after plucking each petal. Crystal brushed her hair softly, "Prosperity, love, luck, and honor." She spoke faintly. Moon assumed she wanted to get something off her chest and didn't know whether she was being cryptic or talking about her. "What's that?" Crystal kept brushing her hair, not losing a pep in her step, and smiled. "It's what a peony stands for. My parents used to give us all one for each meaning. Sometimes in different colors."

"That was loving of them."

"For the most part, yes."

"What were the colors?"

"Pink for love and prosperity, red for honor, and yellow for luck. Nine times out of 10, they would give specific ones to us, knowing that was the only way they could give us the affection we needed. Knowing they were not around to express them." Moon raised her eyebrows and let out a sigh. She knew how they felt. Absent parents were her forte, but her grandparents made up for that in many ways. She thoughtfully said, "If only my mama thought of that. It would make up for her not being around. Not entirely, of course."

Crystal smirked. "Trust me. It doesn't help, but at least we knew they thought of us, but for all we knew, they had the servants put them out."

"Yeah, there's that option. But what color did you get?" she giggled.

"Summer got yellow because she sucked at everything except dolling herself up. I got red and pink sometimes, but they gave Dawn all the colors, mainly pink, if he was mad at them. He has always been their favorite, and they do not hate me for saying this, but I like to say it's because he is a boy." She knew Crystal and Summer had their ways, but they seemed to be sweethearts deep down, a little broken like most. Their parents could have favored Dawn more because of his sex, but not every sibling grew up in the same household. Being the oldest of siblings and a girl could be tricky. She wouldn't know since she was an only child, but only they knew their injustices and trauma.

"Are you sure? Could it have been more than him being a boy?"

Crystal put the brush on the other side of the bed and went back to playing with her hair. "No. That is not the only reason." Moon stopped fiddling with the peony and quietly listened. "My little brother has been special his entire life. He was a premature baby. He got into many fights. He bruised easily and got his heart broken a lot. He was tended to as if he were a fragile prince. Our parents even had me and Summer shielding him of the smallest things he needed to experience as a child."

"I take it you didn't get the same treatment."

"In a way, no, we did not. We do have this lifestyle, so that wasn't a problem. It was more so of the attention and love we got from our parents. Their love towards us felt like a hammy down. It was second-hand compared to what they gave Dawn. It hurt a lot. Summer used to cry under the bed so no one could hear her."

"And you?"

"That's funny, you ask, because I would do nothing. I would be numb and a pushover. I was the shadow everyone stepped over, but Dawn could beg to differ. I don't blame him; he was younger and had a different side from our parents. He couldn't help that. I love him too much to blame him for any of it."

"Did it get better as time went on? I would hope so."

"The naivety of Summer and me thinking it would, but it didn't. We were the girls, so we only got the attention when Dawn disappeared or got angry with them."

"You're not even a little close with your parents?"

"We were once upon a time before Dawn was born, but like I said, all that changed."

"You never know it could change unexpectedly, but at least you have a family."

She tried not to make the conversation about her. It was nice hearing about others' problems for a while. Their family had a love for each other and disdain, as she could see. It was primarily because of their parents, but they still had moments and memories of their family's love. She didn't have anything but family albums and possessions. She didn't know where her mama was and If they could still be a family, not that she would want to. It was scary to think she was the last living relative of the family. Everyone was dead to her, but who knows? She could always make one of her own. *Someday. Not now. I'm not ready.* She wondered about where Dawn was and if he thought of the same things. Could he feel the same way as his sister, and could things be mended? Her family couldn't be glued back together no matter how hard she tried, but his family probably could.

Crystal leaned over her and looked down. Moon looked up at her.

"What?" She smiled awkwardly.

"What about your family?"

"What about them?" She looked down, and Crystal leaned back on the bed. "I don't know much about you, and if I'm going to dump my shit onto you, you might as well do the same."

"Oh, I don't want to talk about them right now."

"Too late. Spill doll eyes." She grinned.

She hated talking about family matters, but an eye for an eye, right? She stared at the top of the bed, letting the peony hit the floor and calming her feet. She smiled unbearably. She didn't know what it was, but it left a lump in her chest and a hole in her stomach. She only told Dawn vague events about her childhood, but her body wanted to blurt everything out to Crystal. She barely knew her, but it was the same with him. She wanted her to be on her side and not to dig for dirt, not that she would deny anything she said. What better way to shut down pettiness other than owning your shit.

"Not much to say about them. My grandparents. Nana and Papa raised me. My father died before I was born, and my mother left when I was eight. She was a drunk and abusive parent."

Crystal's face turned sincere and grew with pity as Moon had done once for her.

"I'm sorry—" She cut crystal short. "Please do not say sorry. It's nothing to apologize for as you did not do it to me. Anything more you want to know?"

"Tell me something. Who broke your heart the most, and whom you felt close to the most?"

"Wow. Straight in we go."

Crystal chuckled. "Yes, you are a mystery, and I like to get inside people's heads."

"Something we have in common."

The questions felt insane. She did not know what to do. She could not approach the question from the right angle. Who hurt her the most was undoubtedly her whole family, but she was close to her nana the most. It was undeniable. She couldn't say her mama because they stopped being close when she turned six. She could not remember anything younger than six. She should not be pondering this question as if in court before a judge.

*Does she know what I want to say, or does she think she knows?*

She could give an easy answer, but the absolute equation was, could she dig deeper?

"Without a doubt, I was close to my nana and mama. My papa was heavily religious, so we couldn't connect with most things in life. I never met my father, as I said before."

"What about your father's side?"

"Good question. They were never brought up. The only thing I knew was that my daddy ran away from home at 17 but kept in contact with his mama, but over time, they stopped."

"Do you tell my brother these things, or is it too hard to?"

"No, we have talked about it. He knows most of everything there is to know about me."

"Okay, good. So, why were you close to your mother and grandmother."

She knew Crystal wanted to pry and get to know her more, but it seemed invasive. She could not talk about her family, especially to Dawn, without crying or her body shutting down. It was like a manual response. She was panic-stricken, so she gave distant answers to compensate. However, it seemed Crystal was the type of girl who wanted real answers.

*I know she doesn't owe me anything, but I'm dating her brother, so why not investigate the girl he was so-called in love with?*

"My mama was raising me with the help of my grandparents. She was my idol. She was my angel. She was so sweet, caring, and the most optimistic about life. She mirrored Nana in that way, aside from the bullheadedness. I was closer to them because I was with them all day, every day. She was my mama until she wasn't. People asked me what happened, but no one knew. One day, she stopped being herself and resided in the darkness she could no longer leave behind. So, she left and never came back. Nana took over my care and loved me the best she could. She was my nana. She raised me into the young woman I am today, and we did everything together." She swallowed her pain. The uneasiness was hard to hold. She didn't want to show emotion because she knew it would stay with her all day. She did not want her day ruined and to have Dawn isolated or far away from her. She bottled all of it up.

"I feel for you. My mother was my idol, too. I used to watch her all day for no reason, like a pest. She was everything to me. I couldn't live if I didn't see her smile, brush her hair, or smell a hint of her perfume. It was addictive. I never knew why, but it was all worth it at the end of the day when I got to lie next to her in the bed, in her mother's embrace, when my father was away on business. It made me feel—"

"Loved." She looked over, and Crystal smiled. "Yeah, loved."

Moon sat up and pushed her hair to the side. "No need to tell me who broke your heart. I could tell by your answer who broke it the most."

Moon furred her eyebrows in confusion. "Do you know?"

"Yes, I do. I would have guessed they both broke your heart, which is accurate. But it is always that one heartbreak that controls you for the rest of your life."

"Dare say who?" Moon's heart pounded to figure out if she knew the answer. She almost sunk into the bed in anticipation. She hated it when people tried to figure her out, but more so when they did. She didn't know what it was about the Wolfe family, but they could spot your deepest, darkest secrets from a mile away. It was exhausting. She wanted to know because she didn't have the answer.

"I do not think you need me to tell you that."

"No backing out now." She pried.

"Okay, I would say your mother." She frowned and was going to refute Crystal, but she hurriedly changed the subject. "How do you like it here so far? Though you have been here only for two days."

"I like it here. It's quiet and isolated. It's a dream for a loner like me. I cannot wait to explore and go into the city with everyone."

"I'm so happy you said that because I and Summer want to take you shopping tomorrow. It will be fun, and you can even bring our idiot brother. What do you say."

"Well—I."

"Say yes, we will even show you some hot spots. Please!"

She snickered, "Okay, I'll go."

Crystal jumped off the bed in excitement. Just in time, Summer appeared at the doorway wearing the same bathing suit as them. It was clear that she was part of the sisterhood. She smiled at the fact that they all had matching outfits and felt a sense of sisterhood. At least they would be able to get their tans on the yacht. Moon felt like she was growing pale and was excited to see Dawn finally. He had already left when she woke up, but his big sister was kind enough to keep her company and help her prepare for the family day out.

Summer was in a cheery state, "I've been looking everywhere for you two! Everyone is ready to sail!"

"Okay." They both replied.

"By the way, where is Dawn?" Moon eyed Summer.

"Man! You have some big eyes!" She giggled.

Moon laughed and said, "Summer!"

"Oh, right! He is on the yacht with our parents. They are waiting for us, so hurry and collect your things!"

"Thank you," she said with a smile.

"You're welcome. Now, let's get this show on the road! And you guys look fucking hot!"

Moon and Crystal shook their heads and laughed.

She was immersed in writing in the journal she had brought along, sitting at the end of the yacht by the pool. The water looked like a hot crimson due to the red foundation, and the seats were positioned on the side of the pool, allowing her feet to remain in the water. The yacht was black and gold, vast and spacious, and the skies were clear and bright. She could hear the ocean as they cruised along the coast, and the wind tried to tug her pages out of the journal. The water beneath her was warm, and she noticed that her pen was running out of ink.

Her thoughts were interrupted when Dawn suddenly grabbed her ankles and pulled her into the water. Her hand, holding the journal, was left in the air, and she felt disoriented. She didn't know whether to be angry or surprised. Dawn took the journal from her hand and threw it on the seat. She was in disbelief as he smiled and playfully tossed her over his shoulder. Unexpectedly, he started spinning around, then dropped her but caught her. Her legs wrapped around his waist, and her arms around his neck. His hands firmly held her as if their lives depended on it.

"There you are." He looked endlessly into her eyes.

She didn't know what to say back. He could be playful sometimes, but she hated it when he would roughhouse like that, especially off guard. She wasn't scared but startled and a little unsettled. The yacht had come to a stop and was anchored into the ocean.

"Dawn! You know you cannot rough house with Moon like you do us! Play nice!" Summer was yelling from the front of the yacht. She was sitting with her legs crossed, holding the reddest of wines, and gossiping with someone on the phone. Meanwhile, Mr. and Mrs. Wolfe rested in the yacht's cabin. Crystal was lying on the top of the yacht, right at the front, getting a tan.

He looked at Summer and rolled his jewel of eyes. "You make it sound like I'm attacking my girlfriend! Mind your business, princess!" Summer flipped him off and continued her conversation on the phone.

He carried her to the water and sat her on his lap. He smiled, but Moon just stared at him. "You know you could have called my name if you wanted my attention." She said gravely.

His smile faded. "I'm —I'm sorry. I thought it would be nice to disrupt you from your thoughts and get you to have some fun."

"Mm-hmm," she said as her big brown doe eyes looked off. She never understood some of the things he did, but it could be what he was used to since he was the center of attention as a child. This was fine with her, but sometimes, she wanted him to be subtle about things. However, who was she to judge when she had her frantic moments?

"Look, if you are angry with me for what I did, I'm sorry, and I will leave you alone if you want." He appeared hurt, and she didn't like that. This is what she meant when she told him she wasn't good at things like being a girlfriend. She had to remember that other people were in her reality, too.

"No, I'm not mad. You startled me, that's all." She kissed his nose, and he lit up like a Christmas tree.

"You are sure?" he smiled, "Yes, love," she smiled.

They kissed briefly and then played in the pool. They splashed water at each other, kissed twice, and gazed at the ocean from the balcony. Dawn's parents woke up from their nap feeling hungry, and his father decided to cook in the kitchen. Crystal joined him, and Summer bonded with Moon and Dawn. Summer sat on a chair while braiding Moon's hair into a ponytail. Dawn sat before her, wearing jet-black sunglasses, smoking a cigarette, and rubbing his temple. He winked at her, and she kissed him while Summer made a throwing-up sound in displeasure.

"Smoking is bad for you."

"For me?" He asked, pointing toward himself.

"Yes."

"Why is that? Wait! Let me guess. Cancer?"

"That's one reason."

"And What is the other reason?"

"I detest smoking, and If you ever want me to kiss you again, you will stop." She smiled.

"Oh, is that why now?" He raised an eyebrow and smiled, blowing smoke out of his nose.

"Yes, love."

"Yeah, D! What are you going to do?" Summer mocked.

"Shut up, Summer."

"Make me!" Summer blew a kiss.

"Don't make me push you over the railing."

"Well, baby." She asked as she bit her bottom lip.

"Anything for you, rose," he said, tensing his jaw and flicking the cigarette into the ocean.

Moon smiled proudly as Summer finished styling her hair. Then, she relaxed with Dawn and basked in the sun together.

"I will head off and see what they are doing in the kitchen. I'll let you love birds have your alone time."

"Okay, later." She looked at Dawn, but he said nothing and wrapped his arms around her.

"We are alone at last."

"Yes, we are, and I sensed some tension earlier."

"That was nothing. My sisters always get on my nerves."

"Okay. I didn't want another repeat of two days ago."

He chuckled. "No, you won't see anything like that for a while."

She was running on empty, or more like her mind was. Usually, she had so many questions to ask, but she didn't have anything to say for some reason. She wasn't a chatterbox like most, but she could converse. Minus the sun, he felt great to lay on. The lingering smoke faded away, and she was able to breathe again. She kissed his chest twice, and he hugged her tighter. She took a deep breath, exhaled, then smiled. It was nice getting fresh air. They had only been with his family for two days, and the engagement party was already happening. They only had three more days left, and it didn't feel like enough.

The trip was supposed to help them get to know each other better, which it was, but it was moving so fast. It was even weirder that Bronte was supposed to come later with his fiancé, whom no one even talks about. She found it peculiar, strange, and downright suspicious. Her senses were tingling. Either his fiancé was a bitch or such an angel that they would have you meet her to bless someone with such grace, then just talk about her. Odd indeed.

Her feet rubbed against his feet as he hummed a song. It sounded familiar, but she didn't bother asking about it. Instead, she wanted to know about the mystery woman coming to Wolfe Manor. She loved juicy information, and Bronte seemed like a sweet guy, so she wanted to know what women he liked to bring home. She knew she should have asked his sisters, but it didn't cross her mind then. She questioned why. She sat up, and so did he. He continued to hum.

"So, tell me about Bronte's lovely fiancé. I noticed no one ever talks about her, which is weird because it is the woman he will marry." She squinted with a hand over her eyes because the sun shone brightly. Before responding, he walked over to his sister's bag and took a pair of sunglasses.

He handed them to her and said, "Put these on." She hesitated because they were Summer's, but she wasn't there, and the sun was killing her eyes, so she put them on.

"As for Bronte's fiancé, she has worked for us for some time. That is how he met her, but she retired from us before they started to date. She has a flower business. She owns three shops," He coughed, "She is kind, beautiful, is about in her late 40s like Bronte." The woman appeared simple but was surprised as she expected a sophisticated, wealthy party girl. But don't judge a book by its cover.

"How does she look? Is she pretty?" She popped gum into her mouth and leaned against the seat, "She has blond hair, brown eyes, an hourglass figure, and an average style of dressing. I don't know," he chuckled. She nodded and asked, "What did she do? Like, what was her job here?" He looked over at the ocean as if impatient. "She was a nanny, occasionally cooked and helped with the garden. Anything my parents wanted her to do." She nodded again.

"Why?"

"No reason. I've been curious about it since you invited me out here, that's all."

"That's normal." He smiled. "Anything else you want to know about her?"

"How did he propose?" She played with the gum in her mouth.

He put his hand over his mouth. "Baby, I feel like he would tell that story better," he said, laughing loudly.

"What? What is it?" She hit his leg. "Nothing. It's comical and romantic, but I wouldn't do it justice."

"Do not make me ask your sisters or parents." He taunted her with an air kiss.

"Be my guest. They will not do the story justice either, and I'm sure he will tell it again at the party."

She rolled her eyes and pouted. "You're so close-mouthed."

He rubbed her chin. "All things come in due time, and everything does not need to come from the mouths of others." She nodded in the boredom of the same ambiguous answers. "Whatever you say, handsome."

He laughed and pulled her onto him. "Yeah. Whatever I say."

They returned to basking in the sun, but their time was quickly interrupted when his sister called for her to help put the food on the table, and Dawn's parents called him over to talk.

The girls put on some music as they set the table. Dawn and his parents headed into the cabin. They laughed and threw napkins at each other while stopping midway to dance in the middle of the platform. Crystal and Summer danced as if they were experts. They were being sexy, and she moved around gracefully. They took each other's hands and danced in a circle, singing loudly and laughing. Dawn's sisters turned red from losing breath, and then Summer pulled all of them into the pool. All they could do was laugh in extreme bliss. The sisters sat and relaxed in the water while Moon merely dangled her feet into it. She felt a splash of water coming towards her.

"What's on your mind, Moon?" Crystal tilted her head back. "Nothing."

"Liar!" Summer smiled and nudged Moon.

"Don't tell anyone I told you this, but I like you better than my brother's last girlfriend." Crystal smiled.

"I do, too." Summer piggybacking.

"That's sweet of you," Moon said, still focused on her feet.

"If we feel that way, I'm sure my brother does. Has he told you he is in love with you yet?"

She looked at Crystal and said, "I mean—"

"Well!" both sisters smiled with intrigue.

"Did he, or didn't he?" Summer said as she swam backward in the pool.

"Uh—uh—Yes. But please do not tell him I told you." His sisters laughed.

"We know our brother; it was only a matter of time, and trust me, Dawn is not afraid of anyone knowing, but we promise. Right, summer!"

"Right, ladies!" Summer floated.

"Thanks! And why did you ask?"

"I worry about him and sometimes need to check on him."

"Trust me, he is okay. I worry about him myself. But he is okay."

"I can tell he is smitten with you more than anyone else he has dated, so I think that is good."

"Me too. I sometimes don't know if I can live up to being "Dawn Wolfe's" girlfriend. And I'm not saying that because of who he is but more so of how I am."

"You will be fine. My parents didn't let me date unless we had the full background check, meetings, and votes." She laughed. "I've only had one serious relationship that ended badly because I wasn't confident in my capability to love and be loved. You will get there. We all have years ahead of us."

"Damn, Crystal! I didn't know you could be so deep." Summer laughed.

Crystal splashed her with water and rolled her eyes. "Pay no mind to her; she tends to fall in love with everyone." Summer flipped her off. "I do not!"

"You have had about eight true loves and ten soulmates by now. And that is me just guessing!"

Moon laughed. The sisters got into a water fight.

"Guys!" Moon shouted, amused. They stopped splashing water at each other.

"Maybe let's get back on topic, shall we."

"Stupid!" Crystal shouted towards Summer.

"You're stupid! Nun!"

Crystal clapped her wet hands. "Oh! Such a fucking burn!"

"Go back to your corners, ladies!" Moon signaled her hands.

 Crystal swam towards her. "Hey! Um— as I said, you will be fine. Don't overthink it. Okay."

She smiled. "Do you love Dawn too?"

Moon leaned back and kicked her feet in the water—a sign of ignorance on her face.

 "I don't know."

"Mm— that is normal; you cannot rush love." She slapped her leg. "You will know soon enough."

"I hope so, for my sake."

Summer smiled. "Our brother won't rush you. It's not his style!"

*It's been six years, so how would they know? But people do not change much, or do they? I hope they were right because I would be in a tough situation. However, the trip was to get to know each other, and we had just started dating. I doubt anyone will fall in love within weeks. Well, at least someone like me, but Dawn, on the other hand, was a quick hand. He was in love with me, and I don't know. I know he makes me feel safe, and I like him a lot. I hope being on two different pages doesn't get them ripped out altogether.*

The girls returned to soaking up the sun and reveling in silence, enjoying each other's presence. The servants took over setting the table as she realized she was starved from such a strenuous evening. The smell of potatoes, meat, and roasted vegetables made its way to her nose. She had all her attention focused on making ripples in the water with her feet as she thought of eating and how it was becoming late into the evening. The loudness of whistles and claps brought her back. It was her mystery man trying to get everyone's attention. His grin was greater than the sun, but his parents' faces differed when they returned from the cabin. They appeared happier than the first day she saw them. She and the sisters looked at each other as they tried to figure out what talk made them full of such harmony. It was as if no more fights and more laughter were on the horizon, promising delightful evenings and days.

He stood 10 feet tall over the pool, his sun-baked tan glistening; he winked and said, "Is there a party going on out here or what?" Moon smiled at him, noticing his tattoo, "Virtus amorem alat" (virtue nourishes love), across his left chest.

His sisters replied, "It wasn't hard to miss. You know us party girls." They both kissed him on the cheek and headed for the table.

"What about you, rose? Are you a party girl?"

She slid into the pool and strolled towards him. "Baby, you would be surprised about what you don't know about me." She knew full well she was not a party girl and hated parties. You would only see Aira Moon at a party to eat food and then leave. This wasn't even close to a party, and they had food. He saw her slip up at the library as a party girl, and it didn't go well, so it wasn't for her. However, she didn't mind teasing Dawn.

"Oh, yeah, I know how much of a party girl you can be." He laughed.

She rolled her eyes. He lent her his hand and helped her out of the pool. She dried herself, but he decided to lend her a hand with that, too. "If you wanted to touch me. You could have just said so." She smirked and looked into his eyes intensely.

"I know, but what's the fun of that?" He smiled seductively.

She twirled his hair with her finger as he dried off her legs. "What would I do without you, love."

He smirked. "I have absolutely no idea, but it would be similar to being like a cup only half full." She chuckled and looked over at everyone eating.

"I'll make you a plate." Summer said cheerily.

"Okay, red! The full works." She winked, and Summer winked back with a mouth full of food. She looked like a chipmunk with food in its mouth. It was sweet.

"I noticed they have taken a liking to you."

He was still bent on one knee and looking up at her.

"Matching gold bikinis gave it away."

"What can I say? I'm likable." She shrugged playfully.

"Great, it's just what I need. A likable and charming girlfriend." He joked.

"Mm-hmm. It's so heartbreaking." She playfully whined. He stood up and threw the towel over his shoulder. "If I weren't so hungry, you would be my meal. I would throw you over my shoulder and devour you downstairs, but my parents are aboard, so I will have to play nice." He licked his lips.

"Mm-hmm. I wouldn't mind being your prey, but like you said, you must be a gentleman." They laughed lightly and headed over to where everyone else was.

"Why don't my sisters make me a plate? I'm hungry, too." He teased

"Mother and father always make your plate, you, big baby." Crystal teased back.

Moon and Summer laughed as they went back and forth, teasing each other.

Then, Dawn's father whispered to her, "Thank you for coming. It's what he needed, and so did we. Thank you." She was stunned since his father barely spoke two words, ever. She put her hand on top of his.

"You're welcome. Anything for Dawn." She said warmly.

The discussion he and his parents had must have been lengthy for his father to acknowledge her to this extent. But she was exhilarated that they were finally getting along. If it meant her presence being there did that, so be it. She was just happy to be around a family again. She did not have anyone anymore except Marleen, but even then, she was a great distance away. Moon is a family-oriented type of girl, or should we say, a young woman. Though she was petrified of love, she did hope to have a big family someday. It's unknown if it was a gene passed down or what she went through in childhood that would make her want such a thing. It was obtainable, but for how long? It was desired now, but what about later? Minds change all the time. The mind of Aira Moon changed like the moon cycle when it came to many things. Indecisive, she was but determined indefinitely. She could see down the road.

In the back of her mind, maybe the middle, well- whatever section of her endless brain, she imagined what it would be like being married to Dawn, even having kids together. This thought was so far ahead of itself because it would be years away. And that is if they would even still be together. Imaginably, he would have grey hair like his father and be much older, and she would be in her late 30s. They would have a farmhouse somewhere isolated. A greenhouse would not be too far away. She would plant roses and tulips. She would even grow fruits and vegetables to try and be organic. Open fields where their children would play. Their children would be three and six years old. She would love to have girls, but boys would be okay too. It didn't matter what their kids were as long as they were loved and cared for by them. The farmhouse would have five bedrooms, a cellar, a big kitchen, and a large dining room and living room for guests and future grandchildren. They would have a massive library for him to dabble in his reading. She would have her own trophy and writing room for poetry. The room would have all her awards across the wall for a magnificent display. Her sorrow would have to go somewhere. His family could visit occasionally, and Marleen.

She was tickled at the idea. Being pregnant in the future, barefoot and glowing, he couldn't resist pampering her. He would be busy fulfilling her pregnancy cravings and showering her with baby gifts, along with his family. The baby shower would be a simple gathering with close family and friends. Summer and Crystal would argue over who had the best ideas and who would handle the decorations. He would carry her around to prevent her from straining herself while caring for the baby. She planned to have a home birth, as she liked the rawness of it - the blood, the baby's head popping out, and all the crying. It intrigued her like nothing else.

Then something happened. *What about our wedding?* She didn't even think about how he would propose, but knowing Dawn, it would be so intimate that the story would be told for generations. She chuckled in the back of her mind and smiled. Undoubtedly, the ring would be stunning, though she did not care for those things. For her engagement, she did. Why not express your love grandly to the world? What girl wouldn't? Imagine herself walking down the aisle in an extravagant wedding. She would be marrying a Wolfe for love, being carried over the threshold of the farmhouse he had secretly bought, and his tears at the altar from the sight of her beauty. Roses would descend from above as they said their vows, kissing passionately and vowing to each other. She could envision it all. Growing old, peaceful days, children, all of it.

He would want the same. Even as these things danced around in her mind, they settled in his; he always knew what he wanted. Her wish would be for her nana and papa to see it all, if only in spirit.

Dawn whispered in her ear. "What's going on up there?" She shook her head and smiled. He placed his arm around her and kissed her forehead. A tiny rosebud sprouting into a rose, at least for her.

# 13. A Haunting Past

Her feet swiftly pranced across the room as she prepared for the engagement party. She wore nothing but panties and cotton, white socks on her feet. The dress she had chosen to wear lay across the bed. She stood in the bathroom mirror, applying black lip liner around her lips and eventually adding lip gloss. She decided not to wear earrings as her hair hung long behind her back, puffy and curly. She ran to one of her suitcases to decide what shoes to wear with her dress. Tossing a couple of gold rings on her finger as she did, Dawn entered the room and smiled. He stretched his arms and sat on the bed. He liked watching her. Whether she slept, ate, or sat in complete silence, he liked watching her. It never felt sexual but more of appreciation. As much as he was fascinated by her, she was of him.

She heard a click. She quickly lifted her head and looked at him. He had a camera in his hand. She tilted her head and put her hands on her hips. "Is there something you would like to tell me? Or ask me?" she said curiously.

"I mean— no and yes. Would you mind if I take pictures of my breathtaking girlfriend?" He asked hopefully.

She cheesed. She had never met a man so captivated by her beauty, but maybe it was his love for her. She knew love made people do many things, but it could create a vision of another person, that the other could become obsessed. Not saying he was obsessed with her, but it was something she picked up on. He adored her to the fullest, and she enjoyed it. She never did care for such things because she saw what they did to her mother; however, it wasn't because of the beauty of her father that drove her to be an alcoholic. It was love or what she did with it.

"My love, as you wish." She winked. She picked out a pair of silky slip-in flats. He kept snapping pictures as she moved around the room. "Do you need me to pose, too, while you're at it?" She asked as she laid the shoes beside the bed.

"I'll follow your lead, rose." He smiled; his face was behind the camera. She pushed her dress to the side and climbed on the bed. "Now we are talking," he said.

They stared at each other flirtatiously. She was on her knees and playfully reached towards the camera. After posing on the bed a few times, she pulled him onto the bed. He then lay down with the camera beside his head.

She sat on his lap, hovered over him, and smiled. "I think that is enough photos from the paparazzi today. Don't you think?" He smiled and threw his head back on the bed.

"Yes, Ms. Moon. I do believe so."

"We should be getting ready for the party." She wisely suggested.

"They are still setting everything up outside. There is no rush." He smacked her butt cheek, and she flinched a little. "You can say that because you are dressed already." She quietly stated.

"Yes, I am, but I wanted to play a little before the love festivities."

She rolled her eyes. "You always want to play, but I think we played enough; I'm not entirely sure about my outfit, so since you are here, you will help me to decide."

*He might as well be a judge and jury for such a crucial decision.*

"Anything for you, rose." They kissed briefly.

She climbed off his lap and began to get dressed. He offered his opinion on several dresses she pulled out of her closet, but it didn't matter because she disliked all of them. She was picky about her style, even though most of her clothes came from her mother. At that moment, she wished she had something more stylish, as the clothes she had brought were either comfortable or new and elegant, and she wasn't feeling them then. She became grumpy because she felt she had nothing to wear.

"They all looked great! I do not see how you didn't like them, Moon." He let out a sigh in confusion, and she pouted.

"You don't understand. I always feel lucky when dressing for events. And I must have a drought today because nothing I brought is working, especially with the shoes I want to wear." She was restless.

Little did she know that a surprise was waiting for her. He grinned mischievously as he held her in his arms while they sat on the bed. He kissed her collarbone. "I wanted to wait to give you this present, but it seems you might need it sooner than I thought." She looked at him confusedly. "Before you ask, it is a dress you can wear, and I think it will match your shoes."

Desperation crossed her face as she hoped this item could take her breath away because she would not go to the party if she didn't love it. Dramatic, she knew, but dedicated she was. He quickly dashed to the closet and returned to her with a bright yellow box, placing it on the bed in front of her. The smooth cotton box had a purple silk ribbon around it. She admired its texture as she caressed the box, leaving fingerprints. Upon opening it, she pulled out a dress. The dress dropped to the floor as she held it up in front of herself. Both of them smiled, but one seemed unsure of the other. "What do you think? He foolishly asked, hoping she would like it enough to attend the party. She bit her lips and took the dress into the bathroom with her. He sat quietly, awaiting her answer while she did a few spins in the mirror. Out of nowhere, he heard loud bursts of laughter. He jumped off the bed, and she glided to the door.

She couldn't contain her smile. "I love it!" She twirled and twirled. "It's something I would so wear!"

He smiled out of relief. "I'm happy you like it, rose."

"I'm happy, too." She kissed him briefly, then sat on the bed to put her shoes on.

"Thank you, love." Her face was buried in trust.

A knock came at the door. She flipped her hair back and forth to set it completely. He answered the door. It was a party worker telling him that his mother requested him downstairs. She was ready for the party but planned to sit in the room until it was time. However, she wanted to do it with Dawn, but it seemed he would be occupied. It might give her an excuse to explore the mansion some more.

"Okay, tell her I'm coming."

"Yes, sir."

"It seems duty calls for whatever apparent reason. Will you be okay? Would you like to come help?"

She shook her head and said, "No, no-I will just sit in here until it's time."

"Are you sure?"

"Yeah! I might call Marleen and see what she is up to."

"Okay, well, tell her I said hi."

"Okay, love." She blew a kiss, and he did it back. He opened the door midway but stopped.

"You look striking, by the way." He winked and left the room.

She always looked alluring. Why wouldn't she unless she did it on purpose? The dress was prepossessing. It was a pitch-dark silk cotton dress. The sleeves reached her wrists, the middle of the dress exposed her stomach, and the top exposed her chest and neck. The rest of it lay at her feet. She stood in the same spot he left her and pressed down on the dress with her hands. She didn't plan to stay in the room like she told Dawn. You would think they were attached at the hip whenever one another wasn't busy, but that's relationships. She hoped not to be found exploring the mansion. She didn't think anyone would be mad, but she wanted to be cautious because of the remodeling. No matter, though, she overthought everything. She exited the room and slowly strolled the halls. She pushed through the plaster that hung from the ceiling. It was all demolished and half-painted, and construction supplies were everywhere. She was about to head back when she saw one room untouched.

The door handle was shaken to check if it was locked. Fortunately, it was. She flicked the light switch on, but only a simple lamp came on. The room appeared to be an old bedroom, with dark blue walls, wooden furniture, white cotton sheets, and a single cream flower-patterned wooden chair in the corner. There was also a dark wood table with an old television set. The walk-in closet was empty and in disarray, but the room seemed well cared for, with no dust in sight. The windows had dreadful silk-yellow curtains, and the floor was marble. What caught her eye was a single photo on the dresser, showing Dawn and Rainy Crow—his ex-girlfriend.

She raised an eyebrow. The picture depicted him hugging her from behind as she smiled. Rainy was slender, tan, and dirty blonde with a pixie cut. Her eyes were droopy, but they had a kindness behind them. Her face was slim; her nose was pointy, and her lips were small. She had on his college sweatshirt. She seemed average in Moon's eyes, but she was like his entire world back then. Dawn looked younger than he does now. He had the look of a baby, new and fresh. His style was even different. You wouldn't catch him in a collared polo shirt, baby blue, nonetheless. The image of them together made her upset. She rolled her eyes and slammed the photo face down. She didn't want to think about his past with her and how he was once happy with someone else. She felt heavy for him, and it swelled her heart. She didn't know why, but he was hers. The thoughts of him with others could hardly cross her mind, and when they did, it made her angry, not in the sense of jealousy entirely, but more about how they spent time with him before she did. She hated it more when his heart was broken. The name *Rainy Crow* swam around in her head, making her uneasy even though she was out of his life for good.

She sat down in the far corner, leaning back in the chair. She realized she had slammed the picture hard enough to break it, but she didn't mind. It felt like she was helping him put the past behind him. Breaking a picture or two wouldn't hurt; it might even help heal, at least for her. She reached over and turned on the television. Only one channel worked, showing static, so she hit it three times. A video of Dawn appeared: he was a lively child at his birthday party, and his family seemed happy. She smiled as she sunk into the chair, her legs sprawled open. Twirling the end of her hair, she sat there watching the television. The video played in loops, but she didn't mind. It was something new and historic.

There was nothing to search through because all the drawers were open and empty. There was little evidence of his old life. Her eyes roamed the room as she hummed a song, eager for the party to begin. She didn't know how long she could last before falling asleep or scavenging for food. She didn't want Dawn to know she was in his old bedroom, as he never got mad at her, but he did about his past. She ran her fingers across the television screen, her doe eyes full of love. She turned the television off and sat in the chair with her arms lying on top of the chair arms. She crossed her legs and swung her ankle endlessly, staring at the piss-yellow curtains, her mind drifting off as she closed her eyes.

"I see you found lost treasure." Her eyes sprang open out of fright, and she sat up. She knew that voice by heart. She didn't even hear the door open. Betrayal of the senses was the worst because her body wanting to rest left her at her most vulnerable.

"How did you—" She was flustered and scared. "How did I find you here?"

She just nodded in agreement. He chuckled. "Well, you weren't in our room nor with my sisters, so I asked myself where Moon would be. And I thought you are a curious little thing, so I decided to check this side of the house." She was unable to speak. "This was the only one not touched yet, so I knew you had to be here."

He didn't appear angry, but she didn't want to risk it. "I'm— I'm sorry. I was curious and bored. I hope you aren't mad."

His eyebrows furrowed but were tender. "Baby, I'm not mad. Why would you think that?"

She was hesitant to say but wanted to be truthful as they agreed. He stood in the doorway, both hands in his pants pockets. "I know you don't like bringing up the past, so I thought you finding me here would upset you."

He took a deep, heavy breath. "No, this would not make me mad." She could see he noticed the picture turned face down, but he treated it as nothing and walked towards her and knelt.

"Don't apologize when you've done nothing wrong." He smiled and kissed her ankle. She felt a slight relief that he wasn't angry. She knew he could never genuinely be angry with her. She smiled and relaxed.

"Did you find anything of worth?"

"Nope."

"Okay, baby." He laid his head on her lap like a cat deprived of love. She smiled and rubbed her fingers through his hair as carefully as possible, as if she had claws.

"I could never get angry at you." He smirked. "Frustrated but never angry."

"I know love, I know." She said confidently.

"This room should have burned a long time ago, along with everything in it."

She looked straight ahead, attentive. She continuously played with his hair slowly. "I'm sure it should have."

He smelled her and smiled.

"Did you spend much time in this room?" she asked.

"Yes." She raised her eyebrows again. "Did you with her?"

"Who?"

"Rainy Crow?" He lifted his head, and she retreated her hand. "Why do you ask?"

She made prolonged eye contact. "I'm curious, that's why?"

He was calm. "Okay—"

She deep breathed. "It was just a question, Jesus."

*I was busted.*

"Rose," he said softly, "She was in here most of the time while we were dating. Are you happy?"

*Of course not!*

She was dissatisfied with the vague answer but realized that she often did the same thing when people asked her questions. She wanted more information. He had left the picture years ago when he left abruptly, but why hadn't he thrown it away or burned it? Maybe he had a movie moment, like in TV shows where they go for good and stand at the door, reminiscing about leaving things behind. He definitely wasn't Miley Cyrus, and this wasn't television. She hoped he hadn't left the picture behind, hoping to meet again. She hated overthinking, but her brain was on high alert when she saw the photo.

She folded her arms. "Fairly," she smiled satirically.

"As suspected." He smirked intriguingly.

He stood up, crossed the room, and sat on the bed opposite her as if anticipating something. They stared at each other briefly before she mustered the courage to ask him anything else. She knew they had spoken about it before, but she wanted to see if he was truly over her—a childish tactic but more human than anything.

"Did you love her deeply?" Her ankle swung harder.

"I thought I did. Or at least I did years ago. I already told you this."

She nodded in agreement. "Yeah, right—Did you find her beautiful?"

It would be wrong to think of Rain in a negative light, but she couldn't help it. Her emotions weren't her own. She knew he loved her but wondered whether he still loved Rainey. Love doesn't just wither away. It was young love, but it still was love. Her heartbeat was fast.

He nearly smirked. "Yes."

She grew anxious. "How beautiful?"

"Not as beautiful as you." He said observantly and with sureness.

She rolled her eyes and said, "Okay— and sorry about the picture frame."

She wasn't even bothered about it. She was internally smiling.

"It was an old photo that should have been thrown away. Don't worry about it." He played with his ring, "I assume finding this picture has sparked these questions."

Guiltiness was written on her face. She smiled nervously. "If they did?" Maybe she was more territorial than she thought.

He smiled big. "It would be okay."

She played with the ends of her hair again.

"I love you, Moon. Okay, there is nothing to worry about, especially some old photos."

"But you would tell me if you still had feelings for her?"

He rolled his eyes. "Cross my heart!" He traced the letter x over the middle of his chest.

Worry lifted from her shoulders. "I know. I do not even know why I worry sometimes."

"It's just you, rose." He smiled.

"Yeah, it's just me."

"So! shall we go back to the room or—"

"Where is everybody?"

"My parents are downstairs greeting guests. I forgot to let you know that everything had been set up. Summer is somewhere running behind her friends, and Crystal should still be in the pool room. I was just there with her."

"Yeah. Um— we can —" She was cut off by Crystal appearing in the doorway.

"Sorry to disrupt, but Uncle Bronte is back." She smiled.

"Really?" He asked loudly in excitement.

"Excited, are we? Little brother."

"I am excited. And that Moon can finally meet his fiancé."

Crystal chuckled. "That's reasonable enough." She walked further into the room by Moon. "You will love her. We have known her since we were kids. She is so sweet and down to earth."

"I hope so, but I like to think I'm good at making new friends."

"We like you, so that's good enough." They all laughed. "Well, Countess is getting ready for her party, and Bronte is downstairs. He missed you guys and told me to come get you."

"Sure. We were just about to head down there." Moon smiled. "And her name is Countess?"

"Yep."

"That's a rare name," she said, though it sounded familiar.

Crystal grabbed her hand. "Well, let's get you acquainted downstairs."

"Are you trying to kidnap my girlfriend?"

"Now that I think of it, yes, since you seem to hide her more than show her off."

He scoffed. "I do not. I merely wish to introduce her to everything slowly, but Moon is an adult. She can do what she wants."

Moon rolled her eyes. "What does it matter? Let's go." She said hastily.

# The Wolfe Family

Crystal quickly pulled Moon downstairs at lightning speed, with Dawn following close behind. Dawn found it amusing that his older sister was in such a hurry, given that she was more eager to show off Moon to their friends and family than he was. On the other hand, Moon was excited and didn't mind the attention. She enjoyed being appreciated, as she was often in the shadows and admired from afar. It was a nice change to be the center of attention. They positioned themselves in front of Mr. and Mrs. Wolfe, and Crystal greeted them with a kiss on each cheek.

"Well, don't just stand their Moon." Mrs. Wolfe said tenderly.

"Hi, Mr. and Mrs. Wolfe. You both look great!" They looked flattered by the comment.

"Aww! Thank you, sweetheart."

"Yes, thank you, Moon."

Crystal raised Moon's arm and spun her around. "What do you think, mother and father? Is she bewitching or what!"

Mr. and Mrs. Wolfe laugh lightly. "Moon, you look amazing! I knew you had a figure but such exquisite taste in the span of two days in a row. Wow! Just wow!"

Moon blushed hard. "Thank you, Mrs. Wolfe."

Mr. Wolfe winked at Moon. "My son might have to hide you, young lady." He took a sip of Gin in a marble glass with ice. His ring made a clanking sound against the glass.

Moon laughed. "I'll make sure to let him know."

He smiled. "Oh, I think he knows, but if you ladies excuse me, I have some business to attend to."

He kissed Mrs. Wolfe and headed over to talk to a guest. She seemed full of joy.

"Don't mind him. He is always discussing business with company partners. Now, where is my son." She inquired, clasping her hands together.

Mrs. Wolfe felt a light breeze behind her. She looked to the side of her, and it was Dawn. She became giddy and smiled. "There you are, handsome." She hugged him from the side, and he wrapped his arm around her. "Here I am. Did I miss anything, ladies?"

"We were just talking about you." Mrs. Wolfe pinched his arm.

"Mm-hmm— What was said?"

"How childish and highly impulsive you are." Crystal taunted. Dawn mean mugged her and rolled his eyes.

"Crystal, stop bothering your brother." Crystal laughed with her hand over her mouth.

"What was really said?"

"Nothing. We were wondering where you were, love." Moon smiled and looked over at Crystal.

His mother smiled. "And why have you been hiding this gorgeous specimen." She pinched Moon's cheek.

"Oh, I do not know. Maybe I wanted to keep her all to myself. I know how you all can become obsessed." He playfully joked.

"Yeah, keep telling yourself that." Crystal playfully rolled her eyes.

"Oh, to be young and have fun." His mother reminisced. "Moon, my son tells me you do poetry. And I know it is late, but I thought you could recite something for us on stage." Mrs. Wolfe clasped her hands together in desperation and ground her teeth.

"I don't know— I'm not good with crowds." Moon stuttered.

He looked at her. "No, Mother. It's too late. What would she write on such short notice for Uncle Bronte and Countess? No."

His mother let out a deep breath. "Quiet Dawn. I'm asking Moon. It won't be too terrible. It can be just six lines. Please! It would be great for a soon-to-be bride. And, who knows, it might help you with your stage fright," she pleaded.

Dawn wanted to speak again, but Moon shook her head for him not to. "I'll think about it. I'll have an answer before guests take their seats."

His mother clapped twice. "Oh! Thank you, Moon. Now I have to help with the flowers. Enjoy yourselves and mingle!" She said as she walked out of the front door. Crystal stretched and stood in front of them.

"You do not have to say yes if you do not want to. Don't let my mother guilt trip you into it." She raised her eyebrows.

"Exactly. I agree with My sister." He threw his hand in the air in disbelief. Moon laughed.

"It's okay. I'll think about it. I'm a big girl."

She wasn't one for stages or crowds, but facing her fears would be great, too. It would be a nice gift for Bronte since it's his special day. She had a lot of thinking to do, but it seemed Dawn was doing it for her because he didn't like it. "It's okay, love."

"It's not. It's last minute. I hate it when she does that. And I'm sure it is to announce you as my girlfriend."

"D? You know it is, but I might as well. You won't!"

"Why do you guys keep saying that? I barely know any of these people. Why Would I introduce Moon?"

"You know a couple of people here."

Moon felt like most of their arguments were childish and unnecessary. Who cares if everyone in the room knew her? It was like she was the new jewel on the black market. She wished his family would leave it be. It wasn't like she was his property. She belonged to him when she made it so.

"Crystal, it doesn't matter. I'm not dying to meet everyone here anyway."

"And I bet that is my brother speaking."

Moon chuckled. "No, it's me speaking. They have eyes and can see me. I'm not going anywhere."

"My rose has spoken." He smirked, putting his arm around Moon.

"Whatever! I still stand by what I said." Moon fixed Crystal's bun.

"As do I. If they want to know me, they can introduce themselves. I'm not a pet." She smiled.

"Right. Of course." Crystal avoided eye contact because she was embarrassed.

"My best friends do not live here, and I will introduce her to them, not these congested snobs."

"Ouch! Prejudice much."

He laughed sarcastically. "Very much."

Crystal flipped him off.

"Moon, the perfume you asked me about earlier is in my room, so you can use it if you want."

"Oh, yeah, I almost forgot. I would love it so much. It smells delicious!"

"I could show you, or my big-headed brother can." She shook her head. "No, just give me the directions, and I'll get it myself."

"You're sure, rose?"

"Yes."

"Okay. Go upstairs, then go left, then go all the way down the hall till you see a door at the far end, and that's me. The bottle will be on top of my dresser, but if not, it might be in a pink round fabric box underneath my bed." She kissed Dawn on the cheek and hugged Crystal.

"See you in a little bit."

"We will be outside, harassing Bronte!" Crystal yelled.

# The Engagement Party

She took her time climbing each step as she went upstairs. Hitting the left corner, she faced a long hallway and multiple bedroom doors. There were two doors at the far end, but Crystal didn't clarify which one. It wasn't even a tiny clue to tell the doors apart. All of them were plain, black, and had a wolf for a door handle. She stood in front of the doors. It was like flipping a coin; though she did not have one at the moment, she had a solution. Heads for the left door and tails for the right. Removing her shoe, she threw it in the air, and if it landed on the heel, it was tails, but if it landed on the front of the shoe, it was heads. The shoe nearly touched the ceiling, flipping in the air as if in a hurry. She closed her eyes and waited to catch the shoe. Bam! It hit her in the head, and it hurt like shit. She bent down in pain and rubbed her head, but at least it landed. "Fuck!" she whispered repeatedly. She stood up and saw that the shoe had landed on the front. "Left, it is, then?" she said defeatedly.

Upon entering the room, she didn't see a perfume bottle on the dresser. She would have to look for the pink box Crystal mentioned. As strange as it sounded, she heard the shower, and the room felt hot. Did Crystal let one of her friends or a family member use her shower? Who could it be? She didn't ponder it too long since it wasn't her room or business. Maybe it was a hidden boyfriend. If it were a guy, she would tease her about it later. She would be so busted. Dawn would have a field day with that information. She laughed slightly and continued looking for the box but did not see it anywhere. She looked through each drawer. The only option left would be the closet, so she hurried over before whoever was in the shower came out.

The closet door creaked open, which was not good. She stopped for a second just in case she was heard, but she was not. It was a walk-in closet, and most of it was white, grey, or pink. She did notice one item similar to what Crystal described. She grabbed it and opened the box, but to her astonishment, there was no perfume bottle. It was just old photos. She found them to be cute and sweet. She flipped through them. Strangely, she landed on a photo of her grandmother, who seemed to be in her 20s at the time. "What the fuck?" she said, puzzled, and written on the back was "JJ- Janey 1974- Nashville, Tennessee/ Birthday Girl" She was happy and seemed to be at a party, with her hand full of cake and surrounded by laughter. She heard the shower stop and a woman's voice as she questioned what was happening. "Bronte! Is that you, baby?"

The stupidity set in as she realized she was in the wrong room; so much for directions. However, the wrong room or not. Why does Bronte have this picture in his closet? Did Dawn have him investigate her and her family? She was going around in circles but had to leave before she was caught by who seemed to be Bronte's fiancé. "Bronte?" she called again. She would find out what was happening because how could they have gotten that picture? Everything was put back in place, and she ran out quickly. She entered the other bedroom and found exactly what she needed. Her gut felt something imprecise when going back downstairs. Marleen had to have given him that picture; no one else could. Unless they found her drunk of a mother on the side of the road somewhere, and she wouldn't put it past them. She needed answers, but that would mean admitting to being in the wrong room. How would she bring it up or even accuse them of snooping in her life? Dawn and she promised to tell each other the truth always. Could he be lying to her now? She didn't know. She didn't know anything anymore. She wasn't angry but more confused and felt out of the loop.

She stepped outside, needing space to process her thoughts. The manor had a medium-sized navy blue tiled fountain with aquamarine water. Three deer were connected in the middle, and water spurted out of it. Only koi fish were at the bottom of the fountain, but that would change because she was about to join them. She felt weird, the only word she could think of. The pit of her stomach turned as she hoped the photo didn't prove her suspicions right. She didn't want to go through any trials like Rainy Crow. She wasn't her, but Dawn probably didn't know that. He had to be innocent. It was just a photo. For all she knew, it could be an item of her nana that had been lost or given away by mistake. It didn't have to be negative; it could be a positive coincidence. She could ask once the day ended. She placed her hand in the water to pet the fish. They were so wet and small, which made her mood lighter.

From a distance, all the guests were taking their seats, mingling, and drinking. She could see Bronte and Dawn talking. Bronte waved, and she waved back and smiled. Dawn did not take his eyes off her as she played with the fish.

He strolled over eventually and asked, "What are you doing over here? Come say hi to Bronte. He missed you."

"I will. I just wanted some alone time." She said in a sulky tone.

He sat down in front of her. "What's wrong?"

She looked at him timidly. "You don't have anything to tell me, do you?"

He sat his drink down behind himself. "No—no, why?"

*I know you are lying. You have to be clueless, if not, at least.*

She looked back down at the water, her fingers making circles, and said, "Are you sure?"

He looked offended. "What is wrong now, Moon?" He sighed. "Did I do something? Hmm? — What did I do now?" She looked at him quickly, shook the water off her fingers, and smiled.

"Nothing, love. You didn't do anything." She kissed him. *Bronte? It has to be.*

"Okay. Are you sure? If you do not want to be at this party, just let me know, and we can go."

She mustered up the energy to speak. "Love! I'm okay. See! I'm happy." She forced a smile once more.

"Let's say hi to Bronte and see what he is doing." He picked his drink back up and headed over to Bronte with her. "You smell delicious, by the way."

"Thank you, love." *He is such a cutie pie.*

Bronte whistled as they walked towards him. Moon did a small pose, then smiled shyly.

"A real beauty!"

"Thank you, thank you." She did a bow.

"This is the dress you got her. If I didn't know better, D."

"If you didn't know better? What?"

"That you want to lose your girl tonight." He smirked veraciously. "Come on, girl, give me a hug." She rolled her eyes and hugged him. "See that, easy squeezy lemon, Peezy!"

Dawn shook his finger at him. "Good one." He seemed unimpressed.

Moon was still not in the mood, but she appeared chipper for appearances.

"Oh, an inside joke won't kill you every once in a while."

She sharpened her hearing. "Is that what has been going on with everyone?"

"Yeah, just a little joke here and there, but that doesn't mean you aren't radiant."

It had to be about the past, she thought. His ex, perhaps. A bit cruel, she thought.

"How can I not be?" She did a shoulder pose, put her hand under her chin, and looked up adorably.

He grabbed Dawn's shoulder. "This fellow right here won't stop talking about you. It's cute, honestly." He laughed and drank some champagne. "I need a best man who is positive and in love. Unlike my playboy friends who don't care about me."

She could tell he seemed nervous about tonight. She wanted to ask him about what. She wanted to ask him about the picture, but it weighed heavy on her that it might be nothing, and she didn't want to ruin his party over anything. But how could it not be? It was Nana's picture. Her nana's, and they had it. It was wrong. It was not nothing to her, but she chickened out. She would try after the party and explain it to Dawn, and maybe they could get to the bottom of it together. She kept her composure because, unlike everyone else, her face couldn't lie.

She nodded. "Mm-hmm. I know how that feels. It's all like a merry-go-round."

He snapped his fingers and said, "Life, am I right?"

"He's had a bit to drink, and hopefully, that's the last one because Countess won't be happy with you."

"Shit! You are right. She will be pissed."

He took one last sip from the champagne glass and placed it on the table.

She noticed that the table had assigned seating, with a long white tablecloth and gold name tags. Orchids were placed in the center of the table, and bright yellow lights hung from wooden posts overhead. She expected to see a photo-op of the couple on the stage, but there wasn't one. Instead, a buffet table of finger food indicated that the main meal would be served later. There was also a minibar. On the stage, two chairs looked like thrones, each with its microphone. Bronte's chair was a classic gold with a red pillow, while Countess's chair was a lighter gold with a hint of pink and an embroidered white pillow. Even the microphones matched the thrones.

"You guys didn't take photos?"

"Yeah, we did, but she changed her mind. She thought it was cliché, so we had it taken down."

"I cannot wait for you to meet her. She's my baby! You know, you remind me of her."

"Oh, really?"

"He is just saying that. He thinks a turtle and a crab are the same."

"Says you! One, they're both nosy pants." She scoffed. "Two! You both have this freeing aura and weirdly enough smile just alike."

"I highly doubt it, Bronte." Dawn drank some of his wine and seemed tense.

"No, let's hear him out. Any other ways we are alike?"

"Yes." He leaned forward. "You both have the same taste in men."

He busted out laughing, and she just nudged him. "Very funny. We both are dating Wolfes. Ha—ha!"

Bronte stretched, then got a text on his phone and smiled. "Well, let's get this show on the road. The woman of the hour is ready to go!"

She took hold of Dawn's hand and kissed him on the cheek. "I guess that means we go to our assigned seats."

He nodded. "Mm-hmm. Are you going to recite something on stage?"

"No, and sadly, I will have to tell your mother." She smiled hesitantly.

"Mother will be disappointed but alive," he shrugged. Bronte slapped his face in a sad attempt to get sober and smoothed out his suit. "Wish me luck, but I'm sure she can smell the champagne on me. See you guys."

"Later!" They spoke as he walked away.

He walked toward the manor to find Countess, and they took their seats. Luckily, they were seated next to Dawn's sisters, and his parents were at the end of the table. She knew she would have Dawn by her side, but strangers would still surround her. She would make it through the night if they weren't intrigued by her, but who knows? She was more of an introvert than anything. She hated having to pretend to be Little Miss Socializer. She grew nervous and played with the silverware. She drank some water to calm down. Her emotions had been up and down for the last minute. Anytime she felt calm, another feeling popped up out of nowhere. It was like being on a roller coaster. She told herself to be normal, but what human could stick to that? Her boyfriend seemed to be Mr. Cool, talking to his sisters, but she felt trapped. The guests began to sit down, and it wasn't as big as you might think. Only close family and friends were invited, though the table stretched far and long.

As the time approached, her legs couldn't help but bounce under the table. Everyone was talking and laughing. Bronte was sitting on his throne, waiting for his queen, Countess. Moon was sitting back in her chair, bouncing her legs, when Dawn put his hand on one of them.

"If I knew. We would have had our very own private party at the manor."

She smiled genuinely. "I bet you would have. I'll be okay."

He smiled. "I see. I'm here with you; there is nothing to be nervous about. Remember what we talked about."

She nodded. "If I feel uncomfortable, just wink."

"Right." They laugh at Bronte on stage. "You see the king on his throne."

"It's a bit much, isn't it?"

He shrugged. "It's their engagement party, but Bronte has always been over the top."

"Yeah, I see." Summer peaked her head over and waved at Moon excitedly. Moon waved back. "Summer seems to be having the time of her life."

He bit into a strawberry and said, "She helped plan it."

Moon looked shocked. "Oh, right."

He asked Moon if she wanted a bite of a strawberry, and she accepted. Then, she received a text from Marleen. *"Hope you're having a great time. Send some pictures and call me later sometime this week. XOXO"* She smiled and wrote back. *"I'm having fun and will call as soon as I can. Send some pictures later. XOXO"*

Everyone started to clap as Countess walked towards the stage. Moon and Dawn were further down and could barely see anything. Countess was a dirty blonde with a head full of large curls covering most of her face. Her dress was violet and satin. It was spaghetti strapped and a half-cut by her upper thigh. She had classic, shiny pumps to match. Her hands had a layer of silver rings and bracelets on her wrist. She wore a silver sapphire stone heart necklace. Her make-up was light and natural. She was pretty tall and slim. The only thing left she could comprehend was her chocolate brown eyes, and that was it; they were so piercing under her curls. She sat on her throne, and the event commenced. Bronte made a few jokes on the mic, and friends of theirs made speeches and told stories. It was entertaining and okay for Moon. It was wholesome to see such honest love between many people. It was different for her, but even she was experiencing it. She and Dawn whispered comments about everyone and speeches in between getting a few laughs and gossiping.

Thankfully, it came to an end, and food was served. Dinner was chosen for the guests—grilled chicken with roasted potatoes and pesto, broccoli, and potatoes. A chocolate-coated cake filled with vanilla cream and raspberries was on top for dessert. The cake brought a memory back for Moon as that was her mother's favorite cake. She would want a chocolate cake with raspberries every birthday, holiday, or event. She found it humorous because it was the fourth of July when her mother was a child, and Nana had baked a chocolate cake. Her mother, being a child, went into the kitchen to sneak a taste of the icing, and there were raspberries next to the cake. Somehow, she knocked it over on the cake, and Nana caught her mother and was furious, but the show had to go on, so she pretended it was something new she tried. Some people hated and loved it, but her mother was obsessed. Ever since it had been her mother's signature cake, she almost felt a speck of happiness thinking of her. It was a lonely feeling, as if she would be the only one left to love her. Nana and Papa were gone.

While most guests were still eating, others finished their plates early and headed to the dance floor. The dance floor was cherry wood, and the edges were covered with orchids. They even had a DJ, but Bronte and Countess had the first dance, which they did. It was pure and lovely. The night was going flawlessly.

"They are so perfect." She said admirably. Dawn kissed the top of her hand.

"Yeah, they are. You are perfect, too." Moon blushed. "He was lucky to meet her the way he did."

"Yeah." She said, mesmerized, then asked, "Wanna dance?"

"Oh, no," he laughed.

"Why not?"

He smirked. "I'm not up for it tonight, but you can," he said.

She took a bite of her cake. "You are so boring."

He laughed out of amusement. "You cannot bait me in with that one." She waved him away.

"I'm stuffed, rose. You can dance with my sisters." He yawned. She felt he could be a grandpa sometimes, but who better be bored with? It wasn't like she had such an exciting life or personality.

"No. I'll sit next to you and keep you company." She patted his thigh and blew a kiss.

"And I'm grateful." They kissed, but Moon got a speck of chocolate on his face and laughed.

"Oh, sorry, baby." They started to laugh again when Summer rushed over from the dance floor.

"Moon, come, some people want to meet you."

"Who?"

"Some friends of mine who think you aren't real."

"Summer?"

Summer whined. "Please, I cannot help it if I like proving people wrong and that you aren't a myth!"

She tugged on her arm. "Go away, summer!"

Summer looked at Dawn crossed. "Shut up! It wouldn't hurt if you walked around and introduced your girlfriend instead of sitting over here like a damn hermit!"

They could smell the wine on Summer, but what's the point of a party if people don't harass you? Moon never liked parties for this reason—drunk people.

"I'll be back, love." Summer jumped up and down with excitement.

"Thanks, Mo."

Dawn shook his head. Crystal laughed from afar, talking with some guy. Moon smiled and waved at her. Crystal rolled her eyes playfully. Summer pulled Moon out of the seat, but Dawn grabbed her from behind before she could run off with her.

"If she goes, I go! Now let go of her Summer!" Summer turned around, irritated but happy they would prove her friends wrong. They all walked over to her friends by the dance floor and conversed. Summer gloated in victory and won a bet, too. Her friends were tired for the night and decided to head home.

"Thanks, you guys. They were assholes, right?" She slurred and tripped over her ankle slightly.

Luckily, Mr. Wolfe appeared behind her and caught her. "Come on, baby girl." Mr. Wolfe said, humored.

"She had a little too much to drink."

"I see. Thanks for keeping her company."

Dawn smiled. "Welcome."

His father nodded. He helped Summer to the mansion with her slurring words, and Mrs. Wolfe met him halfway, stunned and fussed at her. Crystal seemed occupied with the guy still.

"Want to dance, now?"

She tilted her head silly. "Oh, now you want to dance?" She seductively smiled. "But yes, I would love that."

"May I?" he said flirtatiously.

They trickled onto the dance floor and emerged into their bubble. Things started to get hot and heavy. Their bodies moved to the music, seducing one another. She turned backward towards him, and they danced gradually. His hands rubbed all over her as she had them trace her body. His thumb circled her stomach, and her back arched. They were the embodiment of lust. Their bodies became bonded and entranced into each other's existence, and the night, illuminated by a mixture of overhead lights, resembled the northern lights. He flipped her around, and they kissed nonstop, their bodies continuously grinding. Eventually, the music switched to upbeat, and they danced erratically. He moved smoothly across the dance floor with the trick of his feet. His muscular physique bumped to the loudness of the music, mainly his hips and butt. She was like a model on stage. It was as if she commanded the room itself. All eyes were on them, but mostly her. It was like she let loose a cannon and was immersed in her world. Dawn and she came back together, and he picked her up. She danced while sitting on his waist, and both just shook and pumped their hands in the air. The DJ eventually took a break, prompting them to come to their senses.

They laughed as they went to the mini bar for some refreshments. They sat at the bar to rest for a little.

Sitting face to face, He leaned in closer and said, "Want to get out of here?"

"No! Are you tired already?"

"Yes!" he laughed. "Are you not?" He rubbed her waist as she drank her ice-cold water with lemon.

"Mm— I'm not ready to go to bed yet. The night is still young."

"We will have plenty of nights like this." He caressed the side of her cheek and kissed it.

"Yeah, yeah. No." She laughed. "You can go if you want. I want to enjoy the night some more."

"Why do you have to be difficult?" His hands rubbed his face.

"Because you love me for it." She chuckled mischievously.

"Yes, sadly, I do." They kissed, and he tickled her.

"Dawn!" She sat her glass down on the bar, amused at what he did. "You almost made me spill my water."

"It's just water." He scrunched his nose at her.

"It's the principle."

"If you say so!" He said unserious and pulled her onto his lap. She twiddled her finger in his hair. "I love it when you do that."

She smiled. "I know."

"I bet you do." He smiled. They placed their foreheads together.

"You have such dreamy eyes."

"All in thanks to my mother," he said as they laughed.

The DJ continued the music, but they were spent. She wrapped her arms around his neck and his around her waist. They sat there and listened to the music, enjoying each other's company. "I texted Marleen."

"That's good. What did you discuss?"

"Nothing. She wanted to see how I was doing and to call and send some pictures when I could."

"The only pictures you have are the ones I took of you."

"Exactly! So, it will be no time soon, but I will call her tomorrow."

"Just imagine seeing her face if she saw a picture of you topless." He chuckled and kissed her on both her collarbones.

"Oh god! Pure disaster and a thousand lectures on what men "really" want." She laughed. "Your sisters invited me to shop tomorrow and said I could bring you too."

He looked uninterested. "Is it possible for you to come?" She gave an innocent look and bit her lip. She expanded her doe eyes for effect.

He smirked. "I do not know. Shopping? With my sisters?"

"Please! It will be a bonding experience for all of us." She did a puppy dog look. "I'll think about it; besides, you do not need me. We can always hang out afterward."

"But! I want to hang out with you tomorrow shopping. Besides this trip, it will be our first official couple thing to do."

"Okay, I'll give you an answer in the morning."

She cheesed heavily and kicked her tiny feet.

"Thank you, love!" She kissed him multiple times on the face, and he smiled.

It was getting late, and they decided to return to the mansion. She gently jumped off his lap and stretched. He left a tip at the bar and walked over to the DJ to also give them a tip. Somehow, he ended up in a conversation with the DJ. The party guests started to clear out, and she realized she had left her purse on the table and walked over to get it. As soon as she grabbed her bag, she stepped into a puddle of something unknown. It seemed slimy and smelt terrible. The first thought that popped into her head was that it was someone's bodily fluids. She let out a deprived sigh. "What the fuck! Can my day get any better?" She didn't see a waiter, so she took a napkin off the table to wipe her shoe. She sat in a chair at the end of the table and cleaned her flats off. It was so gross to Moon. She loved that she got to spend time with everyone and have fun but hated the part of the parties where people pissed, puked, and got into fights, especially all the drinking. The mere napkin didn't do, so she had to grab another.

In the middle of cleaning, Bronte approached her with Countess. She was so focused that she didn't notice until she spotted their shoes.

"Hey!" She didn't look up. "Hi! Bronte. I would have thought you left already."

He laughed. "Oh, no, I promised you that you would meet my fiancé, Countess." Whom she encountered by the classic purple pumps on her feet and the distinctive rock of a diamond engagement ring on her finger with French tip nails. "Oh, Hi!"

"Hello," she said softly.

"I'm sorry we had to meet like this, but someone had other plans."

"What do you mean?" They asked. "Someone puked on the ground, and I happened to stumble in it."

"Oh, that sucks!"

"Yeah, Sorry," Bronte said, rubbing Countess's back.

Moon laughed. "If I didn't know better, you're not from around here, based on your accent."

Countess smiled. "Oh, yes, I'm not around from here."

Moon was still focused. "This shit is tough to get off but dare I ask where from?"

"Nashville, sweetheart."

"Really? That's funny, b—" Dawn rushed over. "What's wrong? Excuse me, Bronte and Countess."

"Oh, nothing. I stepped into some puke, but I think I got the last of it." Moon sat up.

Dawn was blocking Bronte and Countess. She smiled. "It's okay. I'm fine. All clean now, and Bronte brought his lovely fiancé over for me to meet."

"Oh, yeah, Bronte! Finally, an introduction." He smiled, crossed.

"Well, I know it feels like a century, but we did it."

"I was just telling your lovely girlfriend that I'm from Nashville. And by the way, I didn't get your name, sweetie."

"Hold on just for a second, okay, Countess. It's nice to see you again, by the way."

"Okay." She nodded anxiously.

"Rose, can we go talk for a minute."

He was still blocking her view. "Yeah, but can you hold on for just a minute? I'm talking to Bronte and Countess."

"Baby—" He looked nervous and worried. She wanted to know what was happening with Dawn and why he stood in front of her. She stood up. "Is something wrong?" He was at a loss for words. "Love? What is it?" Bronte moved him to the side, and Dawn seemed shocked, removing his arm. "What's wrong with you son?"

Bronte looked baffled. "What are you whispering about?"

"Like you care. I need to talk to her." He looked concerned and nervous about something.

"Okay, calm down, D." He was becoming agitated. "You calm down!" he whispered.

"My name is Aira Moon, but I prefer Moon." She said, walking past Bronte and Dawn's shenanigans. She held out her hand for a shake as she got closer, and then her smile dropped faster than her hand.

"Moon," Countess repeated.

Bronte and Dawn stood to the side with bizarre looks on their faces.

"I think we should talk. Moon! Moon?" Dawn moved past Bronte.

"Why are you being weird?"

"Moon?" Dawn asked again. "Moon? I'm so sorry!"

He tried to touch her, but she moved away. She couldn't fathom what was happening. It couldn't be. She had to be dreaming or going insane. How could she not see it? How could she be so stupid? Her mind was going in circles again, and the dots started to connect. The picture. Her name. The cake. It was so unbelievable. Her legs were stuck to the very spot where she stood. She was dumbfounded.

"Can y'all give us girls a minute?" Countess said sweetly.

"I don't think—" Bronte cut Dawn off. "Sure Baby."

"What the hell?" Moon said, out of sorts.

"I think you both have much to discuss—"

Dawn pulled on Bronte. "Stop it, now."

"No. What—" Dawn became frustrated. "You know what you are doing!"

Bronte face went pale. "It's okay! She deserved to know." He held on to Dawn's waist. "You may be drunk, but you sure are a fucking idiot and an asshole!" Dawn whispered and pushed him back.

"I can live with that." Dawn gripped the back of his shirt.

"This isn't what we talked about!" Dawn whispered again. "I know, but—" Dawn's grip grew stronger on Bronte. "We need to—"

Countess looked at Bronte and Dawn sweetly. "Please, y'all! Can you give us a few minutes?"

Dawn seemed uncertain.

"I don't think that is a good idea until I talk to Moon!" Moon was frozen. "Let them talk!"

"Shut up, Bronte!" He said angrily. "Moon! Moon?"

Bronte laughed as he held him in his grasp. "Let it happen, son!"

"She will be okay! Y'all! She will be okay!" Countess looked at him gently.

Dawn hesitantly gave in. "Sure," Dawn said tensely.

Bronte looked victorious but still drunk. "Okay!" He waved his hands in the air. Dawn let go of him.

"I'll meet you up in the room. Give me a few." Countess said with her southern drawl.

"I'll take him, but I will be close by for Moon." Moon was silent and just nodded in compliance while they walked off.

There they were all alone. She couldn't believe it. How could she not see it? She wanted to believe her mind was playing tricks. She placed her hand on her stomach because she felt ill. She had to be deluded. Maybe she was second-hand drunk, though it was impossible and doesn't exist. She didn't want to talk. She didn't want to admit it. She didn't want to see it, but deep down she knew. Countess moved her hair out of her face and wistfully smiled.

There she was. She shed tears, her body became like cement, and her neck hair stood up. She didn't understand how this could happen. The memories of her life flashed before her eyes, but its very presence stood in front of her. The myth. The legend. Her mama Angel Countess Moon. She didn't believe in God, but she wanted any existence of a being or the universe to strike her down if what she was experiencing was a lie itself. Nine times out of ten, she was not. She walked slowly towards her and poked her hand.

"You are real." She said, disgusted.

Angel stood there smiling and crying. "Yes, I am real."

"Is this a coincidence or what?" Moon clutched onto the sides of her dress.

She was feeling miserable and began to cry. She tried to wipe away the tears from her eyes, but they kept flowing, and she desperately wanted them to stop. As a child, this situation would have been a dream come true, but it felt like a nightmare as an adult.

"I wanted us to talk without all of them around," Angel said with tenderness in her eyes.

"Did you—did you—" Moon put her hand over her mouth and cried more.

She didn't know what to ask or say. It was as hard as anything could be. She never honestly asked her mother for anything other than to be her mama. Everything didn't seem real anymore. She was a small web in the grand of bigger webs, but this moment seemed like a grand web.

*Wait? Did he know? Did they both know when they met me? Did they plan this? Did she plan this?*

"I know. You want to know how this all came to be. We can talk, or I can just talk if you allow me."

Moon stood there silently.

"I want just to say that Bronte and Dawn had nothing to do with this. Mainly Dawn."

She smiled timorously. "Bronte didn't know who you were until he brought me back, and he didn't tell me anything until before the party. But that's Bronte over the top and late regarding certain things." She explained nervously and walked closer, but Moon stepped back. "I was so happy when he told me that you were here. I felt it was a miracle baby. It was a miracle! My little girl was brought back to me, and with Mama and Papa's deaths, I thought I was lost to you forever."

She took a breath and stood up straight. "Did you even attend their funerals? It was incredibly tough being young and holding a broken family together for fifteen years."

*She had the nerve to stand them like Mother Teresa.*

"I imagine it was hard."

*No fucking clue. It might as well have been child labor.*

She grinded her teeth. "It was exhausting! That night you left, I hoped my mama was coming back, but you were gone forever! You know, I would think that the earth swallowed you whole, or you died on the streets, or the worst of them all, left us for another family. I had so many scenarios racking my brain. It was not enough that you had your parents to raise me. It was hell!"

"I know." She said, her voice trembling. "I came to the funerals. I stayed far back behind that big oak tree. You looked good. You seemed healthy. You seemed better off without me. You were just a tiny thang, too. I wanted to talk, hug, and kiss you so badly, but I knew it best I didn't."

*You can stalk your child but not take responsibility for them as a parent. I got it!*

"I was— I was not okay. I needed my mama. But It seems you have been living it up ever since!"

"Hold on now. It wasn't like that. I sent cards. I made sure to let you know you weren't forgotten."

"I don't care! It was not enough! It was— It was not enough."

She used her finger to twirl the ends of her hair. She needed to calm her nerves.

Her mother looked at her, hurt. "I love you and have missed you since that day, baby girl."

"I bet you fucking have." She rolled her eyes and mocked. "It will take some time, but things will get better, and you will understand over time, well, at least I hope so."

*Trust me, it won't, mamma, no matter how much you try to make it so.*

"You hope? I understood since I was eight years old that my mama was a drunk who only cared about herself. She sent postcards, got clean, and then got herself engaged to the wealthiest bachelor! She didn't come to get her child or check up on her child! Not only that, but you also played nanny to my boyfriend and his sisters!"

"Baby!"

"Now— that's fucking ironic!" Moon walked over to the bar and drank some of the water she had left over. She placed both hands on the counter and took a deep breath. She paced back and forth. She could hear her mother weep and try to compose herself. It's not like she had fifteen years to do so. She would not go easy on her. Her life wasn't easy. She understood being an addict, but she didn't have an addiction at some point, so why didn't she just come back and get her? It hurt to know the most who created you, barely thought of you, or felt leaving you was much better. She turned and looked at her mother. Angel Moon. An angel she appeared to be.

"You know, mama. I thought of this exact moment a million times. What I would say or do, and it never came out quite right because I knew back then that you would always be my mama at the end of the day, and my love would outweigh the bad. Then, again, that was then." Moon looked down to the side. "You look beautiful."

Moon scowled. "What?" *Did she just compliment me now? I just want to strangle that bitch!*

"I've been dying to say that since I saw you when I stood on that stage. You didn't recognize me, but I will always recognize you." She wept small. "You grew up to be a charming woman, and I thank my mama for that. She did right by you."

Moon walked over to her quickly and came to a stop. They were now face-to-face as the rain began to pour down and thunder roared in the sky. There they stood, both soaking wet, trying to find some level of understanding between each other after fifteen years. "Thank you, mama. I look just like you." She said with sarcasm. "Oh, but don't forget I will always have the charm of Daddy too, or did you forget about him too? You know the man that made you a drunk!"

Her mother's expression turned tenderly mad. "Stop! Okay, stop."

She tried to keep her composure, but her body was tensing up. Moon did not care if she was hurt or sad. She wanted to offend her. It gave her satisfaction to let her mama know she was the reason why she was broken and how her abuse made a little girl want to shrivel up and die.

"I'm sorry."

"Yeah, that's not going to cut it!" *Sorry, my ass!*

"I'm sorry! I'm sorry! I'm sorry!" her mother pleaded. "I'm sorry. I do not know what else to say!"

Thunder roared in the sky, and Moon looked up. They felt the surge through each of their bodies, and it powered them to express how they had felt for years without each other. It was a coincidental night indeed, but forced destiny at best. She looked back at her mother and waved her hand for her to stop.

"Why did you leave?" Moon said, exhausted. "I had to leave. I had to get out of that house and away from everyone."

Moon laughed angrily. "No, you did not have to leave your daughter?"

"Oh, sweetie, but I did. It was the hardest thing I had to do besides get clean."

"Why even have me if you were going to leave all along?" she looked for some clarity. "Hmm?"

"You reminded me of him. The only thing left to remind me of him. You were a part of him and me. I couldn't leave him behind. You were made from our love," She choked. "You were the purest form of our love. I thought having you would be the best thing for me, and that would be what he wanted, but I was young."

*So, I was a mistake?*

Moon laughed hysterically. "Wow!" She shook her head. "Well, you did leave."

Both of them paused. "You did leave behind the love you and Daddy had, which was me. And I know it was because I was the child that reminded you most of it. The mistake!"

Sadness shot across her mother's face. "I guess I did. Little Rosie, I guess I did, but you were never a mistake." She looked down with guilt.

"What did you call me?"

Her mother looked fearful. "Little Rosie is what I called you."

"No, you do not get to call me that — you have no right. I have no mama, so just don't!"

"I'll always be your mama, Aira." She said softly, reaching for her hand. Moon flinched back and looked at her mother with a cross. "It's Moon! It's fucking Moon!"

"Moon! I will always be your mama!"

"Not to me—" Her voice cracked and was shaky, "Not to me!" She swallowed her agony. "I do not care that you left. All I know is I want you to stay gone." Her voice left after all the yelling. *I am exhausted.*

She did not know what to say. All she knew was that her worst fear had come true. Her mother was alive and well. She was living great without her. She felt like that damaged little girl from years ago. She couldn't breathe. It was as if a tornado ripped her world apart. Someone else had her mother's love, and she didn't. She was spiraling.

The rain fell even harder. They could barely see each other. Dawn called out to Moon, but she paid no attention. She was just as blurry as that night.

"We should go inside; it's getting bad out here." Her mother cried.

She was freezing but did not want to go anywhere with her mother. It did not matter. Dawn appeared drenched in front of them, and thunder was louder than any of their voices that tried to cling to her ears.

"We should go inside Aira!" Angel screamed. "Aira!"

*I just want her to shut up for three seconds and let my mind, and even my heart, rest in peace. I hurt.*

Her mother begged while she shook her head and stared intensely at Dawn, blinking twice.

"Go ahead. I'll get Moon." He nodded to reassure her.

He handed her mother an umbrella. Her mother looked back but knew she needed time, so she headed to the mansion. Dawn took off his jacket and gave it to Moon. Her teeth were chattering, and she felt icy. He made her hold the umbrella as he picked her up into his arms.

"Rose?" She didn't speak. "Okay, let's get you inside."

He rushed toward the manor and kissed her on the forehead. She began crying again, this time for a much longer, and buried her face in his chest with her eyes tightly shut.

# Aira Moon

He laid her wet body on the bed and ran into the bathroom for towels. She curled into a ball. Her eyes were still shut, and her breathing was shallow. She could hear him moving around, trying to find whatever he was looking for, which she assumed to be a dry set of clothes. She was blindsided, but she was too weak even to express any more emotions, to attack those who injured her. He stood like a giant in front of her and demanded she let him dry her off. She sat up in haste, letting him dry her entire body, and let what needed to be done be done. She had minimal fight left in her. He sat behind her as he patted her hair dry.

"Did you know?" She said, drained and lowly.

"I—found out last minute before the party began. I hoped to stop you from meeting Countess before the party was over." She played with the ends of her hair again. He set the towel to the side. "How did you find out?"

"I overheard Bronte and her talking, well arguing because he told her at the last minute that the very girl I am dating happens to be her daughter, and they needed to figure out how to avoid you or approach you."

She closed her mouth tightly so as not to cry again because a headache was coming on. He hugged her from behind. Her head lay on his shoulder while his thumb circled her lower stomach. "It's all right if you want to cry. Cry all night if you have to." He kissed her forehead, and the tears streamed from her eyes. A million thoughts ran around in her mind, and a thousand daggers were in her heart. She felt betrayed, even by him. If she could move with such pain in her body, she would leave. She would go and never come back, but, in the end, she had to lean on him. "Please say something, Aira."

She whimpered lowly. "I trusted you, and you let this happen to me. You let them do this to me."

"I'm sorry! I thought I could intercept it. I confronted them, but, in the end, we had to figure out a way to tell you. They decided on the party, but when we talked, it would be the day after for an easier approach."

"That's all everyone has been saying, sorry, and that they didn't mean for it to happen this way."

She removed his arms from around her and grabbed the dry clothes off the bed.

"I'm going to change." He sat there defeated. He knew he didn't do anything immoral, but maybe the strategy was wrong. He couldn't sit there and wait for her scolding, so he changed out of his wet clothes into just a pair of briefs. He waited and waited until she came out of the bathroom. Her hair was still damp and curly, and she wore a white oversized t-shirt and dark brown cotton socks.

He smiled worriedly. "Are we going to discuss tonight or just—"

She didn't look at him and sat on the side of her bed. "It's been years since you have seen your mother. I know it must have been gut-wrenching."

She barely had a voice left over. "Why? Why do we need to talk about it? People have been discussing me perfectly fine without me there." She curled up under the covers as he sat halfway off the bed. His back to the headboard. Her back was to him.

"Because you have to talk about it, and you will see her for the rest of the weekend."

A sharp sting went through her body. "Don't you think I haven't thought about that?"

"Well, I'm just stating the obvious. And think you shouldn't bottle your feelings up."

She rolled her eyes. "So, not only am I not getting rest, but I have to talk again!" She snarled.

Her eyes were full of fury and heart of doubt. "Let's talk!" She pushed the covers off and turned toward Dawn.

"I want you to know I love you. I love you and didn't know what to do."

"You should have told me so I would not have been ambushed like that."

"If I did! It still would have the same outcome, but instead of just us four, knowing the whole family would have."

"I do not care. We promised to tell the truth to each other, and you didn't. You waited until the last minute when they approached me, and why would Bronte act like he didn't know what was going on?"

"I do not know! I assume he was playing it off, so it would not be as bad as it was, but it backfired. He probably thought he was doing a generous thing by you."

"Mm." She deep breathed.

"There were no ill intentions. That's the point, Aira! God! I get you are mad, and they lied, but everyone found out today! We couldn't think on our feet like Houdini."

She sobbed again. "You could have thought of me." She shrugged.

He looked at her heartbreakingly, pulled her toward him, and held her face.

"Aira, we did think of you, but no matter what, it ended the same: you were hurt and devastated." He kissed and hugged her. "If I had all the power in the world to make your pain go away, I would, but for now, all I can do is eradicate it humanely next to you."

She smiled sadly and kissed his chest. "I just want to breathe for once in my life."

He sat back on the end of the bed, and she coiled up on his lap like a cat. He stared at her from above like a god overseeing his fragile human. "We can manage that." She held his hand, and he caressed her hair throughout the night.

Two hours had passed, and she awoke. She rolled over to her side and stretched her arms and legs. Dawn was still asleep, his back to the bed headboard. She felt scarcely better. She was in no mood for any more tears. She didn't want to lay down any longer, so she put her hair in a lazy bun and left the room sneakily. She didn't care what time it was because of how she felt; it didn't matter, nor could she measure the grief she was in. She knew she could never get rid of that little girl who was heartbroken all those years ago, but life could challenge even the strongest souls. She stood at the end of the stairs, deciding which door, room, or way to escape. The reality she lived in had to be a hoax because not only was her mother alive, but she was torturing her from the inside out. She had to escape; no one could fix that, not even him. Maybe some alone time with herself would do her good. She brought her phone with her. She placed her earphones in her ear and blasted every song that spoke to her soul, heart, and mind.

She walked through the dining room, to the pool room, to the main entrance, and the living room. Eventually, she wandered through a door that led to another door that led to the kitchen. Which is a place in the mansion she had never seen, but Dawn was right. It was a hallway by itself. It still had gold decorations here and there. It was no longer black but pallid and white. It had what most kitchens have: two stoves and ovens. Pots and pans hung everywhere—luxurious cabinets and counters. Family photos and staff photos hung all over the wall. Then, more things that made a kitchen a kitchen. The only thing that caught her eye was the height measurements and the names next to them on the wall. She bent down and used her finger to follow along, tracing each measurement and smiling at how much the Wolfe siblings had grown. She couldn't believe how Dawn grew to be five-nine. It was charming to her. Based on how Dawn described it, she didn't expect their manor to be homely. She assumed it would be a big gallery where they showcased their expensive belongings to others for status and nothing more—metaphorically speaking. At least their childhood home didn't have a big hole in their closet for a memory.

Next to the wall was a kitchen window the size of a door. It had seashell-white curtains and a window bench with pale pink cushions. The window was cracked open, so she took the chance to revel in nature and the impulsiveness of her thoughts. She sat in the window with her knees to her chest and music blasting. She could see the stars and moon, but they were out of reach. She smiled at the memory of her being drunk, asking Dawn to bring her the stars and the moon—such a silly thing to ask for. No one could do such a thing.

*I wonder if he still laughs about it to this day. I haven't drunk anything since then. It gives me an aching stomach just thinking about it, other than losing my virginity, which was unexpected but fun.*

She smiled again, but it faded as she recalled the events with her mother.

*It's good he is asleep because I couldn't handle the interrogation. When he was the one who lied, but he was right about one thing: I would be hurt no matter the outcome. My anger hasn't gone away, but the temperature is low. I shouldn't be so harsh on him, but I hate lying. I do it sometimes, but it's more of an omission of the truth. I don't know what to think about the whole ordeal. My mama married his uncle and raised him and his siblings. She is their aunt! She is a part of their family. I mean, to think about what happened to her over these years, knowing she cleaned up and could wiggle her way into a wealthy family.*

*Suppose that's not the cherry on top of the cake. She attended her parents' funeral secretly. It makes me think about Nana's nights crying over her daughter and arguments with Papa about it. She wasn't the only one crying over Angel Moon. She looked good. She looked angelic. She looked like my mama. I still have a headache from all that crying and yelling. I sometimes think this has all been a dream, and all I have to do is fall out of the window and wake up. Did Bronte and Dawn know about me since I was a child? Did they find out about me today or realize I was her daughter until today? Who knows what anymore? These questions should be steered toward my mama and Bronte, but I have to think. I do not even know if I want to stay this weekend or head home early. I don't want to say it, but I feel like this trip has been ruined for me, and if that is me being melodramatic, oh well.*

She opened the window wide, closed her eyes, and let the wind wash her clean once again.

*I miss Nana and her jokes, hugs, and just seeing her every Friday at the diner. It's been so long, but not really. It's unbelievable how someone can be with you one day and gone the next. Is it immoral if my mama switched places with my nana? It would be unholy, like my papa would say, but I could never help express my feelings. Deep down, I know she would want me to make amends with my mama, but how could I? I gave her the benefit of the doubt for eight years, but after that, I gave up. I knew she wasn't coming back, and we were alone. All I see is darkness; even the night beauty cannot help me eliminate chaotic feelings. I can feel the anger boil up again. I can't think. I can't think. All I can do is question and feel! It's putting me on edge. I don't like it. This night keeps replaying in my head, over and over and over. I know it's not black and white as I thought. Bronte loves my mama. He loves her and wants to marry her. Since I was a little girl, she would say that my daddy was her one true love, but I guess not. It's odd that someone besides me, my grandparents, and Daddy loved my mama. Well, he loves the "sober" her. It's unfair, I like to say. They got to have the sane, lovable, and beautiful Angel Moon, while I only got her for a time. I was left with the damaged, torn, and drunk version. Did she even tell them about me? Or did she find her new kids to love and be a mother, too? How can this be? It was better when she was a ghost, nothing but the past.*

*Now, I am sitting by the window, consumed by thoughts of her and our situation. I know Dawn's sisters and his parents will have questions if they don't already know. I'm just going to assume I was the last to find out. My chest aches, as does my heart. Tears blind my eyes, and my body feels frozen in time. I can't help but cry into my legs so no one can hear my unraveling. It's not fair. What has she been doing these past 15 years? She missed everything. We used to be the best of friends. We had our faults and quarrels, but she was like a mother to me. Mama? Mama? Why? I'm lost. Lost as I can be and don't know what to do. Did she take fancy trips, fall in love, see Paris, tell people, "Let them eat cake," and form strong bonds with new people while I cried my eyes out every night, struggled in school, and attended a funeral with little to no family? My body is burning hot, and all I want to do is drive a car into the mansion, right where her room is, and demand reparations* for my traumatizing childhood. Understand me. My nana did an excellent job raising me, but it wasn't her responsibility. We had a close relationship. I did everything with Nana. It was like we were joined at the hip. We were practically twins. And to think about Dawn. He is so perfect, but he's dealing with my issues when this trip was supposed to be about us bonding, having fun, and me figuring out my feelings for him. He is my love. He has this sweetness about him. He can agitate me and make me want to jump his bones simultaneously. His love can make my heart float out of my chest. He is my everything.

I hope we can move on from this. I know I scolded him earlier, but he didn't know, right? He is innocent in all of this, even Bronte. I guess I am just angry at her and her very existence. She is like a virus I want to cure. Somehow and someway, she haunts me everywhere. Bronte, be warned. If you have any children, she might abandon them too, even start drinking if it becomes too hard. I wonder how long she has been sober. It has to be for years that she has been sober now. If not, that wouldn't be a shocker. She had the nerve to call me Aira. Shit! She had the fucking nerve to call me little rosie. I felt disgust for her trying to find a middle ground between us. I will never forgive her. She would need a gravestone next to Daddy's if she wanted to talk to me. There is so much she has done to me that I have not spoken of, but she might have told them all about it and made herself a saint out of all of it. She had a way of doing that. I can't talk to her again; it's too much for me. I do want her dead sometimes, but it looks like it's not going to happen.

I cannot help but think about that one time she was sober for a month. It killed her. She could not survive if she did not have one drop of alcohol. Around that time, I was naïve and was six years old, so we had not gotten into a routine yet. She was not herself. She didn't smile, laugh, or cry. It was like she was an empty glass. Not even half full. I like to say my daddy's death finally hit her. I felt so sad for her, so I secretly brought her a bottle of whatever if it meant she would be a little lively and not a corpse. That day, I left her alone and returned to the noises of Nana and Papa, who were trying to calm her down. She had broken the bottle and dug some of it in her wrist. She said she wanted to join Daddy, but luckily, Papa got a hold of her. Nana made me leave the room, and that is when they stopped forcing her to be clean, even for my sake. It was hell from the beginning.

She sat up and wiped the tears from her eyes; in doing so, she saw a shadow behind the curtains. They approached her slowly. She gripped her phone tightly just in case she had to fight. She asked who it was, but the shadow didn't say anything, then she realized her music was still playing. She turned it off and asked who it was again. The figure near her said, "It's okay, beauty. It's me." It was Bronte. She knew his voice anywhere. She cracked the window back and moved from behind the curtain. It was him, and he was alone. She looked at him differently.

He seemed more serious than usual. "Can we talk?" he pointed to the kitchen table.

"Sure." She said calmly. "What about?" A blank stare on both their faces.

"The events that happened earlier tonight." She took out her earphones, laid them flat on her phone, and sat across from Bronte at the table. He looked as if he didn't know what to say. She rolled her eyes and clasped her hands together. "If you came to tell me that it wasn't her fault and that everyone found out at the last minute of knowing about my existence, then you're saved because Dawn told me."

Bronte looked satisfied but still unsure. "My only question is, do you know everything?"

She looked confused. "What do you mean?" Her palms sweated. She became nervous.

"We did find out you were her daughter at the last minute, but more so as you are now, not when you were a little girl."

"Ah! I see. You knew of me for a while but only saw me as a child. Correct?"

"Yes. She talked about you a lot and even showed me photos."

"Mm-hmm." She could feel the stress boiling inside her, and she knew Bronte felt it, too.

"Do you know about her past? Who she was? Why she was the way she was?" she picked at her nails.

"Yes. When our relationship moved past just employer and employee, she told me of her past, mistakes, and a drinking problem."

She folded her lips. "Well, I'm happy for you." She placed her hand on the table in a loving manner sarcastically.

He sighed. "Look! I get it. You and your mother are not on the best terms, which has uprooted your life. But please do not take it out on Dawn. He didn't know, and neither did I, okay."

She looked up at the ceiling as she did as a child. Their ceilings were smooth, but you could notice small cracks in the foundation. "I am just saying think before you act; if you want to keep your distance, that's fine. If you want to leave early, that's fine, but if you want to enjoy the rest of your weekend with Dawn, Please consider sitting down with your mother and coming to an understanding. That way, you can go your way, and she hers or who knows." He smiled hopefully, his gold tooth bouncing off the moonlight.

"You know you are asking a lot of me, especially since you have no right to."

She challenged him with a side eye.

"Oh, I know, but I am anyway for the woman I love and the young woman I adore."

She tensed up. "Bronte."

"Please— please just think about it, and when you do, she will be waiting for you whenever you are ready to talk. There is no rush." She nodded. "Okay, but do not think I will do this for her."

He smiled. "Whatever you want, beauty."

She let out a sigh of relief. "Did she talk about me much?"

He looked at her, smitten. "Yes, she did, dear. She would have fits over you and sleep with your picture next to her heart. She would write to you night and day."

She looked back down at Bronte. Her chin was on her shoulder. "Fits?"

"Yes, it was the longest she had been from you, so she would have episodes."

"Serves her right." He looked uneasy when she said that. "What did she tell you about me?"

"She said you were very bright and smart for your age, not that you didn't have to be, but she would tell stories. She even called your grandparents about you, but she wasn't as sober as she wanted to be, so she avoided contact."

Their eyes watched each other. "I know." She smiled with disdain. "Look, I'll think about it, but you and her can know that I'm pretty fucked up right now, so who knows."

He didn't flinch at one word she said. "Like I said, I understand. We all have fucked up families. Mine is no stranger to it, especially Dawn." He sat there with self-confidence. His ring finger caught her attention as it pecked the table.

"I've heard."

He patted her hand and got up from the chair. He turned and looked at her. "He loves you."

"I know he does."

He sucked his teeth and rubbed his nose. "Do you love him?"

She looked down because she could not answer his question. She did not know.

"Isn't that for Dawn to find out."

He nodded and said, unsure, "Yeah."

She looked at him and asked, "Do you still love my mama?"

The question took him aback. "Always."

"Does she feel the same?" He put his hands behind his back and stood firm. "She does."

"She does, or do you hope so?" Her eyes lowered.

"I know she does."

"Then we both know all there is to know."

He smirked and winked at her. "You're right about that, beauty," he said, knocking on the kitchen counter.

He left the kitchen, and she sat there feeling the chilliness of the room. She hoped he could live up to the image of her father because when it came to the truth, he was just a distraction at best, no matter if she considered Bronte a friend. But how could she know it could just be her hatred for her mother talking? She pretended she had all the answers for the night, even though she didn't. The mental and emotional gymnastics had worn her down for the day, so she stayed in her same cold spot. The quiet helped her, but her jitteriness and emotions were still screaming. She didn't know what to do.

This was the only alone time she had got to herself since the first day at Wolfe Manor. The kitchen was dark, the only light coming from the window, and a lonely girl sitting in it. She would have to go back to bed soon because Dawn would notice her missing, but sadly, she didn't care. She was a shadow at most, trying to find a spark of light. She knew she would have to talk to her mother again and dreaded the very thought of it, or she could leave and not have to worry about the judgment and forced truce. She would still be a lonely girl sitting in the dark. Her only solace in life was to be closed off from the rest of the world.

# 14. Mommy Dearest (Flashback³)

T he lights from the cracked bedroom door blinded me as I awoke. My eighth birthday party took place earlier in the evening, but just by me looking out my window, it was night. The house was quiet. I lay on my side, head still intact on the pillow. Long naps never served me because I always slept till night. Sometimes, I would sleep to escape my problems and sleep so much that I was too tired for them. I sat in my bed, took a second to see my surroundings, and stretched. I rubbed out the leftover crust in my eyes with my hands. Strangely, the house had this stillness because it was its duty to be chaotic. Why was everyone so quiet?

My party went well. It was a peace I had never known. Nana, Papa, and Mama were getting along—no talk of religion. No passing out drunk and no screaming. I had family and friends over. I never had an infinity for sweets, so they gave me a small cupcake to blow my candle out on, and it was the number eight. We sang songs, danced, and we kids played because adults don't do that. At least, that is what Papa says. He said that as an adult, I would outgrow most things, even the ones that make me who I am. I like to think he was being a sourpuss. He always was. It was hard getting Papa to enjoy life; he usually sat around brooding like a Paul Newman character. He looked just like him at a young age. You would swear they were twins, and he thought he almost met him once, but it turned out to be some random guy who looked like him from the side. Mama was all smiles at the party and acted like a mother for once. She kept her eye on me and consumed water for the entire party. I am proud of her, though it was the bare minimum she could do. When the party ended, I fell asleep helping everyone clean up, so Papa put me to bed.

I got up and put my bunny slippers on. I opened the door lightly, not to wake anyone from their sleep. All I wanted was a glass of water. My mouth felt so dry. My room was next to the kitchen, so it wasn't a long walk. Nana and Papa slept at the end of the hall, and Mama in the middle. The whole house was dark, which meant everyone was asleep. I was surprised at best because Papa was always still up watching his recordings of TV shows or sports he missed.

As I turned the faucet on, it made a jumping sound that could spread through the house. Something had to be jammed in it, or it was time to replace the faucet again. We lived in a farmhouse just a short distance from the city. It was an outdated farmhouse, by the way. Everything needed fixing. Papa and Nana fixed everything because my mama couldn't dare break a nail. It didn't register later that everything she touched broke, so how could she fix anything? I shut the shouting faucet off after two glasses of water, and when I exited the kitchen, I managed to trip over a duffle bag. A loud thud rumbled through the house, but no one seemed alert. It hadn't been there before. Who bag was it? It had to be my grandparents because they leave bags around the house for their handy projects, so much who can tell the difference. I paid no mind to it and went back to my room. I decided to lie back down because I had school tomorrow.

However, I could see a shadow at my door before I closed my eyes. I squinted to see who the shadow was, but no luck. It wasn't like I was scared because I had not been scared of the dark since I could remember. It had to be Nana or Papa checking up on me. I didn't make any noise while tripping over a bag of theirs. I waited a minute just in case they barged in and asked me if I was all right. It was their routine. I pulled my pink comforter to my neck and became comfortable. The door began to open, and I yawned. To my surprise, it was my mama, but I didn't say anything because she never came into my room unless she had an episode. She had the dark green and black duffle bag on her arm and sat on the floor next to the door. She walked over to me and sat beside my bed.

A feeling came over me that this night would be different. Not just any difference, but a feeling that made me blue and my stomach drop. Mama whispered, "Are you awake?"

I smiled faintly. "I am Mama."

I didn't know why she would ask like my eyes weren't wide open and shaped like immense gumballs. She acted as if she was hiding something. She was anxious and a bit jumpy. Her demeanor made me worry. She didn't smell like alcohol. I sat up on my elbows, and we talked face to face.

Mama rubbed my puffy cheeks and smiled. "I wanted to see you and give you your birthday present."

I squinted in confusion. "Why didn't you give it to me at the party?"

She looked down at the duffle bag and wrestled a poorly wrapped present out of it. "I felt silly giving it to you in front of everyone, so I decided to do it now, okay."

I smiled with pity. "Thanks, Mama."

I put my hand out, and she handed me an object wrapped in birthday paper. Birthday balloons and confetti images were all over it, but they were wrinkled. Only tape held it together. I flipped the present around twice and then started to open it. She threw the pieces of wrapping on the floor beside her.

Her face lit up. "What do ya think, baby?" she asked.

It was a golden locket. It was smooth, plain, and oval-shaped. When I opened the locket, I saw a picture of Mama and me, but I was a baby. I let my finger trace the image and smiled genuinely for once.

"I love it, Mama."

The veins in her neck and forehead became more prominent as she started to cry. And I have seen my mama cry, but not like this. "What's wrong, Mama? Is everything okay? Did you get into a fight with Nana and Papa again?" She laughed as she cried and wiped the tears from her eyes with chipped black nail polish.

"No, baby. I'm just happy that you like your present."

"Umm—okay."

"I want you to hold on to that. Mama is going away for a while, but I will be back." We both nodded.

She grabbed the end of my hair and twirled it with her fingers. "I always liked how brunette your hair was. I never liked my blond hair. It made me feel ditsy, and it made me look like Papa."

"I like your hair, Mama. It reminds me of the sun and Goldilocks!"

She put her finger over her mouth and said, "Shush! Not so loud, baby. We do not want to wake your grandparents." I smiled innocently. "Let Mama help you." She winked at me and placed the necklace around my neck.

"There," she smiled with her hands in front of her mouth. "It looks good on you."

Tears still rolled down her eyes, and I didn't know why, but I assumed she was being sent back to rehab. She felt ashamed talking about it; there was nowhere else to go. I wiped her tears with my thumb.

"It's going to be okay. I know they are sending you to that place again."

She looked up, tense and sad. "Yeah, they are sending me back to that nice place for Mama to get better."

"How long this time?" she kissed my forehead. "More than last time. It's a lot longer, but I want to know if you will be okay with that. Say you will be okay," she said, concerned.

"I will be okay, Mama."

No matter what she made me agree to, I felt pity for my mama. She was always on edge. She never had a day of peace in two years. She is a former ghost of herself. She needed help, and I was happy that she would get it. They thought I didn't know that they sent her to rehab. They hide these things because I am a child, but, in this day and age, children my age know more than they let on. They would whisper or quit talking when I entered the room as if the arguments didn't damage me enough. The only thing that was off about this was that it was night, and she was leaving. She usually left in the mornings, and Nana or Papa drove her to the place.

"They are not taking you this time?"

She had a look of guilt on her face. "Oh, no, no, not this time, baby. Yall can visit." Her hands twitched, and her skin was full of sweat. "I will send you postcards and call when I can."

I hoped again that this time would be entirely different and that she would be my mama again once she got her treatment. It grew in me like weeds. I always gave her a chance because it was instinct at best. A bond shared between Mama and daughter that I couldn't explain. I hoped so much that it drained me. I wanted to give up, but I couldn't because what kind of person would I be if I did? Nana and Papa didn't, so why should I? If it took a million years, I would wait. I would wait till she came home herself. My heart felt heavy for my mama, but I had no tears left to cry for her. It was her turn. "Do you have to leave tonight? It's freezing outside and dark, mama."

Her face was pink from crying. "Yes, they are expecting me, but like I said, I will keep in touch."

"Okay, but can we go to King's when you come home? We can order one slice of chocolate cake and eat it."

"Rosie—"

"Please, Mama! It will be nice to go out together by ourselves again." I asked lowly. My mama smiled and pushed my hair off my shoulders. "It's just that you do not like sweets much."

I rolled my eyes. "Who cares? I would do anything if it meant doing it with you." She hesitated to answer. My eyes are proud with harmless intention. "A deal on one condition."

"And that is?"

She laughed. "That you do everything your grandparents say and do not get angry if everything does not go how you want, and that I take you to the aquarium instead."

I scowled. "Yes, Mama."

"Good! I wouldn't want our day together to be about me." She kissed me on the cheek.

I would do anything for my mama, even if that meant she would give me her love. She gave her love willingly, but it didn't feel like it. Sometimes, I would have to fight for it like a soldier going to war. It was like a line drawn with my mama. I never knew why. I could say it was her parents or my daddy, but she had many secrets. I just rolled with the punches she gave. She zipped the duffle bag up and shoved the leftover paper on the floor into her bright yellow jacket. She stood up; her denim blue jeans and jewelry sparkled in the night light. She had her favorite faded and dusty cowgirl boots on. The shoes made tapping sounds as she walked over to the other side of my bed.

"I can tuck you in if you like."

I rolled over and smiled big. "I would like that."

She smiled and started to tickle me a little. "Little Rosie!" she said with happiness.

Eventually, she stopped and asked if I wanted to hear a story. It had been so long since she had told me one. Her stories soothed me every time. They mainly were memories of our family and Daddy. They made me feel closer to her, and I liked to think they eased her pain about him.

I placed my bonnet on my head before she tucked my sheets over me. She sat close to me, her wild, curly hair hanging close to my face as she slightly hovered over me. "What would you like to hear?"

I knew I wanted to hear any story she would be willing to tell. I never paid mine if they were the same ones. I was happy to be close to family in a way. Before she started, she grabbed my bunny off my dresser and placed it beside me. I took it into my arms. She put her hand on its face and rubbed it.

"Did I ever tell you the story of candy?"

"No."

"Well, your daddy bought it for you before you were born." My eyes grew wide and intrigued.

"Mama, you never told me. Really?" She nodded. "Mm-hmm. I was about six months pregnant."

"Cool!" We both laughed.

"Your daddy, lucky, had this gift of picking out presents for others." She used her finger to trace over my locket. "I do not know what trick he had up his sleeve, but he did it. He could pick out an item, and the person he got it for was in love with it every time." I hugged Candy tighter. "We were at the fair, and somehow, we lost Nana and Papa. But we parked our butts in front of a game stand." I yawned. "It seems you're more tired than I thought. Are you sure you want to hear this story?"

I nodded hard. "Yes, Mama!" I smiled.

"To keep the story short, we threw rings around some glass bottles and won a blue bunny." She paused and looked towards the door as if she heard something. "Sorry." She looked back at me.

"I was initially going for this hideous bear that I found cute, but he stopped me. And I asked why. He pointed towards this blue bunny that reminded him of blue cotton candy, and it was his favorite color," She flipped her hair out of her face, "I hated bunnies. They always scared me since I was a little girl, but he wanted it for you. I saw it as some plain stuffed bunny with a stitch in the middle of its chest, and I thought we could find something better, but he said no, you would love it." She paused again, rubbing her hair. I could tell the story was a sore subject. It was one she never told over and over. "I went along with it because he had his way about gifts, though we were on a date. He tells the guy he will take the bunny, and we leave."

"That's it," I say disappointed.

She giggled. "No," she said with a smile. "Lucky stopped about five feet from the stand. Mind you, I had no idea what he was doing, and he took the bunny from me, and I was confused."

"Why?"

"Well, he just snatched it out of my hand, and I think he was nervous or anxious because he suddenly knelt on one knee." My eyes lit up. "He took out a knife and cut the bunny in the middle of its upper chest and pulled out a little black box."

"Daddy proposed!"

She smiled. "Yes, he did. He opened the box, and there was an engagement ring."

"What did you do, Mama?"

"I was in shock for 10 seconds before saying yes and crying my heart out." I giggle with candy covering my mouth. "Not only did the guy not know your daddy snuck an engagement ring in his stuffed animal, but he foolishly hoped no one would win that bunny, for it would be yours."

"What did he say?"

Mama raised her eyebrow. "I don't think you want to hear it."

"I do! I do!"

Mama chuckled. "You know, curiously enough, I asked him why now when we already got a baby on the way. He said I love you, angel, and baby or no baby, I would marry you in a heartbeat. All I could do was stand there and cry while people applauded us."

"What else did he say, mama?"

"I'm getting there!" She smiled. "He shed a few tears but said that he loved me more than anyone he had loved. I was his blessing from the high heavens as he was a simple man. With the ring he gave me, we would swear to die before we fell out of love, and he would love me no matter the obstacle. He said— I was his one true angel."

She bit her lip and sighed with her eyes closed. "Then he put the ring on my finger and kissed my belly."

She said in a baby tone as she squeezed both sides of my face with her hand.

I didn't know what to say. Who would have thought my daddy's love was so great? I knew from tonight why she did what she did, but it was no excuse. She still had responsibilities, especially to herself. I mean, how could she let go of herself over love? I have yet to know what it is to be in love, but it was outrageous. I love my mama, and she loves me, though she has ways of showing it. I don't want to be like her. I don't want to be buried by a past love. I never knew Daddy, but he was a fantastic man and loved a lot. That love did not stop him from dying and me from being shielded from years of pain when I was born. My life was hard enough, and I didn't want it to be any harder when I became an adult. But I am curious if she pities me like I do her. We are two shadows doomed to be in the dark together. I just hoped she didn't stay gone long. I want to repair whatever relationship we have with each other.

I yawned again.

She smiled and rubbed the tip of her nose against mine, and I did the same. "Okay, I have to go! Goodnight, baby girl."

I had that harrowing feeling again. It felt like all my feelings hid under my bed and left me empty. I had to be overthinking again. I smiled and said, "Goodnight, Mama." She kissed me on the forehead. She picked up her duffle bag and stood at the door for all three seconds before cracking my bedroom door.

She had this regretful look on her face. And it was a look I could not forget. She was unlike herself, not that I knew her apart from all the drinking. She seemed gloomier than she already was. I tried closing my eyes and wished my brain would be quiet. But my body, against my better judgment, instead gave me images of my mama and how the fear on her face haunted me. I wasn't the only one to feel this way because I could hear Nana and Mama talking. It was so muffled that I couldn't make it out. All I heard was the front door slam, which woke Papa. He rushed to Nana to see what was wrong. They were in the living room for a while, discussing who knows what, and I could hear small sounds of crying coming from Nana. I didn't know why. We would see Mama, but then again, I never could understand adults.

I heard footsteps approaching my room door and closed my eyes. I could feel their presence in the door. They whispered my name to see if I was awake, but I didn't answer. I didn't want to have to answer their questions, nor did I want to partake in their "childish talk" about serious matters with Mama. They whispered again, but I tuned it out. I felt kisses on my cheek, and then the noise disappeared to the end of the hall. I opened my eyes again. I let out a sigh. I was ready for all of this to be over. For my nana and papa to have their daughter back and me my mama.

I wanted to be able to sleep at night. I wanted to be able to go to school and make friends without lashing out about rumors of my family. I wanted a crush, regular holidays, and pretty much anything a kid would have. I do to an extent, but material things were nothing compared to emotional support, which I got from my grandparents sometimes. I didn't know how long she would be gone, but hopefully, the wind would take her somewhere fantastic. I rolled over in bed and stared out the window. It was beautiful for the moon to keep me company. The only existing being that didn't abandon me and treat me as if I was fragmented.

# 15. Angel Wings

Small pieces of star fruit were placed down her lower leg. The baby turtle looked like an inanimate object as she put it on herself, and before she knew it, its head peaked from under its little shell. Its tiny body wabbled as it moved down her leg and ate lunch. One leg perched under the other. She was leaning back onto the couch pillow, absorbing the fact that she had been gifted an adorable piece of nature. Summer and Crystal accompanied her to the living room, each immersed in their worlds. Crystal was in the chair, tending to her company documents while listening to music in her ear. She had rarely seen Crystal so dressed down except when she was in a bikini. She always wore professional, casual clothes, but today, she had Hello Kitty pajamas, plain white slippers, reading glasses, and a bony ponytail. It is not of her character that she knew of, but then again, whoever knows themselves. People change every second and hour of the day. Nothing was ever permanent.

Then, there was Summer, who was napping on the sofa. She had a terrible hangover from last night, and it didn't suit her at all. Dawn had given his little sister his cocktail, but she threw it back up and decided to sleep it off. She wouldn't dare to drink more than eight shots again, though Crystal and Dawn found it funny. On the other hand, Moon knew it would be a long day. She didn't want to stay in the same house as her mother, although she and the girls were supposed to go shopping. It looked to her that it wouldn't happen if Summer was hung over and Crystal deep in files and notes. She didn't get an answer from Dawn if he was coming, and she grew restless because as much as she loved their beautiful mansion, she didn't want to be confined there, especially with her contemplating talking with her mother again.

He wasn't upset at Bronte and her mother anymore. In his eyes, none of this was their fault, which it wasn't, but the surprise attack on Moon was. He and his uncle went to make amends by going to spar in a boxing ring. This is a tradition for any time the men in their family come to a disagreement. The women, on the other hand, would challenge each other with horse riding. But, if it was man against woman, the only option was to talk it out or play a good pool table game. She found the tradition insane but appropriate. Where she is from, people go through a screaming match or fight until they're bloody.

It's been hours since Dawn and Bronte left. She hoped they were okay and didn't hurt each other. Because if not, then they would have to explain to his parents why when they came back into town. Mr. and Mrs. Wolfe left again for a major company meeting but would return tomorrow. She knew her grandparents worked a lot but still had time to be home more than his parents. Dawn and his sisters described their childhood: the staff practically raised them, and their parents were mere decorations. It was sad, and she understood that sadness. But who could ever really hold their family incompetent when their love overshadowed it?

She left the couch briefly to put Lin back into his tank by the entrance to the living room. She knew they would be companions for a while, and he would adjust nicely when she returned home. She lowered him into the tank and petted his shell. The tank was the size of a small box and had half a portion of water. It had pebbles and rocks at the bottom, trim bushes, and green plants, a large brown rock to the back of the tank, a rock for Lin to rest on, and three rocks stacked on each other, and the top of the tank had two large lights indicating a source of light for it. To add a little sparkle, there was a miniature picture of Moon for sentimental value. Luckily, Dawn had already set up this tank for Lin before they arrived at the mansion.

Before she could sit down, Dawn and Bronte dashed through the front door. They laughed and hugged before Bronte hurried upstairs, and Dawn headed to the living room. He was sweaty and tanned more than ever. Both smiled at each other. He walked over by her, bent down, and tapped Lin's tank glass.

He said, "Hi there, little fellow. Is she treating you right?" But Lin just retreated into his shell.

She giggled. "I guess that answers your question." He stood back up and rolled his eyes.

"Did a turtle just diss me, or am I overthinking it?"

She smiled big. "He has to get used to you, that's all. He has become accustomed to me."

"Yeah! Like in a day." They laughed at each other. "Did you name him yet?"

"I did. His name is Lin."

"Lin?" he said, unsure.

She smiled. "After my daddy. He reminded me of him because he is so charming."

He looked at her dotingly. "Lin it is, then."

He took her in his arms, and she practically squealed, waking Summer.

"Dawn! You are sweaty, and you stink!"

He smiled. "That's the smell of a man, baby! The smell of a man!" He laughed and kissed her cheeks.

She blushed and accepted defeat. "Great! Now, I am going to have to shower again."

He smirked. "You are lucky you're cute." She scowled.

"Boyfriend privileges." He said as she smacked his arm.

"You guys are so loud!" Summer said, raspy, as she pulled the blanket over her head.

"Sorry." They replied in a whisper.

"I thought you girls were going shopping?" He pried.

"Us girls?".

"Well, I mean, I know you want me to go, but—"

She pouted. "No buts! Please!" Her doe eyes expanded.

"Okay, Okay. Did they mention anything about it yet?"

"No, this has been the action all morning."

He released Moon from his arms and winked at her as he snuck behind Crystal and snatched her laptop out of her hands. Crystal was stunned, pulled out her earphones, and turned around to see who had taken her laptop.

He smiled and said, "Hello, sister." She let out a long sigh and held onto the chair's arms.

"Dawn, I am in no mood for games. I have things to do." She said tensely.

"Yes, I know you do, but one of those things on the list is taking my girl shopping."

She looked confused, then looked over at Moon defeatedly.

"Oh, I forgot, Moon. I'm so sorry. I got so caught up in my work. Maybe—"

"No! There are no rainchecks. She was looking forward to shopping with us."

"Dawn, I understand that but—"

"It's okay. I'm cool with just us going."

He shook his head. "No! You and Summer promised my girl a girl's day, and she will have it. And, as much as I love seeing her in those skin-tight, rolled shorts all day," Moon threw a pillow at him, and he laughed, "I have to think what is best for her and you guys, which is a day out of craziness for once and besides your work will still be here." He smiled at her awkwardly. It was apparent he wasn't backing down. Crystal silently nodded her head. "Okay, so good! We leave soon!" He clapped his hands and ran over to Moon in a funny manner and slapped her butt. She threw another pillow at him as he laughed and ran. "Love you too, rose!" He said content.

She smiled, her heart filled with happiness. Crystal and Moon looked at each other and laughed. Summer woke up shockingly, and she looked like a hot mess. Her hair was tangled, she had leftover dry makeup, and she was paler than ever. The only thing she could do was burp in response to the glances at her.

"What time is it— or more like what day is it?" she said, dazed. Crystal walked over to Summer and helped her off the sofa.

"It's time to go out like we promised Moon, so let's get ready."

"But I don't feel good." She whined.

"I know, sweety, but some fresh hair will do you good— and a shower!"

"Mm!" she said with dry vomit on the side of her neck.

"You can sleep in the car if you like, okay."

Crystal was put off by the stench coming off of Summer, and Moon followed behind them upstairs. She realized Summer was still in her clothes from last night and reeked of alcohol.

"It's okay, Summer. We will clean you up and get you some fresh air. It will do you good," she said soothingly, rubbing her back.

Summer mumbled, "If you say so, pretty—pretty Moon." Then, she smiled slightly.

# The Melting-Pot

The girls waited outside in front of the mansion while Dawn went to get the driver, but to their disbelief, he pulled up in a 1967 Chevy Impala that was a glossy dark chocolate. The seating and steering had the same color pattern, while the rims and car lights were silver. The license plate on the front of the Impala read BigD#93. The girls looked at each other, confused. Summer just moaned and hopped into the backseat while Crystal and Moon questioned Dawn with their eyes.

"Wearing all pink, are we? If I didn't know better, I would say I am being left out of the dress code."

Moon shook her head and chuckled. "On Wednesdays, we wear pink!"

He chuckled. "Let me guess. It was Summer's idea since it is her favorite color."

Crystal winked and sat in the back seat as well. "It was the only way she would come with us."

Summer slid her shades up and said, "Nothing is better than pink, and it might make me sober faster than your terrible cocktail." She threw the same blanket she had earlier over her to block out the sunlight.

"You are such a baby." He said while rolling his eyes.

"Summer! The point of coming is to get fresh air, not hide from it," Crystal said as she tugged at her.

Dawn's eyes were focused on Moon. "Looking good, baby!" He winked.

She giggled. "You like? Since we were going out, I thought I might as well throw this baby on," she said with a smile.

She wore the fur coat Dawn got her for her birthday, a skin-tight pink dress with the shoulders out, and brown stiletto boots with a pink bottom. That wasn't the only thing he noticed about Moon. There was something majorly different about her, and he couldn't pinpoint it until she did a spin for him in her coat, showing off her outfit. "Your hair is—"

"I decided to do something different. Do you like it?"

"It looks different but beautiful." His eyes were wide and full of glee for her.

She smiled and giggled with excitement. She loved how he got excited whenever her looks changed.

"It's not bony though, thank God, because I wanted it to be managed but still have volume." She said as she got into the passenger side of the car. "And, why didn't you tell me you had another one of these cars here at home? It's much nicer than the other one in Boston."

"Well, you look great, girly, and I am sure Dawn cannot wait to spend a fortune on you," Crystal said as she leaned forward and kissed her brother's cheek.

He side-eyed his sister. "Code for spending a fortune on you and them." He laughed as he started the car.

"I like that code since I'm short on funds," she said, laughing with Crystal.

"It's going to be a day." He sighed jokingly. "And to answer your question. I didn't think I was coming home, so it never crossed my mind."

"Mm-hmm."

"He would have come home eventually, trust me!" Crystal rolled her eyes as she sat back and enjoyed the wind on her face.

"Whatever you say, Crys!" Moon smiled, and so did Dawn.

"I like the whole bang thing going on. Did you do that too?"

"No, Crystal helped me."

Moon put her hand on his leg and winked. He took one of his hands off the wheel and held her hand. She squeezed his hand tight. "You know D jealousy doesn't suit you," Crystal smirked.

"As if! If anything, I am Happy Moon is making friends, even if that is with my nuts of a sister." He smirked.

"You're lucky you are driving," Crystal whispered in his ear. "You are going to have so much fun because we know just where to take you, and I expect you to have a buttload of shopping bags when we return home, okay? No being polite." She fixed a piece of Moons' hair, then leaned over to turn on the radio.

"Sure, Crys," Moon said sweetly.

"My sweet rose," Dawn said, smitten.

The ride was smoother than she had expected. She had anticipated endless roads and trees, but then they entered the city. They drove past many attractions and neighborhoods before reaching the shopping center. She could see that it extended beyond where Dawn had parked the car. Each storefront and building was pristine white with black trims, palm trees dotted the landscape, and the streets were bustling with people and vehicles.

They could spend days shopping there if they wanted to. She felt a bit nervous because she had never been around so much wealth, and it seemed that the people who frequented most of the stores in her sight had money. Although it didn't matter to Dawn, his sisters, or herself, it was overwhelming to think that people might secretly judge her for it. She hoped that other people would be as welcoming as the Wolfes were.

She was aware that her Boston accent made it obvious that she wasn't from there. She took short breaths to calm her nerves as she found herself in unfamiliar territory. It felt as if she were Alice in Wonderland or Dorothy in the Wizard of Oz, except she couldn't click her red shoes together. She just had a boyfriend with a private jet on standby. She let out a small chuckle because of how ridiculous she sounded. She wasn't heard due to the radio being on and Dawn and Crystal debating which store to go to first. She turned to the side and let go of Dawn's hand, which caught his attention immediately. She raised her hand slightly and suggested eating food before their adventure amongst the masses of stores. They agreed peacefully. Summer decided to stay in the car, and Crystal agreed to bring her some food back. Dawn raised the car hood and rolled the windows up.

Crystal stood outside the car, waiting for them. She was about to open the car door when he stopped her. "Are you okay?" he asked, and she smiled. "Yeah, I'm okay. A bit nervous but okay and starving." She laughed.

He sighed with relief. "I wanted to make sure." He kissed her briefly and told her to wait.

He exited the car, ran to her side, and opened the door. "What a gentleman!"

He bowed. "A rose as sweet as you! Why wouldn't I be?" He smiled. They held each other's hands and walked over to Crystal.

"Okay, we have three choices. The vineyard, Melting Pot, and Lily."

Moon thought all the options sounded terrific, but she would let them decide since they knew the place better than she did. "How about this? We let my rose decide."

He winked and put his hands behind his back. She didn't know which place to choose. All of them sounded decent. "Let me think." She looked down at the ground and ran over the names in her head again until she said, "Melting Pot." They laughed and said, "Our go-to spot!"

She felt at ease. She picked up their signal, but the name intimidated her less, and it sounded magical. They crossed the street and headed towards Melting Pot. Dawn pointed to a place that was similar to a cottage. It was garden—pink and had a hanging teapot as a sign. Various pots of small trees were in front of the place, and two large windows had dishes and cutlery sitting idle. As they walked in, she could see it was a small breakfast and lunch spot. It displayed more serving dishes, pictures of random people around the wall, and awards. They all sat down at the table shaped like a teacup. As they decided on what to eat, Moon spotted an old couple across from them sitting at the window and a small child reading a book as her parents silently argued with one another. Everything on the menu was expensive, down to the tea.

"Who pays almost twenty dollars for tea? It must be a big cup of tea." She whispered.

Crystal smiled. "It's worth it! I promise. If you want to order some, it's the freshest tea you ever drank."

"Yeah, everything is good. Are we eating lunch or breakfast because either way, I'm starving?"

Moon smiled. "I usually don't eat breakfast, but I'm feigning for some waffles."

"I think I will just have some tea. I'm not really hungry."

"Comes with the territory when only business deals quench your hunger." He laughed.

"Yes. I'm skinny alone on the paperwork." Crystal rolled her eyes. "I will get summer a Frenchie sandwich, fries, and some water." Crystal tapped her finger on the table. "She needs it after last night."

"Baby, ask for some strawberry jam; you will love it on your waffles." He smiled.

"Okay," she faintly smiled.

Crystal smiled. "Young love. It gets me every time." She wiped a fake tear off her face.

"Yeah, laugh it up, but I don't want to hear a peep when you're in my position."

"You won't." she blew a kiss.

The waiter walked over and took their orders; then Crystal headed to the car to check up on Summer. Dawn gently caressed Moon's chin, her smile radiating effortlessly as she held his hand. A few moments later, their food was brought to them. Crystal returned to the table to grab Summer's order before leaving again. Her tea sat there piping hot. Dawn threw a napkin on top to keep it from getting cold. The breakfast on his plate consisted of a classic American spread: bacon, sausage, eggs, biscuits, and gravy, but it was dressed up fancy with a cup of strong black coffee. Every item on the table seemed to be placed to perfection. Cream, butter, extra tea, strawberry jam, and their plates angled as if in a food magazine.

She had two waffles stacked on her plate with heart-shaped butter placed in the middle. She scraped strawberry jam onto her waffles as Dawn talked about his time in college debates and being a bookworm. She smiled as she reminisced about her college years of being alone and focusing only on her studies. She knew it wasn't the same because he still managed to have friends and a life outside of his studies. She wondered if her life would be different now if she had friends and hobbies beyond watching TV or writing mediocre poetry. But it was too late to know, and she had little time to dwell on it.

She took a bite of her waffle, leaving jam on the side of her mouth. Using her finger to wipe her face, Dawn passed her a napkin. Crystal sat at the table again, taking a drink of her tea in one sitting, appearing frustrated.

"I take it Summer is causing trouble." He said, biting into a piece of bacon.

"I love our sister, but her melodrama when she is sick kills me!" She said furiously. "She had the nerve to nick-pick what I ordered for her and demanded I get her something to cure her headache." She sipped on some more tea.

"Code for you put her in her place, and she cried." He smiled while drinking coffee.

She let out a sigh. "I wouldn't say I made her cry, exactly— let's just say she will be more understanding from now on."

"Did she eat—at least?" Moon said, worried.

"Yes, thankfully."

"Good. I don't want her puking in my car." He said, annoyed.

"She should feel better after she eats, but enough about Summer." Crystal smiled at Moon.

Moon put her fork, knife, and napkin on her semi-eaten waffles. "I'm full."

Full of anxiety, she was, and food could not cure that.

"I feel you there."

"You only had tea, Crys."

"Which was all I needed. Besides that, I'm ready to shop. It will clear my mind." She said, dissatisfied.

"And rose, you barely have eaten your food. Full?"

"I'm full! It doesn't take much to fill me up, love." She looked at him innocently.

"I see I'm the only one with an appetite at this table," he laughed. "However, I can finish early since everyone is ready to leave." Moon rubbed his hand thoughtfully.

"No one is rushing you, Right, Crystal?"

Crystal forced a smile. "Right!"

"It's okay. I think I have enough in my system."

Crystal looked relieved, "Great! I'll call for the bill."

Dawn kissed Moon's cheek longingly, and she kissed him back swiftly on his. He footed the bill, and they headed outside. They checked on Summer one more time before venturing further down the block. Crystal ahead rushed to a clothing store while they held hands and took in each other's presence and gorgeous scenery outside.

# Ethereal

Their first stop was Ethereal, a fancy clothing shop, which was quite underwhelming. The selection was limited, with clothes scattered on racks. The interior was just as dull as the exterior, all white and lacking character. The furniture was uncomfortable, and there was no music playing. Only a few customers would come in, make a quick purchase, try on an item, and leave. The employees seemed lifeless in their all-black uniforms. It wasn't her favorite store - not terrible, but cold and uninviting. She couldn't understand the appeal, but she knew Crystal loved it for its corporate aesthetic. Dawn was again preoccupied on the phone, unaware of who he was talking to, but the person on the other end seemed upset. Slowly, he stepped outside to continue the call.

Moon turned her attention to Crystal, who was trying on various clothes, from professional casual to party dresses. Moon gave her opinion several times but wasn't very into fashion due to budget constraints. Most of her clothes were thrifted, gifted, or lost without any brand name. She watched as the store employees catered to Crystal's every need, making her a top priority. Crystal's generous tips and the employees' brightened eyes at the mention of her name emphasized her status. However, Moon felt overwhelmed by the constant opening and closing of the dressing room curtain. Fortunately, she knew of other stores that might better suit her style. The current situation was quite disheartening. Crystal was wearing a long-sleeved jade-green velvet dress, twirling in front of the mirror and expressing her desires to the tailor.

"Moon?" she called. "Yes?"

"What do you think? Sleeves or no sleeves?"

*If I sit here for one more minute, I might bite everyone's head off. And my eyes are hurting from all this white in the room, and he has disappeared again!*

"I don't know. I'm not going to be the one wearing it." She chuckled, annoyed.

"Ugh! Okay. Leave the sleeves. I'm not a skin type of girl." She said sure of herself.

"Is this the last dress?" Moon whined.

"Yes, I promise." Crystal laughed.

"Why haven't you tried on anything." She said curiously.

"Well, I am too curvy for these clothes, for one, and I don't see anything I would wear."

Crystal looked confused, as if she hadn't thought about it. "They have clothes in the back for VIPs. We can have a look and have them tailored for you." Moon hesitated. "I— don't know—"

"No worries! It's a perk being a VIP." She smiled. "Okay!"

Moon smiled at her.

"Mary, can you bring some dresses from the back for us to look at?"

"Yes, of course."

Mary brought back three racks of clothes. Moon looked puzzled as there was no way she could fit all of that. Crystal changed back into her previous outfit and sat down next to Moon.

"Your turn, pretty."

"My turn?"

"With pleasure." Crystal winked.

Moon approached the racks and perused the clothing, hoping to find something stunning and more her, but most of the clothes were disappointingly generic.

She didn't find anything, but before she could express that, an arm extended in front of her holding a dress. She looked over, and it was Dawn.

"I was way ahead of you." He smiled.

"How? —you were on the phone."

"A hero never reveals his secrets unless you're Louis Lane and I'm Clark Kent."

"Or Peter Parker and Gwen." They laughed.

"Nice choice, D!"

"Yeah, this is so nice. I like it, finally something."

"Nobody knows my rose more than me." He kissed the top of her head. "Go try it on."

"Yes, please!" They smiled at Moon.

"Okay, okay."

Hiding behind the dressing room curtains, she felt like she was on a stage. Bursting out from behind them, she proudly displayed every outfit she could find. It was a miracle because she had struggled to find even a single outfit until now. Suddenly, clothes in her size and style appeared from the back. It was as if she had a clothing fairy godmother. She was grateful, but she couldn't expect Dawn to buy all of these clothes for her. In her mind, she had to choose only a few because she didn't like accepting handouts, even if they were gifts. Despite her usual fleeting happiness, today was different. She felt like she belonged and had made friends, especially the one she loved the most. The mirror became her constant companion, as she couldn't tear herself away from it. The dressing room was filled with piles of clothing, and she knew which ones she would take home. She glanced at Dawn to signal that she was finished and ready to leave. He winked at her.

"Mary!' he called.

A short, older woman with a grey bob and silver glasses hurried to him.

"Yes, Mr. Wolfe."

"We would like to purchase my sisters' items and the items in the dressing room."

"Yes! Of course, Mr. Wolfe." She smiled.

Moon, nervous and frightened, said, "No! No!"

Dawn gave a confused look. "I'll just take a few dresses. It's wrong of me to ask you to do that, Dawn."

He winked at Mary. "Give us a minute." She agreed and went to ring up Crystal's clothes.

He held her tenderly from behind and asked, "What's wrong? Why are you being so—"

"So what?" she looked at him reservedly; her feet were on his sneakers.

"Difficult." He whispered in her ear.

She resisted even though she knew what he was saying was accurate. "I just don't want you to go out of your way. You already do so much for me and buy me things." She smiled, feeling the coldness of his silk shirt on her bare back. He embraced her more firmly, his family ring against her navel, while giving her a brief kiss.

"I love that you think of others and how grateful you are for things you already have."

"Mm-hmm." His denim blue jeans brushed roughly against her thigh.

"But I would also love for you to accept the gifts I give you without a fight. I get it! You're used to doing things your way, but it is okay for others to give you things, even love."

"I know."

He chuckled. "Then why fight me every step of the way? — wait— don't answer that. I know why, but I'm asking that you put things aside and enjoy yourself. I'm offering, and there will be no objections!"

"I—" She let out a sigh.

"I love buying things for the ones I love, and I love you, and I like spoiling you, so let me," He whispered.

"Let me okay," He whispered again and kissed her cheek.

"Okay, love. I'll try not to be so—"

"Stubborn."

"Afraid."

His smile fell, and he became quiet.

"D!" Crystal called.

"I'll go pay for everything, and you just wait here and look pretty!" He smiled with concern.

She observed him going to the cash register before glancing back at her reflection and smiling at her beauty. An employee assisted her in unzipping her dress, after which she changed back into her regular attire. She stood at the store entrance while Crystal directed the store employees to the car. Dawn was finishing up at the check-out counter when Moon noticed someone watching her through the store door. The only feature she could make out was blonde hair.

She ignored it at first, but the figure did not move. Intense blue eyes looked back at her when the sun shone on the door. Between Crystal and the employees passing by, she did not want to alert anyone but wanted to be assured she wasn't going nuts. So, she quickly checked behind the door. Not one person was in sight, but people were walking the streets. She felt tricked by her mind and a bit stupid. She felt someone holding onto her wrist and looked behind her; Dawn was smiling and quick to kiss her hand. Looking out onto the street again for clarity and not finding evidence in return, she left with Dawn and his sister.

# <u>Sol-Mate</u>

"Mr. Wolfe!" sprang from the jeweler's mouth as they entered the store.

"You know I hate it when you call me that!" Dawn uttered in discomfort.

"I had to give it a try, my boy. Welcome!"

They both laughed and hugged. "It's been a while. Last time I saw you, you were just a scrawny young man."

"Eh! You know things happen, but I'm back now. How have you been?" He asked, while Moon stood behind him quietly and listened.

"I've been good, I've been good! Orders here and there, tourists, you know." The jeweler rubbed his hair back out of his face, showcasing his wide-shot and natural black smokey eyes.

"How've you been? The family?

"I was stagnant for a while, but I'm here and happier than ever. And it's been some years, but I kept in touch. The family is doing well as expected."

"That's good. Tell your mother and father that we should catch up sometime, especially your angel of sisters," He winked.

"I will. I'm sure they would be splendid to see an old friend." He chuckled and moved to the side so Moon could no longer hide behind him. He placed his arm around her waist.

It didn't occur to her that her beloved boyfriend hadn't been home in so long, which she knew, but at least it answered why people were so gleeful and doting towards him. His name was added on for effect, of course.

"Hello there! Who is this?" The jeweler gave a creepy smile, but he looked uncanny when they entered before. He exuded an unsettling aura.

Dawn kissed her on the cheek, and she said, "Moon. You can call me Moon."

The jeweler clapped his dry hands and smiled eerily again. "Such a pretty name for such a pretty girl."

"Thank you," she said, spooked, but Dawn was comfortable with him. "And what is your name?" she asked as she and Dawn approached the jewelry case.

"Bob," he said as he pointed toward his name tag.

"Oh, right." She said slowly under her breath. "I know. It's not the name most people expect me to have."

"I didn't—"

"It's okay, really." He smiled again. "I have such a plain name!" Dawn voiced with Bob, then laughed.

"He's like an uncle to the family, but mostly he is an old friend."

"I've known this boy since he was in diapers, his sisters as well, but such a lovely boy he is."

"I've missed you, Bobby." He smiled.

"I've missed you too. Don't ever wander too far again." He smacked his cheek lightly.

"Let's proceed then."

Bob stood behind the jewelry counter, pulled out a display of rings, and then motioned his hand for them to proceed with a decision. "Just like you like it, we made sure to get the ring size right."

Moon knew they were shopping but didn't think they would have anything ready on the spot.

"So, let me get this straight. You gave them my ring size, which I do not know how you know." He winked at her and Bob. "Does that mean you miraculously had all those clothes appear in my size at Ethereal?"

"Yes, to both questions." She slowly smiled, then bit her lip. "Why? — How?"

"Like I said before, I have a habit of doing things for the ones I love, and why not?"

"I'm not complaining. I wanted to know if I was imagining things or if I had a fairy godmother, but I see it was a fairy godfather/fairy god boyfriend." She laughed.

"You can say I am both." Moon nodded her head in agreement and rolled her eyes.

Bob elaborated on the meticulous effort to craft each ring and design; however, Moon could not resist scanning the store. The walls were painted in a deep shade of red, decorated with portraits of unfamiliar faces scattered across the room, except for one, which was the Wolfe family. To the left of Bob, a black door marked "employees only" stood, while Remington Chesterfield furniture was placed for customers to relax, with complimentary alcohol on the right. Classical music filled the air from the speakers mounted on the walls. The room was so chilled that Moon could see her breath, and the windows were concealed by curtains, letting in only a speck of light through the store. She wished she had never left her jacket back in the car, but what could she do? At least she looked good in her dress.

"What will you be buying today?"

"It's up to my girl."

Bob smiled. "Ah! Okay." He noticed she was a little distracted.

"Moon?"

"Mm."

"Moon! Moon!" he called as he tugged at her waist, snapping back into reality; she turned her head slightly and looked at Dawn. "Did you hear anything we said?"

"I heard you calling my name." She laughed nervously.

He shook his head. "She tends to wander off up there, sorry, Bobby."

"No worries. We all do it sometimes. But How about Ms. Moon? What will you be choosing today?" Dawn caressed her back gently.

She was a simple girl, not too flashy and not too common. It had to be rare and still catch the eye. All the rings were out of this world to her, but she couldn't choose. It was hard for someone who didn't wear much jewelry, only the things gifted.

"All of them are stunning. I wouldn't know how to pick."

"I can just buy them all."

she laughed. "Right! Most of these are close to a million dollars."

"And the problem is?" she grinned from ear to ear, but Dawn gave an impression of seriousness.

"No! no."

"Then pick one or two or three!" he said comically. *He is such a showoff!*

"Okay, okay." She snickered lightly.

The back door opened and shocked everyone but Bob.

"Mr. Price, a client is calling."

"Tell them I'll call back. I'm with customers."

"But they want to talk to you, and I already told them that. They said to mention it's the Ivories." He took a deep breath and stood straight. "Okay. Give me the phone." She handed him the phone, and he covered the mouthpiece. "I'll be right back. Take your time."

He whispered to the girl and then left. She stood behind the counter in his place. The collection of rings featured graceful designs with a mix of gold and silver bands. Some had a modern vibe, while others exuded a vintage charm.

"I can help you decide if you want." The girl, dressed in a denim jumpsuit and with her hair pulled back into a ponytail, said while popping gum.

"What's your name?" Moon smiled.

"Birdie!" She shrieked with excitement.

"Oh, okay. Nice to meet you, Birdie, and I would love your help."

Moon looked at Dawn. "It might be a while because I'm so taken with them all. I might get one, two, or three."

He smirked. "Yes, rose." He kissed her on the forehead and made his way to the couch.

After an hour had gone by, she finally settled on two rings, but only on the condition that Dawn also had a matching set. It wasn't up for debate since he agreed so readily. She envied him for it, especially when throwing out money like candy. For someone to ease through life with such a mindset was blissful because she never cruised through life. She always had to hit a bump in the road, be rational, or be of due diligence. She was thrilled to have a sentimental gift between her and Dawn; it meant much more than anyone could imagine. That's why she had the exact jewelry for years; they were gifts from people who meant the world to her, and even beyond items, she would carry them in her heart, gift or no gift. She would wear it every day until it became one with her skin. She knew it was over the top, but anything less than that wouldn't serve her, would it? What better way to show someone you care for them than a bond of significance? If it were up to him, he would likely have their faces plastered on billboards as a couple or her name tatted across his back. And she wouldn't like that much attention, but subtle hints are the best in any relationship; at least, that is what she thought.

Bob received an update from sweet Birdie regarding the requested order, and Birdie also took the time to wrap Moon's new rings. As a token of appreciation for Dawn's loyal patronage, he was given a gift on behalf of Sol-mate. Unfortunately, she didn't get a chance to see what it was as he was whisked away to the back by Bob before Birdie finished wrapping everything. However, she didn't mind because she had company and a viable conversation that didn't make her eyes bleed and her brain want to pop.

"How long have you been working here, Birdie?" Her ponytail flipped back and forth as she thought about it.

"I think four years, but it might be shorter than that." She laughed.

"Cool."

"So— what's the tea? How did you get an eligible bachelor of the Wolfe family to date you? Cause, I mean, every girl has been dying to infiltrate such an elite family." She handed Moon the Sol-Mate bag as she leaned in closer, with just a small enough gap of two inches separating their faces.

*So, he does have a fan club. I am not surprised at all.*

"He approached me." She said, relaxed.

"No!"

"Yes! He did."

Birdie practically jumped the counter while squealing. "Tell me the story!"

"I don't know. It's cheesy, really." She said awkwardly.

"No love story is ever cheesy." Birdie licked her braces.

"Okay." Moon sat the bag down on the counter. "We lived in the same apartment building for a year, I think."

She smiled. "forced proximity."

Moon laughed. "Something like that. We passed by each other now and then."

"Yeah," Birdie said enamored. "One day, I'm trying to move this plant. I started crying because it wouldn't move, and obviously, he swoops in and saves the day."

Birdie slapped the counter. "Why cry over the plant not moving, or are you just highly sensitive."

Moon said, stunned, "I had a family member recently pass, so it was the icing on the cake, I guess."

Birdie became sad. "I'm sorry for your loss."

"It's okay." Birdie nodded in agreement. "My place was a mess, and I still let him in, and of course, he didn't care. I asked him how I could repay him."

"He asked for a date." Moon snapped her fingers. "Yes! It surprised me because he was a stranger and not my usual type."

"What! He is so handsome!" They laughed. "I didn't deny that, but not to go into it. I just felt he wasn't for me, but anyway, I agreed, and he gave me his number."

"Then what happened?

"Nothing, but the funny part was I didn't even ask his name. I only knew his apartment number. I assumed it was the same with him."

Birdie leaned back from the counter, blushing, and hearts in her eyes.

"If it makes it better, the date was great and romantic."

Moon appeared flushed as Birdie gently grasped her hands.

"You are so lucky to run into Dawn like that. I couldn't get a guy to come ten feet of me."

"I don't believe that."

"I think it's the braces. A metal mouth isn't so cute." She laughed hysterically.

"You'll find someone. You can't rush love."

Birdie gasped. "Are you in love?" *Define love.*

Just as she was about to say something, the store door swung open, and out of nowhere, Birdie let out a scream. Birdie ran from behind the counter and hugged someone. Moon casually leaned against the counter, holding her shopping bag. There was a sense of recognition in the air, but when Birdie stepped aside, she said, "Moon, meet Rainey! My bestie in the whole world!" Moon's expression turned icy, and her posture became rigid.

"Hi!" She put her hand out for Moon to shake.

Rainey appeared identical to her photo, except she was thinner, and her hair was a darker shade of blonde.

Moon could not gather her thoughts, but she managed to shake Rainey's hand.

"Nice to meet you."

"You are not going to believe this!"

"Birdie, no." Moon shook her head.

*Birdie, I thought you were more civilized than this.*

Birdie shrugged her shoulders. "Moon is dating Dawn!"

"Wolfe? Dawn Wolfe?" Birdie was jumping up and down again.

Moon smiled strenuously. "That's the one."

Rainey chuckled and said, "Yeah, yeah! I've seen you in one of the magazines at the gas station. It said he had a new fling. You guys were on the yacht his parents used to use every blue moon unless they wanted to impress guests." Moon stayed quiet.

"I doubt you know who I am."

"I think she does." Birdie smiled. "Right, Moon? Or did you not talk about it yet?" Birdie smiled obliviously again.

*Will she shut up? Clueless.*

Moon became calm and collected. "I know who you are."

"Do you?" Rainey raised her eyebrow.

*Of course! I know you.*

"Yes." She let out a sigh. "What brings you out here?"

"Rainey is supposed to be taking me to lunch."

"Sweet! I hope you have a wonderful lunch." Rainey sat down in one of the chairs. "When is your break, Birdie?"

"Now! I'll run back and get my things. And it was nice meeting you, Moon." Birdie hugged Moon and went to collect her belongings, leaving her and Rainey alone.

"It's just as awkward for me being here with my ex's fling, so no worries." She fiddled with her nails, which were a dull shade of grey.

"I'm not a fling." She made direct eye contact.

"Hmm?"

Moon walked over to the couch and sat down. "There is no "fling." We're in a relationship."

"Oh, I'm sorry. That magazine must have been stuck in my head."

*Such a cliché! You fucked up with him and want to step up to the plate. A race you will not win.*

"It can do that to people who like trashy gossip, no worries. I was in that phase in high school, maybe middle school." Moon laughed with harshness.

"Is he here with you? Or are you shopping by yourself?"

"No. He and his sisters are with me. They are showing me around."

"They never did that for me." She said under her breath. "Hm?"

"Nothing." Moon rolled her eyes. Only a second went by.

"You're pretty."

*Why wouldn't I be?*

"Thank you," Moon said sarcastically and confidently.

"I never thought he would find someone after me, especially so attractive. He had flings here and there, but wow! He found a real beauty!" She smirked, wearing ripped denim shorts, a cropped short-sleeve sweater, and sandals.

Moon just nodded.

"Tell his sisters I said hi."

"I sure will."

"We all were friends with Birdie before the breakup." She whipped out a tiny mirror and applied clear lip gloss. "I don't know if they told you, but we used to wild out together, especially Crystal, and she wasn't too stuck up as she is now. But, life happens, you know."

*You're like a speck of a memory. I just want to rip my fucking eyes out.*

"Yes, I do."

Rainy placed the mirror back in her bright yellow purse. "You don't talk much, do you?"

She looked at Moon curiously as if she wanted to read her. "I rarely talk to strangers. That's probably why."

"I—" Birdie came rushing out the door, Dawn and Bob following behind.

"All set!"

"Okay, birdie."

Birdie had to drag Rainy out of the door since her feet wouldn't budge. Moon knew her desire to see a glimpse of Dawn, but he didn't bother to glance at her. Only Bob greeted her with a wave as she exited the store with Birdie. His eyes remained only on Moon as he stood tall, concerned for her well-being.

Fondling her hair, he kissed her atop the head and asked, "I hope I didn't take too long. Is everything okay?" At that moment, she wanted her nana and how ambushed she felt again. The happiness didn't dwindle from her body, but the peace was disturbed.

"I'm fine." She said tensely.

"What did she say?"

"Nothing."

"Aira? What did she say?"

She stood up from the couch.

"I'll leave you guys to it. If you need anything else, I'll be in my office."

Bob disappeared through the black door again. She wasn't too hurt, but it would have been nice to know that his ex was in town. Maybe he knew, perhaps he didn't, but she despised unnecessary surprises.

"She just boasted about the past, being petty and messy. It was nothing I couldn't handle." She smoothed down the collar of his shirt. "I'm sorry. I didn't know she was in town."

"It's fine, love." She smiled exhaustedly. "I'm just ready to go."

"Okay, we can go."

"What did he give you?" Dawn grinned, lifted his hand, and showcased a diamond carved into the shape of a wolf.

"Oh, it's—" He laughed. "It's a joke between us. I'll explain some other time." He dropped the little wolf into her shopping bag, placed his arm around her neck, and they left the store.

# The Social Club

Close to where they were headed, they saw Summer strolling in front of a spot known as The Social Club. Moon shouted, "Summer! Hey, Summer!" At first, Summer acted like she didn't notice them, but when she recognized Moon's voice, she swiftly turned around. A wave of bliss overtook her as she embraced her brother and Moon.

"I'm so happy to see you guys." She exclaimed, wearing an all-pink sweatsuit with Chanel sandals.

"Where's Crystal?"

Summer rubbed her temple. "I do not know. She said she would meet me here, but it's been a while since then."

They both smiled. "We are here now. Let's go inside." Dawn said, holding the door open for them.

As they entered, the place was a combination of a tattoo parlor and a bookstore.

Summer rushed to the register and asked, "Do you guys serve food?"

The cashier nodded and smiled. "Yes, we do; just sit down, and I'll bring a menu."

Summer desperately reached the table and rested her head on it. Moon couldn't contain her laughter at the sight; she had never seen someone so hungover and thought Summer would feel better by now. She sat down next to her and caressed her. "It's okay, Summer. Let's get some food for you, and we can go home."

Summer lifted her head slightly and said, "Home!" playfully.

Dawn shook his head. "When you're done eating, let me know how much the bill is; I'm going to roam the book stacks, and please do be inclined to join me, baby." He kissed Moon on the cheek.

The book stacks were like a circle of time. They were formed in a circular pattern, shelving leading into one another and extending farther back. There were only a couple of dining tables and lounge spots for customers. It was small in comparison to the massive tattoo parlor opposite it. She assumed it was because it made less earnings than the tattoo shop. It was a peculiar business idea, but why not? It's not every day you have spontaneity.

Moon's phone rang, and it was Crystal. "Hey!"

"Hi! Mo, are you at The Social Club with Summer?"

"Yes, we are; we found her standing outside."

Summer mumbled. "She's a terrible sister for leaving me."

"What did she say?"

"She said she loves you."

Summer lifted her head in confusion. "NO! I didn't, and tell her fat ass to get here, or I'm going to tell Mother how she snuck out, her first college year to meet a BOY!"

Moon tried to calm Summer. "Shush! We are in a quiet environment. Enough!" She whispered sternly.

Summer laid her head back on the table. "She's excited that you're coming."

Crystal burst into laughter. "I know my sister well enough to know she is pissed, but I am on my way."

"See you soon!" They both blew a kiss before ending the phone call.

"When are you going to be sober again?"

Summer let out a chuckle. "That's the problem, I am sober," she remarked, lifting her head and forcing a smile through the discomfort.

Moon would rather be in the book stacks with Dawn. She could pick a few books to take back home to keep her busy, but she foolishly volunteered to keep an eye on Summer. Not openly, but by her actions. She sat still as a rock as Summer quietly ate her food. She pondered about the tattoo parlor across the way. It looked decent enough to inspect. She did not want a tattoo, but she did want to take risks on the trip. She wanted to try new things she never felt confident enough to pursue. Moon's eyes wandered to where Dawn was, and she immediately saw him reading a book in one of the bookstore chairs. She wanted so badly to join him but didn't want to leave poor Summer alone. She would strike up a conversation; however, Summer didn't look up for it, so she just sat still.

She took a short, deep breath, stood up, and stretched. Summer looked up from her plate, wiped her mouth with a napkin, and said, "You don't have to watch over me. I'm fine now." Moon's body jumped with excitement.

"Are you sure?"

"Yes." Summer said lowly. "I'm sure my brother is waiting for you to suck up his air."

Moon grabbed Summer by the face and gave her a wet cheek kiss.

"Okay. I'll just be over there."

Summer wiped her cheek. "Yeah, yeah, love bird." Moon smiled at her before heading Dawn's way.

His legs were crossed, book in hand, and his face buried between the pages. She walked toward him at a slow pace. He dropped the book and pulled her into his lap. She was startled, hearing him laugh. He kissed her on the cheek profoundly and said, "About time." She glanced at his partially opened shirt and began toying with the buttons.

"I missed you from afar, love."

"Babysitting Summer isn't so great, is it?" They glared at each other for confirmation, then snickered.

"No, it isn't. I love her, but she is such a drama queen." She whispered amusingly.

He displayed an ardent smile.

"That she is, but she cannot help it, so we just leave her alone. Not when she is intoxicated, I'm not that shitty of a brother." He said idiotically.

"What are you reading?"

He waved the book as he spoke. "Percy Jackson."

She looked at him with a sense of contentment. "What is it?" he inquired.

"Nothing." He glared at her pressingly. "It's—"

"It's what!"

She chuckled and said, "It's nice to see someone reading something other than the classics."

"Uh-huh."

She rolled her eyes. "It is!"

He tongued the inside of his jaw. "You can easily say these are classics."

"Fair." She smiled jubilantly.

"These are considered children's books but still are a big deal amongst the average reader."

"Duh! I'm just saying that it can be a bit much seeing the same books get all the attention. There are plenty of other genres that deserve recognition, too. Not every book has to be a huge ordeal. Sometimes, it's nice to read something that's not considered "overhyped.""

"Ah yes, the personification of literature waging wars, I see."

"Very! Especially in categories."

"You don't say?"

"Yeah, the classics, smut, romance, and self-help books."

"Self-help makes the category?" He said, intrigued.

She nudged his chest and giggled. "Maybe." They kissed.

"You want to read Percy with me. I promise I am a good narrator," he grinned tenderly.

"I don't see why not." She winked.

Crystal bolted through the door. Moon and Dawn glanced her way, and she waved. Summer was unimpressed and looked back at her phone. Crystal lectured Summer, and as soon as she sat down and paid the bill, even though Dawn was supposed to, he kept quiet about it. His attention was on Moon, and hers on him. They read about forty pages of the book before growing bored, especially when everyone could hear his sisters arguing. He politely carried her in his arms to the stacks with him. Laughing, she was overjoyed at the time they spent together, no matter how long or short. He let her down from his arms gradually. She held on to his arm as he was putting the book away. What she didn't anticipate was for him to press her against the bookshelf and for them to share a fiery kiss.

His hand hiked up her leg, pushing her dress back slightly, caressing her thigh. She didn't move an inch with her hands close to her heart, letting him take charge as his other hand cupped her face, his thumb slowly rubbing her cheek. She then wrapped both her legs around his waist. Their mouths were hot with passion and moist with each other's saliva. He pushed against the lower portion of her body, the bulge of his jeans rubbing against her panties, making her moan and slippery wet. Moon's nipples became tender and rigorous, her vagina becoming soaked by the second, and Dawn's body exuded an immense amount of body heat. Dawn's breath was warm on her neck, his hand venturing toward her soft breasts and stroking them intensely. She let out a small moan that no one could hear.

Dawn whispered in her ear to be quiet, but it seemed impossible for her state. Her legs were still wrapped around his waist, but he managed to hike up her dress more and slip a finger into her vagina, their faces pressed against each other. His kisses became more profound and chaotic. She couldn't help but arch her back and grab onto the bookshelf, her eyes rolling, and Dawn took in her enjoyment. His finger moved faster, which had her on the verge of cumming, their kisses continuing to be sloppy.

They were entranced with each other, taking in every second of intimacy, showing their love for one another. Then, a pile of books dropped, and they turned their heads in sync. There she was, Rainey Crow, watching them as they were indisposed, but she quickly turned around, covering her eyes. Everyone was in shock, but Dawn and Moon quickly gathered themselves. He blocked Moon as she adjusted her dress and fixed her hair. Rainey turned around to speak as Dawn sucked the taste of Moon off his finger and wiped it on his jeans.

He looked unhappy to her, which Moon felt was understandable, but it wasn't Rainey's fault. They were in a public place. He glared at her with an empty expression.

"Sorry—sorry! I didn't know anyone was back here." Rainey urged.

"It's okay, neither did we," Moon said while standing behind Dawn. She peaked her head from beside his body and smiled embarrassingly.

"Are you going to pick up your books?" Dawn inferred, narrowing his eyes.

Rainey looked taken aback that he spoke to her. "I—yes!"

He turned his back to her and checked in on Moon. "Are you decent?" he smiled.

"Yeah, yeah, I am." She smiled back. He kissed her on the side of her forehead.

"We probably should get back." Moon nodded her head.

"Yes, that we should." Rainey picked up her books, but before leaving them, she stared at Moon.

Confused, Moon asked her, "What is it?"

"If I can say something before leaving," Rainey uttered nervously.

"Sure."

"NO."

Moon side-eyed Dawn. "She has something to say, let her."

*I want her to have the audacity to act like she did in Sol-Mate.*

He looked uneasy. "Give us just a second." She grabbed Dawn's arm and dragged him to the opposite side of the stacks. "Why not?"

"Because! She wants to—"

"Wants to what?"

"I don't know! But she is not good company, and I can't stand the sight of her, and it's unfair for you to ask me to."

Moon smiled with pity, fixed her hair, and said, "You're right. You're right. But what if she wants to talk to me? I can speak to her alone."

He rolled his eyes and threw his hands in the air. "I thought you didn't like her."

"I don't like her, but she wants to get something off her chest so bad that she ran into us fucking in a bookstore." They busted out in laughter.

"Okay, but I'm not leaving you alone with her," he frowned, "You know— my fingers still smell like you." He smirked.

She shook her head in disbelief. "Don't be a pervert. Come on!"

She pulled him along as she made her way back to Rainy. Clutching the books tightly to her chest, Rainey's nerves were palpable as she swallowed audibly, the sound carrying through the room. Her mixture of anxiety and excitement was evident in every fiber of her being. Meanwhile, Moon and Dawn stood firmly between the rows of bookshelves, their hands intertwined, creating a sense of unity and support.

"We are listening," Moon noted.

"And please don't make a full speech. We are on a time crunch." Dawn exclaimed rudely.

*Nicely said, love.*

Rainey stood tall; they could give her that, but she still seemed unconfident. "I just wanted to say to Moon that I apologize for earlier. I tend to get feisty around certain matters of the heart and welcome you to this part of town." She sneered ingenuine.

Moon realized that her sudden apology was a direct result of someone discovering the conversation she had with her earlier. She couldn't possibly be afraid of Dawn, so the only logical conclusion was that Crystal was the one who found out. Moon noticed that for a brief time, Crystal had disappeared into the library stacks just before they did.

"I really didn't mean what I said earlier," She gave a doe-eyed look," But! be warned like me not to step on any toes in this city. Outsider to outsider." She warned. Moon did not know if it was goodwill or not.

"Apology accepted," Moon said, shrugging her shoulders.

*Bitch is such a liar!*

"As for the warning, thank you sincerely." She put her hand over her heart mockingly.

Rainey's unspoken words were evident in her eyes, but before she could voice them, Dawn swiftly grasped Moon's hand and led them away. He intentionally left Rainey behind and cut off any remaining connections to the past. Once again, Rainey found herself abandoned, left to confront her emotions alone.

"Goodbye!" Moon heard from afar as Dawn pulled her along.

Dawn stopped in the middle of the bookstore, looking for his sisters, his eyes landing on them in a tattoo parlor. He kept pulling Moon along quickly as if he was running away. Crystal stood beside Summer, holding her hand as she got a tattoo. She looked up briefly to smile at them, then back at Summer's new tattoo, which appeared to be a dark pink dolphin. Despite being such a drama queen in everyone's eyes, Summer was taking the pain quite well, and the tattoo screamed soft-hearted brat.

"Crystal? I need to talk with you." He demanded.

"Okay." Crystal smiled broadly. "Can you hold her hand for me?"

*He is pissed, but why? I hope he doesn't argue with Crystal. If anything, she took up for me, not that I needed it, but Dawn has his hero complex. He likes to defend me more than he would like others to—sorry, Crystal.*

Moon said, with a tight-lipped smile, "Mm-hm." They both walked off, and Moon ran lightly to Summer's side.

"What made you want to get a tattoo?"

"I don't know. Boredom. I needed something different." Summer said with a gentle smile.

"Is she almost done with your tattoo?" Moon's gaze focused on the ink penetrating Summer's skin.

"You have eyes, Moon. You can see where the ink ends." She laughed.

"Right," Moon said, jittery.

*I hope I didn't cause too big of a commotion.*

Summer gripped Moon's hand tighter and said, "Want to get one?"

Moon's eyes bulged, "NO!"

Summer sighed. "You're such a baby." She laughed.

"I think you would look sexy with one. I think you should."

"Summer—"

"Come on! What harm could it do? You can always remove it later in life."

Moon played with the ends of her hair, zoning out into the tattoo, debating the option. It wouldn't cause her harm; she wasn't worried about an infection or appearing ugly. This was her body, a temple she was talking about, and she couldn't just tattoo any image. The tattoo had to have meaning, a significance that she could carry by her side for a long time. The needle stopped digging into Summer's skin, leaving the tattoo swollen and areas around it red. Some cold jell and plastic were wrapped around her ankle.

"It looks good!"

"It better have." Moon helped Summer off the table. The tattooist ran to the back for more ink, sitting Summer in the chair and perching her leg on a stool. She asked, "Are you going to get one?"

"No."

"Why! Why!"

Moon couldn't help but laugh. "I cannot think of a tattoo on the spot. Maybe another time."

Summer frowned at Moon. "You are just chicken shit because you would look so hot with another one."

"I highly doubt it."

"My brother would even tell you to get another one." Summer exaggerated her smile.

"Nice try. Also, if you know your brother so much, you would know he would let me choose."

"Well, Moon— I am disappointed because I thought you would want to venture out of your comfort zone today, but slow progress isn't no progress."

Moon bit the inside of her cheek. "What does it matter? It's not like I have an idea for a tattoo."

She crossed her arms and sighed.

"Think of a family member or event you cherish."

"No."

"What about you? You are a meaning, an image, a symbol?"

"No."

Summer looked defeated. "Fine. Whatever!"

Moon gazed up at the ceiling and shut her eyes. She was hesitant about getting a tattoo just because Summer wanted her to get one. While it wasn't a significant issue, she promised to leave her comfort zone during this vacation. Standing at a crucial decision point, Moon understood the significance of getting inked and felt unsure about what design to choose. Names were out of the question, and the pre-made images on the wall didn't resonate with her style. But she had already said no; she didn't want to backtrack. She looked back at Summer, her legs incessantly bouncing and arms still crossed.

Summer smiled and said, "Yes!"

Moon gave Summer a lack of eye contact, agreeing non-verbally to a tattoo, hoping it wouldn't come to regret.

As she settled into the tattoo chair, she prepared for the inevitable pain. The mere thought of a needle penetrating her skin brought to mind her grandmother's many tattoos. Moon chuckled at the recollection of her first tattoo at eighteen. The pain was unbearable, leading to her shedding tears in her nana's arms. The memory made her cringe with embarrassment; she was a teenager, but that moment made it seem as if she were a whiney child. She realized that with Nana's passing, there would be no more cherished memories between the two, only the ones they already made together. She would no longer see all the new memories she would make. It made her dreadfully sad.

*What would I suggest? I can tattoo an animal like Summer. A quote would be cute, maybe something random. I would need at least a few days to decide what to get tattooed. Summer is such a brat! And that makes me something worse: a pushover. I said yes just to shut her up and for her to stop staring, but I've been meaning to get a tattoo, so I'm guessing today is the day. What can I get?*

"So! What are you going to get?"

"When are Crystal and Dawn coming back?" Hesitation was written on her face.

"Don't worry, you do not need them. It's best to stay clear of them when they have their "usual" heated discussions."

"Yeah?" She asked reassuringly.

"Yeah!" Summer offered her hand to Moon.

Moon gripped Summer's hand and said, "72." Summer cocked her head. "72?"

"It's the tattoo I want. It's how long she had been on this earth."

Summer kissed Moon's hand. "Great pick." She smiled with moist eyes.

"Don't crack up on me, Summer." Moon giggled.

"How can I not?"

When the tattooist returned, she stated what she wanted. The pain was bearable this time, which she assumed was because it was placed on her shoulder, and Summer was by her side. Dawn and Crystal wandered back into the store and were in utter displacement, seeing Moon getting tatted. Dawn looked straight at Summer with a tilted head, pressing his lips together. He walked in a quick stride.

"Shut up if you're going to complain." Moon looked over at Dawn's displaced annoyance. "I decided to get one; I'm an adult, after all, love." His demeanor softened, and his ears grew red. "I would like your support if you're willing to give it."

I never stopped."

Moon smiled, overjoyed. "Then come watch me get a tat!"

His dimpled smile caught everyone's eye.

"You do not have to ask me twice, Mo," Crystal confessed as she sat in the waiting chairs.

"Yeah, dimples! Take a load off and let your girl exercise her right to scar her body."

"Who—"

"It's not the end of the world. It's a tattoo like the one on her wrist." The tattooist winked.

"Why didn't you say he was such a cutie." Everyone laughed in the room.

"I like for the people to be amazed on their own." Moon chuckled.

Dawn smirked. "I just wished you had told me. I would have been in here instead of outside."

Moon rolled her eyes. "It's not a death sentence; besides, Summer was here." He hovered over Summer's shoulder.

"I'm not moving from her side. So go endure over there by our lovely sister."

He nodded and kissed Moon on her cheek. "72—" his eyes became sad, and so did his smile, "She would have loved it." Moon's heart skipped a beat as she knew he would comprehend. Their bond, more profound than most days when he didn't, was a testament to their understanding of each other.

The needle sent a jolt across her skin, cascading as if she were a slab of meat, bleeding for a loved one. The numbers seven and two were embedded into her like a brand. The statement was no shorter than the reward of remembrance, a memory forever with her and of Nana. She had grown accustomed to being inseparable from her, making it difficult to connect with others, but with Dawn, it was a different story. Maintaining a facade with him was challenging as he could see through her, and she appreciated that. "Easy" wasn't a word that could capture her feelings for Dawn. Forming an attachment to him, like a slug, was an intriguing experience.

The completion of her tattoo was near. Summer sat beside her, happy, and Dawn watched her like a hawk. His overprotectiveness of her was sometimes over the top, which she could understand; it was what a boyfriend was supposed to do. Dawn was a different breed because he would overextend himself when it wouldn't even be needed. She felt the needle lift from her skin, the tattooist hovered the mirror over her shoulder, and she saw the glory that was #72.

Lightly sliding her index finger across it, she felt the soreness of her skin. The tattoo was not just a mark on her skin but a testament to her love and loss, a memory she would carry forever. Moon's face lit up with relief and joy, and she said, "Perfect," in a small whisper.

Summer and Moon made direct eye contact and squealed.

"All this over a tattoo?" Crystal asked.

"Well, maybe you should be next." Summer smiled.

"Not today." Crystal sighed. "I'm going to sit in the car. I have a call to take."

"Bye!" Summer and Moon shouted.

"See, it wasn't so bad, girly." She nudged Moon.

"I see," she said with a smile and an unfocused gaze.

As her shoulder was wrapped, she observed Dawn and said, "See, love. It wasn't so terrible."

"Mm-hmm." His hands were crossed over his legs as he was bent over.

"That will be a hundred and twenty dollars." The tattooist stated.

Dawn pulled out a credit card. "Here you go."

"D?" Summer called.

"No." he took a quick look at his phone. "But?"

"Summer, you can't convince everyone to get a tattoo. I get you want to bond, but no."

"You're no fun." She pouted.

"Be happy you bonded with Moon, okay." He pinched her cheek, then kissed Moon.

Summer rolled her eyes, "Okay, let's go already!"

He shooed her away while continuing to kiss Moon. Summer pulled at the back of his shirt until he broke away from Moon, laughing.

"Okay. I get it." He helped Moon out of the chair and held her hand.

As they left, Rainey moved away from the register, walking past them. She didn't even look at them as she quickly went through the door, leaving Summer astonished. Dawn smirked slightly, turning Moon around, her side against his chest, her body leaning back, and his hand on her neck. His gold chain was the only thing visible in her sight. Summer followed them, limping.

"Dawn! Really?" Summer exclaimed.

Moon held onto his inner arm and smiled. "Love!"

He kissed her and asked Summer, "Take our picture."

"Really?" Summer said, inconvenienced.

"Yes, hurry! It's about time we left."

Moon complained, wrestling with Dawn and giggling, "You didn't inform me!"

He smiled, "I just wanted to capture us." He winked at Moon, then stared into the camera.

"Besides—doesn't Marleen need some pictures."

Moon's grip tightened on his arm, and she said, "One for Marleen and us." She looked up at Dawn and playfully blew a kiss, and Summer captured the moment in photos.

# 16. Blossomed

Arriving back to the mansion, everyone scattered to their rooms. Dawn placed the shopping bags on the bedroom floor; Moon placed the rest on the bed and searched through the sol-mate bag for their matching ring sets. Suddenly exhausted, Dawn plopped down into the chair and said, "I do not know how you are still standing." She placed the bag to the side and opened the ring boxes. She placed her rings on her finger and then handed the other box to Dawn. "Put yours on love." He didn't want to move an inch further.

"Dawn?"

He sighed, grabbed the box, opened it, and put on the rings.

"Happy?"

"Yes." She said with a joyful smile. "I wouldn't want any less." He winked.

The pair of identical sets were both made of gold, with one being a delicate gold band that looked like a miniature crown and the other being a wider band with their names elegantly written in cursive on the surface. Inside the rings was a quote engraved: "You're mine—a rare longing." Moon charmingly rotates the rings on her ring finger using her thumb. She leaned back on the bed with her elbows and crossed her legs. She smiled endlessly because she had an almost perfect day, and with all the drama with Rainy and Summer, she could take her mind off of deciding to have that discussion with her mother. She did not know how to approach the inevitable. What would she even say to her mother? She could barely stop crying the last time they talked. It would just make her even more angry than she was by having another discussion with her. Only this time, it would be of her own free will. She sank into herself just by thinking of it, and avoiding it wouldn't help. She was at a crossroads again. Her mother was her whole world as a child, even when she would abuse the relationship they had, but at the end of the day, she loved her, and it would break her heart to never see her again without saying a word. She needed closure, and who better to do it than herself? Though sad about it all, she felt a surge of impatience and giddiness when making her decision. Moon's nerves began to be at an all-time high again as she rotated the rings on her finger even faster.

"Dawn?" she said lowly.

"Yeah?" He answered tiredly.

"If you had the opportunity six years ago to resolve any misunderstandings with your parents, would you have taken it?" He looked over at Moon.

It took him a minute to answer, but he said, "The truth?" Moon nodded gently. "If I had to do it over again, I would have responded differently, but I would still have left home."

"Why?"

He sat up straight in the chair, rubbed his eyes, and said, "Because I needed that time away from my family to discover my own identity and allow myself the opportunity to comprehend who my family was."

She smiled with uncertainty. "And— Did you?" She looked into his eyes for answers.

"Nobody truly knows who they are. You change every hour of the day. I did somewhat find myself. As for my family, they are just a product of their environment and, in a way, tried to protect me. I do wish I left home on better terms with them. We still have things to work on, but only time will tell." He smiled softly.

It wasn't up to him to decide if she wanted to talk with her mother, only her, and this conversation didn't help. Dawn walked over to Moon and bent down by her legs. He took one of her hands and kissed it. They both smiled. "Is this about your mother?" She nodded without saying a word. "I see. You're trying to see if it is worth your time to even talk to her." She nodded again. He stroked her cheek. She delicately brushed his hair aside and was entranced by his captivating green eyes. He looked at her with sympathy.

"I know— I know it's for me to decide. I thought—"

"If you heard my piece about my family, it might help you decide about your mother."

"Something like that." She grew pale in the face.

"You have all the time in the world."

She rolled her eyes. "How? We leave tomorrow."

His face became tense, and he couldn't look her in the eye.

"What?"

"About that— it turns out the jet's engine is having some problems, and we will not be leaving until the day after tomorrow." She looked confused. "There is such thing as the airport." They both giggled and smiled.

"Yes, but—"

"Do first class if you have to —but please do not tell me I must endure another day with that woman."

He looked at her with sympathy again. "You'll have to endure another day."

"Why! Airports exist."

He let out a sigh. "Because my family is here and does not want to attract attention, it's safe to say that we will take the jet once it's fixed. Everyone knows I am home now; headlines and news reports are everywhere."

She laughed frustratedly. "Okay," she bit down on her bottom lip, "And Marleen has faithfully sent me those articles." Dawn stood back up and sat next to her, and Moon was upright beside him.

"That's good you're aware."

"It is because paparazzi would trample clueless ole me." She laughed. He shook his head.

"Yeah, it's been a good six years of being invisible, but returning home has changed that, especially going to public places more." They kissed briefly and tenderly, gazing into each other's eyes and smiling.

"It's been a long day. I'm going to shower and get ready for dinner."

"Okay."

"Are you coming?"

"To the shower or dinner?"

"Both."

She smiled shyly. "Dinner. I'll wait to shower after you."

He smirked. "You're no fun." He blew a kiss, and she playfully caught it.

He stopped midway through the bathroom door and looked back slightly at Moon.

"I think you should talk to her. She owes you that much."

She looked down disappointedly. "Yes, she does—I think I will. The only question is whether I will do it tonight or before we leave." She fearfully chuckled.

"Whatever you do, I will be here to support you." He winked, then closed the bathroom door.

Sitting on the bed in complete and utter panic, she took a deep breath and left the bedroom. She tiptoed through the hallway, barefoot and clueless about the approaching conversation with her mother. Overwhelmed by anxiety, she halted before she reached her mother's bedroom door and sat in the middle of the hallway. Something was holding her back. She couldn't get to the door, the very door where her mother resided behind, and it was a few feet away. She could not move; the spot she sat in was a haven; it kept her sane. She tried not to have a breakdown. Talking with her mother last time wasn't easy, but she didn't have the strength this time. Every muscle in her body burned with the desire not to move. She twirled the ends of her hair, trying to calm herself once again and do what needed to be done. This was impossible because she had to confront the very person who was her first heartbreak. Flashes of her childhood warped her mind; she could not think, even breathe. Her body rocked back and forth as she buried her knees to her chest. The walls seemed to close around her, and the floor felt rougher than usual. The air slowly became unbreathable. She hummed to herself, a song she had known for a long time but couldn't remember where she had heard it. It gradually but surely began to calm her nerves.

It didn't alleviate all the pain, absence, and fear she felt because of her mother. Trauma can cause significant damage, with only a tiny fraction of the reward for enduring. Moving back and forth didn't provide much relief, so she curled into a ball on the floor, chanting, "You're safe, you're loved, you're okay" repeatedly.

She took slow breaths, allowing herself to relax and feel grounded. Before Nana passed away, she taught her to believe in herself. She said that whenever she felt unsteady, she should calm her mind and imagine that she was controlling the force that was making her feel unbalanced. Amongst the grief that has haunted Moon about her nana's death and reconciliation with her mother, she realized what she wanted from her was more than an apology, but a crucifixion. A begging for forgiveness and recounting all the sorrow in her life, she hoped it would not only make her mother feel terrible but also ease her heartache about the difficult life she had been given, even though she had a few bright spots among the chaos. Her cherry-red nails dug into the floor panels in the hallway as she gathered the strength to walk to her mother's bedroom door. The mansion was eerily silent, with only faint laughs coming from downstairs. A deafening entrance of despair she felt. She was passionate about drawing out her anger for her mother as long as possible, but she could never truly hate her mother. No matter how infrequently they saw each other, Moon's love for her mother triumphed over any pain that might seep through.

She managed to rise to her knees, fix her hair, smooth her dress, and stand up. Walking towards the door, she said: "You're safe, you're loved, you're okay." She knocked twice on the door, preparing for what would come, and stood tall. In a quick encounter, Bronte swung open the door and found herself face-to-face with him. A silent sense of relief swept over her face as she realized there was another obstacle between her and the conversation she dreaded having with her mother. Moon and Bronte make intense eye contact, causing palpable tension between them. She didn't know where she and Bronte stood after their last conversation, so she prepared for the worst: a door shut in her face. As many negative thoughts crawled to the surface of her mind, Bronte shockingly smiled and hugged her. It took her a minute to adjust, but she hugged him, awkwardly patting his back. Her eyes caught her mother approaching as she emerged from the closet.

Bronte released Moon and turned to her mother, saying, "Look who's here."

Her mother and Brontë had broad smiles. "All dolled up!"

He walked over to her mother and kissed her cheek, "I'll go find something to distract myself with," leaving them alone.

The expectation she had was completely shattered. She encountered no obstacles; she was surprised that Bronte was the "cool uncle" and didn't hold grudges as she had thought. He was mature. She had expected him to at least put up a front at the door, but he welcomed her with open arms, throwing her into the ring with her mother. The both of them did not know what to say at that moment. The elephant in the room was more extensive than either of them could handle, and staring at each other with weird glances and small sighs would get them nowhere.

"We can talk in the sitting room." Angel smiled as she tucked her hair behind her ear.

Moon clasped her hands together, hesitantly speaking, and nodded. She followed her mother from the closet to an office and then through a door to a sitting room. She was amazed at how spacious her mother and Bronte's room were. She could only imagine the number of entrances the room had. The luxurious room was spacious, resembling the size of a well-appointed studio apartment. Every surface was painted in a pristine white hue, consistent with the overall aesthetic of the manor. Dominating the room were two elegant doors leading to a charming balcony overlooking the expansive estate. Furnishing the room were two comfortable sitting chairs, a plush sofa, and a grand fireplace graced by a mirror. The color palette consisted mainly of white and cream, accented by delicate touches of gold in various room parts.

A state-of-the-art portrait TV stood alongside a neatly arranged yoga mat and a sophisticated nail station on the other side of the room. However, the most arresting feature of the room was an imposing closet. Ornamented with intricate carvings of cherubic angels and delicate roses, the pristine white closet featured two doors at the top and bottom. It stood imposingly across the room and captured her gaze. She had never seen anything like it before but thought it was the most elegant piece of furniture she had ever seen. Her mother had taste in décor and clothes like no other; she could admit that, but she had lousy parenting skills.

"Please, make yourself comfortable, baby," Angel said eagerly, her eyes sparkling as she gestured towards a plush sofa. Two exquisite golden earrings in the shape of roses hung from her ears, each featuring a lustrous oval-shaped pearl at the end, glistening in the dim light.

"Thanks." Moon plopped down onto the sofa, placing the throw pillows to her side, leaning back.

Her mother sat in one of the chairs across her, smiling edgily and twiddling her fingers. She opened the side table's drawer and pulled out a pack of cigarettes. *What is it with this family and smoking? How stressed can they be?*

Tapping the box on the palm of her hand and pulling one cigarette with her teeth, she stopped in haste of realization. "Baby? Do you mind?" She smiled with the cig between her fingers.

"I do, actually, and since when did you smoke?"

She shrugged nervously. "I guess I traded one habit for another."

Moon slightly rolled her eyes and let out a sigh. "Yeah."

Her mother threw the box and cig back into the drawer and closed it. She reached for a piece of gum from the candy tray and chewed it instead. Moon and her mother did not know how to start the conversation. Who should speak first among them? Moon thought her mother should speak first because if she did, she would not know where to stop, and it might end up with her screaming out everything she felt. The two couldn't maintain eye contact for long in the tense atmosphere. Moon anticipated their second meeting with concern but needed to address unresolved issues on her terms. Emotions swirled around her, leaving her torn between wanting to confront her mother, embrace her, or vanish from the room.

Under the evening light in the room, her mother appeared striking despite her inner turmoil momentarily masked by her enduring beauty. The same could be said for Moon; beauty and torment were passed down to her as if she were a prodigy in her family. The questions churning in her mind for fifteen long years suddenly vanished without a trace. It felt like her very being was being pulled in two different directions. She found it baffling that her reality consisted of reclining on the coziest sofa, wrapped in the burdensome presence of her mother. But, she knew, even without speaking, how her mother could see the pain she left stained on her daughter. Her lips quivered as she struggled to part them, attempting to form words. However, the only sound that filled the room was her heart's rapid, booming beat echoing in her chest. Her mother's eyes became glossy as she could see Moon's attempt. Spitting out her gum into a napkin, she said, "Aira? — I mean, Moon, it's okay, baby. I'm not going anywhere, okay? Take your time." Moon's heart burned as if inflamed; her vision was hazy, her throat parched, and her hands were like overbearing humidity on a summer day. She was crashing across from the person who could crush her into a million pieces or, given the courage, save her. Moon involuntarily burst into tears, her vision clouded, and her body wracked with discomfort.

"Moon? —Air—" Angel rushed over and hugged Moon, embracing her daughter as she had always dreamed, with no resistance, as Moon grew smaller and smaller in her mother's arms. Closing her eyes, she took a deep breath and surrendered to the flood of emotions inside her. It was clear that any resistance was futile. She couldn't bring herself to harm her mother. She recognized that her mother was the only "family" she had left. Her mother's cloying, overpowering scent of roses annoyed her the most. *She feels like home.*

"You've always been the silent type," Angel gently caressed Moon's arm as she spoke.

"The brightest kid in the family, so sweet and innocent," Angel cried alongside Moon. "Expressing yourself was the hardest thing you could do, but when you did, you set the room afire." She giggled. "I used to be afraid when you spoke your mind because you always saw through the lies and called me out on my bullshit."

"Ma—mama." Angel's eyes widened with hope.

"Yes," she said; her dark mascara accentuated her brown eyes.

"I can't—I can't," Moon cried.

"You can. Go ahead, tell me, tell Mama what you feel."

Moon whimpered sadly, leaving her mother's arms. Hurrying to the other side of the sofa, she said, "It's nothing I haven't said a thousand times in my head and to you."

Angel nodded, wiping away the tears. "I thought I had more questions or jabs to take at you, but if I'm truthful, I just wanted to see you again."

Angel's face was puffy and eyes red. "I wanted to see you again, too."

"I wanted closure, and it's not happening anytime soon," Moon sniffled.

"Okay," Angel said with a downturned head.

"We might not even have a relationship after today, but I just wanted to see your face. I've still not forgiven you, and I do not hate you because I will always love you." She fidgeted with her dress.

"Can I say something?"

"Yeah."

"For the past fifteen years, I felt like a deadbeat leaving you the way I did, but even if now you do not see it as in your best interest, it was, and I will stand by that. Your grandparents sent me pictures and kept me up to date on you. I loved reading your response to my letters, knowing I made the mistake of telling you I wasn't coming back even though I did not know If I was or wasn't yet," Angel said with a tight-lipped smile.

"It's fine—I know it was for the best."

"Whether it was for the best, I am sorry. I apologize for all the missed holidays, birthdays, achievements, everything. I am sorry, baby." Moon nodded, trying not to cry again.

"I'm happy you're here."

"Me too," Moon said, giving a restless stare.

"I don't know if you know this, but I attended your graduation. You looked so lovely that day, like an educated young woman." She cheesed as she wiped another tear away. "I wanted to approach you but saw how happy you were. I always saw how content you were. I didn't want to disrupt that happiness, so I secretly gave your graduation present to your nana and left." She exhaled. "Believe me when I say I've always been there for you more than you know."

"Good to know. There are so many small truths," she said as she rubbed her hand across the left side of her chest.

"Ever since you were a child, I noticed that you would have bursts of energy, and the only way you could calm down was to twirl the ends of your hair. It never dimmed the light in your big, brown eyes," Angel said with a smile as creases appeared around her mouth. "You did the same thing at your graduation, and it tore a hole in my heart to know I would never be able to experience that with you. My baby girl— my little rosie," Angel said as she put her hand over her heart.

Moon shook her head and said, "Yeah, I remember, but I'd rather not reminisce. It might get bleak from where I'm sitting." Angel nodded, her overlapping curls of hair bouncing. "How can you say that Aira—Moon? Your life was never too bleak. Our family had our chaos but happy moments more than anything."

Moon sarcastically laughed and said, "Let's just not, okay, but thank you for "being there" for me."

Angel looked at Moon regretfully, caressed her hands, and said, "You can be angry at me as much as you want, and I will happily love you still. I deserve whatever you throw at me, Moon." Angel removed her hand and stood up. "I promised to help with dinner. You can come help if you like."

"No, um— I have to wash up, so I should be getting back to the room."

"Okay," Angel said, disappointed.

"I didn't know you cooked."

Angel smirked and said, "The perk of connections is you learn to cook. I make a mean meatloaf."

They both chuckled. "I'll see you at dinner," Angel said, her voice trailing off as she gracefully left the sitting room. She wore a stunning red long-sleeve silk shirt and casual yet chic blue denim shorts. The outfit was completed with elegant white kitten heels, adding a touch of charm.

"See you at dinner," Moon replied in a monotone.

# Dinner

Dawn and Moon headed into the dining room, where a full dinner spread was on the table and chairs, ready to receive them. Everyone was at dinner, awkwardly enough, including Bronte and Moon's mother. The tension in the room was not too explosive but very present, and everyone at the table felt it. The food was passed around, and some began to eat from their plates; Moon felt all eyes on her. Well, not just her, but her mother as well. Which made it evident that the news spread through the house that Angel was her mother. She should have known because of the roaring silence and small talk that ended in seconds. She hoped her mother was still on good terms with the Wolfe family because no matter how furious she was, they had no right to shut her out; it was only the privilege of Moon because she was the one abandoned. She and her mother exchanged a few glances, adding to the room's unease, a heavy discomfort in the air.

Feeling the weight of everyone's gaze, Moon found solace in Dawn's comforting presence. As he kissed her cheek, a small smile crept onto her face. His presence was a reassuring anchor amid the tense atmosphere. While serving himself more meatloaf, he subtly attempted to break the silence, "Is it just me, or does it feel hushed in here tonight?" His smirk was a brave attempt to lighten the mood, but it was met with eye rolls from Crystal and Summer, a sigh from Bronte, and blank stares from Mr. and Mrs. Wolfe. Moon, however, couldn't help but laugh.

"Maybe no one has anything to talk about," Bronte said as he bit into a piece of broccoli.

Summer played with the food on her plate and said, "D is right; we usually have lively conversations, and everyone is so quiet."

"Most of us know why," Crystal said under her breath, her words carrying a weight of knowledge.

"What?" Dawn asked.

"Nothing," Crystal replied with an attitude.

Moon looked at her mother, who looked ashamed. Bronte reassuringly kissed her mother on the mouth.

"I'm going to say this once: mind your business; that goes for everyone at this table." Bronte's tone was firm as he took a sip of his wine.

"Leave what alone?" Summer innocently asked.

However, Crystal quickly shut her down, throwing a napkin at her and mouthing, "Shut up."

"I wanted to know why it was so silent, Bronte; I didn't mean any harm," Dawn said, rolling his eyes.

"I hope not."

"Don't we all." Dawn and Bronte stared at each other.

"You know I love you, D, but sometimes you can be a real—"

"A real what?"

"Piece of shit," Bronte smirked.

"Takes one to know one." Dawn cocked his head, twiddling his fork in his hand.

"Dawn." Moon gasped.

"He started it."

"Bullshit!" Bronte pointed at Dawn and then chugged the rest of his wine.

"Stop it!" Crystal and Summer pleaded. Moon's mother looked at Bronte to calm him down.

"There he is. The great Bronte!"

"A child will always stay in a child's place."

Mrs. Wolfe continued to eat off her plate.

"Oh—oh, now I'm a child!"

Mr. Wolfe slapped the table, causing it to tremble with great strength and presence, shaking everyone to the core. Everyone's frightened look was evident except Dawn's and Bronte's.

Mrs. Wolfe patted her husband's hand and said, "I think dinner is over; girls come with me." Everyone was still glued to their seats. Dawn's mother pushed her hair back. "Summer and Crystal, with me now. I'm asking nicely." Mrs. Wolfe bellowed harshly.

Mr. Wolfe looked around at everyone irritated and said, "Go ahead, girls." Crystal and Summer left the dining room with their mother. Mr. Wolfe sat at the head of the table, looking down at everyone in the room, disappointed.

"Moon, I assure you I am not angry with you. The girls do not know about the situation—well, Summer, at least. Only my wife, Crystal, and everyone in this room do."

Moon smiled lightly. "Thank you."

"Welcome—Now, I will take this as a misunderstanding because these two grown-ass men at the table decided to have a battle of the egos."

"Atlas, please!" Bronte looked off.

"Don't!"

"No, you don't! I love your asshole of a son, but it was clear he was taking shots at my future wife. By the way, no offense, Moon, is a low blow!"

"I had a genuine question! I did not try to disrespect Moon's mother when she is in the same room as me, not that I would ever."

"He didn't mean anything by it." Moon insisted.

"Didn't seem that way to me."

"Well, it seemed to me that everyone else was quiet for that reason, so I decided to find out, and here we are!"

"Who cares!" Mr. Wolfe yelled. "Moon and her mother settled it last night; earlier, did they not?"

"Yes, we did," Angel answered, and Moon nodded.

"There you go. So, there is no reason for you two idiots to be bickering other than your pride."

"Atlas—"

"No, little brother! I let you have your way, but I'll be damned if you ruin the rest of this weekend! Your weekend!"

Mr. Wolfe looked over at Dawn angrily. "What? You're going to lecture me."

"Dawn!" Moon gasped again. "Shut up for once." Dawn looked at Moon mischievously.

"It will do me no good. You know that." Dawn shrugged his shoulders.

"I love you, James, but grow up." Before Dawn and Bronte could say anything else, Mr. Wolfe said, "Let's move on, if not for your sake, your women." He winked at Moon. "Leave that shit for outside the dining room."

"Thank you." Both Moon and Angel replied.

"Now, let me talk to my son." Mr. Wolfe rolled up his sleeves.

Dawn leaned back into his chair and threw the napkin over his plate. "Talk?"

"Yes, James, I want to talk."

"For what?"

Mr. Wolfe left his seat and walked over to Dawn. Bronte instantly jumped up and stood near them, just in case, and Moon didn't know for what. Dawn looked unsettled, but Moon held his hand. His father leaned over beside him. "Do I have to ask, James?"

"Dawn? —Mr. Wolfe—"

"It's okay! I want to talk to him. I'm not going to kill him." He laughed, then kissed Dawn on the forehead. Bronte giggled nervously, and Angel gripped the table for dear life.

"Yes, we can leave. Just let me know when you're done, my love, or —"

Dawn smiled and kissed her. "I'll be okay. See you in a minute."

Bronte looked at Dawn and asked, "Are you sure?"

Dawn nodded, "I'm okay," he said.

Bronte and Angel left the dining room, but Moon didn't. She was hesitant. Her boyfriend seemed uncomfortable and wouldn't leave her in such a state if it were her.

Mr. Wolfe sat down next to Dawn, waiting. "It's okay, he will be fine," Mr. Wolfe grinned reassuringly.

"We all can pinky promise on it if you want," he said as Dawn did a slight smile.

"No, no, but another time."

After kissing Dawn's cheek, she exited the dining room. The servants closed the imposing, thick doors behind her, and she carried her concerns with her as she left. Even though she was worried, she held onto the hope that everything would be all right.

# The Fountain

The vast emptiness stretched as far as the eye could see. The main entrance gate surrounded the entire estate. All that could be seen was the night sky with the stars shining brightly. The horses stirred in the stables, cars were parked, the garden flowers swayed in the way of the wind, and the owls sang in the distance. Servants retired to their rooms while the driver took a smoke break—the gravel crunched beneath her boot as she walked over to the fountain and sat down.

The bottom of the fountain flickered with brightness as the koi fish swam in unison. Just as her thoughts became a prison, thinking about what Dawn and his father were discussing and why her mother and Bronte were frightened by it. She knew Dawn didn't tell her everything about his relationship with his family, only the surface-level stuff. His parents seemed decent to her, but who knew their full character but their children? They all loved each other, but she had seen over the past few days that it could only do so much. As she stuck her finger into the water, all the koi fish rushed towards her, each fighting to nibble on her finger, although it felt like a gentle kiss. The flicker of brightness came from the pond as the koi fish swam in unison. Her internal conflict intensified, adding to the complexity of her emotions.

The chilly wind gently caressed her skin as she concentrated on the graceful movement of the fish and the ambient sounds surrounding her. Tired of the fountain's allure, she shifted her gaze upward, captivated by the ever-changing sky. The driver stood by the gate, unnoticed by Moon, staring and smoking. She crossed her legs, adjusted her skirt, and ignored him. She wanted to enjoy the night but was preoccupied with the approaching driver. Her unease with his presence grew, and she began to think of ways to escape, even considering harming him. He only spoke to the Wolfe family and ignored her. She entertained the idea of using her heel to defend herself. She pretended not to notice him, but he halted as if a boundary existed between them. He stood there, staring and smoking, which made her increasingly uneasy.

She sat firmly and asked, "Can I help you?" Lights were coming from the manor, but it was pretty dark outside. He entered the dim light and said, "I don't know. Can you?" She couldn't make out his face, but he was average, with a crooked smile and a blue buzzcut.

"No. I can't help you," she said with a sigh.

The driver smirked. "Do you even know my name?"

She shrugged and said, "You never told me, nor did I ask."

He let out a laugh and said, "Damn." He put out his cigarette, closed his coat tighter, and smiled. "I see your nights not going well."

"It's not going bad at this rate, but talking to strangers at night, I would say it might seem a bit off."

She tightened her lips and smiled, "Can I help you with something? Weirdly, a man approaching a woman late at night screams stranger-danger."

He laughed and said, "I'm just making small talk. I'm sorry if I scared you."

"Mm-hmm," Moon said as she glanced at him suspiciously.

"You were all alone. I thought you might want some company. I know how the Wolfe family has so many arguments it would make anyone want a breath of fresh air."

"Here-say—and we're good as long as you stay where the imaginary line is."

"Got it," he smiled.

"What's your name," Moon smiled.

"Troy."

"Nice to meet you, Troy—I'm Moon," she said as she fiddled with her nails.

"So—what was the fight about? I'm assuming it was between you and Dawn."

She raised her head quickly, frowned, and said, "It's none of your business."

"Yeah! You're right. Sorry," he giggled.

"Don't make a habit of saying sorry too much."

"If it keeps me from getting fired."

Moon looked confused, "I would never— you do not have to worry," she said with a smile.

She looked at the sky, counting the stars, knowing no definite number existed. He side-eyed Moon, hoping to figure out why she was staring at the sky, eventually falling victim to the stars, too.

"Troy?"

"Uh-huh?"

Moon looked at him sadly, "I'm confused," she said.

Pointing back her way, "Confused about what?"

"Love, feelings, relationships—everything," she said as she rubbed her face.

"I thought it was none of my business," he smiled.

Moon sighed and said, "Never mind."

Troy laughed and said, "Okay, okay, I'm listening. Sorry."

"Mm-hmm."

"What exactly is making you confused?"

"I don't know. It's Dawn."

He smirked and said, "Okay, let's start there."

She nodded, grinding her boots into the dirt and gravel, composing her feelings. "I—I like him a lot, more than usual. I do not know how to describe it, but every moment is consumed with him. He means everything to me. I live and breathe him, I don't know," she laughed, confounded.

Troy scowled and said, "It seems you know how you feel."

She shook her head and exclaimed, "No!"

"Then what? Are you confused if it would last?"

"What do you mean," she said with a pout.

"Are you scared for your relationship? Do you like him or love him?"

"All of the above." He laughed and pulled out another cigarette.

He blew smoke into the air and said, "This will be a long night."

The manor door swung open as Bronte appeared. He called out to Moon. "Moon? They are still talking." Moon smiled at Bronte and said, "Okay. Just let him know I'm outside when he's done."

He nodded, "Are you okay? Troy is not bothering you, is he?" Troy flipped off Bronte.

Bronte laughed and said, "Troy—Troy, my boy!"

"Mr. Wolfe," he winked.

"You're in good hands," Bronte said with a smile as he put his hands in his pockets.

"I see," Moon said with a sarcastic smile.

"I won't be too far. And, Troy, you will pay heavily for that later."

"Yes, sir!" They both laughed.

"Hope you like shoveling horse shit," Bronte said as he walked back into the manor.

"Love it," Troy yelled.

Moon started to get cold feet as she discussed her dilemma with a stranger. What advice could he offer? Ultimately, she realized that she alone held the answers to her questions. Deep down, she knew this, even if it wasn't apparent. Moon needed to find clarity, not from Dawn but within herself. She realized she needed to search within herself to find the answers to her questions. She became overwhelmed thinking about the subject. She was used to giving vague answers to her problems, but now she craved knowledge. Dawn was someone she had wanted to be with for a long time, but she knew that just liking him wouldn't be enough. Friendship was great, but it wasn't her long-term goal. There were different types of love— friendship isn't bad, but it is not her long-term goal. But how would she know?

"Back to regular scheduling—look—I've been in relationships, and yes, I am single, but I can give you some advice," he said unconfidently.

"Are you and Bronte close?"

"No, but we fuck with each other here and there. He's the coolest employer of all of them; no offense."

"No offense taken," she waved her hand dismissively.

"Okay, so from what you said, things are going well."

"Yes," she said as she bit her lip.

He chuckled, "So, what is the problem exactly," he said with a look of concern.

She looked back down at the koi fish huddled together.

"There is no defining problem."

"Then I cannot help you."

"Fine! Fine! Fine," she looked at him hopelessly. "I do not know if I'm in love with him."

"But you like him."

"Yes, I like and love him, but I do not know if I'm in love with him," she said, her eyes full of worry.

"Only time can tell— and only you can decide that."

A tear ran down her face, and she said, "But—he is in love with me, and I'm scared of hurting him."

Troy painedly looked at her and said, "It's okay, Moon. You guys just met. And if you're wondering how I know, it's because we gossip a lot around here, more like eavesdropping, but that's not the point. There is no rush, especially if he is not. It's not the end of the world."

Troy could have been more helpful. She tried not to cry because it seemed like all she was doing was crying these past few days. She was ready to give up. There was no divine revelation for what she felt. He didn't understand anything. It's not that she felt out of time; it's that her heartbeat for him and her thoughts jumped around at the sight of him. Dawn made her question things and did things she wouldn't normally do. He was not an obstacle or problem; she felt she wanted to escape, but she was the one holding back. It was a challenge to put how she felt into words. While she loved Dawn and even found him likable, she struggled to overcome her inner instability. Accepting this, she desired to voice her feelings or find someone to support her.

He could see the distress on her face. "How about this?"

She wiped her doe eyes and said, "Yeah?"

"Say I like Dawn."

She laughed and said, "Are you serious?"

"Yes, say it."

She scoffed and said, "I like Dawn."

He smiled. "Okay, good—I love Dawn."

Moon rolled her eyes and said, "I love Dawn."

"Again."

"I love Dawn."

He nodded and said, "Now, say I'm in love with Dawn."

"This is stupid!"

He shrugged, "If it's stupid, why ask for my help?" He blew smoke into the air again, "Say it!"

Moon, frustrated, said, "I'm—I'm in love with Dawn."

He threw his cig to the ground and used his sneakers to put it out.

"Great, now repeat that and see how it feels— I'm going to head to bed. It's past my bedtime."

"Okay?" she replied in confusion.

Troy winked at her and said, "You will thank me later, trust."

"I'm sure I will," Moon said, annoyed.

He yawned, said, "It was nice chatting with you," and walked off.

"Yeah, it was nice," Moon smiled. "And no talking about this with the others," she shouted.

Troy looked back, crossed his fingers, and said, "I promise!"

To her, saying nine words out loud wouldn't resolve her issues. Once again, she was in solitude, enveloped by the night and surrounded by its elusive inhabitants. These creatures seemed to navigate life effortlessly, driven by instinct rather than reason. It was a stark reminder of the primal power of nature over structured logic. On that basis alone, she, as a human being, should know whether she truly loves Dawn or not. After all, aren't humans mammals? She sat next to fish that had no problem being huddled together as if they couldn't live without each other. In their way, she imagined they told each other they were "in love." The situation was challenging, and it hurt her deeply. Dawn didn't expect an "I love you" from her immediately, but she knew it had a more profound significance than the words alone. She yearned to say those words with conviction and unyielding strength that filled them with deep compassion.

Refusing to lose hope, she walked around the fountain, contemplating Troy's request, and decided to comply. As Moon ran her bejeweled finger over her lips, she slowly parted them, the glint of the rings adding charisma to her every movement. Mustering the words, she whispered, "I'm in love with Dawn." She repeated the cycle of walking in circles around the fountain and saying, "I'm in love with Dawn." Each time, the words grew louder and more confident, filling her with giddiness and causing a grin to appear on her face. She paused as she sat on the steps of the manor. The quiet made everything more intense for her as her feet kept time with her chanting.

"I'm in love with Dawn."

Her heart gave no warning; suddenly, she stopped speaking, her eyes widening in alarm. A chill ran over her body, causing her heart to beat steadily. Her face flushed, and everything around her seemed to grow still and quiet, heightening her senses and intensifying her feelings of remarkability. She had never experienced this before, an indescribable sensation. Epiphany—no, Awakening—no, Realization—no. She couldn't quite put her finger on it, but context clues seemed to fit the puzzle together. Her essence was disturbed—no—alive!

She placed her hand inside her blouse where her heart was supposed to be. As the drumbeat of tenderness echoed in her heart, she closed her eyes and listened intently. At that moment, there was no concept of time, no distracting sounds, and no other people to cloud her thoughts. With deliberation, she said again, "I'm in love with Dawn." The declaration caused her body to jolt in astonishment. She clenched her fist, nodded, and kept her eyes closed as tears welled up, feeling a sense of relief as she knew exactly what she felt—the *words*. With a trembling mouth, Moon said, "I understand now."

# 17. Fallen Dominoes

The sun peeked from behind the bed curtains, causing her to squint. She lay naked in bed, with her head resting on her crossed arms. The pillow beneath her was softer than a feather. Her hair covered most of her back and shoulders. She dared not move among the wrinkled sheets, with a vigilant eye, hidden behind sheer, white curtains with a wide opening. The same eye managed to catch a glimpse of Dawn standing naked in the window, observing the outside world as if hidden behind the glass, invisible and trapped in the very bedroom he could quickly leave. He stood tall, devoid of body hair except for his legs. His well-defined muscles glistened in the light, and his buttocks were firm. Though not in a rush, she wrestled with the thought of moving; she couldn't stay in bed forever. She flipped over on her back in one take, then sat up with her hair mess and was more tired than usual from last night.

Last night, amidst numerous existential crises, Moon was relieved to learn that Dawn had a meaningful conversation with his father. She had expected a negative outcome, but it was a heartwarming father-son exchange. This realization lifted her spirits, and as she brushed her hair back, hoping to dispel her sluggishness, Dawn seemed to notice her and briefly glanced in her direction. His jade green eyes, with specks of gold around the pupils, shone brilliantly, casting a radiant glow in the sunlight that seemed to draw you in and hold your gaze captive.

Moon instantly smiled and said, "Morning love." He winked at her and said, "Morning rose."

Dawn walked over to Moon, his penis on hard, pushing the curtains on the bed back. She gestured with a pat on the bed, inviting him to join her, and his response was a warm smile. He jumped onto the bed, landing on top of Moon, and in response, she giggled endlessly with love. He used his hands to tickle her, pulling her out of her body slump. When he stopped, he traced kisses around her face.

He managed to take a breath only to say, "It's family day."

Moon affectionately smiled in confusion. "What is family day?"

Dawn smiled again and said, "It's when my family spends an entire day together. We choose places to go hang out and bond." He rolled over and lay beside her.

"Oh, right! You told me about that. It sounds fun."

He rolled his eyes, "Yeah. It is fun when we don't fight for only two seconds."

Moon rolled over and wrapped her arm around Dawn, kissing his chest gently.

"We'll have fun, you'll see."

Dawn smirked at Moon tenderly and said, "Okay."

Moon closed her eyes and embraced the warmth emanating from Dawn's body. Her bare nipples were soft against his skin. His fingers slowly caressed her lower back.

A knock came at the door, and Dawn yelled, "Who is it!"

"Your darling mother! I just wanted to say that we will leave in an hour!"

Dawn smiled and said, "Thanks!"

Mrs. Wolfe did a faint sigh and said, "Welcome!"

Mrs. Wolfe's footsteps gradually faded, creating a faint and distant echo. Dawn whimpered loudly and embraced Moon tightly, causing her to chuckle while he kissed her on the top of her head. He used his hand to caress her bare ass in gentle circles before lightly tapping it and saying, "Let's get this show on the road."

As Moon and Dawn sat on the bed, he quickly picked Moon up into his arms and got off the bed. He appeared to be in great spirits, and she knew it was partly because of his conversation with his father. Among their many discussions, he mentioned that he loved Wolfe Family Day because it allowed him to see his entire family together, especially spending time with his parents. Her heart swelled with joy as she watched him in this state, starkly contrasting his usual nonchalance toward his family. He was genuinely ecstatic, reminiscent of a carefree child at play.

Moon giggled, then said, "Happy, are we?"

Dawn shrugged. "I will say this—I am looking forward to the day. Everything else depends on the circumstance." His eyes lit up with cheerfulness.

Moon kissed the bottom of his chin and said, "Okey, dokey! —love."

"But I'm not the only one happy. If you know what I mean," he smirked flirtatiously.

Moon blushed as if she had a crush and said, "I think you and him had gotten enough happiness last night," she giggled. He kissed her on the lips faintly, "The future can always change, baby, by sheer will," he jokingly said.

He spun Moon around in his arms as he headed for the bathroom. Her little feet were kicking, free from care, as her last day at the Wolfe Manor would be splendid. Dawn was happy; family issues had settled a little, and she realized something about herself she hadn't noticed before. She hoped the day would stay peaceful and quiet, but as Dawn said, "Everything else depends on the circumstance." She would graciously tolerate her mother's company for the day, determined to savor what was left of the paradise within the walls of the Wolfe Manor. She cannot say anyone can fix their family trouble in a day but wants to anticipate some closure for her and Dawn. And she would undoubtedly be willing to repair whatever was left of the relationship between her and her mother.

# The Beach

The Wolfe family had purchased the beach for the day to have privacy, but little did Moon know that this had been a tradition since Dawn and his sisters were kids. She never liked being around strangers, especially when Dawn became touchy-feely. It was like an apocalypse had cleansed the world, leaving only the Wolfe family and Moon. She had never been to the beach nor stood in the sand. It was like the world was for her taking, especially with such a bright turquoise, massive, shallow ocean. The warm sand stretched out in front of the family as they set up their beach spot, using colorful sun umbrellas and comfortable beach chairs to mark their territory. Strangely, the family had hired servants on call, tirelessly serving and cleaning up after everyone. A fully equipped outdoor kitchen had been set up for the chef to prepare delicious meals, and a charming little minibar was on hand to quench everyone's idea of a beverage.

The Wolfes had more family members than Moon realized. Suddenly, cars appeared, and unfamiliar faces emerged on the beach. Dawn's parents were ecstatic to see them all, while Crystal and Summer briefly paused their tanning to acknowledge their relatives. It seemed like a large family reunion as more than 25 people of all ages arrived on the beach in groups. Moon and Dawn set themselves near the pier on the beach but not directly under it. Music started to play, frisbees were thrown, people laughed and drank, and introductions were made as the beach came to life.

Sitting on the beach chair, Moon put her hair into a claw clip and said, "Wow! I knew you had family, but not like this. Is this why you were always excited about family day?" she smiled.

Dawn's chiseled muscles moved as he placed the sun umbrella in the sand and giddily smiled.

"Well—yeah! I get to see my cousins, uncles, and grandparents whom I haven't seen in years."

Moon giggled in shock. She had never seen him so happy. "Mm-hmm," she smiled. "I'm going to lay in the sun for a bit, so your time is all yours— for now."

He winked and kissed her on the cheek, "I love you," he said and smiled. "I'll see you in a little bit."

She smiled at Dawn as he ran over to his family. As time passed, Moon gradually drifted into a nap beneath the shade of the sun umbrella, the glisten of her sunscreen leaving a sun-kissed glow on her skin.

Her senses sharpened when she heard footsteps in the sand drawing near, then weakly opened her eyes. Suddenly, her body was lifted from the beach chair, jolting her awake, and she was baffled. Her heart was racing, and her mind was elsewhere, but she managed to grasp her surroundings. She knew she was still at the beach but was being carried. Once her eyes landed on a familiar face, Dawn, his dark green eyes made her settle into ease. It took her a moment to form words as he carried her across the beach. As they inched closer to his family huddled together, she could see Crystal and Summer jumping for joy.

Wrapping her arms round his neck tighter, she asked, "Where are you taking me?"

Dawn's dimples became visible as he smiled and said, "The family wants to meet you." He kissed her on the nose. "I'm sorry for waking you. I just thought you were soaking up the sun."

She groaned, "No, I was sleeping, but yeah, no, meeting your family is so much better," she said as she rolled her eyes.

He laughed, "I'm sorry, Rose," then stopped walking. "I can tell them, right now, that you're not up for it. Besides, I did rudely wake you," he said as his face grew disappointed.

She faked a smile to avoid suspicion. "I am awake in your arms, just an inch away, so I cannot refuse. Would you mind asking next time before eagerly taking me somewhere? Okay?"

He nodded happily. "Yes, Rose."

He kissed Moon and took a few more steps before helping her into a beach chair beside his mother. She gently adjusted her posture as she straightened up. She noticed everyone's eyes were on her, making her feel nervous. The children were off playing, and about half of the adults were observing Moon, with some smiling and others looking serious. Crystal and Summer sat on the other side of their mother. Mr. Wolfe was nowhere to be found, and Bronte and her mother were still on the other side of the beach. Dawn smiled relentlessly as he sat beside Moon, but he still noticed her nervousness and held her hand. His demeanor was bubbly and carefree as he introduced Moon to his family. He answered questions swiftly without revealing much. Everyone was making jokes here and there. Moon mentally prepared herself to answer questions because she knew there would be some for her. She had already had enough of everyone staring and giving mass compliments, though they were mainly towards Dawn and more so slyly to question their relationship.

The family seemed dominated by red hair on his mother's side. It was as if that was the only hair color she had ever encountered: the vibrant reds, the soft gingers, and the striking grey gingers. Dawn and his mother had an unmistakable similarity in their striking green eyes, a rare trait within their family. Observing that few family members had black or brown hair, she inferred that the captivating feature likely originated from Dawn's father's side of the family. No blonde was in sight, so Crystal was the odd man out.

"James! You are so pale!"

"It's because he never goes outside," Smokey taunted.

Dawn laughed, "I do," he said, then smiled.

"You don't handsome. I'm surprised we got him out of the manor this week," Mrs. Wolfe laughed.

"How long are you going to be here?" Cousin Adrian asked as he stuffed his face with steak.

"Yeah, we missed you, James," Cousin Connor said, softly punching Dawn on the arm.

"You should visit more!"

"Your car is hot shit! I haven't seen you drive in so long."

Mr. Wolfe appeared behind Dawn, "Woah! Back off of my son! One question at a time," he said as he placed his hands on Dawn's shoulders.

"Thanks, Father." Dawn smiled shyly in relief.

"They are just excited to see him," Mrs. Wolfe voiced.

Moon kissed Dawn on the cheek, noticing how cute he looked as his family interrogated him. They seemed normal, not too harsh, but that could be what six years apart does. Dawn kissed her back, and everyone started swooning over them like celebrities.

"Aww, they are so cute!"

"She's so pretty! James, how did you pick her up?"

"He stalked her. It's a Wolfe mentality," Crystal laughed.

Dawn tossed sand at her, "Ha, ha!" and rolled his eyes. Crystal threw sand back at him, and Summer got some in her eye and screamed. "Okay, okay, stop throwing sand," Mr. Wolfe demanded. "Crystal, help your sister get sand out of her eye before she collapses."

Crystal sighed and said, "Fine. Even though he was the one to throw the sand!"

Summer started to whimper. "It hurts! I hate you guys!"

Crystal smirked and said, "Come on!"

"Sorry, sis!" Dawn shouted in regret.

"We know, honey," Mrs. Wolfe said with a smile.

"Yeah, whatever!" Crystal shouted back.

"No more sand, please, James," Mr. Wolfe scolded Dawn.

"I said sorry," he said with a shrug, his arm around Moon's waist as she rested her head on his shoulder.

The circle tightened, and two older women positioned themselves in front of everyone, exuding an air of control over the space. Everyone who was yapping at first moved to the back of them. Something ominous was imminent, and the tingling at the end of her toes warned her to dread it. Moon tugged at the claw clip in her hair, feeling uneasy. Mrs. Wolfe helped her remove it, and Moon shook her head, letting her hair fall onto her shoulders.

Mrs. Wolfe said, "Is that better?"

Moon nodded and smiled. "Yes, thank you."

"Moon, is it?" The older woman asked.

"It's okay, rose; these are my grandmothers, Pearl and Cora."

"Yes, Pearl is my mother," Mrs. Wolfe smiled.

"And Cora is mine," Mr. Wolfe frowned.

"Nice to meet both of you. And—I am Moon," she said as she smiled.

"What is your Last name?" They asked.

"Moon." Both women laughed at what she said. "Your name is Moon, Moon?" Cora Asked.

Moon was embarrassed but said, "No—um, my full name is Aira Moon, but I prefer people to call me Moon."

"Aira is such a pretty name."

"Yes! I don't know why you would prefer Moon over it."

"It's a long story, Grandmothers," Dawn said sweetly.

"Understood!"

"Mm-hmm—so is this serious?" Cora asked firmly.

"or just for fun?" Pearl Asked.

"Grandmothers!" Dawn shouted.

"Mother! Pearl!" Mrs. Wolfe shouted.

Mr. Wolfe just sighed as he sat next to his wife.

"What? Are we not allowed to ask questions," Cora said nosily.

"I—" Dawn stumbled with his words.

"It's very serious, and we love each other," Moon interjected, "No, I'm not using your grandson, nor do I plan to. I'm from Boston, and I've never had a boyfriend. I am a Virgo. I have a moon-shaped birthmark on my lower back. My favorite color is red, and I'm not too fond of winter. Does that answer most of your questions, or should I keep going?" Moon said, staring at Cora and Pearl with curiosity.

Cora smirked proudly and said, "I like you." She pulled out a cigarette, and Pearl lit it. "Spirited!"

Pearl laughed and said, "Our grandson is a Wolfe. We know all there is to know about you— and what our beloved children sent us. No one comes into the family without background checks. We wanted to see what you were like." Cora passed the cig for Pearl to smoke.

"That's good to know," Moon giggled.

"Gorgeous, too!" Cora said as her ginger-grey bob moved effortlessly.

Pearl blew smoke into hearts and said, "Better than any others we met." She grinned, her two gold front teeth showing. "You're lovely as well," Moon winked.

Cora chuckled, "Well, thank you, we try to be."

"Now, tell us everything!" Dawn's grandmothers lovingly grasped Moon's hands, forming a touching connection.

Everyone's faces began smiling again, and they huddled around Moon and Dawn, asking more questions, sharing stories, and making plans for the future. Summer, who returned with an eye patch due to irritation from the sand, decided to stay at the beach.

During the Wolfe's family day tradition, they held a castle-building competition. Moon wasn't interested in architecture, so she hoped Dawn would take the lead. Initially, Moon tried to excuse herself from the competition, but everyone insisted that she participate and assured her that she would enjoy it. Each team represented a family, and the winners received a prize of $100,000 along with bragging rights. The entire family had to participate, and there would be a total of four rounds, with each round involving building the castle from the foundation and upwards. Before the competition, Dawn and his sisters disagreed over strategy, but his mother assured Moon that they did this every family day. She was used to their sibling rivalry; if anything, it made her laugh.

Out of the corner of her eye, she caught sight of Dawn's father engaged in a heated argument with his mother, and the exchange didn't appear to be agreeable. She couldn't help but wonder whether anyone else had noticed, but it seemed to be a widely held assumption that Mr. Wolfe harbored a profound dislike for his mother, evident solely from his demeanor. On some level, she could relate to Mr. Wolfe; not everyone's first love is their mother or father. Sometimes, a person's worst enemy is their parents upon their first breath coming into the world, before their feet even touch the sacred ground they call earth.

Mrs. Wolfe, standing next to Moon, affectionately wrapped her arm around her and drew her close for a gentle side hug, "You're doing great, so don't worry," she smiled.

"Thanks, I'm just nervous about the competition; I've never built anything before."

Mrs. Wolfe laughed and said, "I never will, as often as we have done this competition. I can never say I built a sandcastle, but I still try."

"At least I'm not alone," Moon said as she laughed.

."We are all in the same boat, except for my children, who are adept at this. It's nice because, for once, we did something right by them."

"I'm just happy to be out of the manor and to meet everyone. I hope I wasn't too energetic back there."

"Oh no! You were great! Our mothers have been like that forever. Our family has grown soft over the years, so you are safe. Imagine the Wolfes and Hawks 30 years ago," Mrs. Wolfe smiled cheekily.

"If only. And— not to pry but —"

"My husband and his mother have been like that for years."

"Oh, okay. I know how that can hurt."

"Do not worry! Atlas instructed everyone in the family not to intervene. But who doesn't have parental issues, am I right?"

"Right—" Moon nodded.

"Not to be insensitive of your case, of course."

Moon laughed, "No offense taken. And where are their grandfathers, if I may ask?"

Mrs. Wolfe chuckled violently, "Mines is somewhere in Europe with his new wife, and younger if I may add," her face riddled with disgust, then softened, "My husband's father, Dawn's real grandfather, died on his 49th birthday. A heart attack." Both of them were silent. "My condolences to both of you."

Mrs. Wolfe laughed again but lightly and more genuinely. "Thank you! It's hard losing family. I know Atlas was closer to his father than his mother. Not that I do not love Pearl, but she can be more of a sergeant than a mother."

"What was his father like?"

"He was down to earth, kind, and well-spoken. He was an angel, truly, and there is no other word to describe him."

She lightly fiddled with Moon's hair. "My condolences for your nana. I heard she was a lovely woman."

Moon smiled, then said, "Thank you, and things will work out."

Mrs. Wolfe nodded and took a sip of her martini. "We can only hope."

She glanced at Moon enduringly, "Good luck on behalf of my husband and me, little rose," she said, winking, then walked over to Mr. Wolfe and his mother.

As the family gathered around, one of the members enthusiastically grabbed the microphone and began explaining the game's particulars to all the participants. Anyone eager to join was allotted ten minutes to prepare and take their designated spots. Amidst the growing anticipation, Summer stepped forward to kick off the first round. Meanwhile, Dawn pulled Moon and Crystal aside to discuss game strategy. After huddling up like football players, Dawn clapped his hands together, and they broke apart to cheer on Summer. Moon thought he looked attractive when serious about competition. It was the most carefree she had seen him. Everyone didn't seem cold towards each other anymore, and like children, the way their eyes lit up for the game. He jumped around with his cousins and father, shocking Moon. Their team was ahead of everyone, but she needed to figure out how long it would last because she wasn't sure if she could lead them to success after Crystal or Dawn's turn.

Summer and Dawn swiftly switched positions as the second round of the game began. Dawn charged into the game with determination as if preparing for battle. However, there was a subtle yet significant handshake between Summer and Dawn as they swapped out what caught Moon's attention. This small gesture reflected their strong bond, a connection that the Wolfe family may not have fully realized. Moon couldn't help but smile at the interaction between the two. Summer hugged Moon, kissed her cheek, and said, "Good luck, lovely," before rushing to Cora, her grandmother. Summer slid onto her grandmother's lap like a child, her grandmother playing in her hair and speaking in a foreign language. Moon couldn't understand, but it sounded like Latin or Spanish.

As Crystal clung to Moon's hand, a sense of calm washed over her, infusing her with the hope that she would swiftly secure victory in the final round after Crystal. Leaning her head on Moon's shoulder, she managed a serene smile while maintaining her unwavering focus on Dawn and whispered, "You're worried about the game?"

"Somewhat. I'm not good with crowds and competitiveness," she said through gritted teeth.

Crystal chuckled, "No one truly has confidence, Moon. You'll do great; besides, I'm freaking out about going next."

"Really," Moon said as she turned to look at Crystal.

"Yeah! I hate this fucking game ever since we were kids, but it always brought us together, so I suck it up and play to my best ability. Can you believe that?"

"Yes, I can, but I can't believe I'm going to build a castle from sand." Moon giggled.

"They didn't tell you?" Crystal lifted her head and looked at Moon.

"What?"

"You didn't pay attention to the instructions, did you?" Moon shook her head.

"The last round is a race to put your team's flag on the castle, not building, so— there isn't much to worry about."

"Race? Running? I think you all want to kill me." She said, inconvenienced and nervously.

"No. We want you to lose weight." Moon pushed Crystal's shoulder lightly, and Crystal laughed.

"Not funny!"

"Lightened the mood, didn't it?"

Moon rolled her eyes, smirked, and said, "You can say that."

Crystal leaned back against Moon's shoulder as they watched the competition. Dawn was focused as he smoothed the castle's edges and created new pieces. The enlargement of his dark green pupils revealed his determination to win. The veins in his hands bulged as he manipulated the sand as if it were nothing, highlighting the sharpness of his jawline. The definition of his chest was accentuated with every breath he took. His hair was disheveled and damp, and his tan was darker than before. He was a work of art to her, and she adored it. His beauty was unyielding, and she could gaze at him every hour and every second of the day. Moon licked her lips at the thought of his hands all over her. She would be the castle if she could, but at least it was safe to say that he finished ahead of the others before the horn blew. The sound of the horn snapped Crystal into action as she transformed into a beast, sprinting with all her might toward the castle. On the other hand, Moon was left alone and watched as Crystal ran ahead. Feeling nostalgic, Crystal then performed the same handshake that Summer and Dawn had.

Dawn rushed over and hugged Moon from behind, kissing her cheek. Moon stood on her tippytoes, her feet no longer feeling the scorching hot sand. She smiled as she welcomed Dawn's warm embrace, hoping to be in the moment forever. As everyone became more tense as the last round was nearing, Crystal looked at Moon for reassurance, and Moon gave her a thumbs up. Crystal smiled and moved faster than ever, making Dawn grin widely. Moon placed her hands on top of his, her thumb caressing his hand, daydreaming about life.

He hugged her tighter and said, "It's almost time."

Moon's heart started to race again. "Is it too late for me to back out?"

Dawn laughed, "Yes, unfortunately."

Moon could feel her palms beginning to sweat and her ears becoming hot.

"Please, Dawn," she pleaded with fear in her eyes.

"Hey—hey, it's okay, baby," he said as he kissed her forehead.

"I'm scared. It's like the horse all over again."

He smiled and said, "Did you not prevail in that?" She nodded in agreement. "It's not over yet, but you are ready, and I believe in you. There is no judgment if you do not win. It's for fun."

"So, you say."

"It is," He turned Moon around to look at him, "You have to be confident. Believe! In yourself!"

The horn sounded, signaling Moon's turn. They embraced each other once more, sharing a hug.

"Do us proud." He patted her on the ass as she ran to her place. Crystal stopped her midway to do the handshake, and surprisingly, she caught on quickly.

She strolled over to the imaginary starting line, joining five others already in their places. She got into the runner's position. Fortunately, she had some experience in track for a short time, so the race should be a piece of cake—assuming her anxiety didn't initially overwhelm her. The ringing in her ears grew louder, especially as she could hear Dawn and his family cheering her on. It was heartfelt for her to hear that. She squinted and saw her mother and Bronte standing next to Dawn. Then, her heart swelled with happiness. They had walked over to this side of the beach to watch her. She felt a mix of emotions - indifference and pride - which made her want to cry.

She shook her head to refocus, holding back tears until later. The countdown started, and Moon glanced at her opponents. Two were teenagers, two were middle-aged, and one was a child. There was nothing remarkable about them except that they might have a talent for running. She turned her attention back to the castle, repeating to herself that she would win if she just believed. As she took two full, deep breaths, feeling the air fill her lungs and centering her thoughts, the sound of the horn pierced the air, signaling the start. With a burst of energy, everyone surged forward, propelled by the wind.

Everything and everyone moved both fast and slowly at the same time. Her body's energy surged as she ran, and she felt proud that her legs didn't buckle in the fight. Even as both opponents stumbled in the sand, Moon didn't mind. She ran blissfully, smiling and carefree, leaving one opponent far behind and going toe to toe with the other. She turned her head to smile at her competitor, and it was the child, and they smiled back. They were nearing their sandcastles, and Moon seemed to enjoy the friendly competition, so why not try harder? With all her might, she pushed her legs further and picked up the pace—harder and faster.

She clenched the flag in her hand like a cherished treasure. The kid and her were neck to neck, but they parted ways and ran to their team's sandcastle. She dropped to her knees and hands, racing to plant her flag in the sandcastle as if her life depended on it. She sat before the sandcastle, closed her eyes, and hoped she wouldn't disappoint anyone. When she peeked over at her opponent, she saw that he was crying, but she heard loud cheers behind her. She was too afraid to turn around, fearing that her opponent might be weeping for victory, and she didn't want to break her own heart. The thought of seeing the disappointment on Dawn and his family's faces was crushing.

So, she waited. Someone stood behind the child and hugged him. Moon, in doubt, was then swung into Dawn's arms, to her surprise. People surrounded her with cheers, smiles, and laughter because she had won. She could hear Summer shouting, "The Wolfes won for the first time in 3 years!" Not only did she win, but she made history, and who couldn't be proud of that? Dawn's family took turns congratulating Moon as he held her in his arms. She felt as if she was a chosen Messiah by the way everyone surrounded her, and, if she wasn't mistaken, someone called her a "Queen." Dawn briefly lowered Moon so she could hug Crystal and Summer.

Moon jumped up and down, "I won," she shouted joyfully.

"We knew you could!" Summer smiled.

"Queen!" Crystal shouted.

Moon laughed and said, "Why are you calling me that?"

"It's what we call champions. If a woman, then Queen of the Wolfes, and if a man, then King of the Wolfes until the next champion."

Moon smiled and said, "Queen?"

Dawn pulled Moon back into his arms and said, "My Queen! My rose! Mines!" and ran off with her towards the ocean. The ocean appeared vast and greenish blue, allowing the human eye to perceive even the tiniest creatures in its clear waters. Moon bounced as Dawn ran into the sea, closing her eyes out of fear of falling. However, Dawn held onto her tightly. She could hear everyone telling Dawn to be careful. He spun her around quickly and then left the ocean. Moon opened her eyes again, felt Dawn lift her in the air, saw him smile, and then he placed her back on her feet. She saw that he had calmed down and went in for a kiss. Moon pushed him back and stepped backward,

"You have to ask nicely," she smirked flirtatiously, short of breath.

"Oh, really," he grinned.

"Yes, sir," she said with a smile as she twirled. Her body was wet, and her bikini clung to her skin.

Dawn stood tall and confident as he declared, "I have to request a kiss!" he announced to the crowd.

Everyone shouted, "Ask the Queen!" Moon and Dawn laughed at the joke but now had to stand by it.

"What if I just take my kiss?" he sneered.

She waved her finger and said, "Un-uh!" He smiled while out of breath. "You're going to have to ask."

He shook his head and looked back at everyone, then said, "Really?"

She gestured her hands to the ground in front of her, giggling. "Really."

He took a second, looked at Moon playfully, got onto his knees, and pleaded. "Queen of the Wolfe's, the rose to my heart, the love of my life, may I please share a kiss with you," he said, licking his lips flustered.

Moon pondered momentarily, then said, "Your request is granted, my love," she smiled, her heart and stomach fluttering with butterflies.

Dawn whistled as he jumped up and enthusiastically kissed Moon. He held her down on the sand as they kissed while the others cheered in the distance. He eventually turned over, and Moon was on top, his hands cradling her ass, both covered in sand and seawater. He held her up and carried her back into the water. The waves broke apart as they enjoyed the sea together. Dawn slowly lowered Moon into the water, wetting her hair, and their faces met as they gazed into each other's eyes. Her arms were around his neck, and she gently rubbed the side of his face. As people left and others looked on, Dawn whispered sweet nothings into Moon's ear, and then she kissed him passionately, making his lips tender and raw. The waves became calmer as the golden sun set behind them, casting pink and orange hues across the sky. Instinctively, they lingered in a gentle embrace.

# The Aquarium

Crowds of people hurried into the Aquatics heritage site. The sound of shoes squeaking and bodies brushing past each other filled the air, and then, Moon emitted a piercing scream of excitement and leaped onto Dawn's back. This surprised the people around them, including Dawn's family, who all stopped to stare. The place had families, couples, and fascinating aquatic life specimens. Moon was thrilled to be at such a large aquarium, feeling like a little girl on a memorable field trip. As they waited in line, Moon's eyes widened with anticipation. Dawn's cousins teased him when they saw Moon on his back, and she laughed. Dawn had two younger cousins and one his age, not particularly close, but close enough to feel like family. The place had given out bubbles at the door entrance, and Moon couldn't help but blow them onto Dawn's cousins and up into the air. His cousins were popping bubbles as they flew in the air, but Summer and Crystal managed to wiggle their way to the front and join in on the fun.

It was heartwarming to see everyone having a great time, especially Dawn; she had never seen him laughing and smiling so much around the family. His dark curls brushed against her inner thighs as he planted a kiss on her knee, causing Moon to blush. Summer kept blowing bubbles in her cousin's faces while Crystal teased them. Dawn was talking about a nightclub with Adrian, one of his younger cousins. She peeked behind her and saw Bronte and her mother debating whether Twilight was a movie for teens or adults, which she felt was for both, and waved hesitantly at them. Their eyes lit up with disbelief and hope. Mr. and Mrs. Wolfe paid for access and counted each person while Pearl hovered over them like a shadow. Surprisingly, Cora was beside Moon and Dawn, quiet, while the rest of the group made much noise. She was reading a book while in line, which meant she had a mind of steal because it would have been impossible for Moon to read with all the noise around them. She must have felt her glances because she immediately looked up, startling Moon.

"Jumpy, are we?" Cora smiled friendly.

Moon, then smiled, "N—no. Not when it comes to you."

"Good," Cora winked. "The name is Anna Dressed In Blood."

Moon scowled, "Isn't that a kid's book."

Cora smirked, "Somewhat, depending on how you view reading books."

"I didn't mean—It's a rare read. I doubt many people know about it."

"You will be surprised, honey; my book club goes crazy over books like these."

Moon cheesed at the fact that Cora was far cooler than she thought. She always thought Pearl was the more relaxed, but people tended to prove her wrong. She looked at them both and wondered about their lives before their family and duties. Did they have tattoos, let loose, have multiple loves, travel, or even battle between age and politics? When she glanced at them, she saw her nana, what could have been, and her life. Though their appearances differed from her nana, she could feel nana near, whether by touch or by the people she was destined to meet. It made her heart swell, like a welcoming calm that overpowered every fiber in her body. Moon looped her pinky finger under Dawn's ring finger while keeping her eyes on Cora, who was immersed in her book. For some reason, she wanted to rant about her nana and how she was feeling to Cora, but she stopped herself. It wasn't her right to; no matter how much she missed her, she tried not to cry by looking forward.

The line started to move as they finally went inside to see aquatics up close, maybe even a dolphin showing. Cora tapped Moon's arm and said, "Are you ready for the show? Hmm," she smiled.

"Yes—no excited," Moon said as her shoulders danced.

"That's my girl," Dawn said as he chuckled.

"Dawn!"

"What? You're so cute when you're excited."

Cora laughed with her book over her mouth and said, "She sure is."

"Okay, I'll take it as a compliment."

Dawn rolled his eyes, "It is a compliment, baby." He smacked her thigh faintly.

Moon bent forward, kissed him, and said, "My love."

Cora put her book away and said, "See you later, love birds." She winked as she rushed over to Dawn's parents and Pearl.

"What do you want to see first?" Moon asked. "Maybe we should roam around first or not—um."

Dawn laughed and said, "You're more excited than me."

"I can't help it," Moon chuckled excitedly as she slowly hopped off Dawn's back.

"I'm up for anything," he said, taking her hand.

Moon smiled, "Me too; let's look at rockfish." She pointed to the glass.

She savored the final drops of her refreshing raspberry slushie as they exited the dolphin exhibit and descended the staircase. The display of nature never failed to captivate her, and while she knew that dolphins weren't exactly angelic beings, she couldn't help but find their natural charm endearing. Her highlight of the day was interacting with one of these incredible creatures, and to her delight, Dawn purchased a dark purple stuffed dolphin for her at the concession stand. Its one-eyed appearance struck her as unusual, but she quickly realized it was likely due to manufacturing imperfections. The unique, mismatched nature of the plush toy appealed to her, reminiscent of a black sheep standing out amongst the crowd.

Tossing the cup into the trash, Moon held onto Dawn's hand and rested her face on his arm as they walked far behind everyone. Her dark brown eyes were large and round, and she gazed at him with a doe-eyed expression, giving him a gentle smile. Dawn didn't notice as he was on the phone, ensuring everything went smoothly for their plane ride tomorrow. The day wasn't over yet. They planned to watch the turtles before leaving with the others. She wished she had brought Lin along because he would have enjoyed seeing the other turtles. Maybe next time. As he hung up the phone, he looked at Moon and smiled, scrunching his nose and kissing her forehead.

The hallway was dark like the others, with tanks the size of trucks and open for people to stand around and watch. They stopped in front of the glass, her finger lightly tapping it. Among the turtles, there were various sizes and ages present. Some were small, others big, and some were in-between. Some turtles were old, while others were young or just babies. However, the tiny baby turtles were tricky to spot due to their small size. Excited as usual, Moon couldn't contain herself, and she fawned over them and ranted to Dawn that someday Lin would be the size of an average plastic cup. He didn't say a word, letting her rant and taking in the joyful energy she had. She was adorable to him, making him fall in love with her even more.

Moon didn't want to forget such a spectacular day, so she pressured Dawn into taking photos, even the off-guard ones—but he agreed only on the condition that she let him grab her ass in at least one photo. She agreed, happily, since it turned her on most days. Everyone else was preoccupied with the other species, and Moon wasn't. She wanted to watch the turtles until they left. Summer was flirting with a man old enough to be her father while Crystal followed her parents and grandmother around. Bronte was with his nephews joking and poking fun at the aquatics, while Moon's mother disappeared. She secretly tried to keep an eye on her because she wanted to speak to her—not about past offenses but new beginnings. She was scared to admit she missed her mother every second of the day, but her pride wouldn't let her—it didn't mean she would jump into it right away.

Dawn embraced Moon from behind while they watched the turtles. He pushed her hair to the side and kissed her neck, leaving Moon with a smile and a potential hickey. "Dawn! People are around," she whined.

"We should care because —" He fondled her breast.

"I care, that's why," Moon giggled.

Dawn sighed disappointedly, "Okay, I'll stop," he said with a chuckle.

"They are such a peaceful species. How can people not be fascinated?"

Dawn shrugged, "Who needs people when they have you watching."

"Aww—my love," she caressed his face and kissed him.

While kissing, Dawn's cousins Adrian, Smokey, and Connor called him. They wanted him to join in on the childish fun they were having. Moon left the kiss, giggled, and motioned to his cousins to give them a minute, but Dawn didn't stop cuddling her and said, "What!"

Smokey smirked, "Come over here! We want to show you something."

"You can leave your girl for two seconds, can't you." Adrian taunted.

"I mean, she is prettier!" he taunted back.

Moon giggled again, "Just go. I'll be right here."

"Are you sure? I'd rather spend time with you," he hugged her tighter.

"Yeah, I'm sure. Alone time wouldn't hurt, and your cousins miss you. A lot!" They both laughed.

"Dawn! Come on!" Smokey yelled. Dawn looked at Smokey and flipped him off.

Dawn released his arms from around Moon and playfully smacked her on the ass.

"Don't wait up," he winked, then joined his cousins.

She realized she wasn't alone when she shifted her focus to the turtles. To her surprise, her mother wandered over. Moon attempted to appear composed, yet her heart raced within her chest. She had grown accustomed to her mother avoiding parental responsibilities and not embracing them. She could feel the cold breeze against her black mini-skirt as she crossed her legs. The silence between them was exhausting—her mind was ridden with what to say, but she was unclear on how to say it. Angel moved closer to Moon and switched her purse to her other arm. Awkwardly, Angel moved Moon's hair from her shoulder, afraid to touch her because it's been fifteen years and she was not the Mother of the Year, but it could give her the courage to spark conversation.

"You've always loved turtles—I've never known why," Angel smirked.

Moon didn't respond. "You look pretty today—well, every day. I'm used to your hair being curled. I like the bangs. It's different. They look nice on you." Moon still didn't respond. It wasn't to be cruel but to understand—or at least to grasp what reality she was experiencing. "I understand if you don't want to talk to me. I'll leave."

Moon grabbed her hand and said, "I like the family dynamic and the fact that they are peaceful. It calms me," Moon smiled.

Angel chuckled, "Ah, I see. They are beautiful."

Moon turned back towards the glass. "Are you having fun?"

"Sure, I was until Bronte ran off with his nephews."

Moon chuckled and said, "They stole my boyfriend too."

Angel laughed and said, "I guess it's just us two then."

"Someone can enjoy such profound nature alone. I have for years."

"Mm-hm!"

Moon smiled and started to twirl the end of her hair. "I don't know if you know this, but Dawn bought me a turtle."

Angel smiled, "What is the turtle's name?"

"Lin, short for Lincoln."

Angel held her breath, "After your daddy?"

Moon nodded, "Yes. My sweet daddy."

Angel giggled, "That's nice, baby, real nice."

Moon noticed she was still holding her mother's hand but, weirdly enough, didn't mind. It could be a start to a clean slate, not to forget but to forgive over time. "I never asked you this, but how did Daddy die?"

"Nana and Papa didn't tell you?"

Moon shook her head, "No. Every time I asked, they would change the subject."

Angel was not shocked, "Suicide. At first, they told me about a car crash to not upset me because I was pregnant, but I just knew something wasn't right, and it wasn't until you were born that they had told me it was suicide." Moon's heart fell into her stomach. "I—wow." She whispered.

"Yep. I was devastated when they told me, but I was not surprised because your father was a happy person but sadder than anyone I knew. His family, though estranged, tried to get him some help, and I did, too, but it happened—the inevitable." Angel nodded her head for comfort. "Do you want to know how?"

Moon looked at her mother sorrowfully, "No. I have no need."

Angel smiled sadly, "Okay."

"Is that what made you sad in the long run?"

"Yes and no. I lost the love of my life and carried around this enormous guilt for most of my life. I just—" she sighed, "Finally broke down." Moon held her mother's hand tight. "You would have loved him."

Moon and her mother stare at each other tenderly, then break apart. Angel sat on the bench, and Moon leaned against the wall across from her mother and crossed her arms.

"Do you love him? Do you love him just as much?" Moon asked wholeheartedly.

"Every day, but not as much as your—daddy," Angel said with a wink.

"I figured." She said condescending. "But I wanted to tell you that I am open to mending things—over time."

Angel smiled, "I am too."

Moon looked away, "No promises, okay."

"Okay." Angel stared at Moon enduringly as any mother would.

"Can I get a hug?"

Moon hesitantly answered, "Sure," then shrugged.

Angel rushed over and hugged Moon. Moon's arms stayed to the side of her, and her eyes wandered around as if under suspicion. "You can let go, now."

Angel, embarrassed, stepped back. "Sorry."

"Thank you." Moon stared blankly, "I'm going to look for Dawn. I'm finished here."

Before Moon could walk away, Angel said, "I suggested this place to Dawn's parents."

The cold air in the hallway made Moon shudder as it teased her through the unbuttoned, thin, white cotton long-sleeve shirt. Her crimped hair framed the delicate initial necklace peeking from beneath her shirt.

She turned her head only to speak, "Why?"

"I promised when I came back that I would—but you came back first."

"I forgot about that. You didn't have to; there was no point. I was a child, then."

Angel looked down, "I still had a promise to keep, regardless of the fact."

Moon looked forward, "Thank you for upholding your promise."

"No, a thank you is not needed. I wanted to spend the day with my daughter, and I did, even if it was only for a short time." Moon rolled her eyes.

*Why did she have to make things difficult for herself and still be Mother Teresa?*

"I feel the same way." Moon looked back at Angel and smiled, then walked away.

"Love you, too," her mother mumbled.

Moon encountered Dawn and his cousins, who indulged in onion rings while participating in an eating competition. He and Adrian were chewing endlessly to see who could eat the most onion rings while Moon stood there and chuckled, waiting for Dawn to finish. After a while, they noticed that Moon was there. Moon waved as Dawn glanced at her; somehow, he managed to smile with a mouth full of onion rings. Dawn and Adrian were tied until Moon blew a kiss, and Adrian choked on an onion ring, leaving Dawn as the winner. Dawn grabbed a water bottle and washed down the last onion rings in his mouth, smiling as the water trickled down his chin. She didn't care as she boldly walked over and kissed him, tasting the leftover onion.

"Dawn has his own personal napkin." Connor laughed.

Moon winked, "That's not so bad," she kissed Dawn again, this time with her tongue.

Connor waved a white flag by walking away.

Dawn hugged Moon, "Have fun with your little friends?"

"Mm-hmm—I missed you," she said as she nuzzled under his chin and rested her head on his chest.

"I missed you too, and I am a champion of bragging rights," he said with a laugh.

"That's my Wolfe," she said as she laughed, making Dawn blush.

"Not for long, cousin!" Adrian rebutted.

"We'll see, boys!" Dawn said as he walked off with Moon.

Dawn's grandmothers announced that it was time to leave, and the group began discussing where they should go to eat. Moon observed her mother and Bronte quietly slipping away from the crowd while Dawn's sisters bombarded their parents with questions about who would get to drive. Dawn's arm was around Moon's neck while they tried to reach the door. "What are you hungry for?" Dawn said as he sucked on his bottom lip.

Moon rubbed her lips with her cherry-red nail and said, "Whatever looks good." She laughed. "I'm starving. That slushie and popcorn didn't quench my hunger."

Dawn looked at Moon tenderly. "Okay, rose," he said. "Let's get my baby something to eat," he teased.

"Can we invite everyone?"

Dawn scowled, "Who is everyone?"

"Your sisters, Bronte, Countess, and your parents."

Dawn shrugged, "Okay, that sounds fine to me—but I might as well invite my cousins, too. One of them owns a restaurant, so that would be perfect."

Moon gave a bright, kind smile and said, "Great!"

"It's good that you are including your mother."

Moon's smile dropped, "Yeah. We talked, and things will get better over time, of course. But better," she said.

Dawn kissed her cheek. "I love you," he said, kissing her cheek again twice, causing Moon to giggle like a child.

After leaving the aquarium, they found their family members in their designated cars. Dawn quickly approached his parents and sisters to ask about dinner, while Moon hurried over to Bronte and her mother to invite them to join. They agreed, which made Moon's heart flutter with excitement because it meant they were making an effort. Everyone planned to head home, change their attire, and reconvene at the restaurant. Dawn gleefully hoisted Moon onto his shoulder and returned to the car for the journey home, causing Moon to laugh and his family to exchange playful banter and affectionate comments about them. The ride home would be long, but at least the day would end on a good note.

# Mustang

It was the end of their meal; as the waiter placed the bill on the table, a bar of delicate, palm-sized chocolate shaped like a rose appeared as a surprise. Intrigued by the gesture, Moon and everyone couldn't help but wonder about the sender's identity. The waiter presented the plate of chocolate in front of Moon and handed her a note. She glanced at everyone, particularly Dawn, seeking clarification. Moon considered whether Dawn's parents might be the reason for the gift, as they were sorry for missing dinner but had arranged to catch up with everyone later at Adrian's nightclub. The note was on beautiful, pristine white paper embellished with intricate golden roses shimmering in the light. Not to her surprise, no name was found on it, adding an air of mystery to the elegant note.

When she opened it, she read:

*"For the prettiest rose— from your devoted and caring boyfriend—soon-to-be future husband.*

*- D."*

Moon gazed directly at Dawn and smiled. It was evident from everyone's expressions that she had discovered the identity of the gift-giver without needing to ask. The chocolate was so beautiful that eating it seemed almost a shame. Shaped like a rose and dyed red, a gummy substance oozed out when Moon broke off a piece to taste it. It had a delightful flavor of strawberries and chocolate, which she found pretty pleasing. Although she wasn't particularly fond of desserts, she appreciated the thoughtful gift from Dawn, her devoted boyfriend, who always expressed his affection openly and never shied away from anything.

Dawn grabbed Moon's hand and kissed it. "A rose for the sweet rose in my life," he said.

Moon grinned and said, "My love," with hearts in her eyes.

Angel smiled and said, "You spoil her."

Moon nodded in agreement as she broke off another piece of chocolate.

"I'm happy to do so when she means everything to me."

"Please—please do not get all mushy around us," Crystal complained.

"I think it is cute and so romantic!" Summer said, obsessed.

"Thanks, Summer. At least someone around here is romantic."

Bronte chuckled, "You are second in line, young blood. I've been in this game longer than you."

"We have yet to see it," Dawn taunted.

"I'm working on making it public, but I'm more of a private man."

Angel chuckled and said, "Then I am a nun."

Everyone laughed, but Bronte protested, saying, "Hey!" He laughed. "I will get some practice in now since I am to be Moon's father-in-law." Everyone went silent. "Too soon?"

Dawn and Moon nodded. "It's too soon," They spoke.

Bronte laughed, saying, "As long as you call me Bronte, we are good."

"No problem. I always wanted someone to pay my rent." Moon laughed.

"I would, but that is what rich boyfriends are for—right? D?"

"Nothing I can't handle," Dawn said while flipping Bronte off.

Bronte responded by silently mouthing, "Fuck you too!"

"That's fine with me," Moon said. "Now I have two men who can pay my rent." Moon winked and playfully flipped them both off.

Summer looked up from her phone, "Wait? Father-in-law? Did I miss something?"

"We will explain everything on the way," Crystal reassured Summer.

"But—"

"It's a long story and better fit for a conversation in private, don't you think?" Moon asked.

"Um—yeah." She said, unsure.

Moon smiled and said, "Okey, dokey."

Summer returned to texting, and Crystal winked and blew a kiss to Moon for support and comfort.

"I'm ready to party!" Crystal whined impatiently.

Bronte paid the bill, and everyone made their way to the door. It was warm outside, but the ground was wet from the earlier heavy rain. Moon and the girls started talking about Bronte and her mother, and Summer felt confused and conflicted by the end, but she was caught up in everything. Moon wanted to discuss Rainey Crow with them but didn't want to ruin the mood. Rainey wasn't too important to her, but being able to rant about her jealousy and fears to her friends helped with the irrationality in her head. "Bitter" was the only word that could describe Rainey Crow, nothing more. Sure, the girl is human just like anyone else and may even love to the point of self-destruction, but the things she did yesterday were spiteful.

Moon almost tripped thinking about it, but by favor, Dawn caught her—his hands held her waist, pulling her into his arms and safety.

"Moon? Are you okay?" Angel asked.

"I'm okay. There's nothing my big, strong man couldn't solve," she teased.

Angel chuckled, "Of course." Dawn smirked and continued to hold Moon.

They stood outside the restaurant, waiting for the valet, each engrossed in their conversation. Bronte and her mother began kissing, which made Moon feel awkward. She wasn't ready to see her mother being intimate, even though she showed affection frequently in front of her mother. Seeing her mother loved by a man who wasn't the father figure she had imagined was strange. Bronte, in Moon's opinion, wouldn't make a terrible father. He was handsome, kind, and serious about her mother, but he wasn't Lincoln Bowie—and never would be, not even in her mother's heart. However, they would love him to some extent. It was close enough to accept.

Moon's thoughts were racing, and her pinky traced a heart over Dawn's hand.

Dawn whispered, "I love you too."

Moon whispered back, "My love."

The valets arrived promptly, gliding up to the curb with a line of sleek, polished cars. Moon's mother and Bronte were the first to reach their awaiting vehicle, their footsteps quickening in anticipation. Meanwhile, Dawn's sisters stood by, exchanging excited chatter as they patiently waited for their car to pull up. Finally, with a graceful swoop, Dawn's car arrived, ready to whisk them away to their next destination. Dawn rushed to the passenger's side and opened the door for Moon, but she was hesitant to leave his sisters alone.

Moon was tentative. "I think we should wait until their car comes before we leave," she said.

Dawn was unbothered. "They are going to be okay. There are lots of people in the restaurant and outside," he said.

"I don't know."

Dawn sighed. "You just don't want to leave your friends behind," he said, then kissed Moon.

"You are correct about that," Moon snickered.

"Go! Moon, we will be fine."

"Are you sure?"

"We are going to the same place, are we not?"

"Yeah—yes."

Summer giggled and said, "Okay, we will see you there unless you want to ride with us."

Dawn quickly responded, "NO! She is riding with me," he declared.

Moon laughed, "At least let me answer first," she insisted.

Dawn closed the car door and placed his hands on his hips. "You're riding with me," he said.

"I didn't say I wasn't."

Crystal, annoyed, said, "She didn't say she wasn't."

Dawn glared at his sister, "I heard her, Crys," he replied.

"Big bad Wolfe!"

Moon was incapable of another fight and said, "No arguing, please!"

"Sorry, lovely."

Dawn's demeanor softened. "Sorry."

"There is no need. Look!" Summer pointed to the valet that arrived with their car.

"See, there baby, now can we go." Dawn massaged his face, feeling stressed.

Moon smiled, "Yes! Sorry, sorry." She spoke.

Moon hugged his sisters. "We have a club to get to," Moon said.

Dawn's two sisters ease themselves into their gleaming, sunflower-yellow convertible, luxuriously appointed with seats wrapped in soft, brown fur. Meanwhile, Moon and Dawn climb into a vibrant cerulean-blue 1960 Ford Mustang with the convertible top down. They steer straight into traffic, with Dawn's sisters ahead of them. As they drove, Dawn glanced at Moon in the driver's mirror. The bustling city lights and the steady stream of cars kept her too occupied to notice. Her rose-cheetah dress was sleek and form-fitting, the fabric wrapping elegantly around her neck and extending into long, snug sleeves. The back of the dress was open, adding a touch of allure to the ensemble—The back of her lustrous, shiny black heels featured glossy golden heart-shaped bottoms that didn't kill her feet but mainly were for sitting and short walks. With attentive eyes, he gazed at the advancement of her portrait while remaining vigilant behind the wheel—her curled bangs graciously veiled her stunning chocolate-colored eyes, and the vivid cherry red lipstick on her lips emitted an aura of bratty confidence.

It wasn't a secret that he adored Moon's beauty; it wasn't hard for her not to notice. She looked at Dawn and smiled affectionately—their eyes meeting but for a moment lovingly. Eventually, her eyes fell on the rings on Dawn's finger, which reminded her of her rings. She rotated the rings around her ring finger with her thumb. She sunk into the car seat and kicked her heels off in anticipation of arriving at the club. Adrian, his cousin, owned Red Dawn, which was named after him. She questioned the symbolism of the word "Red" in the name. The breeze was invigorating as Moon rested her eyes, savoring the quiet ride with the Mustang's top down. Dawn seemed to be anywhere Moon was, and he enjoyed her company. He reached out to Moon but noticed her eyes closed, so he touched her thigh. He smiled slightly at her peace, and then Moon held onto his hand.

However, his hand was not in place to be gentle but disruptive. His hand moved up her dress, caressing her inner thigh, and she offered no protest—moving it closer to her clothed vagina. Moon's legs moved farther apart, and everything below her stomach felt hot. His middle finger gently caressed her vagina before moving her panties to the side and entering with his finger. Moon's body arched, her eyes still closed, and her mouth making small whimpers. His pace was gradual but increased. The motion of the Mustang added more friction and intensity to the moment. Moon's hands clawed at the car seat due to the sensation between her legs. Her eyes opened to glance at Dawn and his smirk, realizing he was turned on. She hoped she could orgasm before the next traffic light.

She tried her hardest not to scream. The lump in her throat was driving her mad. It was hard not to express how good she felt. They were fighting against time as he fingered her—they were near the next traffic light, and Moon could only move her hips. Dawn had an evil grin as he pleased her. He saw they were near the light, so he tried his best to make her cum quick as he added another finger to speed up the process. He could see Moon trying not to moan loudly, but it made her more beautiful and desirable in his eyes. Moon clasped his hand, feeling she was near an orgasm, adding more pressure and picking up the speed.

The car came to a stop, and Moon was about to cum when Dawn's cousins appeared in the vehicle beside him. He removed his hand and hastily pulled down Moon's dress. Moon was stunned by what happened, and then she saw his cousins in the distance. Annoyed, he smiled at them so as not to draw suspicion, while his cousins goofed around in their car. Adrian alone stared at Moon. Amidst playing around with his other cousins, Dawn noticed, and so did Moon. It wasn't just any stare but something more familiar in a way she had seen before.

He didn't look disgusted or intrigued but instead concentrated as if he wanted to hold her gaze in his hands. She couldn't quite describe it, but she felt his eyes piercing her. She wasn't sure if Dawn noticed his cousin staring, but she tried to hide behind him. She never paid Adrian any mind; if he wanted to be seen, he was because he made her feel indiscreet. Not to imply that what she was doing with Dawn was sinful, but the way he looked at her made her feel exposed.

Dawn snapped his fingers at his cousin to catch his attention.

"Hey!" Dawn yelled.

Adrian's gaze shifted to Dawn as he said, "Yeah, cousin!"

Dawn smirked curiously, "Do I need to cut your eyes out of your sockets, or are you going to stop staring at my girl," he demanded strongly.

Adrian chuckled, then smirked, and said, "Sorry! I couldn't help but take a look at your rose!"

"Mm-hmm—well, stop because you're making her uncomfortable!"

"Sorry!" Adrian raised his hands in surrender. "Sorry, Moon!"

Moon nodded forgivingly. "Happy now, D?"

*I didn't know he could be such a weirdo and confident about it, too.*

"Yes! Now, keep your eyes on the road!"

Adrian's pale hazel eyes met Dawn's gaze, creating a standoff. Since their arrival, Moon, aware of the underlying competition between Dawn and his cousins, seemed to bring them back to the beach with their games and aquarium. Moon did not take their rivalry seriously since they appeared so close to each other, even more so than his other cousins. She placed her hand on Dawn's leg, catching his attention and smiling in return.

"Everything okay," Moon asked, worried.

"Yeah," Dawn grinned.

"Okay," she smiled, "The light is green," Moon said as she pointed at the traffic light.

"Sorry, rose." He said and kissed Moon on the cheek.

"D?" Adrian called.

"What!" Cars behind them began to honk. "Follow me to Sharks station."

"Why?" Adrian rolled his eyes. "Just do it! I have something to show you!"

Another car honked its horn, so Dawn and His cousins honked back.

"It can't wait until the club. It's down the road."

"No! I have something to show you! Come on." Adrian whined while Smokey and Connor were getting high in the backseat.

Dawn looked at Moon and said, "It will take just a second."

Moon hesitated, "I don't know," she said worriedly.

"I can drop you off, then return," Dawn suggested.

Moon held his hand and shook her head hard.

"No, I go where you go. Never suggest that."

Dawn laughed and said, "Yes, ma'am." he looked at his cousin and said, "Okay."

"Alright!" His cousins cheered.

Dawn allowed Adrian to lead the way to an old, abandoned building called "Sharks." It seemed to be an old car repair shop; they weren't the only ones there. A group of people, some of them unfamiliar, had gathered around as several vehicles, including vintage cars and sports cars, were parked. Money was changing hands between the drivers and other individuals. They drove cautiously into the area, following Adrian until he pulled over and exited his car. He then walked up to Dawn's car window. Moon was confused about why Adrian wanted to show Dawn a bunch of people who were about to race illegally.

Dawn swiftly rolled down the window, grabbed Adrian by the ear, and whispered, "Why the fuck did you bring me out here!"

Adrian mischievously pleaded, "D, I know you're mad, but I thought for old-time sake that we let some steam off."

Dawn let go of his cousin's ear and asked, "Did you two know?"

Smokey and Connor broke out laughing, high as kits, and shrugged. "No!" They both spoke.

Moon was confused and said, "You're not a stranger to this." She wasn't angry but shocked that Dawn did things like this, which was the opposite of his character.

Dawn stuttered, "I—uh—yeah, when my parents and I became estranged six years ago. I started to venture into many things that weren't good for me," he said nervously.

Adrian smirked. "Listen, Moon, he was the man! He won every race and did every drug and girl," he said as he hit his chest.

Dawn slapped his hand away and looked at him angrily. "My past, baby."

Moon giggled, "I'm not prejudiced, Dawn; I wish you had told me. It doesn't seem like you to race, but I guess I was wrong."

Adrian's smirk dropped, and he rolled his eyes. "Come on, D! Just this once if your rose doesn't mind. It's good money, not that you need it, but it could be fun."

"What about the club?" Moon asked.

"What about it? It will still be there, princess."

"Regardless! I don't want to get in trouble, Adrian, but you should know better."

"What are you afraid of? Mommy and Daddy because they will not find out, and even if they did, you are a grown-ass man."

Dawn gazed at Moon for approval because he was afraid of his own decision on the matter. She felt it wasn't up to her. She wasn't his owner; he could do what he wanted if it didn't dangerously put her in harm's way. She saw racing from a distance in her lifetime and wouldn't mind seeing it up close, but it wasn't her decision. A woman called for the last of the bets and announced that the first set of racers would race in ten minutes. The only thing that worried her was Adrian; she did not trust him around Dawn, and it seemed that Dawn felt the same way.

"Damn, D! What is it going to be?"

"Moon?"

She kissed him on the cheek and said, "It's up to you, my love."

"MY LOVE," Adrian said mockingly, and Dawn smacked his face.

"Stop the bullshit!"

"Ouch! That fucking hurt."

Moon smiled with a chuckle.

"Watch your tone!" he demanded angrily. "You placed a bet on me and told them I would be here, right?"

"I mean, you owe me!" Dawn took a deep breath, bowed his head, and closed his eyes to stay calm.

"It's old news, Adrian."

"Bets! Bets!"

Adrian looked nervous. "Please, cousin! You owe me," he pleaded.

"Why does he owe you?" *There is more I do not know about him.*

"Rose—" Moon put her hand over his mouth.

"I did him a big favor, and he owes me. That's all."

"What favor?"

"Just a favor. It's not my business to tell."

Moon giggled. "Ironically, your family keeps telling me that.

"Baby, we can leave?"

Moon stopped Dawn from starting the car. "He did you a favor, and it seems like a big one, so you owe him." Dawn had a look of guilt on his face. "Yes, but—"

"Do it so we can go to the club before everyone starts worrying."

"Aira." *Does he have to call me that in front of him?*

"Dawn, Adrian, let's do this and get it over with so it won't happen again."

Adrian smiled and said, "Thanks, princess!" Then he ran from the car to the lady placing bets.

"Moon! You know how hard I tried to get away from stuff like this! It ruined my life!"

Moon stared at Dawn calmly, "How would I know? You didn't mention any of this."

"Because it's in the past!"

Moon raised her hand. "Yell again, and you'll find yourself under the car when I win the race." She smiled, though her expression was tense.

Dawn's demeanor softened. "I'm sorry."

"Good. Now, let's race, and you can tell me more about your past later."

"I don't want you entangled in this mess." *It's a little late for that.*

"Just drive, my love," Moon said with a kind smile.

He was silent and gripped the steering wheel hard, "Yes, Aira."

Moon buckled her seatbelt and tried not to let her excitement and intrigue show.

*Sometimes, I think he likes the sound of my name coming out of his mouth.*

Dawn had a conversation with Adrian before he parked at the starting line. He revealed that he had placed a $2,000 bet on the race and already owed about $10,000 for racing. Dawn was shocked but wrote a check for Adrian because his cousin's parents decided to limit his allowance. Dawn made it clear that they would be even after the race, and if he tried anything like today again, he would face consequences. Dawn wanted Moon to wait with everyone else as the race continued, but she insisted on staying in the car with him to experience it fully. They debated the matter, with Moon ultimately winning. She felt it couldn't be too dangerous since she had Dawn to protect her. She acknowledged that love can sometimes involve danger, but she didn't wish to be in danger or to die.

The woman who placed bets asked one of the girls to wave the flag when it was time. She noticed Moon in the car and rushed over to Dawn. She told him it was against the rules for Moon to be in the car, but he waved a fat stack of money in her face and mentioned his name. Undoubtedly, the woman agreed without reluctance. She couldn't even be shocked at what she had seen this past week while vacationing with Dawn. It was new territory, predator and prey, it seemed. The flag- girl stood before the cars wearing fishnet tights, a gold dress, and black thigh-high boots. Her hair was teased wide, and her makeup was heavy and dark. The racers revved their high-performance cars, with smoke billowing from every inch of their sleek vehicles. The girl counted down from three and waved her red flag. The audience roared as the cars sped off down the street.

The Mustang was like a machine, a beast at best, at how fast it was going. Moon was taken aback by how good Dawn was at racing. The car was faster and lighter as he whipped it without a care. He was focused, just like he was on the beach. He made sharp turns, flew over bumps, and went toe to toe with two other sports cars. She smiled as she could feel the adrenaline he felt, especially his outwitting other racers who tried to cheat by taking shortcuts. It was an out-of-body experience. Fun was not the word to describe what was happening. He had to stay focused as he could not check on her, but he asked a couple of times. Cocky as he was, he turned on music to add to the atmosphere, which turned her on. Dawn was an odd creature, making him happier than he could imagine. He was her baby, and there was nothing better to understand than that.

She gently caressed his face when she saw how tense he was. It was between him and another car approaching the final road before the finish line. However, the opposing driver was a challenging competitor. He could keep up with Dawn, which made her feel uncertain about the race. Even though she knew Dawn didn't need the money and was only racing because of his debt to Adrian, she believed in him and forced him to do it. She glanced at his opponent, who wore an eye patch, which puzzled her because she didn't know if it was a fashion statement or if he had lost an eye. But none of that mattered because Dawn was going to win. She always had faith in him, mainly regarding his family.

They edged upon the bustling crowds, tensions rose, and the friendly atmosphere turned sour. Dawn's rival deliberately caused his car to emit smoke, causing Moon to cough, struggling to keep control and avoid being pushed off the road by his opponent. Dawn initially remained calm, but as the other racer closed in and attempted to collide with his car, the situation became increasingly intense. With a reassuring smile, Dawn turned to Moon, gently took her hand, and said, "Don't worry, hold on tight." Understanding the gravity of the situation, Moon nodded in agreement and braced herself, determined not to budge an inch from her seat.

He leaned back in the car seat, and a sense of determination and focus washed over him. His movements were deliberate as he adjusted the gears, and with astonishing speed and precision, he executed a maneuver that sent his opponent's car careening off the road. A crowd quickly gathered around the scene, their concern palpable as they rushed to ensure the well-being of the other racer. Meanwhile, Dawn continued driving across the finish line with a stoic expression, showing no signs of remorse or hesitation. His demeanor was remarkably composed, almost as if he were unaffected by the turn of events.

He tended to be ice-cold emotionally on occasion, but not like this. It frightened her, but she chose to come along for the ride. His cousins ran over to the car, hitting it cheerfully, and pulled Dawn out. They were all jumping for joy and congratulating him. Moon was ecstatic, too, but she kept her distance. Dawn patted his cousin for a share of the money, though he did not need it. Adrian did put up a fight, but Dawn got his share because of emotional distress and his girlfriend being put in harm's way. After being overconsumed by the presence of his family, Dawn snuck up on Moon and hugged her. Moon turned around and kissed him intensely.

"Congrats," She smiled wearily.

"Thanks. Are you okay?"

"I'm fine."

Dawn, skeptical, asked again. "Are you sure?"

"Is that guy okay?" she inquired.

"Ah! He's okay. I know enough to hit a car for someone not to get hurt. At best, he's a little winded."

Moon-side eyed him and said, "You know?"

He nodded, "Look, I told you not to come," he said. Moon looked at him, demanding.

"What?" he chuckled. "You cannot complain about something you begged to experience," he said, raising his eyebrows.

Moon rolled her eyes and asked, "Can we at least take a look?"

Dawn grinned, "Sure, but we have to go after that," he encouraged.

She caressed his face, kissed him, and said, "Okay, my love."

As they approached the crowd, he winked at Moon and gently clasped her hand. Though not severely damaged, the racer's car revealed a leak halfway through the journey. Seeing this, he swiftly scooped Moon into his arms.

"Dawn," she whispered.

He kissed her. "Bear with me. We do not want your shoes getting wet," he said. Moon looked down at the soaked ground with a brown substance on it and couldn't help but smile and think, *"He's such a gentleman."*

# 18. Wounded

**R**ed Dawn was a club with no windows, predominantly made of rough and weathered brick, giving it a formidable appearance. The club sign was large and elegant, with bright red lettering flashing the word "red." A long line of clubbers awaited admittance while Moon, Dawn, and Adrian walked past security. She felt important and, quite honestly, liked that they could skip the line. It didn't make her a terrible person, but did it just a tiny bit?

As they strolled the club, the hallways were a deep red with carmine curtains hanging from the ceiling and matching carpet underfoot—leading into olive-green hued walls with gold and creamy-white human faces wearing golden masquerade masks—making their way into a bar full of people. Crystal chandeliers of various styles hung overhead. The bar was made of radiant mahogany, and so were the chairs and bar stools, the fabric cherry-red. An onyx piano was positioned near the entrance with a sign that read "Only for VIPs," while a bold cheetah print carpet covered the floor.

She could only feel the faintness of the dance floor being so far away. The bass of the music could shatter the floor under them. The music overpowered the club; it made you want to cover your ears, but it was busy with people enjoying their time. Adrian took them onto a long and never-ending balcony, then stopped. If she looked closely enough, each room had vibrant red curtains as a form of privacy and had a VIP sign.

Adrian turned to face Moon and Dawn. "Here we are," he said, pointing to the third room down from them.

"You're not coming?" Dawn asked.

"No, sorry, but some of us have a club to run," Adrian said cynically. "You understand."

Dawn smiled and said, "Yes, I do."

"It was nice to meet you, Moon," Adrian said, offering his hand.

"Same here," Moon replied, shaking his hand.

"Let Michael at the bar know if you need anything, and he will take care of you." Adrian saluted his cousin and Moon and then headed downstairs.

It only took three steps to get to the VIP room, with wide-open curtains covering most of it. The room consisted of a carnelian corduroy couch and a vintage chest box table with an ashtray shaped like a lamp. The walls were detailed with drawings of flowers and dragons. The space was dimly lit but bright enough to see the person sitting beside you. Everyone except Bronte and her mother were inside, smoking, joking, and smiling. It made the wheels in her head turn to where they could be. Dawn and Moon sit on the sofa opposite everyone, and Moon accidentally knocks over the ashtray. Finally catching everyone's attention, she cleaned it up as they greeted them.

She placed the ashtray back on the table and dusted her hands, but she still had remnants of leftover cigarette buds on her hand, so Summer handed her a wipe out of her purse.

"Thanks," Moon sniffled.

"What took you guys so long?" Mrs. Wolfe asked.

"Traffic," Dawn insisted. "You know how it is out there."

"Okay, well, it's good that you made it here on time."

"On time for what?" Moon inquired.

"It's my birthday, dear," Mrs. Wolfe said excitedly.

"Oh! Happy birthday. I had no idea. Dawn did not say a word," Moon nudged him.

"I forgot myself, rose—but my mother usually has it at the manor."

"I wanted to do something new. And me and your father rarely get out of the house unless for work, so why not?"

Moon smiled brightly. "Happy birthday again. It suits you." Mrs. Wolfe leaned over, and she and Moon kissed each other on the cheeks.

Mr. Wolfe smoked a cigar. "Adrian didn't come with you? He's usually attached to your hip."

Moon rested back on the sofa, and Dawn placed his arm around her and kissed the top of her nose.

"Yeah, he had business to take care of, but we came together. We might see him later."

"Mm-hmm, it's nice to see," Mr. Wolfe said as he looked suspiciously at Dawn.

Moon, curious, asked, "Is it bad for them to hang out?"

"Yes! He and James used to get into a lot of trouble together," Mrs. Wolf blurted while swaying her arms to the music.

Dawn became tense, "Can we change the subject, please." His mother smiled, shrugged her shoulders cheerfully, and danced while his father joined in. Summer went to use the restroom, and Crystal sent her last text on her phone. Crystal looked at her brother and Moon, then sneered and asked, "Why?"

"Why, what, Crys?" Dawn said tensely.

"Change the subject. Adrian is—was your best friend."

"Yeah, he was, but he wasn't good for me," he said, his face agitated.

"Sorry. It's just weird."

"What's weird?" Moon asked.

"Well, I have a friend who just sent me a video," Crystal smirked.

Moon rolled her eyes and said, "If it's what I'm thinking, please do not mention it."

"I mean—"

"I'm asking nicely. I was there, and it doesn't matter."

Crystal laughed, "Oh! I know you were."

"Then why does it matter, Crys?" Moon said, annoyed.

"Rose, it's okay."

"No. I love you, Crystal, but please, not tonight. It's your mother's birthday. Pry another day."

Crystal folded her arms, dropped her smile, and asked, "No offense, but who are you?"

Moon was shocked at Crystal's response. She didn't think that would ever come out of her mouth. She was a hurricane, but never towards her. "I'm your brother's girlfriend. That's who I am. And—"

"For how long?" Dawn slammed his hand on the table loud enough to startle everyone.

"Who are you to talk to Aira like that?"

"D—"

"NO! WHO THE FUCK ARE YOU!" He was furious, and Moon tried to calm him down, but he pushed her away. "Wait, Moon—IS MY QUESTION GOING TO BE ANSWERED? IT'S REALLY ANNOYING THAT ADRIAN, MY EX, AND YOU SEEM OKAY DISRESPECTING MY GIRLFRIEND!"

Mr. Wolfe put his cigar in the ashtray, and Mrs. Wolfe stopped dancing.

"Son, calm down."

Dawn gazed at his father heatedly.

"James, calm down."

Mrs. Wolfe took a deep breath and said, "Crystal, apologize to your brother and Moon."

"WHY! I DIDN'T DO ANYTHING ITS NOT LIKE THEY ARE SPECIAL!"

"THIS IS WHY! THIS IS WHY! YOU ARE A BITCH!"

"AT LEAST I'M NOT RACING AGAIN!"

"FUCK YOU CRYSTAL!"

Mr. and Mrs. Wolfe whistled to stop the bickering between them.

"Dawn. It's okay, my love," Moon comforted him while caressing his chest and back.

Dawn and Moon touched foreheads and took a deep breath in unison.

"Oh, Please! When is the wedding?" Crystal stated sarcastically.

Mr. Wolfe took her by the arm and pulled her out of the room.

"Father—"

"SHUT UP!" demanded Mr. Wolfe.

Moon and Dawn consoled each other when Mrs. Wolfe sat at the table. They turned to look at her, and there she was, smiling with a hint of guilt. "I'm sorry, Moon. She was rude."

"Yeah, she was— just to piss me off."

"It's okay—shocking, but okay," Moon lied.

"It's not okay, Aira! She has it out for me, and I do not know why." Mrs. Wolfe kissed her son's cheek. "You know Crystal gets snappy when she is worried, which is no excuse but to be expected."

"My fucking luck!" Dawn struggled not to cry with frustration.

"Your father and I will discuss this newfound information with her and you."

"Oh, please, Mother, I'm a grown man."

"A grown man who could get in trouble running with the wrong crowd."

"I was with him. He was okay, and no one got into trouble."

"And I thank you for that, Moon, but I know he most likely did it for Adrian," His mother reapplied lipstick. "His parents aren't going to like this, but it's life." She laughed and patted their knees.

"It's my birthday, and no one will ruin it, not even your stubborn sister, so hold tight, and the party will be a party again." Dawn and Moon nodded. "Good. Now breathe in and out while I go help your father."

Dawn laid his head on Moon's chest as she caressed his hair, and then Summer walked in amid all the excitement. She was confused about what was happening and asked, "Did I miss something?"

Moon and Dawn sat silently as Summer placed two rosy, pink martini glasses on the table. The drinks looked ice cold. Dawn rolled his eyes while Moon hesitated to smile, uncertain of how Summer felt about them. Summer sighed, crossed her arms, and leaned in to speak to them.

"I know you don't drink, Moon, so I got you a mocktail. This is my brother's favorite drink, the pink kitty, and it's a sweet and sour twist," Summer giggled, then began to worry.

"Are you okay? What happened while I was gone?"

Dawn raised his head and asked with intensity, "What do you think happened?"

Summer, shaken, said, "Not on Mother's birthday."

"She did," he said.

Summer placed the drink in Dawn's face. "There's no better cure than a little fun on the tongue."

Dawn broke a smile, "Summer," he said.

Summer smiled, "Come on! You too, Moon."

"Thanks, Summer," Moon said with a polite smile.

"No problem, beautiful," she said as she sipped her pink cocktail.

She gestured for them to drink, so they picked up their glasses, cheered, and then took a sip. Dawn gulped his drink, which made Moon and Summer even more worried. The pink drink had a playful flavor, but it was the opposite. It reminded Moon of Sour Patch Kids but in reverse. The drink started with sweetness, and then a burst of sourness took over. It was like lemonade for her, but for them, it could have more impact since they had alcohol in their drinks. Dawn asked Summer for another, so she placed an order for more.

Dawn's parents returned without Crystal and took their seats. Moon and Dawn were confused but did not care to ask because of Crystal's disrespect. It was better if she was out of sight and not filling the room with her gloom. "Your sister had to go take care of things at home, so she will not be back." Mrs. Wolfe asserted.

"It seems I missed all the fun, but whatever." Summer danced to the music.

"That's fine with me." They both spoke.

"Great!" Mrs. Wolfe clapped her hands in a fit of joy.

They played a few games and discussed politics, money, relationships, and cars. Dawn had a few drinks, but only because his parents insisted on trying the other two. Moon enjoyed the drink, but it wasn't her favorite, so she didn't have another. She wasn't into sweets, but sour drinks weren't her thing either. Before they knew it, a birthday cake was brought into the room, and everyone sang "Happy Birthday" to Dawn's mother. The cake was white-frosted, layered with an edible flower and five twisted candles. His mother blew out her candles and, per tradition, cut the first slice of the cake.

The only thing next was to hand out the presents, but there had been none since his mother's spontaneous birthday celebration at the club. Everyone sat in the room, immersed in conversations, but Moon's mind wandered elsewhere. What happened earlier between her and Crystal weighed on her heart. She would never think Crystal would dare talk to her that way, especially how welcoming she had been. She could have expressed that she was upset about Dawn racing, and they would have understood. Moon didn't see him racing as outrageous as they did, but then again, Dawn kept many things from her as she did him. Every recap of the argument haunted her like a ghost; the way Crystal's demeanor turned hollow like that made Moon feel like she was nothing to her. Moon didn't expect to be the highlight of her world; they had only met this week, but seeing a potential friend turn into a stranger in minutes was disappointing.

*So, did she put Rainey Crow in her place or tell her to taunt them?*

It made Moon reconsider every interaction they had as an attempt to gather information and made her think that Crystal was acting as a double agent. But was it that serious? She didn't think so until she remembered how they approached Rainey Crow. It saddened her to know the truth, but she would forgive her in a second because Moon never held a grudge. She only hoped Summer wouldn't be the same because she couldn't handle it. It would make her realize that his family, in a way, secretly despised her.

Once again, Dawn was in high spirits, and she realized why Adrian named the club after him. He tended to get heated when angry, and the club attracted many partygoers who enjoyed the excitement of the nightclub scene. It seemed strange for her to think about it now, but it was clear because no one got as angry and lively as Dawn. He leaped for joy as he ate cake while talking to his parents. Moon enjoyed seeing him bond with them; it revealed a different side to him, a kinder side they rarely saw unless he was with her. But even then, this gentler side differed from the one she witnessed. It was like observing a delicate child surrounded by safety compared to a teenage boy with an average crush who wanted to make an impression.

The sudden intimacy between Dawn and his parents left Summer and Moon feeling embarrassed as they stared at each other. Moon wanted to speak but didn't for fear of the reoccurrence from earlier, and Summer didn't because she was afraid of being misunderstood. However, it didn't stop Summer from sitting next to Moon on the sofa. Dawn glanced at them quickly but continued his conversation with his parents. Moon looked down at her nails, picking at the smoothness of her nail buds, while Summer sighed.

"Listen," Summer demanded, "I'm sorry about what Crystal said. There was no excuse, and it was mainly because she is a bitch."

Moon smirked, "Who are you telling."

"She finds people's weaknesses and plays on them. It's her schtick."

Moon sighed, "It was to be expected, but I am not happy that you guys have to apologize for her," she said, then rolled her eyes.

"We are used to apologizing for one another," Summer said, smiling sadly.

Moon held onto her hand, "I'm not mad at you."

"But you are scared that I might feel the same way."

Moon nodded in agreement, and Summer said, "I don't, and you've seen me. If I had, it would have flown out of my mouth by now." Summer chuckled, adding, "I like you, Moon, especially for my brother. He hasn't glowed like this in years, not that we were able to see him."

Moon giggled and said, "You're welcome," implying playfully.

"Enough of wallowing in the past. How about you and me go to the dance floor and release this tension."

"Oh, I don't know," Moon said nervously.

"I saw you on the floor with my brother, and you did great."

"I was in the moment and with your brother."

"Stop making excuses and come with me. I can stand to dance alone," Summer pouted. "Should you ask him, or should I?"

Moon winced. "Okay, okay," she whispered, then glanced at Dawn. "Dawn?" she called quietly.

"Dawn!" Summer shouted. Moon looked at Summer, appearing irritated. "Sorry."

"What is it?" Dawn asked Summer.

"I'm going to go dance with Summer," Moon smiled.

Dawn tugged at his earlobe, but his dimpled smile appeared, and he said, "Okay, baby."

Moon smiled and said, "Okay, see you later." She kissed him on the mouth and then headed to the dance floor with Summer. As Summer stopped in the doorway, she said, "Mother and Father, see you at home," and blew a kiss goodbye.

# The Dance Floor

Stepping onto the dance floor felt like paying homage to the gods. It seemed like a temple dedicated to the God Apollo. The floor had an embedded wolf image of translucent marble, allowing everyone to see their reflection. The room was illuminated with bright, dark red lights that shone down onto the dancers dancing in a circle. The space was expansive, with people spread out everywhere. There was no bar and only a few seating areas. With such a theme, she expected sweltering heat, but it was an overbearing coldness. The people dancing were in trances, their bodies intertwined and kissing, in the moment forever. Others overhead on the balcony were either making out or watching people on the dance floor. She loved red, but everything was a bit much for her; it was overstimulating, and she did not know how people stayed focused. But then again, they were there to lose themselves, not solve crimes.

Summer convinced Moon to join her on the dance floor and groove to the beat. She focused on moving her hips mainly and swaying her head back and forth to the music. Her ginger hair blended with the color of the lights while she swayed her arms to the sounds emitting from the speakers.

She winked at Moon and mouthed, "Dance! Dance!" with a hopeful look.

Summer sighed, rolled her eyes, and pulled them into the middle of the dance floor where everyone was. She placed her hands on Moon's hips and moved them to the beat so Moon could loosen up. However, Moon stood there embarrassed and too afraid to dance in a crowd of strangers. Summer whimsically whispered, "You can't wait for him forever." Moon appeared flushed. "It's okay for you to be sexy on your own."

Moon had her moments, but it wasn't because she was scared to do everything without Dawn. He had no impact at this very moment. She knew people found her beautiful, serene, or breathtaking, but she did not see herself that way. She did not feel comfortable in her skin enough to dance. She smiled at Summer to distract herself from not dancing but bobbed her head to the music. She tried to scan the room and find seating to sit down, which made her a terrible dance partner. If her nana were here, she would support Moon until she danced, although her grandmother would never have been found in a nightclub at her age. Life never goes anyone's way, really, does it? And where was her mother? She felt it was too soon to come out on the dance floor. She didn't mind sitting around looking like a statue frozen in time, but it would mean leaving Summer alone, not that it was hard for her not to get another dance partner.

Moon was unfamiliar with herself, unlike everyone else. She promised to come out of her shell, not be so uptight and boring, to be open-minded, and to explore new ventures. She didn't want to kill the mood, and what happened earlier still tainted her mind, but it didn't even come close to her wondering where Bronte and her mother were. She knew it was stupid, and she could have called them to see where they were and even asked everyone in the room, but she tended to overthink things and miss a few steps. Belief in yourself goes a long way; sometimes, Moon did not have it. She wanted to stop thinking and dance the stress away, but how? She harbored disappointment towards herself, and she knew Summer could feel it. It made her want to cry at the fact that her self-esteem dropped to zero. Defeat didn't win yet because she took a deep breath and thought about what made her afraid, like her nana used to say, and then strived to conquer it.

Moon moved her head up and down to the bass of the music; she copied Summer's movements; her hips swayed slowly, then her ass. Her hands played in her hair as she danced, her intention to forget her surroundings and be one with the music. Summer backed up, taking the lead, Moon following her. Summer then came closer and dropped low, caressing Moon's lower stomach and hips. Then the music switched to another song, and Moon helped Summer up. Then, she spun around her, her hair moving with the air in the room. She grinded as she dropped to the floor, then slowly bent over as she rose back up. They started grinding and sensually dancing with each other, feeling sexy in the moment. Round after round, they danced, the music transitioning to techno.

Moon cleared the middle of the floor, moving everyone on the dance floor out of the way and freestyling on her own. She took the lead, and Summer trailed behind her. Her body bounced, and her arms swayed to the music as she caressed her own body from her breasts to her hips. She lost track of how long they were on the dance floor because she could feel the heat consume their bodies and form sweat. But it didn't matter because she wanted to dance it until her feet bled. Summer unexpectedly kissed Moon on the mouth, but she didn't mind. She knew she was in the moment, and they considered each other beautiful specimens. Even the God Apollo would forge music to their very being. She only kissed her for a moment, then went back to dancing.

She did one fatal spin and saw a familiar face watching from the balcony. It was Dawn, and he had an enormous smirk on his face. She could see in his marvelous dark green eyes that he was surprised to see her let loose like this. She thought, why not entertain him, so she teasingly danced while maintaining eye contact with him, moving her hands all over her body, especially the parts he would love to touch. He bit his lip as he watched her make a showing for him. They blew kisses to each other, and Summer spotted them and then rushed over to hug Moon from behind, laughing. Moon touched foreheads with Summer, giggling at the fun they were having, and when she glanced back at the balcony, he was gone. She looked around on the dance floor and the stairs, but he was nowhere in sight.

She turned to face Summer and grinned, "You were right. Dancing wasn't so bad." She said out of breath.

Summer gave a friendly smile, "I am always, but I have to piss."

Moon giggled, "Do you want me to come with you."

Summer dismissed the question with a wave of her hand. "No. It's all those drinks I had," then laughed, "I am a bit more sober than I was a few hours ago."

Moon laughed and said, "Okay." Then, she bit her bottom lip.

All alone, Moon kicked off her heels, placed them on a chair, and then returned to the floor to dance. She felt unstoppable and wanted, not by others but by herself. Though she could not solve the mystery of Dawn's disappearance, she wanted all this time to herself. It felt good, and she felt confident. She did miss him and his succulent lips with those alluring dimples. The way he would smile would light a fire in her. His muscles and tattoos were just the perfect combination to make her wet, and how his voice cracked occasionally made her melt. He was her weakness, and she couldn't stop thinking about it, which must have been a sign because she felt someone's hands around her waist. And it wasn't just anyone's hands; It was Dawn's. He spun her around and kissed her ferociously. It was sloppy and wet, their bodies dancing to the music, and he held her close to his heart.

She broke away, shaking her ass on him, and he responded by grinding. She then stood back up and leaned on him as they danced. They smiled constantly and maintained unbroken eye contact while exchanging kisses here and there. He spontaneously lifted her into the air in his arms; she flexed her muscles and then laughed. They kissed as he let her back down, but she shortly noticed his cousin Adrian watching from afar. He looked flustered when a blonde girl brought him a drink, and then he walked away annoyed. She paid no mind to it as she did not care to understand him. Some families could never be supportive or loving; it was just how the world worked. Dawn carried her off the dance floor to her chair and sat beside her.

Dawn let out a tired sigh as they rested their bodies. They weren't soaking with sweat but shimmered. He gently turned her chair to face him, then placed her foot on his lap and massaged it. She looked at him wearily and smiled. "I'm glad you decided to join us from your godly heights." She said playfully.

"How could I not, with such beauty in my sight?" He looked at Moon lovingly.

"I missed you, so I must have been heard."

"Haven't you heard I am the king of answering such prayers?" He leaned in to kiss Moon, and she giggled as he did so. After the kiss, they locked eyes as he savored the taste of her lips, quickening her heart. Her nails massaged what was left of his brain as she delicately ran her hands through his hair while his ring hand caressed the side of her cheek. "God," he sighed, "I love you."

Moon blushed and said, "My love."

He smiled intensely and said, "I'm in love with you, Aira. I love you, and I'm in love with you."

He kissed her again, pulling her closer with his arms wrapped tightly around her waist. These kisses were different, and it made her concerned. His kisses were usually light as a butterfly's wings, but not this time. They were rough and forceful. "I'm not going anywhere, Dawn," she chuckled.

His face was filled with uncertainty. "It feels like it sometimes."

"Well, I'm not."

He gave a rictus smile and said, "Tell me you love me."

Moon sighed, "I love you," she giggled with confusion.

She placed both hands on his face and asked, "Are you okay?"

He kissed her twice again and smiled, hoping to understand what was happening. He stared at her with narrowed eyes, searching her face for confirmation of whatever he was looking for.

"Tell me you are in love with me." Moon was too stunned to speak. She dropped her hands and tried to move back, but he wouldn't let her.

"Dawn." She whined.

"Say it."

Moon was flustered, and her lips couldn't move; she could only smile frantically. His grip on her became tighter, and it made her uncomfortable. Dawn's face looked at her with love, but it was something else she couldn't put her finger on. He seemed slight towards her, and she could guess why. Did he need to know right now if she was in love with him? At a nightclub, no less. You would think he would want somewhere else, but no, he wanted her to confess her ever-dying love to him, but it wasn't happening.

"Baby, do we have to do this right now."

Dawn's face became serious, "You can't, can you?"

Moon became fearful, "No—I just don't want to discuss this at a nightclub where we can barely hear over music around strangers."

"But you are not around strangers. You are with me, and I want to know if you are in love with me. It's simple: You either are, or you are not." Dawn gently let Moon out of his arms and sat in the chair.

The distance between them relieved her, allowing her room to breathe and think. She needed him to understand that she wasn't ready for what he wanted, and she knew it would hurt him, but she wasn't prepared. Even though she felt the same way, she couldn't bring herself to say the words. This time, she couldn't take a break from the conversation like she had done in the past. There were no excuses – she wasn't sick, and they weren't in a situation where his family could easily distract them. She felt lost and didn't know what to do.

"Say something, Aira—say something," he pleaded.

Moon was scared and said, "I love you, Dawn, but—" as she fiddled with her nails.

"But what? Huh— you can't say it," he scowled.

"You said there was no rush," her face saddened.

"I did."

"What has changed?" her heart raced in fear of things going wrong, which they were.

"If I am being honest, I said it to appease my insecurities, but I didn't mean it."

"Why would you do that? Dawn! I—" she said, bewildered.

Dawn held his composure, "Are you going to say it?"

"Dawn."

Moon knew this wouldn't go well, but they had multiple discussions on the matter, and that was the problem. Of course, she would love to run around shouting from the top of her lungs that she was "in love." She moved her chair closer to Dawn and tried to caress his face, but he lightly slapped it away. He was making her sad because she did not understand the change in his mood. Where was all this coming from, and why now? She sympathized with him and understood where he was coming from and the need to be loved, but not like this. She wouldn't let any of this get to her and change her perspective on the matter or him. He was hurt, and that was understandable.

Dawn had a guilty look on his face. "I didn't mean to do that," he said, kissing the hand he slapped away. "It's just that I love you so much. I'm afraid to admit this week had its ups and downs, but it made me even more in love with you, and I want to know if you feel the same." His eyes searched hers for answers.

"I had a great time this week, too."

"And that is great." Moon looked at him with sympathy. "It's not that hard to tell me how you feel."

"I know it doesn't seem like it, but it is hard for me, and you know that."

"I do."

Moon chuckled and said, "Exactly! I told you that, so I don't know why we are having this conversation."

He rubbed his eyebrow, disheartened. "When I was standing on that balcony and saw you dancing, I thought, 'Wow, this is the woman I am going to grow old with, have kids with, and marry.' It doesn't take much to know if you want to spend the rest of your life with someone or if you are in love with them," he said, then leaned forward and placed his elbows on his legs.

Moon's eyes softened as she said, "My love," and kissed him, but he didn't kiss her back.

His demeanor was cold. "You are being mean—I don't like it," she said with an unhappy smile.

Dawn shrugged and said, "Well—we can't get what we always want."

Moon was utterly skeptical of her current experience. She couldn't shake off the feeling that it must all be a prank or a joke, as she couldn't fathom why he was suddenly so distant just because of a few words. She had poured her heart out to him, expressing her love in every way possible. Why couldn't he give her the time she needed to process things? It all felt so unjust.

"Okay. I do feel the same as you. Baby, I do." She said as if she was going to cry. She didn't like this side of him, though she had seen it many times, just not towards her. Her doe eyes became glossy, and so did his.

He bit his bottom lip and said, "Okay then! Why can't you say the words!"

"Shush! Before they hear you."

Dawn laughed and said, "Who? Them? People!"

"Dawn!" she yelled with a crack in her voice.

He closed his eyes. "Baby, I'm telling you how I feel, and you are not meeting me halfway."

"I'm trying to my love." Dawn knelt before her on his knees. Moon was shocked and looked around to make sure no one was watching. "Baby! What are you doing?"

"What do I need to do? Huh?" he kissed her hands. "Tell me what I need to do for you to say, 'Dawn, I'm in love with you,' huh?" His eyes were full of earnestness. "Tell me what I must do, baby, because I am giving you my all." He took Moon's hand and placed it on his face, and she could see how he felt through her touch.

"My love, I honestly do not know. I'm not ready. It doesn't mean I love you less or that I don't just because I don't say it."

The atmosphere around them became scorching and unbreathable. Their hearts swell with empathy for each other's situation. He gave her small pecks on the hand. "Dawn, I love you; isn't that enough? —please let it be enough. Everything you said can happen, regardless."

He was consumed with irrationalness, "No."

"Then, I do know what else you want me to say," she pleaded.

Her hand still caressed his face.

"Rose, I would do anything for you," he said, full of love. "Can you say the same?"

Moon smiled affectionately. "Yes!"

"Mm-hmm," he said, then became silent and pulled away from her.

"Dawn?"

She didn't think the night would pan out this way, and it was going horribly. Why did he have to ruin it? She loved him, which was enough for her; why did he need her to shout it out loud? He was not himself and began to scare her. She needed Summer to intervene. It doesn't take that long to come back from the bathroom. This was a battle lost, and he was in denial. They couldn't force each other to do what they wanted, so it was time to leave.

"My love, why don't we return to the room, cool off, and recollect ourselves?"

Moon quickly put her shoes back on, and Dawn stood back up on his feet, towering over her.

"Why do you do that?"

Moon furrowed and said, "Do what?"

"Oh, I don't know. Change the subject or give bullshit answers."

Moon snickered, "You do the same."

He nodded and said, "You're avoiding the truth when my heart is open to you."

Moon scoffed, "Why am I on trial? You're the one being unreasonable." She clasped her hands.

"Please, let's just go. I'm tired," she said, and she could see the wheels turning in his head.

Frustrated, he wiped his face and demanded, "Say it," standing over Moon.

Moon was shocked at the audacity. "No," she said as she got up from the chair and started to walk away.

Dawn pulled her back and shook her by the arms, demanding, "Say it! Say it!"

Moon was terrified and pleaded with him to stop, but he persisted, repeating, "Say it," as his eyes turned crazed, and tears streamed down his face. Moon felt a strong sense of responsibility.

"Dawn, stop! Dawn!" she screamed until Summer and Adrian ran over to pull them apart.

Everyone stared at Dawn like he was batshit crazy except Moon; she couldn't help but cry and look at him with all the love in the world.

Embarrassed, he said, "I'm Sorry," tears streamed down his face.

"My love," she said with pity. Adrian stood between him and the girls.'

"Are you okay, Moon?"

Moon nodded. "I'm okay. It was a misunderstanding," she looked to Dawn for confirmation.

"Yeah, it was," Dawn said, feeling dazed.

"I hope that's all it was, Dawn!"

Adrian put his hand out, "Wait! They said it was a misunderstanding and that it was okay."

"Shut up! Adrian, he was practically—"

"Please! Everyone, it was nothing. Can we go?"

Dawn stood quietly, then walked away. "Dawn? Dawn!" Moon shouted.

"Let him go," Summer insisted.

"It's okay; I will go check on him," Adrian said as he rubbed Moon's chin, and she pulled away.

Summer led Moon back to the seating and checked up on her. Moon filled Summer in on what had happened and explained that it was a highly emotional moment. She understood his pain, but it did not excuse his behavior. When he calmed down, she planned to scold him and make sure he did not do such a thing again, nor feel comfortable doing it. It took strength to convince Summer not to tell anyone else about it and to ensure Adrian didn't either. She could hear his ex and Crystal laughing in victory, but she didn't want his parents involved as it would worsen everything. After that, Adrian returned and explained how he couldn't find Dawn.

What happened didn't sit right with her. He rarely acted like that around her, making her hate love even more. He reminded her of her mother in that moment, of how she would become mad out of nowhere over love. Except with him, he was not drunk. It crushed her to see him that way, but she made it known she loved him, not that it mattered to him. He wanted to hear, "I'm in love with you," but she was not ready, or at least she thought so. How could he have an outburst like that? Now, his sister and Adrian will think he has been abusing her. She hoped she could erase that thought because he would never. This should have happened in their privacy, and now she has to deal with others' emotions on top of hers.

Moon appeared irritated, "I'm not broken, so stop staring at me like I am," she said.

"Sorry. I want to make sure you are okay," Summer said tentatively.

"I've said five million times I am okay. I'm worried about Dawn. Where do you think he is?"

"He probably went home, but then again, I do not know him as well as I used to."

"I want to be alone, okay," she said, curling the ends of her hair.

Summer, determined, said, "Are you sure? We can leave together or look for Dawn with you."

"No. No. I want to be alone and the one to find him."

"Okay." They both spoke.

"Thank you. This is between us, and I will call you when things are settled," Moon said with a reassuring smile and wink.

Moon tried to think where he could have gone. She considered four options: the VIP room, the manor, the bar, and the restrooms. Everyone, including Moon, attempted to call his phone, but he didn't answer. She gathered her thoughts and began looking for him. The bar was almost empty, with only two people in sight. The VIP room was also empty, with the curtain closed, but she checked thoroughly in case he was hiding. She tried texting him again, expressing her love for him and her disappointment rather than anger. She assured him that she would always love him and asked him to let her know his whereabouts so they could go home and work things out. The last place to look was the men's restrooms, which made her feel even more awkward because it was not in her reality to hunt down her first real boyfriend in a nightclub.

She searched the crowd on the dance floor, looking at every face, but nothing. She didn't mean what she said; she wanted him to know she loved him so deeply that she would drown in it like she was trapped in the deep blue sea: no air, no life, all love. She was too afraid to admit to herself, especially to him, that she was in love with him. It took a long time to come to that conclusion until that night at the fountain in front of the Wolfe Manor. It had to be there for a while because she never looked at anybody like she did Dawn. He was everything to her, her a thousand suns but with a beating heart. He was the first for everything for her, from taking her virginity to becoming her first love and providing her with the desire for new beginnings. It took a minute to process things, but she was human. What more could she do but be rational and try not to feel or even think? It was too early, too soon, too hard. The only love she felt was maternal, and it was her grandparents. The amount of fear and doubt that could build up from love like that from a man, a man she was romantically involved with, a man she thought she would never see again after one night, who was now part of her life and whom she did not know how to part with.

Unfortunately, her reality was him and only him. They could not live and breathe without each other in such a short time. If anyone knew, they would call them maniacs.

She walked towards the restrooms and didn't see him but saw a couple kissing. She turned around to leave but noticed it was Rainey Crow, and she couldn't believe it. She decided to take another glance so she wouldn't think she was crazy because this would be the third time she ran into the girl. She could swear she was a stalker. In the corner of her eye, there she was, but it was dark, and it wasn't until she moved into the light that she saw who she was kissing. The man wore all-black attire, with jewelry similar to Dawn's and hairstyle the same way. Rainey's leg was around his waist while he hoisted her up while making out, and she could have sworn she was losing her mind.

It was a fragment of her imagination; this could not be the man who so devotedly loved her and begged for her to feel the same way. It wasn't even a case of him not kissing back because he was, and his hands were caressing her body as if she were his. She had to prove herself wrong, so she lightly called his name. "Dawn," she murmured, then spoke louder, "Dawn?"

The man turned to look at Moon, and it was him. No other man had his exact face: those dark green eyes, chiseled chin, and gorgeous dimples. Rainey had a smug look on her face and kissed him on the chin to add to the horror. Her body dropped into the depths of hell as she grew cold; her eyes blackened. He pushed Rainey away and tried to move closer to Moon, but she stepped back and ran so he could not plead his case.

Everyone dancing was entranced, blocking every way she could run. She wanted so badly to hide and never be found, but she fought through the crowd as there were more people than before. The shoes she wore made her stumble, but she persisted. "Aira!" she could hear him call but didn't dare to look back. "Aira!" he called fiercely. How could she be so stupid? How could she believe he loved her? He was never hers, to begin with, and she fell for it. It was good that she never admitted her true feelings to an extent because it seemed to get her nowhere. And if he did love her, he was royally messed up for betraying her over such a misunderstanding.

She stumbled over a martini glass as she made her way across the dance floor. However, she was determined to leave the dreadful place and escape him. She thought she was getting closer to the stairs but somehow ended up further away, finding the situation insanely amusing. Just as she heard Dawn call her again, she felt him getting closer, but she refused to look back, knowing she would never return to him after that night. She removed her shoes, ready to crawl if necessary, but he caught up. He grabbed her waist from behind, and despite her fighting, she couldn't break free from his tight grip.

The blaring music irritated her ears, and amidst the noise, she could only hear him saying, "Aira, it's not what you think! She kissed me!" Moon struggled to move his hands, but he wouldn't let go. "It's not what you think!" Moon refused to listen to anything he had to say. Her heart, which was filled with love for him, was now full of sorrow as her body ached and her mind collapsed. She fell back, and he picked her up into his arms. The only way she could react was to scream and kick for dear life, begging him to let her go.

She cried endlessly, and his response was, "I love you." His eyes were teary, intense with emotion.

# 19. Collateral Damage

**As** they left the club; Dawn carried her in his arms as they returned to the car in the dimly lit parking lot. However, once they reached the car, she slipped out of his grasp and attempted to flee, only to be caught by him just as she was about to escape. He held onto her from behind, wrapping his arms around her waist tightly, almost like a parasite clinging on. Despite her pleas to be released, he refused to let go. He held her firmly, cradling her like he couldn't bear to be without her. They stood next to the Mustang for what seemed like an eternity, with him breathing in her scent and planting a kiss on her neck.

He cried out to her, "I need you to listen to me," his tears wetting her hair.

Moon did not say a word, but one thing was for sure: she planned never to speak to him again. The brim of her toes pressed against the harsh pavement as she stood on tiptoe.

"Aira? Please say something—anything," he whispered. He wanted her to speak, to do what he wanted, and to control her, but that would never happen. If she were to talk, it would be on her terms, and since he wanted to hear words pouring out of her mouth, so be it.

She licked the tears from her lips and stared at the ground, then said, "I hate you and always will."

Dawn's core was shaken. "You're upset," he said.

She sneered and said, "No. I mean it from the bottom of my heart, not that you care." He dared to kiss her with the same lips that touched Rainey Crow. It made her sick to her stomach, and it made her despise him. Every emotion she ever had was on high at the moment, and she couldn't come down.

"Aira—I know you think you know what you saw, but it was the opposite."

Moon nodded and said, "I hate you no matter the reason because— because you were fucking making out with her!" she screamed to the top of her lungs, then cried again. Her body stopped resisting his embrace, and she became weak, leaning back into his arms, murmuring, "I just want to leave. Please! —Dawn."

He took in her scent again, then said, "Okay, rose, but I'll let you go only if you don't run."

She breathed a sigh of relief and said, "Thank you," her mouth trembled.

"I want you to leave with me." Moon was quiet. "I want you to leave with me, and I can explain everything."

She remained quiet. "Do not leave it like this, rose, please."

Moon nodded to shut him up, knowing she would get away from him as soon as possible when she had the chance. He couldn't be trusted, and there was no logical explanation for what he had done to them. It was like she was on a rollercoaster, begging to be let down. Dawn released Moon and opened the car door, letting her inside. Then, he bent down to be face-to-face with her.

"I'm going to get the things you left in the club, and I'll come right back," he said with a guilty smile.

Moon stared expressionless and said, "They are just things. They have no value, not really."

"No matter," he sighed. "I will get them, so sit tight." He looked at Moon pathetically in love and said, "I love you," then closed the car door.

She never thought she could feel as sick as she did right now. It was exhausting to be in this very moment. She went over every possible scenario as to why he would break her heart. *Did he still love her?* She feared he would do such a thing and not feel bad about it. He loved her, no doubt, but not enough. He wasn't a man. He was a boy. A broken little boy who felt good hurting others. He and Crystal were two peas in a pod. They sought to hurt people with their deepest fear or insecurity. He knew. He knew. He knew she hadn't loved anyone before, and he chose to tap out in the worst possible way from their first obstacle. *I love him so much—why? Why did he have to do this?*

She couldn't breathe and wanted to cry all night. She did not know what else to do but run away. Tears wet her face, and it was as if she could physically feel her heart stop. What made it worse for Moon was that he did this random act without at least still loving his ex—not that she knew if he did or didn't. She clasped onto the dashboard of the Mustang and tried not to have a panic attack, but at that point, it was inevitable.

As Moon's temperature rose, flashes of their passionate encounter came to mind: her leg wrapped around him, their kisses, her moans, her pleasure-filled smirk, and him looking disheveled. Reluctantly, she noticed the rings she had on her finger; she was pissed, so pissed. What would have been their point if your partner had been unfaithful? She snatched the rings off her finger, threw them on the floor, and then cried. The whole trip came down to nothing; that is how she felt. It was all for nothing. She leaned back into the car seat, waiting for him to return. But she needed to get away, and she needed to think quickly. She did not owe him anything and did not have to stay in her position, but it broke her heart to try to leave again. It was unfair to her. *He had the nerve to smile and tell me, 'I love you.'* She placed her hand over her heart and cried nonstop. The moment she needed her nana, she wasn't there. The worst moment of her life, next to her mother reappearing, fifteen years later. Who better to understand than her nana? The only torture she has felt came from the one person she chose to trust with all her heart, and now nothing. Nothing was the word that popped into her head the most because that was how she felt.

The bareness of her feet moved back and forth on the car floor for stimulation since nothing else calmed her down. She closed her eyes, breathing in and out, hoping for a miracle. Everything on her hurt, and she wanted to go home and crawl into a ball. She didn't even have her phone, which was even more torture. She couldn't call Summer or Marleen to save her. She had to do it all on her own, be an adult. She moved her feet faster on the car floor carpet and harder because it was wearing off. She wanted to cry again, but she was tired of constant crying. She looked behind her to ensure Dawn was not coming; she would make a run for it barefoot and strung out. Dramatic it was, but how freeing to be set free from the pain and seeing his face. *I'm in love with him.* She opened the car door hesitantly and stepped out. She looked around to make sure he wasn't coming, and something incredible happened. She bumped into his cousin Adrian, who was not too far from the Mustang, but he didn't see her.

"Adrian!" she shouted with a friendly smile. She was disheveled, barefoot, with wrinkled hair and a puffy face from crying. Adrian looked confused when he saw her standing alone. Moon approached him, feeling exhausted but hopeful. "It's so nice to see a familiar face," she said with a sad smile.

"It's nice to see you too," Adrian said, unsure. "Where is Summer or Dawn? Why are you all alone out here barefoot?" He looked concerned.

"I need a ride back to the manor, and I don't have my phone, so—" she said with kindness. Moon rolled her eyes. "Are you going to give me a ride or not?"

Adrian scoffed and said, "Not until you answer my question."

Moon impatiently said, "Summer left after I told her too because I was going to find Dawn, and I did —"

"And?"

"Please! I need a ride. I can explain on the way." She looked around her, impatient.

"Moon, listen, I'm tired and don't have time for your drama with Dawn."

"Adrian! Please!" she cried out.

Adrian was stunned, "Okay, okay."

She clasped her hands together and smiled, "Thank you!"

They both got into the car, and Dawn appeared outside the club without coincidence. He had Moon's things in his hand and walked towards the Mustang. Adrian spotted him and said, "There is the man of the hour. It seems you don't need me after all."

"Yes, I do. Drive!" Moon said with panic.

"What is going on, Moon?"

"I'll tell you on the way," she said impatiently.

Adrian shook his head. "No."

"What?"

"I'm not moving this car until I know what is going on," his hand on the keys in the ignition.

She knew she had little time before Dawn figured out where she was, so she told the truth the best she could.

"He hurt me, and I need to get away from him as soon as possible, okay."

"Hurt you. How did he hurt you?"

Dawn started to shout Moon's name and looked around the parking lot. She needed to convince Adrian before he spotted them, and she had to endure seeing his cheating and lying face. If she got near him, she feared she might die from heartbreak. "I caught him kissing someone else—happy!" she said, holding back tears.

"Please take me back. Help a girl out." Moon's eyes teared up again.

Adrian was speechless but started the car. "Thank you—Adrian," she deep breathed.

He smiled with pity, "No problem."

Adrian backed the car out of the parking lot, and Dawn saw Moon in his cousin's car. He appeared confused and hurt, but his emotions didn't stop him from running towards the vehicle as Adrian drove off. He pounded on the car, shouting Moon's name and pleading for answers as he ran alongside it. "Moon!" was all she could hear as the car exited the club's parking lot. She felt indifferent to leaving him behind, but he couldn't imagine her pain and how stupid she felt for falling for him. She never wanted to bring others into her mess, especially Adrian, but what could she do? At least he was decent enough to give her a ride, though she had to be interrogated first. It wasn't like he was so innocent. He placed a bet on his cousin and tricked him into racing. He should not be the one to judge on "drama."

The drive started in silence and nothing more. Adrian glanced at Moon in the corner of his eye, and she pretended not to notice. Pity was one emotion she did not want anyone to feel for her. She could handle her own and did not need fake looks and concerns. It was bliss to her to be home free. She had the space to sort out her feelings without being consumed by "him." The thought of coming to terms with what happened upon her return and explaining everything to Summer made her want to shrink into dust. She would tell her mother, but it would be weird and too soon. What if her mother was the only one who understood her situation? Summer stood up for her in the club, but could she do the same under the influence of Crystal? They were still attached to the hip. She didn't know how to approach the situation, but all she wanted to do was to escape it.

She slightly lowered the window, allowing crisp, fresh air to fill the car. Hoping the invigorating breeze would bring her mental clarity, she carefully placed her hand outside the window, moving it against the wind. Adrian chose to take a shortcut to avoid traffic, driving down a long road surrounded by trees with the city visible in the distance. Moon had this hollow feeling, and she didn't exactly know why, but she wondered if this was what her mother felt when her father died. Dawn was not dead, but it felt like it in her heart—or was it her heart that was the one dying? "So—he kissed another girl," Adrian said, unsurprised.

"Yeah," she said with a bitter tone.

"Did you know the girl?" He inquired.

Moon rolled her eyes and said, "It was Rainey Crow."

"Wow! I would have never thought—"

"Yeah, why is that?"

Adrian chuckled and said, "He hated her after what happened, but I saw her at the club. I didn't think she was there for him."

Moon focused and said, "You saw her?"

Adrian nodded. "Yeah, assumed she was there with some friends."

"No," she said tensely.

"It was strange because when I went to look for him, she was sitting with someone in her section, but I couldn't see because of the dark lights, so I assumed she was with a friend."

Moon's heart dropped below sea level, and she was disgusted by her feelings toward the love of her life. To think he took his time with his ex and then went and did what he did was disgusting and diabolical. She wanted to vomit at the thought. She tried to keep her composure, or she would have been crying all night and would have to endure the lectures of "wise" Adrian, who was no better than Dawn.

"Well, thank you for telling me," she swallowed hard as if drowning.

"Happy to add to the drama of Dawn Wolfe's life." He smiled. "It seems my cousin is back to his playboy antics."

"Playboy?" Moon asked, curious.

"Oh yeah, he didn't mention after his "break-up" he fucked every and any girl within a mile radius and got into illegal shit that sometimes landed him and me in jail—good times." He flashed a sarcastic smile.

"That isn't something to be proud of," she said with a judgmental look.

Adrian shrugged and said, "He had to cope with his girl using him, so he did what most kids did, you know."

Moon looked away. "The worst part was the bitch was pregnant with his baby, but the family took care of that."

Moon stared at Adrian angrily. "What?"

"Yeah, um —she was pregnant but lost it."

"Oh my god."

Adrian laughed, "Do not feel sorry for her. She used it as leverage to get a year's stipend of money from the Wolfe family, so they had the tabloids to say it was someone else's and she was fucking someone else while pregnant with his baby. I wouldn't be shocked if it wasn't his."

"Did he know?"

"Yes, he knew about all of it, so I'm shocked she was the one you caught him with."

Moon sighed. "You deserve better, if you don't mind me saying."

"I do, especially coming from you."

Adrian laughed, "I seemed to have touched a soft spot."

"No!" she said with a chuckle.

"I was just saying princess."

"Well, don't!"

Adrian shrugged and said, "You can always trade one cousin for another."

Moon looked at him disgusted and laughed, then said, "You're not my type." She pulled her hand back into the car and sighed heavily. "But then again, that never stopped me," she mumbled.

"Offer stands whenever you grow tired of the "golden boy.""

"Not in a million years and every lifetime," she said with a side-eye.

"I had to try, you know." He winked.

Moon did not say a word. If anything, he and Dawn were alike, except Dawn was better-looking, and his family cared a bit more about him. She wanted the ride to be over, but they had two more miles to go, so she turned on the radio to avoid the silence and avoid hearing Adrian's annoying opinions. Always Forever by the Cults played, which she found ironic and depressing. There was no "always and forever" for her and him. She had her answer to the question she had so dearly kept close to her heart, more than her mind. She wanted to mock it, but it beat her to the punch before she could say, "I'm in love with you." More than anything, she desperately wanted to fade away, but she just listened to the song, imagining what could have been. A short love lived for a week and a day.

It didn't alarm her that Dawn did not tell her anything more about his past. It was not about a baby, but it was apparent he had unfinished business with Rainey, which is why he did what he did, amongst other reasons. *Did he even love me or try to convince himself he did to get over her?* The girl had rotten intentions but still loved him. How could she compete with someone who was possibly his first love and heartbreak—things like that never go away? It stays with you forever, and she knew it but hoped he was strong enough to love her at least more. He should have fought for her instead of seeking comfort in his ex, whom he claimed not to love anymore. It was a devasting thing to process, but the hurt she felt this night could never wither away as quickly as she liked.

Like Dorothy, she clicked her feet together and wished to return home with Marleen, but it did no good. She was stuck in California with a broken heart and an insufferable chauffeur.

"Is there any way you could speed it up, just a little," she asked warmly.

"I can go fast, but it won't change that we have two more miles to go."

She threw her head back against the seat and sighed. "Don't push your luck. We might make it back before he does." Adrian kept his eyes on the road. "Do you need to stop anywhere or need anything?"

"No. I want to go home," she said, looking out the car window.

"Okay, not even shoes?"

"Not even shoes, Adrian," she gritted her teeth.

But with just her luck, they stopped at a traffic light.

"I thought this road passed by the traffic."

"Not all traffic, but it's still like a back road." Moon rolled her eyes and nodded.

The piercing red light beamed onto the vehicle. She couldn't help but lose herself in the light, hoping it would turn green, though it's been red for a second. Would she still like the color red? He tainted the color with his actions. She knew she could have faced her fears and said, "I'm in love with you, Dawn." But she wasn't ready for such a big step; he knew she felt it; why that couldn't suffice for the time being, she didn't know. No matter because the night would not be too long for her, seeing as they would leave tomorrow, she didn't have to speak to him ever again. What woman in her right mind would? The light turned green, and a car zoomed past them at such a furious speed that even Moon was taken aback. "So much for safety at night," Adrian chuckled.

It was only a few minutes before the same car backed up, but they couldn't see too much with Adrian's tinted windows. It was good for keeping people out but never helping the driver to see. Adrian slowed down so as not to get into a crash with the other car; he had to see what they were doing. It was pitch black, so even through the windshield, he couldn't catch a good glimpse. "open the glove box," he demanded.

"why?"

He looked annoyed. "Just do it!" he whispered.

Moon opened the glove department, and Adrian reached over and grabbed a box. It looked like a toolbox, but when he opened it, there was a semi-automatic gun. At this point of the night, Moon wasn't even phased that he had one. Dawn's family was full of surprises.

"What are you going to do?"

He winked and said, "I'm going to go see why this car decided to follow us," putting the gun in his jacket pocket. "And keep quiet. I don't want them to know you're in the car for safety reasons, just in case, okay?"

She nodded. "Be careful!" she whispered.

Adrian gave her the thumbs up and exited the car. She couldn't see a thing, which made her even more worried because she did not want to deal with a robbery or plain death just because someone felt like it. There was nothing at first; she could hear him speaking to someone, but before she knew it, there was yelling. Then she felt a blow to the car, and it wasn't a bullet but a body being slammed. She froze up and didn't know what to do. She didn't know if Adrian was hurt or the other person.

The car took another hit, and she screamed. She then put her hand over her mouth.

Adrian yelled, "She doesn't want to go with you!" It dawned on her who it could be, but it couldn't be Dawn.

They sped away, and there was no way he could catch up to them that fast. She heard someone jiggling the handles of the car doors and pounding on them.

"Moon?" he called. "Aira!" he called again angrily.

And she knew it was him, but she didn't dare open the doors, and it seemed Adrian was on the same page. "Adrian open the door," he demanded.

The voices were so muffled that she was surprised she could hear anything. "No. leave her be—give her some time." After that, she heard Adrian's body being slammed against the car once more.

"Fuck you!" Dawn yelled.

"Fuck you too!" Adrian yelled back. It grew quiet for just a second.

She heard slamming, and then Adrian exclaimed, "What are you doing? What—?"

Moon huddled in the passenger seat, frightened and anxious about what was happening. Suddenly, Dawn's fist pounded against the car window; his knuckles sounded like they were going to break, and the glass was cracking with each blow; his fist turned red, then there was a loud crash as the driver's side window shattered, scattering glass everywhere. With his bloody hand, Dawn reached into the car and unlocked the doors.

He then walked over to Moon's side and pulled her out of the car, kicking and screaming, "No! No!" she cried. "Cheater! Let me go!" He threw her over his shoulder and said nothing.

She saw Adrian bleeding from his mouth and looking pissed. Dawn placed Moon into the car by force, and his hand was still bloodied, though she did try to put up a fight.

He glanced at Adrian, "Don't try it again!" he pointed at him with one of his bloody fingers.

Adrian smirked and said, "Fuck you!"

Dawn laughed and said, "Fuck you too, stay away from me and MY GIRL!"

"She won't be for long!" Adrian stood outside his car, rubbing his temple and feeling frustrated.

Meanwhile, Dawn got back into the Mustang in silence. His hand was bleeding all over his lap, which made her heart swell. She hated seeing him like this, knowing he had brought it upon himself. Even now, she worried about him, regardless of his involvement with Rainey Crow. Nevertheless, she said nothing about it. As they sat in the car, both remained silent. He tried to touch her, but she flinched. To Moon, he seemed like a stranger, and perhaps that was who he was. He tested his hand by opening and closing it; the cuts were bruised and deep, with blood spurting out like water. "I told you not to run, and you did it anyway," his leg was shaking, "Why can't you stop for once and listen?" Moon looked at him like he was full of shit. She did not speak.

"Oh, so now you are not talking to me," his eyes were sad. "I'm sorry—" he stumbled on his words and began to cry. "Aira?" Moon looked out the window and settled into the seat, putting on her seat belt. "I love you so much, and I'm sorry."

Moon gave an empty look. "I don't care about you, your hand, and your intentions," she sighed. "Take me to the manor so this night will be over, and I can go home."

Dawn nodded and said, "I didn't mean for this night to end like this."

"Well, we don't always get what we want, do we?" she said, folding her arms.

He brushed back some of her hair with his bloody finger, touching her cheek for a second. She flinched in response to his touch, but it made her heart flutter slightly. He removed his hand, started the car, and said, "Whether you listen or not, I will explain my actions to you; at least give me a chance." He looked at her like a bird with a broken wing. "Don't leave me. I don't think I could handle it, not when it comes to you."

Their eyes met for a longing moment, then Moon looked out the window, trying her hardest not to fall for his act. She could feel his gaze as she tried not to look again. Dawn's bloody hand gripped the wheel and started the car. She just wanted to go home. She never wanted to experience such humiliation and feelings like this again. Did he love her? Could she feel worthy of love like others? Was she one of the women on his list to conquer like the rest? These questions swarmed her mind as he drove them back to the manor. She initially found Dawn mysterious, but now she realized that he was deeply wounded and oblivious to how he inflicted pain on others due to his suffering. It took her a while to realize this, despite the outbursts of anger and not sharing critical points of his life.

# The Truth

They crept upstairs so as not to alert the rest of the household. Neither of them uttered a word to each other during the car ride or after. She threw her things on the floor when they entered the room and sat on the bed, her mind still not quiet. Dawn stood by the door, afraid of entering, hoping she would not start yelling immediately. However, Moon sat on the bed silently, ready to hear his reasons for caressing and kissing Rainey Crow, which he did not have, but she was fascinated to see him try to make up some. He closed the door behind him, went to the chair near the bed, and sat down. Neither of them could stand the anticipation, though they knew the outcome of this night. But they still hoped for a better ending to the mess they endured together. She watched as he reached into his pocket, pulled out the sol-mate rings, and placed them on the side table.

"You forgot these," he said hurt. "I know you are angry, but I hoped you would still want them back," he said with a slight smile.

Moon rolled her eyes, "No. I do not want them or anything else you gave me. I'll return it all, okay." She said with a sarcastic smile.

"I don't want you to." She turned her head away. "These were gifts, and they should stay with you."

"I don't want them, okay? They will remind me of you." Her heart skipped a beat.

Dawn's heart dropped. "Okay, Sorry."

"Let's get this over with. What was the inexcusable reason for kissing her? It had better be a good one."

"I—"

Moon whispered, "You can't, can you." She said with her face covered with repulsion.

Dawn started to cry, and Moon looked away. Her heart was filled with adrenaline and pain, and she couldn't help but hold her chest. It felt like everything in the room was spinning. Dawn covered his face as he cried, too guilty to speak the truth they both knew: He betrayed her with Rainey Crow. She wanted to explode so badly, but she held it together because he did not deserve a reaction from her. It would do her no good either way. She held back her tears as she turned to look at Dawn.

"You're crying when I should be the one crying," she said, gripping onto the edge of the bed.

Dawn wiped the tears from his face, his eyes boiling red, and staring at Moon. "You're right, but I'm just as hurt as you."

Moon shook her head in disbelief. "Hurt? Yes, I can understand that, but it gave you no fucking right to kiss another girl and leave me out in the cold looking for you when you were having the time of your life with your ex!"

He pushed his hair back out of his face, "You're absolutely right," he said, raising his eyebrows.

"Thank you!" Moon clapped while laughing hurt. "You can finally admit it."

"Yeah." He murmured.

"Why?" her doe eyes glossy. "Why? Was it a game to you? Am I nothing more than a toy for you to manipulate? What exactly was it?"

"No. No!" he said while shaking his head, then rubbed his chin. He got up from the chair and paced around the room. Moon slid further on the bed, sitting in the middle, waiting for Dawn to explain his actions.

"When they broke us up, I felt so hurt, yeah, hurt, and I needed to breathe. I just needed a second from everyone." He kept pacing back and forth. "The woman I was in love with just told me she wasn't in love with me, so yeah, I needed some space."

Moon bit down on her lip, tasting some blood, then said, "I did not say that, Dawn. I said I wasn't ready to say it." Dawn sighed and said, "It's the same thing."

"No, there is a difference!"

"Not to me! You're in love with me, or you're not!"

"I love you, but isn't that enough?"

He smiled with rage. "No, it isn't!"

Dawn stopped pacing and stood by the window, his back to Moon.

"I don't know what happened, okay? I went into the men's restroom to calm myself, and when I walked out, Rainey was there. And she started asking me what was wrong and saying she still loved me. I don't know." He turned his head slightly. "I like the things she was saying that I wish you would say, and then one thing led to another. I tried to stop, but—"

Moon burst into silent tears. "You're a piece of shit," she said with a crack in her voice.

"I know I am!" He turned around. "I'm sorry, but you were laughing in my face! You didn't even want to say you were in love with me. I felt hurt and betrayed. I felt played with, if anything, but I'm used to it!"

"I never said I didn't have my faults but don't you fucking dare imply that!" she sighed. "And I didn't laugh in your face. I love you, so what would be the point of humiliating you like you did me."

His face tensed up. "Fair enough, but it felt like it. Like you didn't trust me enough to say it."

"And here we are!"

"I mean, you heard about me, right." He implied.

She scoffed and said, "I heard about you, but did I know who you were? No. If anything, you were another stranger to pass by!"

"Mm-hm," He scowled.

"Very much so, especially from the girls crying at your door and gossiping about you all over the city and in our fucking building. So yeah, I heard about you!" She stood on the bed on her knees and faced Dawn, "So you tell me!" Both of them were furious and crying. Their words barely rolled off their tongues, and their bodies were so shaken with exhaustion that they wanted to rip each other apart. They stared at each other as if in battle, wondering who would emerge as the winner.

Dawn chuckled nervously, "How am I to blame in this? I tried understanding. I tried to understand you and your reasons for shutting me out, but now it has gotten so out of hand. I needed some reassurance, and you spit in my face."

"Out of hand, Dawn? —you—you kissed her! How can you not be to blame for it!"

"She kissed me! Listen—"

Moon was tired, so tired. "You kissed her back and more than that!"

"I try and try, and here I am." She cried out.

Dawn tried to touch Moon, but she smacked his hand away, so he went back to stand by the window.

"You are not the only one who has been trying, and I meant everything that I have said or done for you. I meant everything that I put into this relationship."

"Yeah, you did, but only to mess it up!"

Frustrated, Dawn pulled on his hair and said, "Aira, I'm burning up inside, and all I want is you. Tell me what to do to make it all better. I do not love her. I LOVE YOU! I'M IN LOVE WITH YOU!" he sobbed out.

She looked at him compassionately and said, "I don't know love. I don't know."

Dawn nodded in aggravation and said, "You never know," as he pointed at Moon.

"What?" she said with an irritated expression, her chest breathing heavy.

"What can I say, Aira? You never know if you just like me, love me, hate me, or anything! You never fucking know!" Moon left the bed and stood beside it, holding the post. Her anger escalated because she responded politely to him, but that would stop now.

"You're the one to talk. Mr. I'm alone, and everyone is against me!"

"Says the girl who tries not to cry herself to sleep every night because of her mommy issues and that most of everyone she loves in life is DEAD!"

Moon smacked Dawn across the face. "Stop, okay. Stop!" she shouted, defeated.

"Stop what! It's true. You are a princess who can make mistakes, but everyone else must be a model citizen. Such the little moralist," he said, soothing his face after the smack.

"I can't believe this. You hurt me, and now I have to answer to you!" she cried out, her mouth trembling.

She sat on the bed, rocking back and forth to calm herself. She needed to pretend he wasn't there, or her heart might explode from intense hatred.

"Aira," He called softly.

"Stop!"

"Aira," He called again.

"Stop! You're hurting me—you're hurting me!" She pleaded and cried, looking up at him with surrender. "I—"

He was silent as he gazed at Moon's face, fully aware of the additional damage he had caused and unable to handle it any longer. His face conveyed terror and confusion as though he had reached his limit. Without a word, he left the room, leaving her behind in uncertainty. She longed to follow and press him to resolve the argument, but she was emotionally exhausted, especially in dealing with him. So, she prepared for a good night's sleep. Locking the door for privacy, she picked up the rings he had left on the table and placed them carefully on the nightstand next to the bed. It was not a sign of weakness but a way for her to remind herself of his actions and to never forget.

She curled into a ball under the sheets. The night was silent, and so was his side of the bed. She didn't curse herself for her weaknesses, at least not in private. She turned over and lay on his pillow, taking in his scent. The pretty brown eyes she had were dried out from crying all night. His scent stained her heart, making it flutter once more. She wouldn't be easy on him, but she hoped he would return to her.

*What if it's over? I do not know. I do not know what to do, Nana. It was hard, so hard, to even look at him, but God, it was so refreshing even though I hadn't seen him for an hour. I love him so much. Everything hurts, and I do not know how to soothe the pain. Nana! If only you were here. I miss you and Pa. I want to cry until everything is washed clean around me so that I can start over, but it's not easy. He hurt me, and, like any right-minded person, I responded with my true feelings. I have this weakness of forgiving others so slightly that I cannot let something this big slip. My dignity, heart, and love were betrayed, and he knows it. He dared to question me when he was readily at the feet of his ex. I don't know. To forgive him is like wearing my heart on my sleeve, to be kind to him is like wearing my heart on my sleeve, and to love him is to bear my heart and soul to him without any will because I would be delighted to do so.*

# 20. No More Lies

The loud sound of slamming doors forcefully pulled Moon out of her sleep in the dead of night. Her t-shirt clung uncomfortably to her skin, and her tired eyes struggled to focus. Dismissing the disturbance, she settled back onto the bed, clutching Dawn's pillow. The heat trapped beneath the covers prompted her to cast them aside, commencing a restless cycle of tossing and turning. Eventually, she managed to find a sliver of comfort, with her back turned to the window, a gentle breeze playing against her neck. The room was bathed in the ethereal glow of the night, casting intricate patterns of shadows resembling a sprawling tree. Her feet were entangled in the twisted sheets at the foot of the bed, and her hair cascaded partially out of her bonnet. Despite her best efforts, an elusive deep sleep evaded her, as if her body sensed a lurking presence. The distant noise emanating from the hallway served as an eerie confirmation.

Despite this, she consciously disregarded the unease, succumbing once again to the refuge of her dreams, wishing her problems to dissipate into the night.

Around 2:00 AM, she woke again and turned to the bedroom window. She lay on both her hands, her eyes closed, until she heard a loud thump. Slowly, she opened her eyes and sat up slightly. Her eyes darted towards the floor, and there was a cognac bottle and then a hand reaching for it. The hand was familiar. She questioned how he entered the room when she had locked the door. She couldn't see him because the bedroom chair was pulled into the corner of the darkest part of the room, his dark green eyes glowing as if he were a mysterious creature of the night. She squinted her eyes and said, "Dawn?"

He remained silent, drinking from the cognac bottle and staring at her, so she knew something had to be wrong. Without much context clues, she figured he was still upset from their earlier argument. "Dawn," she called again. Once more, he did not answer, and it made her anxious. His hands were the only things visible. One hand was bandaged from busting the car windows out, and the other was swollen and bruised from the fight with Adrian. She noticed he was still in the same outfit as earlier as well. She sat on the edge of the bed, waiting for him to speak. He leaned forward with the bottle in his hand and liquor dripping off his lips.

"Where have you been?" she asked without hesitation. He just stared at her. "I should be giving you the silent treatment after yesterday, not the other way around." She rubbed the sleep out of her eyes and threw her bonnet onto the bed; her hair cascaded down her back, thick and long. She did not want to play games with Dawn, yet he persisted. It crept her out that he was staring at her, not saying a word, and angry.

*How could he be more furious than me?*
*He turned our weekend into a disaster, and I'm being punished.*
*How selfish can he be?*

"Dawn," she shouted with irritation.

He smirked, then said, "Shush," placing his finger over his lips. "Shush!"

Moon shook her head in confusion. She knew he was drunk. He had to be, and it made her even angrier. Why did she have to fall for such a douche? She didn't know he was one at first, but it made it even harder for her. She was stuck in a mansion with a cheating boyfriend who had decided to drown his sorrows in alcohol instead of talking to her and facing the consequences. "Exhaustion" didn't even begin to describe how she felt. It was more like suffocation from the situation she was in. She had learned enough about her mother in the past two days, and now, just in one day, she had found out that her boyfriend wasn't who he pretended to be.

In a matter of weeks, they were moving too fast, so who would have thought? She laid back on the bed and then looked at Dawn. He continued to drink from the bottle, chuckling and ranting to himself as if he were a madman. She wasn't fazed by it because he was just drunk and eventually would pass out from his hysteria of emotions, but she didn't have to be drunk to do that. At least he was in a safe place with her, not somewhere wasted and in danger. Suddenly, he went quiet and sat back in the chair in the dark. She sat on her elbows and called his name; he did not answer again. Frustrated, she sat up and moved to the middle of the bed.

Dawn began to whistle a tune. The room was pitch black except for the moon's light shining through. He poured more alcohol into a glass and then set the bottle on the table. He drank each glass as if it were nothing.

Swirling the last drop of cognac, he looked up at Moon and said, "You know, you tend to talk in your sleep. I can never determine what you're saying, but I know enough to know you're not having a nightmare," he chuckled—then whispered, "Little rose, little rose, how can this be? Little rose, little rose, I need you next to me. Little rose, little rose, come home so I can tuck you in safely. Little rose, little rose, a gift meant to be."

Moon's heart sank in her chest. The tune sounded familiar, and now she knew why. It was the lullaby her mother used to sing to her, and that wasn't the only time he hummed it. She wanted to ask him how he knew that song, but it was clear that her mother had introduced him to it, or perhaps she had sung it in her sleep that night he stayed over. "Sounds familiar, baby?"

Moon rolled her eyes and said, "You plan on annoying me tonight, I see."

Dawn smirked, "Quite the opposite," as he finished the last cognac in his glass.

"What is this, Dawn? How can you sit here and act like this?"

"Act like what?" he shrugged.

"You already know, and if you're going to act like this, then please leave because I would like to get rest before our flight later."

He leaned back in his bedroom chair. "You're worried about rest and a flight while I'm here?"

She exclaimed, "Yes!" and bucked her eyes.

Dawn nodded his head and quietly placed the glass on the table.

"Not surprised—the princess needs her beauty sleep."

"Princess? Where is this coming from? Huh?"

"I don't know. You tell me."

Moon retorted, "I'm nowhere this spoiled and explosive brat you're trying to paint me randomly. I have been nothing but supportive and loyal to you."

"Mm-hmm," he nodded.

"I mean, what does it matter when you're putting your tongue down other girls' throats? Oh! Sorry! A girl. Your ex. SINGULAR!"

Dawn glared at Moon with his dark green eyes, filled with bitterness, but didn't say another word. Moon felt chills due to his behavior. It was cold and distant, no longer loving and inviting. She longed to run over to him, to kiss and hug him. Every bone in her body wanted to forgive him. She couldn't hate him even if she tried; it felt like a curse. She sensed he felt the same. She noticed he still wore the rings they had bought, and it touched her heart. Her rings were still on the nightstand beside the bed, but he brought misery upon himself. They could have worked things out and reached a reasonable solution, but NO, he wanted to make other plans. She would be a fool to forgive and forget such inexcusable actions, which went against her morals and beliefs. Her heart was broken, but she could not be gullible and a hopeless romantic. Even though she had her limits regarding being 'in love,' she did not want to be all consumed like her mother.

He used his injured hand to slowly open his shirt, taking a few deep breaths as he looked out the window. Tension filled the room, creating a distance between them. He had earlier begged for her forgiveness but now gave her the cold shoulder. Sensing that the situation wouldn't improve, she laid back on the bed, planning to fall asleep in the immense silence between them, although both were aware of an unspoken tension. Falling asleep wasn't easy with him nearby and the overwhelming urge to cry. She longed for the weekend to end, wishing her life could return to normal without him. In the back of her mind, she wondered if he felt the same way.

He continued to look out the bedroom window, his eyes restless and his body sprawled out in the chair. Moon dared not to look at him. She didn't want a stare of a thousand deaths between them, which felt more like death. The agony would be felt, and she did not wish to fault such a beautiful face. He was an asshole to her, but a gorgeous one at that. The man she spent time with was not the one in the chair, one with many demons in his closet and longing for love, not beyond black-and-white understanding. Moon knew they were at a crossroads, and both wanted to solve it, but the only solution would be to part. He broke the cardinal rule. If he were "in love" with her, he wouldn't even think of hurting or cheating on her, regardless of what she didn't grant him.

SUFFOCATED. Her mind was consumed with the same thoughts repetitively. All her peace was gone, and the room felt like a prison. She sat up in panic, unable to breathe. All she could think about was how she was a failure, regretting her choices and the trust she had put into life. Dawn saw tears flow from her brown baby doll eyes and hurried over. He held her face in his hands as he asked what was wrong, but she couldn't answer. It was like her lungs were full of water. He caressed her face, helping her take slow breaths while holding eye contact. He smiled as she calmed down, his first genuine smile since that night in the club. She lovingly touched his dimple, closed her eyes, and savored the respect and love they had left for each other.

When she opened her eyes, Dawn kissed her gently and sweetly. Her body relaxed in his arms, and all her worries melted away. His embrace was worldly, and it sent her into a frenzy. Their kiss grew passionate and intense as his hands tangled in her hair. But with what little strength she had, she pushed Dawn away and covered her mouth. Dawn savored the taste of her as he pushed his hair back. His eyes lingered on her as she looked at him with guilt. Moon averted his gaze, and Dawn played with her hair before he kicked off his shoes and took off his dress shirt. Moon lay on the bed, feeling confused and guilty as he rummaged through the closet for a change of clothes.

Moon lightly touched her lips, thinking about the kiss and how good of a kisser he was. She crossed her legs at the thought of him touching her in all the right places. "Why? Moon? Why?" she said, punching the bed. Dawn walked back into the room with a bare chest and pajama pants. She accepted that he would stay in the room even though there were more guest rooms he could sleep in. As long as he stayed on his side of the bed, she would be fine.

"You stay on your side, okay? I will do the same," Moon said with a forced smile.

Dawn, lost in thought, replied, "Okay."

"Okay?"

He nodded in compliance, still clearly drunk. "Okay," he shrugged.

Moon crawled over to the side of her bed, and Dawn stopped at the other side. She paid him no mind as she snuggled into bed. His arm was on his leg, and his back was to Moon, staring at the rings on the bedside nightstand. "Dawn? Are you okay?" she asked.

He fiddled with the rings, quiet and thinking. "I'm okay," he murmured.

"Tell me what's wrong," she insisted kindly.

He choked on his words at first, then said, "I'm sorry. I know I disrespected you and what we built together. I hope someday you forgive me." He peered back at Moon while crying.

She wiped his tears and replied, "I could never hate you; let's leave it at that." He smiled faintly, wiped his tears, and turned away, with Moon reclining on the bed.

"Some sleep—"

Drunk and interrupting, he slurred, "Do you know how long I waited to meet you?"

"The distance between us wasn't far, so no, I don't," Moon chuckled.

"Not because we were in the same building, but the first time I saw you."

Moon massaged her sore shoulders, indulging his drunkenness, and asked, "Okay, when did you first see me?" with a sigh.

"You were wearing a blue turtleneck sweater. Your hair was messy but freshly washed and curled. You had a prominent and noticeable gold locket around your neck. You were smiling and happy in the picture that your mother had of you, but I could also see a hint of lonesomeness in you." Dawn lay against the bed beside Moon.

She wrinkled her eyebrows and said, "What are you talking about? I thought you didn't know—"

Dawn glanced at her, his face red and his eyes tired. "Your mother kept tabs on you through your grandparents. She had this beautiful little girl she always talked about. She would show us pictures, and I could see why she would smile, joke, and cry over you. You were something so pure and distinct."

"Okay," she said, looking puzzled.

"I mean, I rarely paid attention to your mother, her mood swings and breakdowns. I figured you were lost to her until that picture was gifted on her birthday. I wanted to steal a pack of smokes," he said, slurring his words.

"I thought you said you didn't know."

"I lied, and so did your mother and stepdaddy," he laughed and mocked.

"I don't understand what is worse: your constant lying or that you think it's funny," she said disappointedly.

He laughed again and asked, "What else have I lied about, rose?"

"Rainey's baby," Moon said while she looked down. "Adrian told me the truth about it being yours and how she lost it."

Dawn's face dropped and appeared severe. "Why would he tell you that?"

"I don't know. Maybe he thought I should know." Moon caressed her temple.

"It seems like you place a lot of faith in Adrian."

"I mean, I can't trust you! And it's not like he lied to me, did he?"

"No."

Moon chuckled and said, "Well, there you go."

Moon sat in silence for a moment, and so did he. She pushed the covers to the side and got out of bed.

"I think we should sleep in separate rooms. We are just going to keep going at each other's throats."

"Why?" Dawn asked anxiously.

"You're drunk for one, and I'm too tired to bicker with you. My heart can't take it. I love you and—" Moon paused. "And I need a moment's peace."

"Aira, please! I'm sorry," he whined.

Moon sighed. "We can talk about it later, okay."

Moon walked towards the door, and Dawn blocked her. "It's your mother's fault."

"What are you talking about?" she asked while she tried to move him out of her way. "Dawn, move. I don't have time for this." He gripped her waist so she couldn't move, and Moon's heart started to pound out of fear.

"Dawn! Let me go!" She tried to reach for the door, but his body blocked her.

"It's okay, rose." His eyes grew intense. "I tried to tell you the truth for the longest time, and I never thought you would even date me. Since I was a kid, I knew you were the essence of my heart and mind. Something to never be assessed." Moon tried to push him away, but he was too strong.

She cried out repeatedly, "Let me go!"

Dawn moved Moon away from the door and tightened his grip on her waist. He pressed his face against hers, taking in her scent and pretending not to hear her pleas. He was determined to let her go only after she had listened to what he had to say. "Dawn! —please!" Moon cried out, feeling the pain from his grip on her waist.

"No! You know how long I've been waiting," he replied, their eyes meeting intensely. Dawn fell to his knees but maintained his grip on her waist. "I begged Bronte to keep tabs on you since I was a kid, but he stopped because he felt it was an obsession."

The pain in Moon's waist intensified. "My love, I hear you, but I need you to let me go, okay?" she said gently, tears welling in her eyes as she caressed his face. Dawn refused to release her, and his behavior became increasingly erratic. She felt the same fear she had experienced with her mother's drunken and volatile behavior over trivial matters. At that moment, she was terrified of him. As he continued to ignore her pleas, her fear grew.

"I love it when you call me that, so don't say it unless you mean it!" he cried.

"Yes, my love. I mean every word I do, but you're hurting me!" Moon's hands were placed on Dawn's shoulders.

"I never meant to, but I don't know how." Moon nodded. "I just wanted to meet you because a love blossomed that day. I saw your picture. Seeing such sadness from those exquisite eyes made me want to hold you. You know? It made me want to protect you from the world." He removed one hand from her waist, giving momentarily relief.

"Those big ole brown eyes," he said, stroking Moon's cheek aggressively. Moon squirmed as she cried. "Don't cry. This is a good thing, rose. It's the day I fell in love with you and when I saw you at the diner. I fell in love all over again."

Moon forced a smile. "And I love you too, my love. Please let me leave. Okay? Just let me leave."

Dawn was still on his knees when she noticed the door was unlocked. "Why do you want to leave? I'm just expressing how I feel. So why do you want to LEAVE?" he asked.

"I feel scared," she murmured. "You're scaring me, Dawn! Let me go!" she shouted.

Dawn's face became angry. "I'M TELLING YOU HOW I FEEL, AND YOU WANT TO LEAVE ME!"

He stood up and grabbed Moon's arms. "AHHHHH! I FEEL HURT; LET ME GO! DAWN!" she shouted.

"NO! WHY CAN'T YOU EVER APPRECIATE ME AND SHOW ME THAT YOU LOVE ME BACK—I—"

Bronte rushed into the room and tackled Dawn, waking the whole house as he fought to keep his nephew away from Moon. Her mother stood in the hallway, finding her frightened and crying. She quickly took Moon out of the room. Dawn yelled angrily, "AIRA! AIRA!" She and her mother rushed past Mr. Wolfe and Mrs. Wolfe and took her to Summer's bedroom. However, Summer was not in her room. Her mother sat her on the bed and wrapped a blanket around her.

"Summer's staying with some friends, so you can sleep in here," Angel kissed her on the forehead.

"Lin, Lin?" Moon cried out in hysteria.

"Don't worry. You're safe in here, and I'll bring Lin to keep you company," she said with a concerned smile.

Angel hugged her and reassured her that she would be fine and that everyone needed time to calm down. Her mother cracked the door as she rushed out into the hallway. She could hear everyone screaming and talking, slamming and crashing, and Dawn shouting from the hallway. She felt like a child again in that closet. Dawn was crazed and called her name. She curled up in the bed, crying and covering her ears. The door squeaked, and Moon leaped up in defense, but it was just Crystal sneaking into the room amidst the chaos. It made her cry even more. Crystal walked over to the bed and held Moon as she covered her ears.

Crystal whispered, "I'm sorry. I'm so sorry." Then comforted her some more.

It was a long period of Dawn losing his temper. His father and Bronte had to lock him in his room and guard the door. Dawn spent hours crying out for Moon and for someone to understand him. Moon, on the other hand, was disappointed and frightened of him. It was the second time he had lost his temper with her; this time, he could have hurt her. He was an explosive, just like her mother used to be. He knew how she felt about alcohol abuse and what she endured as a child, and to make her experience it all over again with him clarified why they needed to separate. It was a ticking time bomb. The worst part was that she felt sympathy for him and wanted to say it would be okay. There was so much she could take. But he would not be her entire existence, though he wanted her to be his. The lies, cheating, and outbursts were not on her list of things for the weekend.

*I should have followed my gut. We should have stayed strangers, though I wasn't to him. I did not know that having a stalker boyfriend was on my list. A crazy one at that. Nana? If you're listening, show me the way. I need you here. I wish you were here. What can I do? I'm in love with him. I still am despite him hurting me.*

Moon was sore all over, both in her waist and arms. Crystal had drifted off to sleep on the other side of the bed while Moon was wide awake. Her pet turtle, Lin, was nibbling on her finger as she lay on the bed, feeling completely numb. She felt like a dead weight on a cold slab, heavy with long-awaited misery. She knew Dawn had treated her poorly since last night, turning their fairytale romance into a nightmare. His beauty couldn't hide his flaws for long, but she was relieved to see them finally. The journey back home would be long and filled with the silent treatment she had endured. He wanted her love, and she gave it the best she could – saying "I love you," supporting him, and even meeting his family. What more did he want? She even lost her virginity to him. He needed help, and it was his responsibility to seek it because she refused to be burdened by such a manipulative, insecure man.

The hollowness of the pillow muffled her screams, which she hoped would silence the pain in her head, chest, and body. It felt as if she were collapsing in on herself. Dealing with her own emotions and mistreatment next to Dawn, who was having a breakdown down the hall, was unbearable. Her tears soaked the pillow, forming large wet spots. She didn't expect her love to be perfect, but she didn't expect him to be a harassing and explosive man. He was the opposite of the ideal partner she had hoped for. She wished she could go back and start the last two days over. She wanted it to be a cruel prank, something everyone would take back. She had dreamt of marrying Dawn and living happily ever after, but now they were in separate rooms, realizing they weren't meant for each other. He had pressured her about "destiny" bringing them together as soulmates, but what soul would want this?

Lin retreated into his shell, and then Moon placed him on the bedside table so as not to disturb him with all her crying. Her world was turned upside down, and she didn't know if this would break her. Indefinitely, she wanted the nightmare to end and to go home. She faced the ceiling with a wet face. Her brain flashed with memories of romance and mystery between her and Dawn. It made her heartache at the very thought of losing him and him losing her. It all ended so fast, just as it started. She didn't even get to say "I'm in love with you" to him. Not that she would say those very words to him presently. It would be impossible. It would just remind her of how much of a maniac he could become and hurt her again. The way his face was distorted as he screamed at her burned into her mind. His anger. There was so much anger and misunderstanding between them that she was floating on the surface of her emotions. He understood her most days, and why this was different made sense, but it wasn't right. He wasn't right, she wasn't right, and the moment wasn't right.

The whiteness of her eyes burned red. The bed felt cold - colder than she had ever experienced. The window was open, the wind blowing Summer's tall pink, lavish curtains that seemed raggedy but screamed "70s couture." The color of the room was thin. It was hard to see truly, and the color in the room was scarce. It wasn't the fact that pink and yellow covered the walls, but the color in her eyes left because this night alone determined that they were broken. Sometimes, broken things are not fixed; they are thrown away and never reused.

# 21. The Fog

When Moon woke again, she found a neatly stacked set of clothes on the chair in the room, her belongings placed along the wall. She noticed that Lin was gone but found a note on the nightstand from her mother mentioning that she had put him back in the tank.

Amid feeling comforted by this, reality hit her again as she got out of bed and felt the lingering soreness in her body. She picked up the clothes set out for her and found that her mother had picked out her favorite dress, a red, form-fitting V-neck mini with white lining and a small bow between the breasts. After locating the mirror in Summers' closet, she placed the dress on the chair and searched her luggage for matching jewelry.

Standing in front of the mirror, she appeared lost in thought; she practiced a smile that would not trouble or frighten anyone. It felt terrible because she shouldn't have been the one trying not to hurt anyone's feelings. Brushing the static off her shoulders, she began to remove her shirt. Exhausted beyond measure, she could have sworn she noticed bruises on her waist and arms. She quickly panicked, took off her shirt, and frantically searched her body. Although she twisted and turned every which way, she found nothing. She was just sore and mistook the shadow of her shirt for bruises, then burst into tears.

She stepped into her dress, tears streaming down her face, and placed coffee-ground-shaped earrings onto her ears. Out of nowhere, Crystal burst through the door, catching her off guard and in tears with a tray of breakfast, flowers, and a note. If that wasn't the worst timing, her mother wandered in behind her with cowgirl boots in her hands. They both stared at her with sympathy, hoping she would let them comfort her. Moon turned back towards the mirror, crying and wiping her tears.

She asked, "Is that for me?"

Crystal, unafraid to speak, said, "Yeah. Breakfast courtesy of me and—"

"And?" Crystal sighed and then looked back at Moon's mother. "The letter and flowers are from Dawn," she hesitated and spoke. Moon's body boiled at the mention of his name, making her blood pressure rise. Crystal set the tray on the table and said, "I'll set this here. What would you like me to do with what he sent you?" She reacted slowly and then looked directly at her mother and Crystal. "You can leave them there."

Crystal clasped her hands together and said, "Okay. I will be going and leaving you two to it." She gave Moon a longing hug and left. Angel smiled at Moon and placed the boots on the floor.

"I brought these for you. I realized they would look nice with your dress, so——"

"You didn't have to," she said as she sat in the chair.

"Also, it's something to remember me by."

Moon took a bite of croissant. "They will remind me of you," she chuckled.

"Good," Angel said with a smile.

"It's been years since I've gotten you a gift."

Moon nodded as she took another bite of her croissant and said, "Thank you."

"No one has asked you yet, but are you okay? Well, are you going to be okay?"

Moon felt a chill rise and said, "I'll be okay." Angel smiled, then nodded.

"Let me know if you need anything else," Angel's feet seemed reluctant to move, but she managed to step out of the closet when Moon called her. "Mama?" her mother peeped back into the closet.

"Yes?"

Moon knew that asking about him would only intensify her feelings of hurt and rejection. She resisted the urge to cry and kept her emotions in check. His actions were inexcusable. He was selfish in what he did. Not only did he make her feel inadequate, but he also made her believe that everything was her fault, as if she should have tried harder or loved him more. They both had flaws, but she would never have thought to hurt him like he hurt her.

Angel stood in the doorway, silently waiting to hear the words she knew her daughter wanted to express. Moon gazed at her mother, not uttering a word, but her mother understood.

"He's fine."

Moon sighed with no clear indication of release or sorrow.

"Okay," she said with a slight smile.

"He's sober and feels terrible about what happened."

Moon nodded again. "Atlas will arrange separate travel arrangements, but only if you want that."

Moon leaned back in the chair and said, "Can I consider it?"

Angel's face looked confused. "Um—sure."

"Thanks for the boots and breakfast."

Her mother sighed, rubbed the sides of her pants, and said, "I'll let you get ready." She smiled with tenderness. "And If I don't see you before you go, I love you and will see you soon." Moon smiled and waved goodbye to her mother. "I hope so," she murmured to herself.

After eating breakfast and getting dressed, Moon sat back on the bed, reluctant to read Dawn's note and embrace his gift of ten counts of stunning, vibrant red roses. A knock came at the bedroom door, and she turned to see Crystal again. "Hey, beautiful."

Moon smiled and said, "Hey."

"The jet will be ready in an hour. Okay?"

"Okay."

"I hate to ask this, but my father wanted to know if—"

"Oh, yeah—um, no. I will be fine."

Crystal appeared shocked and asked, "Are you sure?"

Moon nodded. "I am—promise," she said as she crossed her fingers.

"Okay." Crystal winked at Moon, then slightly cracked the bedroom door.

Moon picked up one of the roses and inhaled its scent. The freshness and sweetness of the rose subsided her mind, bringing a slight smile to her face. After returning the rose to its vase, she gathered the courage to open Dawn's note. Like many things on the surface, the letter was extravagant as ever, and she wondered if there was any significance within it. As she opened the letter, she quickly closed her eyes, afraid of what she might read or if she might weaken in the face of the love of her life, who had hurt her in many ways. She took a few deep breaths, then opened her eyes again. The letter read:

*Aira,*

*It's difficult for me to say just how sorry I am. I spent the entire night agonizing over this letter, tormented by my guilt. I realize now that I have been wrong in so many ways - wrong to love you possessively and burden you with my fears and uncertainties. Ever since I discovered my love for you, I've been consumed by a desire to spend my life with you too quickly, too intensely. These recent weeks with you have been beyond excellent, and it pains me deeply to see you hurt because of me. I let things spiral out of control, causing the person I hold dearest to experience real fear, and I cannot bear the thought of you fearing me. I never intended to hurt you, and I'm prepared to face the outcome of my actions. I can only say that you are out of this world; any fault lies with me, not you.*

*I love you. I love you. I love you.*

*Please, I ask you to forgive me in your heart. The decision to remove me from your life entirely or allow me the chance to prove my love rests with you. You are my sole desire and the only woman I love.*

*You are the only person who has left me a wreck. I have been unable to eat or sleep because of what happened. I questioned whether I hurt you, not just emotionally. I did something foolish that a man should never do. What more could you ask for than a loving partner, yet you got a man-child who couldn't see that he was cruel to the one person who loves him the most? I want to hold you again and tell you I love you, even if it means losing you forever. I am a messed-up person, and there is no excuse for anything I have done other than doing what I wanted of my own free will.*

*I promise. I promise.*

*I will never do anything like it again, and you are the one I want, not choose, not desire, not crave, not need, but WANT! You are my rose, my dear, sweet rose. I want to belong to you, marry you, love you. I cannot help but love you. I burn for you! I know you feel the same way, and if you need time to say it, I am genuinely okay with it. I'm in love with you, all of you.*

*It's pathetic how I woke up in our room, hoping to see those big baby-doll eyes looking at me, telling me everything would be all right. Then, I would say I love you, and we could work through anything. Though you are not far away, it feels like you are. I miss you so much, and we have only been apart for eight hours and two seconds. I'm going about my day, but I am in literal agony from not seeing you and not being able to come to you.*

*You may not know this, but I paced the halls approximately twenty times to catch a glimpse of you. I finally saw you briefly when my sister opened the door slightly to leave the room, and you were asleep there. You looked so serene and beautiful—exactly the peace you yearned for. Seeing you like that made me realize how conflicted I had been. I resisted the urge to kneel by your side to take in your sweet vanilla scent, to caress your cute but not too small chin, and to grovel for your forgiveness, but I hope you can see how sorry I am for betraying your trust and love.*

*I want you to understand that I have always understood you and will never stop. I love you. I'm in love with you, and I hope you believe in second chances because I couldn't bear to have a void in my heart where you fill my life. I beg for you, your love, mercy, and forgiveness.*

*—I love you, rose!*

She cautiously handled the envelope, feeling a weight inside as she attempted to slide the letter back in. Shaking it gently, she turned it over, and out fell the delicate sol-mate rings he had lovingly chosen for her. Holding them in her palm, she impulsively slipped them onto her finger, feeling the metal twist and turn as her emotions ebbed and flowed. Overcome with a deep sadness, she removed the rings and tossed them back into the envelope alongside the letter, laying them both on the nightstand. Curling up on the bed, she found herself whimpering at the overwhelming wave of emotions that had engulfed her since she first met Dawn. The pain was insufferable, too much to carry in front of others. Her heart still ached from the loss of her grandmother, and now it was bruised even more by the disappointment of someone she had cared for deeply. This anguish felt painfully ordinary yet so achingly familiar, except this time, it was not the grief of death but the heartbreak of shattered expectations.

She had an hour – an hour to grieve, to succumb to her emotions, to rest. Did she have anything else or anyone else? His sisters, as cool as they were, wouldn't keep in touch unless she was around. They weren't people she would genuinely hang around with every day. Dawn and she were more troubled than ever on the rocks, and everyone and everything hurt her head. It all felt like one gigantic wound. All she wanted to do was rest her eyes. There was nothing else she could do. Everything and everyone was out of her control.

Lying in the room's quiet, she could hear the bustling activity downstairs through the cracked bedroom door. The absence of laughter was noticeable, replaced by the sound of shifting objects and snippets of conversations about their lives, social events, and friends. As she reflected, she realized that the world continued to move forward despite her pain. She pondered the universal truth that everyone endures pain and departs from the world on their terms. However, at that moment, she desperately wished the world around her would stop. The rapid pace of everything left her questioning whether her current struggles were worth enduring for the promise of a better future. Feeling overwhelmed, she closed her eyes, seeking solace in the calm.

# Home.

The staircase in the manor seemed to have more steps than usual in her head. She wanted to go home but avoid him, though she couldn't and wouldn't because she could not shy away from a fight, no matter how defeated she felt. Making her way downstairs, Moon noticed Dawn in the living room talking with his father and Bronte, and he appeared to be happy. It made her skin crawl. How could he be so happy after what happened? It didn't seem he was as hurt as his letter exclaimed. She hoped to slip out quietly as she approached the last step of the staircase, but Summer appeared out of nowhere, rushing to hug and talk to her.

The commotion alerted Everyone downstairs: Dawn, his father, and Bronte turned to look at her. The expression in their eyes was enduring, except Dawn's. His eyes seemed filled with shame yet also brimming with so much love. Moon nodded to them, and Dawn smiled eagerly like an awkward child urged not to speak. Summer hugged Moon, who flinched slightly due to soreness, catching everyone's attention.

She pulled Moon to the side and asked, "Are you okay?"

Moon gently rubbed her soreness and said, "Yeah, I'm just sore from—"

"Him."

"Yeah." Summer glared at Dawn with a death stare. Moon could feel the anger boil up in her, but she was too tired to feel it. If anything, she felt sorrow more than any other emotion, and she felt aching love.

"It's all right, summer, don't kill your brother," Moon chuckled.

"Maybe I should. It would teach him never to put his hands on a woman again."

Moon sighed and said, "It wasn't like that."

Summer rolled her eyes and crossed her arms. "Then what was it? It definitely wasn't a slap on the wrist. I'm surprised he didn't leave bruises."

Moon nodded. "He didn't, did he?"

Moon was annoyed and said, "No!"

"Okay, good." Summer sighed with relief. "He's lucky our uncle and father didn't put him on his ass too hard, anyway," She chuckled.

"Did they fight," Moon asked concerned.

"Not really. They snapped him back into reality, then locked him in the room, but if you look closely, Uncle Bronte has a cut above his eye."

"What," Moon said, astonished.

"It's his fault he shouldn't have touched you."

"It wasn't like that," Moon whispered. "He was distressed and drunk."

"Exactly—if we weren't here just like last night at the club and earlier, who knows what would have happened."

Moon rolled her eyes in frustration and said, "Can we change the subject, please?"

Summer smiled and said, "I know, but —I mean, you have a history of behavior like that. Your Mom and—"

"I know! Can we please talk about something else," she whispered. "If we don't, I swear I will walk out of this conversation."

Summer nodded, "Okay," she said.

"Anyway, Crystal, our mother, and Countess have left, but they did leave a gift basket in the car for you as a last goodbye."

"Where did they go?" she asked.

"I didn't ask with all the ripping and running around the manor, sorry."

"That's okay. It's sweet of them to think of me. Please tell them I said thank you," Moon said, appreciative.

"I chipped in too, of course," Summer said, pulling Moon's phone out of her pocket and putting in her phone number. "Keep in touch, okay?"

"Thank you, and I will," Moon said as she side-hugged Summer. She started to walk towards Dawn, then Summer lightly grabbed Moon's hand and asked, "Where are you going?"

Moon rolled her eyes and said, "I'm not a baby. I don't need coddling. If I'm not going to talk to him now, when will I," she sighed.

"Call me if you need me," Summer said as she let go of Moon's hand.

"Stop worrying so much. It will give you wrinkles," she said playfully.

Dawn was still discussing something important with his uncle and father, which she wasn't too clueless about. She took a deep breath and approached the living room while Summer gazed from behind her. Dawn wore white sneakers, denim jeans, a brown cotton T-shirt with his medallion necklace, and a baseball cap, just like the first time she had seen him. He was hiding from everyone but not everyone from him, which made him look less intimidating, more like the average Joe.

She stopped in the doorway and knocked on its wooden frame. The talking ceased, and all eyes were on her, but everyone knew what she wanted. His father and Bronte patted Dawn on the shoulder as they left the room without saying a word, but they still lingered like Summer. Moon looked back and saw them hovering in the dining room. She knew it was for her safety, but she liked to think he had come to his senses. If he did try again, this time, she would be ready to slam anything heavy enough across his head and pepper spray ready to melt his eyeballs from his socket. It wouldn't be for her enjoyment but for her well-being.

Dawn sat on the sofa, hunched over, his cap hiding his beautiful green eyes. She was still fearful of him but bold enough to sit beside him. She made sure not to sit too close, just enough for them to speak without anyone else overhearing. He tugged on his cap to pull it down further and fiddled with the rings on his finger. Moon sat up straight and pointed her body towards him.

She cleared her throat. "I heard you're sober—and regretful for what happened," she said, secretly mocking him.

Dawn nodded and said, "I am." Moon was quiet. "Did you get my letter?"

"Mm-hm," she said. She could see him smile slightly. "Did you read it?"

"Yeah." Dawn peeked from under his hat and looked at Moon. "I'm sorry. Okay? I'm sorry, that is all I can say, and you know what the letter stated, so—"

Moon sighed and said, "You hurt me, you know."

He nodded again. "You did, and not only that but physically to the point I am so sore it hurts to move sometimes." Dawn lifted his head in shock and said, "Rose? I—I'm so sorry!"

Moon put her hand up and said, "It's okay. There are no bruises, and I will see a doctor when we get back to ensure the pain will subside soon."

Dawn reached for Moon but pulled his hand back, fearing she would not want him to. "That's good."

Moon looked down at her boots, "I read your letter," she said lovingly.

Dawn stayed silent. "You're a romantic by heart, and I wish that were enough for me to forgive you, but I've never been more humiliated and heartbroken. Like I said, I don't hate you because I could never."

He nodded once more, quiet and listening to her speak. "I appreciate the love you have given me, and I'm sorry, but it won't fix anything. Not immediately, anyway."

Dawn cocked his head, "Immediately?" he asked.

"Yeah, I think we need to take some time apart."

"Aira." Moon put her hand up again. "It's not a breakup. Okay?"

"I thought you would never want to see me again after everything."

"I said the same thing, but what can I say? I am just as disappointed in myself."

"Don't say that." Moon glared at him, their eyes meeting, and for a moment, feeling the intense passion they shared. "We will have to see in the long run."

He politely smiled. "How did you find the roses?"

"Reminiscent—" Moon smiled wearily.

"So, what are the terms for us "being apart?" he asked.

"We give each as much space as possible."

"Okay," he said hurt. "I want so bad to hold you right now."

"Dawn."

He chuckled miserably and said, "But here we are stating terms of separating, and all I want to do is tell you how much I love you." He leaned back onto the sofa, resting his head. He looked at Moon, "I love you," he said.

Moon leaned back beside him and said, "I love you too, my love, and always will."

The air between them was heavy with sorrow. It hurt to be apart, but they both knew they needed space. Their romantic relationship had moved too fast, causing chaos. They needed to come up for air and hoped it would help them gain clarity. Being unable to be close and talk as much was difficult for both of them, but they knew they needed to clear their minds and decide if they wanted to continue their connection. They realized that they couldn't move forward while smothering each other. It was a difficult situation that felt like killing two birds with one stone, day and night.

"I fear you will not love me anymore after," Dawn declared.

Moon tried not to cry and said, "If only you knew."

"I have these fears about us. I can't help it."

"You have to because it is what caused this in the first place," she sat back up. "I would give you my heart and sit it in the palm of your hands so you can see how much it beats for you. That is how much I love you," she said teary-eyed. Dawn scooted closer to Moon on the sofa and hesitantly but gently caressed her hand.

"I know that now and feel foolish for what I said—did! I will never do it again." Moon pulled back her hand. "That's what they always say."

Dawn saw his family hovering in the dining room and hallway.

He scoffed, saying, "They act like I'm going to go on a rampage."

Moon glared at him and said, "You did." His demeanor became cowardly and withdrawn.

"Okay. I agree to your terms if it means I have some chance."

"Thank you," she said sympathetically. "I'm not going to lie to you." She looked him directly in the eyes.

"Okay?" he chuckled insecurely.

"I love you, but—"

He nodded his head. "Go ahead, rose."

"I love you, but I don't know if this will last." She put her hand up again before he could speak.

"I'm not psyched about it, but you know, in a day and a few hours, you have potentially lost me. I can tell you I love you, and you can tell me you love me, but it will ultimately fix nothing. Everything in me is screaming to love you no matter what happened, but I know, and you know what happened is wrong and unjustifiable."

"I know that. Don't you think I know that?"

She caressed his hand gently. "I know love. I know, but I don't want to get your hopes up."

He smiled in pain. "My hopes," he whispered. "The way you look at me gives me hope. The way you smile and talk to me gives me hope. Your very presence in front of me gives me hope. I'm sorry, but I can't help but think this is a goodbye."

"It's not, but just in case, you know." He looked down at the floor. "Well, can you do me a small favor before we depart from each other's lives for a short time?"

She nodded and said, "Yeah."

He choked for a mere second, "Don't come away from this thinking I'm a monster because I'm not, or at least I try not to be. I lost track, and I can admit that, but please don't leave thinking I don't love you with the deepest part of my bones and that I am a monster. If you leave me after all of this, please, don't think that of me. I could care less about everyone but you; it would rip my heart in half." He stroked her cheek delicately.

She smiled heartbrokenly and said, "Favor granted love."

He smiled unhopefully and asked, "Promise?"

He was scared, and so was she.

Her eyes didn't leave his. "I promise," she said, sound of mind.

They sat so close that their breath mingled in the air, and the air felt heavy with their unspoken emotions. He gazed into her eyes, and she returned his gaze, each moment stretching out with tension. In a wordless acknowledgment of their separation, they held onto each other's presence in the silence. Dawn inched closer to Moon, her every movement betraying the weight of her emotions, and finally leaned in for a kiss. The remaining perfectly still Moon allowed the connection, hoping that even the slightest show of affection could provide solace.

Closing her eyes, she savored his sweet touch on her lips. It was the most tender kiss they had shared in a while. Their lips moved slowly, caressing each other's mouths with pure love. His hand lifted her chin as he deepened the kiss, and her hands rested on his chest. The kiss became enchanting, deep, and passionate. She felt herself slipping away into his arms and didn't want to fight it. It felt so good, and she was in love. She wanted him, and he wanted her. It felt both wrong and right.

After the tender and gentle kiss ended, they locked eyes with affection one last time. Moon gracefully exited the living room and proceeded towards the dining room, leaving him in solitude. By coincidence, Mr. Wolfe informed her that the jet was prepared, prompting the servants to fetch her bags, but Dawn was quicker. She interpreted this as a gesture to assure her he would not cause discord between them again. Regardless of bidding everyone farewells, they remained, with Summer lingering incredibly long, considering that she believed Summer would have left for an affair by now.

Dawn brought the last bags downstairs, hurried to the car, and placed them in the trunk. He walked back to the door as Summer hovered next to Moon.

"Well, that's it," Dawn said.

"Okay." Moon nodded. "I loved meeting everyone, and once again, goodbye."

When Moon stepped outside, Summer followed behind, confusing Dawn and her.

"What are you doing?" he asked. Summer looked back at her father in the doorway, and he nodded.

"I am to go along for the ride until you guys reach the jet," She smiled nervously.

"No—no, come on! Father, really?"

Mr. Wolfe stared at Dawn and Moon, saying, "It's just a precaution, and it's only on the way there. You will be fine, and it's been decided."

"No one asked Moon how she felt."

"Oh, yeah, sorry, Moon." Summer said regretfully.

Moon winked at Summer and said, "It's okay, but I should have been asked," looking back at Mr. Wolfe.

"Well? Do you mind, Ms. Moon?" Dawn's father stood firmly at the door, awaiting an answer, but Bronte had long been gone. Moon folded her arms, smiled, and said, "No, I don't mind. I'll be happy for Summer to accompany us."

She nudged Dawn. "It's fine!"

Dawn rolled his eyes and said, "Okay, but please, no family stories and talking the entire way."

Summer giggled. "You're such a grouch," she said, squeezing Dawn's face.

"Dibs on the backseat!" Summer said, rushing to the car.

"Wait for me!" Moon shouted.

Dawn stepped in front of Moon and asked, "You're not sitting up front?"

Moon sighed and said, "No, I'm not." Dawn nodded. "You have a problem with that?"

"No." He said cautiously.

Moon walked around him and got into the backseat with Summer. Dawn's father stood on the porch, and as Dawn approached, his father's face broke into a warm smile. He extended his arms and drew Dawn into a tight hug. Leaning close, he whispered something in Dawn's ear, the words soft and intimate. Even after they released each other, the embrace seemed to linger in the air shortly. As Dawn returned to the car, starting the engine, she could see he couldn't shake the feeling of those whispered words lingering in his mind.

The weight on his shoulders persisted, but a glimmer had returned to his eyes. Summer and Moon engaged in lively conversation in the backseat, the sparkle in Summer's eyes betraying her awareness of his gaze in the rearview mirror, but Moon noticed. Summer's enthusiasm brimmed over as she shared her plans for a program catering to pink enthusiasts, drawing inspiration from Legally Blonde. Witnessing someone's aspirations take shape was genuinely heartening to Moon since everything became turmoil for her. Amid their discussion, Summer leaned in to gently kiss Dawn's cheek, irking him but allowing him to steal another look at Moon.

Moon's eyes wandered to the gift basket enticingly between her and Summer, causing her to avert her gaze. The basket, a rich shade of red, was adorned with a gracefully tied ribbon and wrapped in protective plastic. Inside were extravagant items: delicate rose seeds, a luxurious perfume bottle, an array of high-quality beauty supplies, sparkling jewelry, and indulgent snacks. Attached to the basket were two notes from Dawn's sister expressing their appreciation for meeting her and one from her mother expressing love and wishing to see her again.

She smiled warmly at the thoughtful gesture and felt a sense of reassurance, realizing that she wasn't alone after all. It was a comforting revelation that people didn't harbor animosity towards her; instead, they felt a protective instinct. Suddenly, the thought of returning home didn't evoke as much fear within her. However, what truly perturbed her was the prospect of Marleen discovering the details of the encounter between her and Dawn. If her intuition served her right, Marleen would deliver a stern lecture that would seem never-ending. With no friends to confide in back home, her solitude would bring a sense of loneliness, while her rationality chastised her the most.

Visiting Nana at her grave and strolling through the bustling streets among the locals held an allure. No longer a mere stranger, she could find comfort in the city's welcoming. The most striking revelation, however, would be seeing her mother outside the manor and pursuing a relationship, though she might be departing from the manor with a potential ex-boyfriend and found comfort in the newfound friendship and maternal connection she had gained.

The powerful Mustang raced along the walkway, heading towards the imposing manor gate. Moon sensed that her journey had reached its conclusion there. Uncertain about the fate of their relationship, she acknowledged the necessity of taking a break. The harsh reality they faced contrasted with the profound love they shared. Even though instructed to maintain silence throughout the drive, Summer continued talking, finding comfort in breaking the tension. She journeyed towards the jet in peaceful reflection. Yearning for her family and bed, she longed for a private moment to release her tears. Once the gates swung open, Dawn accelerated, eager for the next destination. She keenly observed his struggle to resist talking to her and reaching out. His tense expressions revealed his internal struggle with each conversational topic that Summer initiated, resonating with Moon's inner conflict.

The longing to talk with him ate away at Moon. Their silence felt like a chasm, creating an alternate reality where they were mere strangers. Eventually, she skillfully guided the conversation to a halt, allowing them to bask in silence while Summer dozed off in the car. Moon and Dawn were left alone, enveloped in their love. The wind gushed as she rolled down the window, creating a welcome distraction from the powerful calm surrounding them. Among the moment's intensity, they found themselves unabashedly captivated by each other's gaze. For the first time in her life, Moon found herself at a loss, unsure of everything, yet reveling in the uncertain beauty of the forbidden moment, a moment that was filled with their undeniable love.

# 22. Mirror

It was hard for her to return to the apartment the first night. She was heartbroken and alone. She hoped they would keep in contact, for the most part, because though he hurt her, she did not want him to vanish from her life completely. She made her boundaries known when they arrived home: No surprise visits, No surprise calls, and No meltdowns because he does not get his way. The fear had dwindled for the most part, but she was still cautious when it came to him—four weeks had passed, an exhausting, challenging four weeks.

Within that time, they had talked less than they had before. It didn't come as a shock to Moon that they had little to no communication most days. Everything had erupted in two days, so it would take a minute for them to adjust, especially during a break period of their relationship. She didn't think being on a "pause" would mean he would be so distant that it sometimes took him hours to respond to a single text. She thought at least he would try even harder than before because she did.

The mirror they held up to each other's identities had a crack, which showed their insecurities, fears, and hopelessness. It would take time to fix, but it did need fixing. It showed them their true essence, his to her and him. They had only seen each other twice in person to catch up, but that was the day they arrived back home and another two weeks ago. It frustrated her because she felt he was doing better than her when it came to the break. She lost sleep, barely had an appetite, would peek outside her apartment door to catch a glimpse of him, and pitifully touched herself to the sound of his name on her lips and the image of him in her mind.

It made her feel pathetic because she craved him. She wanted him and no one else. It was killing her, and she tried to brave it all. She was going cold turkey, which wasn't as easy as she thought. Ever since they came back, she had gotten stares from the others in the building. The atmosphere seemed filled with an unspoken understanding of what happened between them, and everyone deemed her brainless for it. The whispers and giggles behind her back and the anonymous gift of a pity pie with a note saying *"Welcome to the club, beautiful"* left before her door were cruel reminders of her perceived shortcomings. The incident left her feeling deeply unsettled, sending shivers down her body and adding to her embarrassment. That day, the weight of it all became too much, and she found herself seeking solace in the work bathroom, the tears flowing as the hurt dug deep into her mind and heart.

What made it worse was that she had not seen Dawn for so long, and he had become a ghost. His family was more present than him. His sisters texted and called Moon almost every day. Bronte and her mother were busy planning their wedding, but her mother managed to see her last week. They had lunch, caught up on life, and discussed their relationship as mother and daughter. It was nice and, finally, something she could solve besides crying herself to sleep and rotting in her apartment. Her mother looked healthy and happy, more than she was. She found it excellent for her mother to find peace, which she one day wished to see. She asked her mother and his family if they had heard from him, but they claimed they had little to no contact. Crystal said it was possible, but it was just a rumor that he left the city and was in Italy— and he said that he liked to travel the world to clear his mind and probably has flown to at least three new countries by now.

Moon had extended family now but wanted more, and that "more" was Dawn. The focus of her mind always circled back around to him: how was he doing, what day or hour would he text her, and did he think of her? Was he even "in love" with her anymore? What more could she feel about besides work and redecorating her apartment to avoid having a breakdown of her own? Sometimes, she would "noticeably" pace by his door to see if he was there, but she would not hear a peep. Maybe he left her for another country, perhaps even found a new girl, a new love. She feared he would come back and hear a knock at the door. It would be him holding hands with a pregnant wife and explaining that she was no longer his "true love" and that she should move on since he did.

She regretted the "break," but she would not falter. She had the right to simmer things down because they were moving fast and dangerously. She hoped his well-being was okay and that his heart would heal just like his bandaged hands. Everyone was moving forward except for her. It was hardening because she was always the one to be doing things, participating, and moving faster than lightning in life. She was initially stuck in one spot, waiting for time to move things. She had a reputation for being the "go-getter." Now, she was the sad girl in the apartment.

When she arrived home, her first goal was to visit Nana's grave. But she did not dare to do so during the day, so she did it at night—the first night. She was never a morning or evening person but the brightest at night. She had energy and this life, so why not visit her grandmother at her best? She had brought her journal with her, so they would write poetry together, laugh, cry, and get angry about the past and present like they always did.

That night, she had never slept so soundly and peacefully as she did next to Janey's grave. She was her one true home; not only that, but her grandfather's grave was right next to her nana's. Also, she never cried as hard that night as any other. It was a safety she missed that her grandparents gave her to be able to conquer anything in life, but it was gone. That night, she fell to her knees, crying and discussing how her life had erupted since they left the earth. She talked and cried until she fell sound asleep. It was like a release of an imbedded sorrow that she could not let go of. It wasn't gone, but a scab of developability grew.

She did not understand, and she did not know what to do. She did not know how to move past such horror in her life, and she could not express that much to her mother because it would not be the same and never would be. She hated it all. When she lay on the wet grass with dirt, worms, and the stench of raw nature, she clawed at the dirt of their graves. Her sobs could be heard a mile away from the way she hugged the bare ground as if the bodies lay beneath her. It shaped her immensely but into what she could not grasp. All she knew was that she walked back to her apartment early in the morning, filthy and in disarray. It was apparent she needed professional help, but when would she be brave enough to get some because she could not cope or heal alone? She was used to being independent, closed off, and free to lie to herself about her sanity. A sanity that was slowly fading.

Moon was not whole anymore. Who was she kidding? She was never whole as a person. She always coddled and cared for others, letting herself go while others benefitted. Yes, people checked up on her but could not cure her illness. She was sick, so sick, and wanted help. A broken heart she was used to, but what she was experiencing added on more and was slaughtering her beyond measure. No one noticed, not even him, because he was gone. Forever gone, she thought. She was better suited alone, never interacting with others much and expecting less.

She would always be "little rosie," a little girl who never had her wish granted for love, peace, and a home. They are three things anyone would want, but they are all incomplete to her. She had to find them in herself, though people drained her for it. Was it horrible that she wanted to be taken care of for once? It would be ideal. It was partly her fault because she sometimes did not speak up, but it was primarily due to being around shitty people. Marleen doesn't even know what happened between her and Dawn. She couldn't bring herself to tell her because she knew it would break Marleen's heart and Dawn's legs. Marleen was very protective of Moon and never shied away from a brawl. She almost killed her grandfather from a misunderstanding between her nana and him.

He would have been one eye short if her grandmother had not clarified things. And she would love for Dawn to keep his life and limbs. Also, she was too chicken shit to explain to Marleen why she would not just break up with him and endure the strongest of pains in weeks for the illusion of healing. It was mind-blowing, but she needed time. Time to figure her heart out, time to breathe, and repeat. Knowing Marleen, she would suck all the air out of the room to get Moon to come to her senses and fight for her life. The life her grandparents so "courageously" raised her for.

Her apartment looked mostly the same, except for the living room. The walls were painted white instead of the old, faded peach color, the carpets were now thrifted Armenian carpets instead of the fuzzy ones, the TV was placed on a sturdy white glass shelf on the wall, and Lin, her pet turtle, had his spot next to the windows in the living room. The bookshelf had gotten smaller since she didn't read as much anymore, especially since she hadn't gone to Little Reads due to her separation from Dawn. She also took the door off the hallway closet and replaced it with a convenient bead curtain. She would never touch her bedroom or kitchen because they were too much of a haven, and it never dawned on her to change those spaces.

She blinked not once but twice as she sat on the kitchen counter, facing the living room. She waited as the steak sizzled in the skillet, browning on one side. Today, she only craved steak and potatoes, something hearty and protein-based. One leg dangled off the counter while the other was tucked under her chin as she painted her toes. The sound of sizzling grease and seasoning filled her ears. Toe after toe, she painted them dark cherry red. The skillet started to smoke, catching her attention, so she set the polish on the counter and hopped onto the floor lightly so as not to mess up her polish. She rushed over to the stove and flipped the steak over. She grabbed a knife to cut the steak slightly to see if the middle cooked enough, but she saw it needed more cooking time.

She turned down the heat and resumed painting her toes. Afterward, she tossed the polish into her vanity drawer and changed into comfortable clothes: a T-shirt and shorts. Pulling the potatoes out of the oven, she sat them down on the stove to let them cool down, grabbed a plate, fork, and knife, and placed them on the table. Then, her phone rang, and she turned to the sofa. She stopped everything she was doing. It was like a flash of fear washed over her at the thought of "who" was calling. She didn't know if it was him, but she wanted it to be him because they hadn't talked for so long. Only four people called her around this time: Her mother, Summer, Crystal, and Marleen.

Ironically, it used to be her nana or Marleen who would call, ranting about their day and making plans. It was unbelievable how everything changed in her life so fast. She wanted her grandmother to be there so badly and to advise her on what to do or how to feel. Though she was there in spirit, she wanted her to be there physically, flesh and all. The phone kept ringing, so she rushed over and grabbed it. She didn't look at the caller ID at first, staring only at the wall, hearing the sounds of her ringtone. She braced herself and looked down at the phone. It was Marleen calling, and her heart sank with displeasure.

How could he not call or text yet? she asked herself. She answered the call, and Marleen responded with glee. She walked back toward the food cooking on the stovetop as Marleen ranted about whatever while on the phone.

Marleen laughed, "Anyway, Mo, how are you doing? How are things between you and—"

"You ask me this every time you call. Nothing between us has changed in the past four weeks, okay? As for me, I'm taking it a day at a time," she sighed.

"Sorry! I just wanted to know. You never know your life can change in a second," she said.

Moon flipped the steak over with a spatula.

"Not when it comes to me," she said unhappily.

"Mo, things will pick up. Sometimes—"

"Things in life take time." She mocked her with annoyance.

"Yes, sweetie." Moon gripped the phone hard and rolled her eyes. "I believe that," she stumbled over her words. "I do, but if love was so real as people say, why is it taking so long for him to meet me halfway?"

"He's hurt and scared like you are."

"It doesn't feel like it."

Moon turned the heat on the stove higher, hoping the steak would cook faster because she was starving. While on the phone, she grabbed a piece of baked potato and bit it.

"Mo, he loves you. I know it. Did you try—"

"I've asked everyone I know and visited his apartment, but nothing," she complained.

"He's an asshole if he doesn't want to see you."

"He is?" she asked. "Absolutely, Mo!" she said, empowering.

Moon grabbed another potato and ate it.

"Can we change the subject? I'm so over the Dawn topic." She said with an exhale.

"Well— I haven't seen you in so long. Can you clear your schedule so we girls can hang out? I want to visit Janey." Moon nodded and smiled slightly. "Yeah—yeah, we can. How about this weekend?"

"I was going to use my day off to clean my backyard, but we can go then. Friday sounds good?"

"Done. I will see you Friday."

"Good. It will be nice to see you again. Now, tell me. How is work?"

"Um—"

She was interrupted by the smoke alarm going off due to the skillet smoking. Moon quickly moved the skillet to another burner and turned it off. Then, she placed the phone on the counter and grabbed a rag to wave in front of the smoke alarm to silence it.

Marleen called her name from the phone, so she briefly paused and said, "I'll have to call you back."

"What? What's wrong?" Marleen said, anxious.

Moon sighed and said, "My cooking set off my smoke alarm, so I will call you back."

"You never could cook," Marleen laughed.

"Says you. But I have to go!" she chuckled. "I will see you Friday?"

"Yes! Friday. You will see me Friday."

"Okay, love you, bye."

"Bye." She said as she hung up the phone.

The smoke alarm finally stopped, and she was able to finish cooking her steak. Sitting at the table, eating and watching TV, she heard a knock at the door. At first, she ignored it because it was faint, so she continued to eat and turned up the TV. Then, a louder knock at the door made her jump. She muted the television, dropped her fork on the plate, and sluggishly walked towards the front door. She looked through the peephole and didn't see anyone, so she unlocked the door. She opened it slowly to be safe, but there was no one. She heard the apartment building door close downstairs. She was going to look, but her foot hit something, so she looked down. There were roses in a black vase, but more than a dozen this time.

A smile came across her face because only one person would send her roses. *Did he come back? Was it him?* It had to be him and no one else, or it would be cruel torment. She quickly picked them up and closed the door. She sat them on the table. A note said: *To the most beautiful rose in the universe.* There was no indication of the sender, but no matter because she knew it was him. It was Dawn. One of her fingers traced a rose before pulling one out and smelling it. They were sweet, sweet as anything could smell. It was a gesture she had wanted for so long, but what did it mean? It never crossed her mind what if he contacted her, how she would react, and what he would say, but this was different. They were flowers, not words, per se.

She stared at the roses as a gift bestowed on her. It gave her some hope even though she didn't know the answer to one question. The question she and Dawn pondered in their time of being apart. She lost her appetite just thinking about it and him. It wasn't fear this time, but life and life would go forward no matter the issue. It didn't even stop for the death of a loved one. It surely wouldn't stop someone from going through heartbreak. She placed the flower back into the vase, returned to the chair, and laid her head on the dining table.

"What am I going to do?" she repeated as she moved her head from side to side on the table.

*Why did he send the flowers? Did he want to tell me something? I need to know what he is thinking. Do we have to decide together, or will I have to?*

She placed her arms under her chin as she sat up and stared at the roses again, the note wide open. She read it repeatedly until her brain turned to mush, and then she heard her phone ding. She ignored it, knowing it had to be Marleen again, but it kept dinging as if her phone would explode. She quickly grabbed it off the counter and saw that it was incoming messages from Dawn, old and new. She started hysterically laughing and crying until she cracked a smile. It seemed she had gone mad, but she was sane, sane with overpowering love for a man.

She couldn't read them all at once as at least a hundred messages flooded her phone. She wondered where he could have been if his messages had not gone through. She wanted him hidden at some monastery or retreat because she would curse him if he weren't. She couldn't contain herself, so she stood up and walked around the apartment, waiting for the messages to be done uploading; once they were, there were mainly two that caught her eyes amongst the poems, ramblings, and constant I love you.

*"I apologize for the sporadic nature of my messages—amid my confusion of emotions. This was to be my journal for my pain and to help me process what I was feeling, mainly the things I wanted to confess to you and no one else. I have been in Italy for some time. I left as soon as possible because I could not bear to be apart from you and near you at the same time. But It is beautiful here. You would have loved to be here, and I hope you will soon experience such a lovely place like this. I wouldn't have it any other way to see you enjoying the sunny beaches, roaming the old villages, and being the beauty of Italy—my rose.*

*I know you have tried to reach out and have been in pain, just as I have. I didn't think it would take long to muster the courage to tell you how I felt. This could be the thousandth message I sent to you. I hate it. I hate that I broke what we had, but rose, if only you knew how much I wanted you and wanted to be near you. As you said, we needed some space, so I took the opportunity to leave, but I think it was enough, don't you?*

*I'll be back in Boston in two days. I wanted to break the ice and let you know what was happening. I love you and wish you the best. You will read all of the messages that I so desperately sent. I hope that they can help you understand me and learn more about what happened that night. Believe me, you have been on my mind and heart since we returned to the city that day. I haven't been able to sleep since. Nothing the other messages haven't conveyed before, but I will say it a thousand times if necessary. I want you and always have wanted you. I will always choose you and choose to love you sincerely.*

*I want you to understand me as I have understood you for some time. I don't want to be alone without you, and I hope you feel the same way. I hope that you haven't fallen in love with someone else or fallen out of love with me. I hope you* returned to your routine but not so typical that you have forgotten me. I love you. There's so much that I can say, but I feel it wouldn't cure as much as we think. Words can only do as much as actions, and I plan to use my actions to prove my love to you.

As crazy as it sounds, please do not leave me. Please do not love any other man while I'm still away. Please—please do not give your heart away as I have not and will die before I do so. I need to believe that you will be by my side forever faintly. Please, my rose, love me forever as I cannot force you to but beg.

Nonetheless, this is no excuse, and I would like to meet you this Sunday at King's Diner at 2 to have an open and honest conversation about our relationship. I love you and hope to see you soon."

-Love D.

# 23. Lost Daughter

**M**oon unwrapped a peppermint and popped it into her mouth while waiting in the car outside Marleen's house. This was the first time she had a car since college. Her nana took her everywhere, and she lived in the city, so there wasn't much need for it because of trains and traffic. Her grandmother had a 1975 Dodge Coronet Brougham that she had bought from an old friend and fixed up. It was plain before Moon decided to make it her project to fix up instead of sell – because why not? It was easier on her pockets than constant walking and train rides. Sometimes, she wanted to be alone in her own space.

She felt as though her grandmother would have been enamored with the customizations she had made to the car, and it encouraged her to start using it despite having to renew her driver's license. The car boasted a rich, dark red interior, complete with plush red carpeting and luxurious red fabric seats. A golden rearview mirror and a striking pink exterior added to the charm. Additionally, intricate flower designs decorated the rear car lights, giving the vehicle a uniquely personal touch. The license plate spelled out: *24ROSYLOV.*

The car would be her pride and joy now, and it was nice to have something in common with her grandmother again besides Marleen. Not to sound mean, but Marleen was not the only thing she had in common with her grandmother because, as much as she loved Marleen, she could be insufferable most days. Aside from her caring and generous side, she loved her nonetheless. Moon rolled down the window and tossed the wrapper out of the car. Then she adjusted the rearview mirror to fix a smear of lip gloss on her lips and glanced over to see Marleen stumbling out of the house.

Marleen's outfit was certainly eye-catching. She wore a long, flowing skirt with vibrant patches of orange that seemed to dance in the light. Her top was a cozy brown turtleneck sweater, expertly layered over an undershirt with white Converse sneakers. Her hands were decked out with stacks of delicate gold rings. Around her neck, she wore not one but two necklaces - a glimmering gold piece and a captivating evil eye necklace—her hair being styled in a voluminous and stunningly bold fashion, with luscious curls flowing in every direction.

If anyone asked, Marleen and Janey were different style-wise, but by the eye's beauty, they could be twins with opposite eye and hair colors, but their facial features were almost identical. And, if Moon were being truthful, she would admit that that's why she found it insufferable to be around Marleen; she reminded her so much of the times with her nana and how they could sometimes be like sisters.

Moon observed Marleen approaching the car, smiling enthusiastically at the window, and then unlocked the vehicle to let her in. As soon as she sat in the car, she tossed a bouquet of irises onto the backseat along with her lime-green tote bag, which had some pins with pictures of her deceased cats. Moon leaned back into the car seat and began to start the engine, but Marleen stopped her hand.

She appeared confused, "What's wrong?" she said, sucking on peppermint.

Marleen observed her and said, "I wanted to get a good look at you."

She put her hands in her lap and rolled her eyes, "You've seen me most of my life. What else is there to see?" Marleen smirked. "Rude as ever, I see, and may I remind you I haven't seen you in six weeks."

She nodded. "Yeah."

Marleen smiled, "Mm-hm," she said.

"I'm sorry about that."

Marlene sighed, "I know. You needed space, so I will not hold it against you," she said as she toyed with Moon's hair. "Well, thank you for not doing so."

She chuckled. "I missed you, especially since our girl is gone."

She looked at Marleen enduringly.

"We need to see more of each other, especially more now than ever."

Their eyes met for a moment. "I agree!" Moon shrugged. "I will try, okay."

"Promise?" Marleen asked, her expression serious.

"I promise," she replied.

"Good," Marleen said, patting her leg. "How's Angel?"

Moon huffed, "She's doing well, better than any of us," she said as she smiled anxiously.

"I would like to see her too, if you don't mind," she asked as she put on her glasses.

She rolled her eyes and said, "I honestly don't care."

Marleen giggled. "Okay, Mo."

"Why do you need to anyway? You have never mentioned my mama once around me."

Marleen pushed her glasses closer to her face, "She was like a daughter to me too, Mo, but it hurt me just as much as Janey and Victor to see her become so broken, so I never brought her up," she said honestly.

"Angel has always been a topic to avoid for most of my life, which I hated because the way she tormented us with her addiction was still fresh in my mind, but everyone could just forget."

"I'm sorry, girly. We wanted life to go as smoothly as possible for you and us, so we did what we thought best." Moon fiddled with her nails, glared out the car window, and said, "It didn't."

Marleen looked at her, confused. "You all gave me a good life, but it made it worse for me because she was my mama. Avoiding her like the plague did not cure me— it only made things worse."

"Janey and Victor would apologize if they were here—and I apologize myself for adding to such a stressful childhood."

Moon shook her head. "My grandparents and you did nothing wrong. I just wish you had approached the matter differently; that's all." She grinned faintly.

Marleen nodded, then changed the subject. "I like your hair like this; I wish you would wear it like this more often."

Moon smirked shyly and said, "Thank you. I've been doing what I can lately." Moon's hair flowed in luscious afro-like curls, framing her face like a halo with a striking black scarf, chosen as an accessory.

Marleen smiled as she took another look at her before saying, "I'll let you choose where we eat this time."

She chuckled, "Let me? Last time you chose, we ended up with food poisoning and on bed rest for two weeks."

Marleen laughed. "It's safe to say there is no choice," she then asked, "What are we in the mood for?"

Moon shrugged and said, "I don't know."

"How do you not know?"

Moon started to become restless. "Can we go, or?" she asked.

"Yes. Yes! I'm ready."

Moon exhaled and started the car. "Finally! And we can figure it out on the way."

Marleen winked at her and said, "Sometimes I wonder where you get that attitude from."

"Who else," she chuckled.

"Janey," she replied in a murmur.

The drive to the cemetery was unexpectedly brief, thanks to the unusually light traffic that day. Typically, the roads were congested at that time, but this particular day was an exception.

With a sense of urgency, Marleen swiftly reached out and took hold of the bouquet of vibrant irises, her eager anticipation palpable as she stood poised outside the car. Moon casually popped another peppermint into her mouth, and as she shielded her eyes with a sleek pair of sunglasses, she emerged from the vehicle. A welcoming smile graced Marleen's lips as she extended her hand towards Moon. Moon gratefully clasped Marleen's hand, and together, they strolled towards her grandmother's resting place, embarking on a lengthy walk.

"Marleen?" She called.

"Yes."

"Is my father buried here?" she asked innocently. Marleen stopped walking and turned towards her.

"Yeah, he is. What makes you ask?"

Moon smiled, "I've been curious about it," she said as she looked down at her boots and smooshed her heel into the grass.

"Oh, okay," Marleen said, inquiring.

"I wanted to visit him today, after Nana."

Marleen's eyes brightened with love. "Okay, that's fine." She pointed North to the graveyard and said, "He should be between those two graves, but I can show you if you like."

She shook her head. "No. I can find him."

Marleen nodded, then proceeded to walk, and so did she.

As they walked towards the gravesite of Moon's grandmother, a gentle breeze tousled their hair. She released Marleen's hand and, with a contemplative expression, adjusted her brown leather jacket. Her fingers traced the outline of a single red rose tucked into her jacket pocket, a tribute to her darling grandmother. Moon then smoothed down her white mini dress, taking a moment to compose herself before joining Marleen in placing flowers at the foot of the gravestone.

"I miss you, sister," she said teary-eyed.

Moon knelt down and gently placed the vibrant red rose on the weathered gravestone, its petals vivid against the muted gray stone. "I miss you, Nana," she whispered softly as she leaned in to kiss the cool surface.

Squeezing her eyes shut, she took a deep breath, feeling the weight of her grief, before turning to hug Marleen, finding solace in the warmth of their embrace. With a heavy heart, she gently disengaged from the hug, using her hand to wipe Marleen's tears. At the same time, Marleen made a reassuring gesture to indicate that leaving for her father's grave was okay.

Moon glanced back as she walked to the northern part of the cemetery. As she ventured farther into the graveyard, her feet felt heavier, and she thought about seeing her father's gravestone. It was as if she was climbing a tall hill. For what reason, she did not know. She had only heard stories about her father but never knew him. She had seen photo album pictures but never smelt, touched, or experienced him truly. "A gentle, kind man he was," they would say about him. There had to be more to him than that, which made it even sadder how he left the world.

He was an average man with lovely brown eyes and a charming smile. He dressed like any Southern man, but from the photos, he liked to wear plaid shirts and jeans with workman's boots. Not to forget the worn cowboy hat he loved to wear. It belonged to his folks but stayed with him after he ran away from home. Her mother did not mention his family other than their only wrongdoing, which was keeping him out of trouble and seeking help for his well-being. She pondered what he liked to eat, how he would sleep, and his childhood. If he lived, would he love her to the fullest or be an absent father? Would he have been too busy chasing around her mother or vice versa?

She understood her parents' love but knew it wasn't the best example. Although they married and had a child, they were wild and caused trouble in their youth. One parent had passed away, and the other was a recovered alcoholic. As she looked for her father's grave, her emotions overwhelmed her. She lost control as her fists became sweaty, her heart raced, and her mind fixated on the name Lincoln Bowie.

As she searched, her foot slipped, and she landed on someone's grave ass-first. She propped herself up with her elbows and turned her head towards the gravestone. To her disbelief, the name Lincoln Bowie was written on it. She laughed loudly at the coincidence of her situation.

She sat up, placed her sunglasses in her jacket pocket, crossed her legs, faced her father's gravestone, then put her hand out and said, "It's nice to meet you, Mr. Bowie. I'm Aira, your baby girl—daughter."

"No words—well, I know it must be a shock, but you have one," she said as she looked at the grave sadly.

"Comments? Concerns?" she joked. "None, huh? I know I wouldn't say I like to talk much, either. I must get it from my father," she whispered.

She ran her fingers lightly over the eroded letters of his name engraved on the cold stone, her eyes lingering on the jagged cracks and the marker's dull, muted color.

The obituary, printed in elegant script, described him as "a *beloved son, husband, and father—a true angel who will be deeply missed.*" She looked around and saw that the place was almost empty. She wanted to talk to her father quietly so no one would think she was crazy. She wanted to tell him about her life, whether or not he was watching over her.

She took a deep breath and asked, "So, where do I start?"

"Well, Nana and Pa are no longer with us, but you probably already know that," she chuckled. "If you are with them now, tell them I said hello and that I love them dearly," she said, smiling wistfully. "Is it crazy that I am speaking with you right now? If someone saw me, they would deem me insane, but who cares, right?" She could feel the tightness in her chest, and her eyes were watery.

"Oh, um—mama is clean now. She has been for some time, but the last time you saw her, she never touched a bottle as much, and she was younger." She picked at the gravestone. "Can you believe she is marrying my boy—Dawn's uncle? She would cry night and day over you. That doesn't mean she loves you any less, trust me. You will be the only man I call father, though I have not met you, but in my heart, I know we would have been closer than thieves in the night," she chuckled again. "But you are her one and only true love."

She debated mentioning the dreaded name but couldn't hold it in.

"Dawn. He is a man I met who has stolen my heart. I didn't think I would fall in love, but I did, Daddy." She said as she nodded. "I didn't know love and the person who came with it would sting this bad. I want to think our love could survive anything, but I don't know. I'm new to this, and he consumes my being. I don't know, Daddy. Our love is worrisome." She placed her hand back into her lap. "If only you could talk back, it would make things much easier and less insane. I want to cry, laugh, and be angry with you. I want to hang out, do daddy and daughter stuff, celebrate Father's Day, and say I will call or tell my daddy about it. But you are not here. And no one, not even you, are to blame for it. Life happens." She bowed her head and exhaled. "Absolutely. Right now, I want to be able to cry to you about my guy trouble and life, the good and the bad. It just hurts, that's all. It just hurts."

She hugged his gravestone childishly. "I shouldn't be here," she said regrettably. She gripped the stone tighter. "I'm talking to a rock, but no matter how I justify this, I'm just a little girl who misses her daddy." It felt like a trivial thing to want her father alive. Selfish. But how could it be to her? She wanted both parents in her life, like any other living human being, regardless of them being "shitty" or broken people. As a child, she saw it as indifference, pretending not to care about her father or his existence. But as a daughter, her mother and father's daughter, she lit up at any picture and story of him.

A simple and gentle man. She wanted to have a father in her life, and maybe she had another chance of doing so with Bronte, but it was hard. She already had a father she wanted to meet. He may be dead, but not to her. She would never call another man father. He was her prince charming, coming to save her, though she knew he would not come. In denial, she was, but at least it dulled the ache of pain until reality set in again. She would sometimes cry, think about it, have outbursts in class, and retell his disappearance without truly knowing if he was dead or did not want her as a daughter.

For some time, she didn't think she deserved one. It sounded horrid, but she did. It made her extremely angry, especially with a mother who was drunk out of her mind, in and out with stories of their love and his life before her. She wanted a simple family life, but it would not come. It was hard for her to express such a feeling to her family. Seeing other little girls with two parents or just their father made their world seem magical, As magical as any child craving to be loved.

She rested her head on the dry, rough surface of the tombstone, trying to overcome the swelling of emotions consuming her. With her eyes closed and a heavy heart, she felt the presence of her father's shadow as she realized how much time had passed since she last thought about him. It sucked, everything sucked. The weight of his absence dawned on her as she considered that he had never been there to watch her grow up, fall in love, and wouldn't be there to see her marry and have kids. The loudness of the pitter-patter of her heart surrounded her in the cemetery.

"I should have the right to miss you. I know you well as the stories recited to me since birth, which is good enough for me," she said as she let go of the stone. "I miss you. Isn't that terrible enough? Such a sad fate for one's child." She smirked. "Such a sad fate for me."

Suddenly, she was startled by the sound of crunching leaves and felt a presence nearby. Turning, she saw a woman standing not too far away. Moon seemed unfazed, assuming she was passing by. However, the woman appeared confused. "Hello?" asked the woman.

"Hi," Moon said, waving and intrigued.

"Who are you, and why are you at my son's grave?"

Moon's heart sank in her chest. "I—um."

"Look, if one of your little friends put you up to this, then gone ahead because I will call the police," she said as she gripped tight to her bible book.

"No, no one put me up to this."

Moon was at a loss for words. After all, as far as she knew, her father's family didn't reside in Boston. She assumed they had visited his grave, but she had never anticipated meeting one of them—let alone her other grandmother. "It doesn't matter. I will need you to get up, little girl, and stop playing around with people's loved ones, okay."

"He is loved," She said, staring at the whiteness of the lady's buzz cut.

"What?" She closed her coat and walked to Moon, bending down.

They were face to face, but she hadn't moved an inch from her father's grave.

"He is a loved one—or more so, my father."

The woman was taken aback. "I'm Aira," she said lightly.

It took a moment for the woman to reply. She examined Moon closely and then suddenly grasped her face, gazed into her eyes, and uttered, "Aira?"

Moon nodded. "Yeah. I'm Aira," she giggled.

The woman stood up, pondering the situation. "Cusp—Cusp Bowie," she said, unsure.

"I take it that's your name?"

Cusp laughed and said, "Yes, that is my name. And you are my son and Angel's baby." Moon nodded again. Cusp exhaled and started to cry. "You know how long—" she choked on her words. "You know how long we have been searching for you, unable to reach Angel during her struggle with sobriety. But my prayers have been answered by God."

Moon stood up from the grave and dusted herself off.

"You and me both."

Cusp opened her arms to Moon, and she politely obliged.

"You are so big, now." She said excitedly, with tears streaming down her face.

"Yeah."

Cusp let Moon out of the hug and placed her hands on Moon's shoulders.

"Let me get a look at ya." Moon smiled. "You could be your parent's twin, my God!"

"Thanks," she said, giddy.

"How's Janey?"

Moon gently removed Cusp's hands, walked over, and sat on the roadside bench.

"Did I say something wrong?" Cusp asked.

"No. It's just that my grandmother died two months ago."

Cusped gasped and placed her hand over her heart.

"I'm sorry, child. My prayers are with you," she said, her cross-necklace dangling as she sat beside Moon, patting her face dry of tears.

"Thank you," Moon sniffled.

"Janey and Victor were lovely people; may their souls rest in peace," she signed the cross.

"If you don't mind me asking—"

Moon smiled and said, "You want to know how she died?"

Cusp nodded. "Heart failure. Ironically enough."

"I'm sorry." Cusp patted her hand.

"It's okay. It's life."

A moment of silence was taken between them for what she did not know, but they both needed it.

"Do you come here to see Daddy often?"

"Yes, every Friday and Sunday." She grinned.

"This is my first time."

"I understand. You didn't know your daddy, so it's understandable."

"Yeah."

Cusp nodded. "Did they talk about him much?"

"My mama talked about him sometimes."

Cusp smiled and said, "Mm-hmm."

"That's good. That's good," she exhaled. "Well, here is my number if you want to catch up." She pulled a marker from her purse and wrote her phone number on Moon's hand.

"Okay," she replied.

Cusp was about to leave the bench, but Moon stopped her.

"Cusp?"

"Yes."

"If you want, you can eat with me and a family friend after visiting Daddy. Her name is Marleen, and she was like a sister to my grandmother, but she is also like an aunt to me," she said hopefully.

Cusp contemplated, then said, "Okay, but I will need a ride. I took the bus here."

"Yeah, that's fine. I have a car." She pointed to her Pink Dodge.

Cusp chuckled, "That's your car?"

"It is, yeah."

Cusp gave a judgmental look. "It's an inquired taste."

She snickered. "It's not for everybody, but what can I say? I love to be daring and bold."

"You are your mother's daughter."

Moon grinned wide. "That's me," she shrugged.

"All right. Give me some time with my son, and I will be ready."

"Okay," she said as she sat back on the bench.

She sat silently, her senses tuned in to the sounds of the world around her, much like a mouse. The gentle breeze tousled her hair as she savored the crisp fall air. The rows of graves around her caught her attention. She only felt cold and blue around the dead, which reminded her how fleeting life could be. It made her think about how someone's memories, warmth, and laughter could be forgotten or buried in a wooden box beneath the earth.

She counted in her head: one, two, three— the number of people who have left her life because of death. Death waits for no one while life continues. It wasn't her time, but she wondered, when it did come, how would she honor the earth with her death? A box or a pile of ashes? She felt a box would be too morbid and hypocritical because it didn't give back to Mother Nature. She would prefer ashes: soft and shallow, and they could feed the earth just by being scattered in the wind. She loved the wind.

With her eyes closed, she clung to the heartfelt words whispered at her father's grave. Every word Cusp spoke seemed to carry her sense of suffering and guilt. She looked over at her, seeing her filled with tears and prayers for someone she had no control over. No one could control sadness, happiness, anger, or bitterness but themselves, including her father. He seemed to carry a different sorrow that he couldn't shake off. Despite everything, they had each other, whether they acknowledged it or not.

She promised to support Cusp from a distance to be a good granddaughter, understanding the pain of losing the two most important people in her life. She didn't count her mother, but in a way, the impact of her mother's absence also took away her childhood.

Her knees were pressed into the ground, and her light purple dress was stained with dirt and grass. Her shoulders drooped heavily as the cold outside started to set in. She wanted to console her, but it was her time at the grave. Disturbing someone else's mourning felt impolite, so she looked ahead, listening to her cries. Strange as it sounded, Cusp cried just as Moon did when she realized her grandmother wasn't returning. It was up to them to move on in life, although it seemed impossible because the crying might stop, but the scar would forever remain. It would heal, but it would be as easy as cutting it again and reopening old wounds that would never return to new skin.

It all seemed unjust. 'Boring and blue,' she thought. Mourning was not easy, nor was it fun. In the 21st century, you mourn your loved ones instead of celebrating them moving on to a better place, wherever that might be. She wasn't a religious person, but very spiritual, so it hurt to hear Cusp pray for her father's soul and for him not to burn for his sin. Sin. What sin? Humans always devised these beliefs and systems to carry them through their shame and wrongdoings, blaming everyone else but never holding themselves accountable. She wanted to pray for his soul, but all Moon wanted to do was scratch the sound of it from her ears.

*Where could they be?* It was interesting to contemplate how one's soul is questioned, but she always felt that one's soul should be its own salvation, not God's. It might sound dreadful to others to hear what she thought, but she had always been a free thinker. This was not to say that no one else used their free will, but it was something that lingered on her mind. He wasn't in flames, but rather a broken soul merely lost. However, Moon continued to let her mourn as she saw fit. She wasn't in a place to judge but to observe what her grandmother was.

Cusp remained on her knees after the whispering stopped. She checked to see if she was okay, then saw Cusp caress the gravestone one last time before gently kissing it. She smiled empathetically and turned back around. Her phone dinged with a text from Marleen, saying she was ready to leave. Surprisingly, Cusp was ready, too.

Walking toward the car, Cusp said, "Ready when you are."

Moon muttered, "I'll never know when I'll be." On her way to the car, Marlene was not too far behind, overwhelmed by everything.

## 24. Faint Heart (Flashback[4])

The theater door closed behind us as we emerged under his umbrella in the rain. After that night, we had been catching up, which I found unusual because I never thought I would see him again. But I guess I surprised myself. His reveal of secretly knowing me was devastating, but when I thought about it again, it wasn't a surprise since I tend to stay in my head and avoid people I don't want to know. It was a silly mistake on my part not remembering him in the first place, but I guess that is what being a hermit does.

He wasn't very tall but still taller than me, so he had to scrunch under the umbrella. You would think he might break his neck or injure his back. It was cold, too—so cold that it made walking in the rain courageous, especially for a second or third date. It felt like my coat was a thin layer of clothing, but his car wasn't too far away. Thankfully, I wore my favorite boots because they could weather any climate, at least in Boston. My eyes fixed on his beautiful dimples as he smiled at me while shivering as we walked. I wanted to hold him, but my body couldn't warm half of his. I closed my jacket and hoped that my teeth chattering would stop.

"Did you like the movie?" He said as his bold green eyes darted towards me.

"Eh—I've seen better." I chuckled while cold.

"I thought it was interesting." He smiled.

"Interesting. And that is it?"

He laughed, "Yeah."

"Okay," I smiled as I chuckled again.

"I'm more into science-fiction."

"Yeah, I understand. I like horror movies more than any genre."

"Mm—a horror fan. What are you into?"

I bit my lip. "Um—monsters, possession, hauntings. Metaphors about life. The works."

"Like?" he laughed.

"Okay—uh, The Conjuring or Bram Stoker's Dracula."

"Good options."

"You?"

"Blade Runner or Alien— no Blade Runner and—"

"Alien!" I whispered playfully.

"Oh—yeah. Those two are the only ones I can think of right now."

"Good options," I mocked.

"How about we just not see another terrible comedy? Ever!"

"Deal." We bumped each other playfully.

We could hear the sky roar as thunder started to come in. The news stated we would have rain but not thunderstorms, and my birthday would be in two days. I'm sure I will still be able to continue the family tradition at King's Diner. I couldn't miss it because of some rain. It would just break my heart because our tradition is the only real thing I have left of Nana besides the car she left behind and Marleen. Besides, it felt like things were turning around. I liked to have things to do besides occupy my apartment with depression and boredom. What was on my mind the most was whether I should invite Dawn. I know we are only dating right now, but wouldn't it be rude not to ask him, or would it be moving too fast? I no longer have friends, and the most beautiful thing about being in a relationship is beginning as friends or at least having the potential to become friends.

I contemplated before speaking. "We can see another movie this week or do something else if you like."

He smirked and said, "I'm up for anything when it comes to you."

"I wouldn't say that is a good thing."

"Why?"

"What if I'm a psycho or a stalker," I laughed.

He nodded. "And if you were?"

"I would want to be as far away from that person as possible." I laughed again.

"I think I will be okay. You seem harmless."

"For now." I squinted playfully, then smiled.

"Uh—anyways, do you have plans for the rest of this week?"

"No, why do you ask." He gripped the umbrella tighter.

I closed my jacket and crossed my arms. "My birthday is coming up, and I want to ask if you want to come?" I said nervously. "But you don't have to tag along at my boring birthday if you don't want to."

He appeared confused.

"Or you can!" I played with the ends of my hair as I quickly looked ahead.

He stopped walking, his car just one block away, and we stood in the cold. He took hold of my wrist, found shelter under an abandoned store, and set the umbrella beside himself.

He smiled slightly and said, "I would love to come."

I blushed. "Okey dokey," and nodded.

"Will it be at King's? Tradition and all."

"Yeah, it will." He took my hands and blew on them to give them warmth.

"Um—" he tended to do such sweet things but in a weird manner. What if I smacked him after this or pulled my hands away in disgust? But that wouldn't happen because I was so obsessed with him that it made me want to puke. His adorable gestures, gifts, and dates. He's the first ever guy to give me genuine attention aside from liking me because of my looks. He was my prince charming.

"Thanks, I guess." I giggled.

"Can't have you getting cold." He winked.

"Is this why we stopped?"

"Mhm?"

"For you to answer my question?"

He smiled and said, "Oh! Yeah, I can't talk and walk in the rain like most people. Also, my neck needed a break."

I placed my hand over my mouth to avoid laughing too much. Isn't it sad how I laugh so much around him, even though sometimes it's because I'm nervous? He understood that because he never made me feel bad about it. I did notice one thing about him. He liked to stare, and I don't mean in a "she's pretty" way but more so in the 'she stole my soul" way. I had mixed emotions about it because I didn't want either of us indebted to one another, especially if we didn't work out. I like him around, even my pest of a mind. It seemed like he felt the same way, but sometimes, I could barely read him.

"The rain is nice. Don't you think?"

"No."

I appeared astonished. How could anyone hate the rain?

"You don't?"

He laughed and put his hands up. "Don't murder me."

I rolled my eyes. "Very funny," I said as I jokingly smacked his arm.

"Well—" He said as he looked to the side playfully.

"Dawn," I whined.

"Okay. I'm more of a summer guy, sun on your skin, sand between your toes, and a good Summer breeze."

"Ew! You're one of those people." We laughed. "Well, I'm a spring girl, but out of everything, cold or wet, I like rain the most. It washes everything clean. I like that." I smiled sharply.

His dark green eyes watched mine. "When you put it that way, it does sound nice," he smiled, smitten. "I'll learn to like it if you love it." He winked.

I asked, "Why? You don't have to like the rain just because I do."

He pondered, then said, "Relationships involve give and take. What good would I be as a future man in your life if I didn't at least attempt to like the things you love."

"If you say so."

"Wouldn't you do the same for me?"

"Yeah— I guess."

He nodded. "Okay. Now stop looking at me like I offended you."

I chuckled. "You're too cute to offend me right now."

"I would hope for nothing else."

"Same." We smiled at each other awkwardly.

He inched closer and leaned on the window. "I want so badly to—"

He sighed, looking at me longingly, and said, "Never mind."

"What were you going to say?"

"Nothing, honestly."

"Okay." I sighed. "But we should probably start heading back."

As I looked up at the sky, it had turned a dark grey-blue as thunder bellowed. The rain continued to pour down heavily, and I knew we were having a moment, but I thought it best to head to the car immediately. The sewers in the city always overflowed and stank severely afterward. We didn't want to be trapped in such a dreary place, regardless of how fond we were of each other. And I certainly didn't want to get my hair wet.

However, the city seemed to think otherwise, as many people were still outside, drinking, dating, and playing in the rain, and we were among them.

He exhaled and said, "Ready beautiful?"

I nodded and kissed his cheek, making him smile.

"I can see." He chuckled.

He placed the umbrella over us, but I swiftly grabbed his wrist.

"What's wrong?"

"Can I ask you something?"

"Mm-hmm." He said unsurely.

The shadows covered us as we gazed into each other's eyes. I struggled to articulate my thoughts. It seemed as though we were concealed in darkness, with only a glimmer of light connecting us. The glare of passing car lights briefly flashed us while strangers hurried past as if we were ghosts. The rain puddles reflected a distorted image of us. The air around us grew colder, but our beating hearts kept our bodies warm. The sound of our shoes moving slightly across the wet concrete made our ears tingle. Our faces felt like frozen icicles; the air would form ice anytime we breathed.

It was hard to resist a human urge while standing in the freezing cold. He was so handsome and relatively normal. I was holding his wrist so tightly that I thought I might break it. I knew what he wanted to ask, and I had been trying to do it since the movie theater. It showed that we both were shy around each other, but he's usually confident, which makes this different. I gently let go of his wrist and moved closer, slowly but lovingly hugging him. We hadn't been intimate for some time, and I'd like to think it was to give each other space to understand one another better and see if we had more than a physical connection. The fact alone that I kissed his cheek was astonishing to me. We were like school kids with crushes. It was sweet—no, lovely. He wrapped his arms around me and inhaled my scent. I felt like a mannequin, not wanting to let him go as I absorbed his warmth.

He caressed my hair. "What is it that you wanted to ask?"

I smirked. "Is it so terrible that I wanted the simplest thing in life?"

"And what's that?"

"A hug," I said, muffled with my heart racing.

He tried not to smile too much. "No. There is nothing wrong with that."

I closed my eyes and exhaled.

"I wanted a hug, too," he chuckled. "We have been cautious of each other lately, so I dared not to ask, and I thought if I did, it would make things weird." He licked his chapped lips.

I lifted my head, and my eyes met with his chin, my breathing warming his neck like a baby bird in a nest.

"I also found it weird to ask."

"I'm glad you didn't." he smiled. "I missed your scent."

I chuckled. "And I missed your hugs."

I bit my lip and said, "Tell me. What do I smell like?"

"Sweet but not like a rose."

"Mhm."

He was focused. "More like a freshly baked cupcake. Yeah. The ones only a person could make at home."

I kissed his chin. "Cupcake," I said as I accepted the compliment warmly.

I loved his hugs, which were always so warm and inviting, but I could never quite figure out his scent, which lingered in the air every time we saw each other. It made me a little irrational, but the only word I could use to describe his smell was "clean." It wasn't unpleasant; in fact, it was comforting and made me feel sleepy. I think most men like to smell like fresh linen or strong cologne. For either to work, it had to be nice smelling, or it would be too overpowering for everyone else. I didn't really care much about how he smelled as long as it was not a strong spice or a foul odor. He could smell like pollen, and I would still be pleased, even if I were allergic to it, just because I like him. It was funny, but lately, I was willing to overlook many things for him.

I lied; even the foulest of odors couldn't keep me from him. His smile, with its warmth and brightness, would effortlessly dispel any unpleasant scent. The gentle gaze of his eyes, filled with understanding and compassion, would soothe any discomfort. His innate kindness, like a refreshing stream, would wash away any lingering traces of unpleasantness.

In the past few days, I had experienced joy— the first emotion I had felt since Nana passed away. It's strange to go through such an event without her. If she were alive, I would call her for advice. She would say, "Aira, you are in a jam now. Who would have thought you would set your sights on that lovely boy we met months ago? Don't forget to bring him over sometime, and then I could sink my teeth into him and see what I can bring back to you." We would laugh endlessly. Then, she would give lectures on love and the lessons it provides by mentioning her marriage to Pa and Mamas to my daddy.

I would lean in close to the phone and say, "Nana, don't worry. I have everything under control. Please don't tell Marleen because I will never hear the end of it. But he's great, so great, and I can't wait for you to meet him. Everything about him makes my body scream with passion. I don't know how to explain it." She would be quiet for a moment, then say, "Aira, love is different for everyone. I'm not saying that you love him, but he seems to make you happy, and that makes me happy. If you feel what you are telling me now, then you don't need anyone's advice or opinion. It's all about you and how you feel. He does make you happy?"

I would tightly grip the phone and say, "He does make me happy, so happy, but you know me, the overthinker." Nana would exhale with her hand across her heart and say, "Then you and I have nothing to worry about. My baby has finally found someone. It brings back memories." I would become overjoyed just as she was, saying, "Long time coming, I know. I promise to be careful. I love and miss you. I hope to see you soon." And she would happily say, "I love and miss you too, Aira."

She would blow a kiss into the phone and hang it up, leaving me to my inconsistent thoughts and feelings. It drove me mad to think we would never have such conversations. She would have loved to meet him again, and by now, she would be picking out a white wedding dress for me as if I didn't daydream enough about marrying such a handsome man as Dawn.

He kissed me on the forehead and said, "It's time for us to go before we catch a cold, rose."

I didn't want to move. I didn't want this moment to leave us or to leave it behind, so I hugged him tighter, my fingers going numb. "I don't want to leave just yet."

The air caught his breath. "It's cold!" he laughed.

"I don't care," I exclaimed.

"You should because, at this point, we will get frostbite."

"What's that?" I joked.

"Aira." He said grave, and I let him go.

I looked at him and rolled my eyes. "I hate when you call me that."

"You wouldn't let go." He kissed me on my bright red nose and smiled.

"I just wanted a few minutes."

"Well, when we get somewhere warmer, we can cuddle for as long as you like."

"Promise?"

He stuck out his pinky finger and said, "Promise."

I curled my pinky around his and winked. "Cool. We can leave now."

"You will always be stubborn."

I shrugged. "Unfortunately."

"Yeah, and for how long?"

"Forever," I joked.

We smiled at each other, and then he quickly picked me up into his arms. Stunned, I looked at him with my big brown eyes. "I will carry you, and you hold the umbrella."

"Okey dokey," I smiled, enamored.

"That way, I won't have to bend my neck so much, and we can reach our destination faster." He smiled without a care in the world. "My sweet rose."

I was all smiles; nothing else would suffice. He began to walk to the car, and I rested my face against him, planting small kisses on his cheek. I inhaled the scent of his face, not knowing what I smelled, but it made me feel connected to him— and, most of all, happy.

# 25. Absent Love

It seemed like the diner had grown bigger and taller since the last time she had seen it. It was still somewhat worn down but had a fresh coat of paint while still maintaining its retro theme. The doors were different, too; they were now made of glass with long metal handles, similar to the ones at the mall. Things changed all the time, but sometimes it felt like a message. If everything and everyone moved on and progressed around her, then it meant that her life would solely but gradually end up doing the same without her permission, no matter how much she hated it or didn't feel ready. It was haunting to know that by force of nature, nothing would be the same, and her nana would forever be gone, possibly him too.

Outside the doors, life bustled: cars passing by, people on their way to work, friends and families going about their day. The diner stood empty, and she sat alone at the table to the far back, where she and Nana used to sit, where she and Dawn first met. She gripped the glass of orange juice for dear life as her nerves heightened. It didn't matter to her if it was morning or evening. She always loved a cold glass of orange juice, especially when it was bitter. Then, again, her taste buds favored sour over sweet every time.

It made her feel like a Martian because people always wanted something sweet when she wanted to chomp down on citrus after dinner. The same thing could be said about life. There were two kinds of people: Sweet and Sour. The sour people were not too badly off. They had friends and family and could love life fully. They stayed optimistic and minded their own business as best they could. They tried to live life to the fullest regardless of the circumstances. On the other hand, there were the sweet people. They were indulgent, selfish, abusive, took advantage of people and things, and were blessed beyond repair but cold. They wanted their cake and to eat it, too. They were people who didn't live life to the fullest but wanted to suck it dry and eat even more, like a black hole. Sometimes, two words aren't always what they appear to be, just like people.

It was 1:30 p.m. on a Sunday. She had arrived early at King's Diner because she wanted every fear and impulsive thought to be proven true when she and Dawn discussed their relationship. It was unbelievable that they were going to have "the talk." It was humorous at best. It could be either bad or good, good or bad. It was like an adrenaline rush waiting for 2 pm to appear on the clock. She had to be a big girl because no one could solve this except her. She thought maybe she had jinxed it by telling him it wasn't possible they would last, and it had been eating away at her since morning. It reached a point where she felt emotions tearing at her heart and extreme doubts filling her mind.

It was the only way she could explain everything she felt—restless and hopeful. It was all she could think about besides him. It's like he embedded himself in her very essence, her very bones. No doubt her heart was first in line. She sat in her apartment that day and read all one hundred of his messages. The words made her feel distant but loved. His words were at the tip of her fingers, behind a screen and on paper, but never in front of her. They were never coming from his soft, pink lips spoken to her. Could it be cruel to want his undying love to be expressed to her in person? Was it wrong to want to be loved up close and not from afar?

Sometimes, she felt he knew what to say, to get her never to leave him emotionally. He had expressed everything he was feeling, but she didn't. The ball was in her park, but it was like a tunnel leading to her heart, and he had access. Sadly, it was not the other way around like she hoped. It felt so strange watching from outside her body the events that led up to the destruction of their relationship. Were they right for each other? It could be her loneliness talking, that one itch begging to be scratched. She missed him, that's all. What better thing to do than what she did best —overthink?

The love of her life, right? It was like everything, and everyone was a distant memory, except she had pictures to remind her of their briefness in her life, dead or alive. He flew back into the city two days ago but did not see her again. She wanted to see him, at least. It didn't mean she forgave him for what happened.

He was a different person, and it scared her. The fear subsided due to their time apart, but it rose again as she sat idle at the table. She was sure he felt the same, not in fear of him but the outcome. Her fingers tapped the table as she slid the glass out of the front of her, leaving it empty. She tried to calm her chaotic brain, but it wouldn't quiet down. So, she looked back out the diner's window, trying to tame the very thing that made her afraid.

Marleen was at the diner for her shift, which worsened things as Moon battled with herself about Dawn. It worsened things because she still didn't know what happened between them. She didn't want another person involved, especially Marleen, who had a habit of prying. Moon had returned to her routine, working, trying to spend time with friends, and reigniting her passion for poetry. It was amusing how, when she mentioned her poetry to others, they expected her to be like Shakespeare and recite on the spot, which she never did. She used to perform on stage, but not anymore. Her poetry was for her alone, and she felt it would diminish her if others even caught a whisper of words she never intended for the world to hear.

She took off her jacket and threw it onto the seat, then checked her phone for the time. Only ten minutes had passed, but it felt like an eternity. She was waiting for someone to come and determine her romantic fate. She noticed Marleen sitting in the back of the kitchen, watching her, and couldn't help but laugh at Marleen's overprotective nature. It was ridiculous how nosy and hovering she could be. Twirling the ends of her braided ponytail, Moon felt her nerves calm as Marleen rushed to her table.

"Is he on his way?" Marleen asked nosily.

Moon chuckled. "Yeah, he will be here at two. We both were supposed to, but I came early to calm my nerves."

"Is it working?" Marleen sat down across from her. "No," she said as she laughed nervously.

Marleen grabbed her hand and said, "Calm down. It's okay."

Moon couldn't help but overthink. Anyone could see on her face that she was losing her mind. It was a habit but something brought on by her mother during her addiction days. She never knew when her mother would be up or down, so it created this cast-like protection of an emotion that she would randomly freak out due to others' feelings. People called it trauma or PTSD, but Moon called it existing.

She gripped Marleen's hand back. "I know. You know how I get—"

Marleen nodded. "Yes. Did you talk to him before coming besides reading his messages?"

Moon shook her head.

"Nope. He didn't even come to see me, but I hope that is because we will meet today," she said, fearful.

"Asshole."

"Marleen!" she whined.

Marleen rolled her eyes and leaned forward. "Is he not? He swears up and down that he loves you but can't see you face to face."

"He is today!"

"Through appointment, but if you say so." She dropped her hand and crossed her arms.

"This is why I don't tell you anything," Moon whispered, playing with her clear-coated nails.

Marleen shrugged. "And, of course, you don't care."

"He doesn't either, it seems." Marleen smiled sarcastically.

Moon exhaled and said, "Low blow." She looked at her, annoyed.

"Is it? I was excited for you and him to be together, but you have to face the facts and signs at the end of the day! But it's your life." She smiled at Moon. "It'll be okay, and you're a grown woman. Don't ever let a man or anyone get you down. But I should be getting back."

She chuckled. "I won't, and you're right. I shouldn't let my emotions run my life, especially over some guy." She winked and gave her a doe-eyed look.

"What?"

Moon smiled. "Can you have Joe cook me up a grilled cheese?"

"Um—"

Moon clasped her hands and said, "Please!"

Marleen laughed. "Of course." She scratched her eyebrow.

Moon jumped with joy. "Thank you."

"Mm-hm. I'll make sure it's extra crispy." She winked and grabbed the empty glass.

Moon leaned back in the booth, pulling her sweater's sleeves down to her hands. "Love you!" she said to Marleen as she returned to the kitchen.

"Yeah, sure! Love you too!"

She experienced a brief moment of happiness in those few seconds, but then sadness enveloped her again. She had twenty minutes left before seeing him again, twenty minutes before they would engage in intense conversation at the table, and these twenty minutes seemed to exist only in the realm of human perception. What should she say to him? How should she act around him? She knew she was in love with him and hoped to tell him one day, but she was uncertain whether she wanted to be with him or missed him. For so long, she struggled to decide whether to be distant or affectionate towards him. Each passing minute made her heart race as she kept a vigilant eye on the door, eagerly awaiting for him to walk through.

One of her biggest fears was that he had played a practical joke on her and decided to live his life with someone else, maybe even Rainy Crow. She could admit that she had the last laugh because of what happened. The events redefined their relationship and now dictated it. It was hard for her to process everything and every emotion she had. It felt like she was sinking and needed saving, but only she could do that. She counted the days and hours in her stuffy apartment when she had nothing better to do. She would lie in the middle of her bed and stare at all the things around her, trying to be thankful even for the breath she had taken, but the depression and anxiety were winning.

It went beyond him, her grandmother, and her mother because something was wrong. She didn't know how to fix it. Her emotions were out of whack, and she could barely sleep, but maybe it was her life she was unhappy with. Time and time again, she blamed others but still had no honest answer to her problem. The only conclusion she came back to was Aira Moon. It became exhausting that this was to be what held her back. How can the only person to ruin your life be you? It racked her brain, and she realized that ever since she was a little girl, she wanted what others had, regardless of the simple pleasures she had in her own life. It could be family, love, money, or anything to distract her from the truth. She was never happy, significantly since things worsened as she grew up without a father or experiencing true love, a love that didn't come from family. It made her want to cry, scream, and give up in the most tiring way possible. She couldn't put it precisely into words, but she felt in her heart that she was never truly free from the emptiness that had plagued her life since childhood. Trauma and absent love were her boogeymen under the bed and in her closet.

A plate of crispy grilled cheese with melted mozzarella and marinara sauce on the side and ice-cold water poured into a freshly cleaned glass was placed in front of Moon.

"Thank you." She whispered to Marleen.

Marleen nodded, kissed her head, and said, "Welcome, beautiful." Then, she tended to other customers.

She tore the cheese toast in half and dipped one end into marinara sauce. As she chewed her food, she stared at the ice-cold water before her. Her eyes followed the water trickling down the glass, one drop at a time, while the ice floated on top like melting glaciers. She looked around and saw three more people in the diner, all alone like her. She broke another piece of toast off and dipped it again, taking another bite. She constantly checked the time on her phone, expecting him to walk in any minute, though she didn't know where he was. If in their apartment building, he would be there in a matter of seconds, but if somewhere else, who knows how long.

She was pleased that the grilled cheese was excellent; it would have ruined her mood if the food meant to cheer her up had been terrible. Finding solace in something so trivial lifted her spirits a little. Sitting and waiting, she kicked her feet under the table, humming. She thought, "What fun," and smiled at the thought of seeing those dark green eyes that first captivated her and those milky, deep dimples that always gave her butterflies. It was no one else but him. Who would have thought Aira Moon would be longing for Dawn Wolfe like a schoolgirl excited to see her crush for the first time?

After eating only the middle of the grilled cheese, she discarded the leftover crust onto the plate. She quickly finished her water and excused herself to freshen up in the restroom. The walls were plastered with old magazine images, a red hand dryer, and gray tiles resembling a pebbled walkway outside a house on the floor. She examined herself in the mirror, washed her hands, smoothed out her hair, and repositioned her clothes. She flicked her hoop earring for effect, and then her phone dinged in her dress's front pocket. She pulled it out and saw a message from Dawn telling her he was five minutes away.

She panicked and quickly sat on the toilet, staring at the message. She didn't know how to feel; a mixture of giddiness and a sinking feeling in her chest reached her stomach. She had only five minutes to compose herself before he arrived. Her legs shook steadily as she bit her nail. Knowing he was about to walk into the diner, her worry started to fade, and it soothed her. She put her phone back into her pocket and sat silently, processing what would come next.

"You're safe, you're loved, you're okay," she repeated urgently while holding her hands together tightly.

The dimly lit restroom had a yellowish-pink hue due to the two lights near the mirror. It lifted her mood temporarily, even though she tended to be slightly sour. She sat in the small bathroom, which only fit one person at a time, gazing at the floor tiles that seemed to blend into each other. If she could, she would smoke to alleviate the stress that consumed her, but she didn't want such poison in her mouth.

After taking a moment, she looked in the mirror again and couldn't see a glimmer of her beauty because the restroom was so dark. She tried to clean the mirror with a wet paper towel, but it didn't work. Frustrated, she grabbed another paper towel, wiped it dry, and looked back at her blurry image. She felt like she didn't know who she was, just like the mirror. In spite of feeling this way, she chose to stay in the restroom rather than face her uncertainties. She would only leave if she had confidence, and she didn't have it. She tapped the glass on the mirror, realizing five minutes had passed.

Composing herself, she chuckled at how absurd her situation seemed and even how ridiculous it was that she was losing her mind. He was just a simple man, nothing more. How could he have so much power over her? Better yet, how could being in love have such a hold over someone? He was beautiful with a beautiful heart, but it shouldn't be driving her this crazy. Her love for him and her fear were bursting at the seams. She smoothed out the dress underneath her sweater, constantly finding things to fix as if he would notice. And that was the one thing she didn't want him to notice: she wasn't as put together as she always seemed, even though he had seen her break down a few times. She had to appear independent, not desperate to consume his every thought. It seemed as though she was mirroring her mother's approach to love, no matter how genuine it was. It was all over. She was tied to him for life, even if she found love with someone else or moved on. Forever bound by heartstrings that could cease to beat in the next few minutes.

It wasn't like she had to answer to him, but more like the other way around. He was the one who screwed up, and she was scrambling. Did he even feel as nervous as her? Unlike most, she hated for this to be her reality. The love she had for him was addictive, and secretly, she wanted to drown in it. It was insane; everything she felt for him in her body was irrational. What is a greater curse than love? Her heart raced faster and faster as she thought about him. If they managed to work things out, she wanted him to be hers and no one else's. It was a definite feeling to make him hers; he could understand better than anyone. She had a certain possessiveness, but overall, she just missed him. The first thing she would want them to do after their talk was to laugh at how hard they overthought everything, tell each other about the new things they had experienced since being apart, and, even better, express how much they loved each other. She felt it would be a splendid thing.

If only he knew how many times in a day she would whisper, "Dawn Wolfe" out loud to herself to ensure he was real and not part of an imagination she created in her head. She found love to not be for her in the past because of how it made her mother nuts, but in the present, she found love to be a complicated thing because it could give you the world but abandon you at your worst at the same time. Love, she said in her head. What is it good for but absolute agony and self-pleasure? She exhaled onto the mirror and drew a cupid's arrow through a heart.

A knock came at the door, and she paused. Growing quiet, she tried to see who it was, and someone knocked again. "Who is it?" she asked. After another knock, she became irritated and walked to the door, asking again, "Who is it?" With no response, she opened the door, and Marleen stood in front of her and said, "Boo!"

Startled, she hit Marleen's arm and said, "You scared me!" breathing a sigh of relief.

Marleen laughed. "I wanted to see if you were okay."

"I am. I was just—" She looked at her, rattled.

"What?"

She sighed and smiled. "Nothing."

Marleen sighed and said, "Well, I wanted also to let you know that your mystery man is parked outside and is about to come into the diner."

Moon's eyes widened, "What! How—when did you see him?"

"I was outside taking a smoke break and couldn't help but notice a gorgeous young man in a lavish car, so who else could it be?" she chuckled.

Moon nodded nervously. "Thanks for letting me know."

"Welcome, honey." She caressed her arm and started to walk off.

"Hey!" Moon called to Marleen, and she turned around. "If he comes in before I leave the restroom, just tell him I will be out in a minute, okay?" she whispered while blushing.

"Okay, I will, and do not take too long. You're scaring the customers," she said as she winked and laughed.

Moon rolled her eyes. "Yeah."

She abruptly closed the door and paced around the restroom about eight times. Eventually, she stopped and stood tall, hoping not to erupt before speaking with him. She saluted herself in the mirror and said, "Fuck it!" as she exhaled. She opened the door slowly, peeked into the diner, and saw him standing outside. She smirked, quickly walked over, and sat at the table, but this time with fake confidence. It was okay for her to feel like shit, but it was too much for her to let him know that. The racing of her heart seemed childish, but it comforted her to know it still pumped blood. It was as if he were a shadow, swiftly moving toward the diner door, opening it, and appearing more important than the ground everyone stood on. It messed her up in ways no one could imagine. She was so in love that it hurt to even gaze at him, although it was something she had yearned to do for the entire four weeks they had been apart.

She bit down on her finger to keep from smiling as he walked through the door, which she found pathetic. She was excited to see and breathe the same air as him. She could see Marleen watching as she tended to a customer from the corner of her eye. Time seemed to drag as he made his way to the back of the diner. Even with his sunglasses, she maintained eye contact with him. It saddened her because she wanted to see his lovely dark green eyes, but it didn't matter; she was sure she would as soon as he sat down.

His appearance was distinctive. He had a tan complexion and a relaxed demeanor. He wore a cream-colored, short-sleeved, collared sweater, navy-blue dress pants, and black shoes with a gold chain. What caught her attention the most was his hair. His beautiful pitch-black hair was gone. He had cut his hair short, which was a sign of change, but maybe too much. It was his body and life, but she wondered why he had to rid himself of such gorgeous hair. Her eyes shifted toward his hands, and she noticed he wasn't wearing his soulmate rings. She had hers in her purse but didn't wear them either and wondered if he had tossed his away or secretly kept them as she did. It was strange for her to think that way, but she hoped.

The sound of his keys clacking grated on her eardrums as he stopped beside the table. He put them in his pocket and tossed his sunglasses on the table. He appeared colossal as he stood over Moon. She looked up at him and smiled, and he smiled back. There was a silent admiration between the two as they smiled at each other, their eyes focused on one another. She looked down shyly, and he kept his gaze on her while she smoothed out her dress embarrassingly. They didn't know who would speak first, but it was evident not soon. She gazed back at him, stood up, and warmly hugged him.

At first, he didn't hug her back, but eventually, he gave into the embrace. They absorbed each other's warmth, scent, and the beating of their hearts that kept the same pace. It felt like they knew each other but were strangers. It seemed like their interaction was something fresh, as if they hadn't seen the most intimate parts of each other or known each other's deepest, darkest secrets. His grip on her tightened as he lifted her off her tiptoes, pulling her further into the hug. Ever so sweetly, he kissed her on the cheek, and she kissed him back on the neck. Each kiss was a quick peck. She gently caressed the back of his head and closed her eyes as he absorbed her scent, touch, and love. She felt his breath on her ear as he parted his lips to whisper but stopped, hoping to hear what he had to say soon.

They both let go of each other, sat down, and continued to stare. She played with her nails as she turned her head away, and he leaned back into the seat, crossed his legs, and exhaled. He fiddled with the menu opening and closing, then tossed it back onto the table. She rested her chin on her shoulder and looked back at him, taking in his new look and losing herself in his eyes. He chuckled as he leaned over and touched her ponytail, finding it different from how she always styled her hair. And not one word left either of their mouths as they found solace in each other's presence.

However, Marleen disrupted it. She observed Dawn at first and then pulled out her notepad to take his order. She asked smugly, "So, you are Dawn Wolfe?"

He nodded. "That is me," he said with a tight-lipped smile.

She extended her hand. "Marleen."

"Nice to meet you." He shook her hand.

"Took you long enough to come." She pointed the pencil towards him. "You know you hurt my Mo, and I should throw you out of here, but—"

"Marleen!" Moon yelled and shrugged in confusion. "I'm sorry." She smiled awkwardly.

"What? It's true! He's an asshole." She laughed as she chewed gum.

"Why would you— never mind. Stop doing what you think you are doing, okay."

Dawn chuckled. "It's okay—Marleen? Right?"

Marleen nodded. "Mm-hm."

"I respect how you feel and promise not to step on any toes while I am here." He smiled.

Moon rolled her eyes. "Okay, Marleen." She piggybacked.

"He's a Gentleman, and it does appear he can communicate."

"Stop!" Moon whined.

"Okay! But be warned." She put her hand on the table and leaned closer to Dawn. "Marleen?"

She ignored Moon. "Between us two, can I give you some advice?"

"Yes, ma'am," he said casually.

"No."

Marleen sighed. "Cover your ears, Mo."

"No!"

"Cover! Now." She demanded.

Moon rolled her eyes and said, "This is stupid." But she covered her ears as Dawn nodded in agreement and said, "It's okay."

"Okay. You love Mo?"

"I do." He smiled confidently.

"Okay, that's good, so act like it, and I know it's none of my business, but that girl needs good in her life, and I will be damned if someone, especially a man, takes that away from her." She tensed.

He nodded. "Yes, ma'am."

Moon's face set with worry.

"She is my family, and I want to see her happy, so do us all a favor and love her here, not from afar."

"What do you mean?" He scowled.

"I mean, decide. And I know this might fall upon her, but I know her. She will be too scared to say it, but she is dying for you both to be together, and she will most likely follow your lead."

He nodded again and said, "Okay," as he winked at Moon to let her know everything was going well.

"Now, make up your mind, and she will too. And don't think I haven't gotten on her ass too. You love each other, so act like it. Love might not always win, but hopefully, it does today." She placed her hand over her heart and smiled.

"I would like nothing more."

"Okay." She side-eyed him.

Marleen looked at Moon, who removed her hands from her ears and sighed.

Moon asked, annoyed, "Did you have a good chat?"

Marleen chuckled. "You can say so."

Dawn smirked, "Very informative."

"I would hope so."

"Are we done here? Marleen?"

"Yes, lovely." She rubbed her chin.

"Thank you."

"I would like to order if you let me, Marleen."

"I want you to remember what I said. Okay, dimples," she waved her pencil.

"Oh my god." Moon laughed and placed her hands on her face in embarrassment.

Dawn looked at Moon smitten, then said, "Yes, ma'am. Can I order now?"

"Sure, what will you be having?"

"Finally!" Moon said, frustrated.

"I will have black coffee and apple pie."

"That's it?" Marleen asked sincerely.

He exhaled and said, "Yeah," while tapping the table.

"Can you bring me another water?"

Marleen smiled at her. "Sure, Mo." Then she returned to the kitchen.

The silence between them returned as their smiles dropped. She wondered who would speak first and about what. They could feel eyes on them as everyone glanced their way now and then. Hesitantly, he reached out his hand in the middle of the table, and she stared at it. It was an invitation, but for what? She placed her hand in his, and he gently caressed it with his fingers, smiling. He then brought her hand to his mouth to kiss it. Moon blushed at the act, making her heart skip a beat. She thought it was sweet of him and his way of trying to make it up to her, but she pulled her hand back.

The tension in the kitchen and the conversations in the diner added to their indecisiveness. Moon and Dawn felt uncertain about the future of their relationship despite still feeling affection and respect for each other. What was preventing them from eloping and saying, "Fuck you" to the hidden rules of it all? They both seemed to be doing well, and she was curious about his time in Sicily. He had a tan, a change of heart, and a clarity in his eyes she had never seen before. She thought it was good for him to get away once in a while, but she felt hurt that he did it without her, as they were supposed to travel the world together.

She wanted to cry because they felt different. There was still a sense of familiarity but a considerable distance. It made her want to pull her hair out, especially since she wasn't as relaxed as him. She could imagine joining him in Sicily, experiencing the culture, and saying "I'm in love with you" for the first time, but she also wished many things were different. It hurt to think about the night on the trip at the manor and wish it had never happened.

He had time to gather his emotions and thoughts; now it was her turn. Dawn had his reasons for what he did that night at the club and the manor, but it stuck with her. They didn't feel good enough in each other's eyes, leading to chaos. He hurt her, and she hurt him, but it wasn't like it didn't cross her mind to compare herself to his ex-girlfriend. Not that she had to because she was average at best, but she must have had something to attract him that night. His words alone would not suffice in Moon's mind. It must be how she looked or kissed because the past shouldn't have tethered him that night. She even thought about cutting her hair and dying it blonde, believable enough, but that's when she couldn't get through their first week apart. It was ironic how she called the shots but felt as if she was being punished in return. She beat herself up every day because of it. To him, it was just an expression of emotion like a lump in someone's throat or just a kiss that felt numb, but to her, it felt like a tight, dry rope around her, pulling and pulling until she bled dry and like a shallow grave that no one cared for, covered up with the dead of night. It was all these things but never explicit, never clear.

Another waitress brought water, apple pie, and coffee to their table. The coffee was scalding hot as he blew on it to cool it off. He poured packets of sugar into his coffee and ate his pie. Moon sipped on her water as she finally mustered the courage to break the silence between them. She placed her glass to the side of her and slowly exhaled to get his attention. He looked up from his plate and smiled. They held eye contact for a few seconds before both stumbled to speak over each other, then laughed nervously. A pile of dishes crashed to the floor, grabbing her attention, with leftover food hiding in the cracks and sticky drinks staining the floor.

As she looked back at Dawn, his attention never left her; he kept staring. It couldn't be too hard to have a simple conversation. They loved, desired, and waited for each other, so how hard could it be? He set his plate and his coffee to the side. She ground her heel into the floor and bit her lip as she thought of what to say. It was apparent he wouldn't speak unless she did. He wouldn't move unless she did, and he wouldn't even break his gaze unless she did the same. They were like robots mimicking each other. She twirled the ends of her ponytail again and slightly began to speak.

She could complain about her broken heart or restless nights. She could rant about how beautiful he looked and how sad she felt when the thought of him never wanting to see her again crossed her mind. She could talk about her desires and lust; she felt only for him, not allowing anything else. She could confess the notes, messages, and flowers weren't enough to ease her aching heart. She could shout that she had doubts and fears about him seeing other women, even choosing his ex over her. The idea of him created so many horrific thoughts and feelings about being worthy of love and of him and him of her. She could express much about what she was going through and how the world stopped because of it.

She could vividly remember the night when he lost his sanity and hurt her. She struggled with whether to forgive him or let love guide her.

In the face of her love for him, she couldn't ignore the pain she had been through in the past few weeks. She found it tough to convey her feelings, and all she could taste was the lingering smell of the diner. As she twirled the ends of her hair, she grappled with whether to stay calm or confront him with her pent-up emotions. He had been absent for a while, leaving her to pick up the pieces. The energy between them was tangible, like scattered fragments, and they both knew it. He should have been the one to initiate the conversation. He wasn't a monster but rather a beautiful, damaged beast.

Envision them on a seemingly endless highway, each longing for the other from a distance. Time seemed to stretch on forever as they gradually drew nearer. She is in an elegant, all-white gown, barefoot, clutching a bouquet of roses while he stands not too far ahead, his features just beginning to come into view. All she could discern were his captivating eyes. When they tried to communicate, it felt like an unbridgeable gap swallowed their words, leaving them unheard by each other. As they met in the middle ground, they could see each other exchanging smiles, locking eyes, and feeling tenderness for one another, causing all their problems to fade away. Looking deep into each other's souls, they stood face to face, hoping to say what the other desired, but the only words they could say were, "Hi." With unfortunate smiles.

www.ingramcontent.com/pod-product-compliance
Lightning Source LLC
Chambersburg PA
CBHW020002120726
47903CB00004B/1100